No Road Among the Stars

an InterStellar Commonwealth novel

A. Walker Scott

This novel is a work of fiction. All names, characters, places, organizations, and events portrayed in this novel are either products of the author's imagination or are used fictitiously. Any resemblance to actual events, locations, or persons, living or dead, is entirely coincidental.

NO ROAD AMONG THE STARS
Copyright ©2018 by A. Walker Scott

An ISC Publishing Book
Published by ISC Publishing
awalkerscott.com
ISBN 978-0-9998995-0-2 (print)
ISBN 978-0-9998995-1-9 (electronic)
First Edition: June 2018
First Electronic Edition: June 2018

For all those trying to find a road among the stars…or elsewhere.

Acknowledgments

This book has been a huge journey. I started my first attempt at writing the story, which later became this novel, decades ago, while I was in my junior year of college in Dallas, Texas. I wrote a couple of truly horrible chapters and worked up the courage to show them to my favorite English Lit prof, Dr. Deborah McCollister. She was kind enough not to tell me right out that what I had written reeked like three-week-old, soured laundry, but I figured it out for myself soon enough. I couldn't figure out how to proceed with the story, so it got filed away for years.

I pulled it back out and reread it one afternoon, sitting in my study in Kaohsiung, Taiwan. I still liked some of the characters, but some of them no longer held any interest for me. I realized that one of the problems with the first failed attempt was that I had tried to start the story on David's first day at Shel Matkei, while the real story needed to start further into his time as a student. I had a number of silly ideas for plot that never felt right. I made several false starts and then filed it back away, having written three or four chapters, not as bad as the first ones, but still bad enough.

Then along came NaNoWriMo, National Novel Writing Month. I had been vaguely aware of NaNo for a few years; I had a few friends who had done it and talked about their experiences. So in October of 2011, I decided to give it a try, but what would I write? I had a half-finished novel I'd been plugging away at for a few years and a stack of story ideas waiting their turn. Then I remembered this story. The one that had been living in the back of my brain for almost two decades by that point. I thought about it. I looked at some of the notes I had on characters and places and read over the scenes I had written for the other attempts at making a real novel out of this idea. And suddenly, I felt like I knew what I had been doing wrong. The story wasn't about beginnings, but endings, and how those intertwine with new beginnings and unwanted opportunities and crushed dreams. And suddenly, November was underway, and the words just poured out of me. I got about 60,000 words that month and thought, very foolishly, that I was nearly done.

At that point, the manuscript was full of holes—plot holes, character development holes, logic holes, deep dark holes that motivations hide in only to jump out when you least suspect. But I kept working on it, because this time I knew I was on the right trail. This time the story was happening. I kept shoveling plot and other missing stuff into those holes till it really looked like a story.

Then I let some people read it. Brave souls every one. There were still huge holes in the plot, still characters that didn't pull their weight, or acted for unfathomable reasons, or…you get the picture. But the comments and suggestions they made were good, and right, and true. So I went back to work on the second draft. And the problems were fewer, but still there, and still needed more attention. And so it went. And so it goes.

This story may still not be everything I once dreamed for it, but it has become what it is. Somewhere along the way, stories take on a life of their own, and like the Velveteen Rabbit, they become real in the process of rubbing all the new off. For me, this story is now done. It is time to turn it over to you, the reader, and hope you find something to enjoy, maybe even something to love. If you do, then I have done my job. If not, I hope to do better by you in David's next adventure. Or perhaps in another universe altogether. Once the story bug has its jaws into you this deep, there is no cure. At least I hope not.

I owe a lot of people for their help in making it this far in my journey:

Dr. Deborah McCollister, for making all those literature classes so much fun, and all the green pens you drained!

All the folks at the CONLANG-L mailing list, for over 20 years of language building fun, and the Language Creation Society, for all you do, especially putting on the Language Creation Conferences. LCC5 was one of the best weekends ever!

Laurie Grey, for leading a really cool writing workshop group. I miss the old gang! You guys were some of the first to know about this book when it started taking its final form!

NaNoWriMo, for giving me the impetus to really get going!

FenCon, for being the best con in DFW!

All my international friends and roommates from college…
Three years in Taiwan…
Everyone on Graciosa Bay, Nedr (Santa Cruz) Island…
    for helping shape who I am!

Brenda Boerger, PhD, for discussions about linguistics and anthropology and TCKs and a chance to play linguist and anthropologist in the real world. You rock!

Lorinda J. Taylor, for hours and hours of fun reading about her Sh'shi, and many long conversations about conlangs, aliens, writing, and life. She was the first person to interview me about my writing and my aliens.

Juanita Redfield, MD, for help with the hospital scene and noticing many errors.

Dr. Mindy Uhrich, for advice on writing the medical scenes.

Diana Lum, RN, for help understanding anaphylactic shock and its side effects.

Derek Hamsho, EMT, for help with patient triage.

Anne Prather for conversations about genetics and Fibonacci numbers (and a little bit of everything else!).

Adrian Puentes, for help with physical training, and enthusiasm. Oorah!

Sergio West, for great workouts, one enormous black eye, and questions about training rank beginners. I still owe you!

Prince Puyos, for encouragement, insanity, enthusiasm, and fan art!

My sister Becky, for loving sci-fi almost as much as I do, for all the hours of shared series and conversations, and quoted lines! And for help with some tricky spots in the editing. Oh the faces!

Brenda Boerger, Dan Boerger, Laurie Gray, Barry Haworth, James McCleary, Jackie O'Connor, Anne Prather, Shelena Szrom, Becky Walker—for wading through the first draft.

Brenda Boerger, Dan Boerger, Devra Carmical, Jordan Curtis, Kathryn Frazier, Laurie Grey, Jeremy Graves, Suzi Hunt, James McCleary, Anne Prather, Shelena Szrom—for commenting on the second draft.

Donald Furnival and Jeremiah Aviel—for reading the third draft in the heat and humidity. How about some tinfis and rice?

Now for the really serious stuff! I, and all my characters, say, "Thank you," in English, Standard, and all their other languages, to Kathryn Frazier, my extraordinary editor, who not only willingly, but gleefully, dealt with this manuscript full of aliens, editing both the fourth and fifth drafts. Her comments, suggestions and questions have made this book a much better reading experience. Of course, any errors or rough patches still remaining are my own stubborn fault.

Thanks to Ashley Mays for designing my logos for this book and for my website.

Thanks to Hannah Lewiston of Carckerjack Arts for the photography.

Thanks to Sarah Anderson for cover design, and Felipe de Barros for the amazing artwork. They are the reason the outside of this book looks so great.

Thanks to Polgarus Studios for doing a great job with the interior design and layout. They are the professionals who made the text look like a real book.

And last, but not least, I want to thank my mother. Science fiction is really not her thing, but nevertheless, she sat through me reading this entire book aloud, while recovering from a major illness. Now that's dedication! She's the reason I've made it this far in life. It wasn't easy raising me, but she never gave up. If it required reading medical books, trying special all-natural diets (with homemade toothpaste!), battling the system, homeschooling, or working long hours to see that I went to college, she did it. And the encouragement and love has never slacked. I love you, Mom. You are my hero.

Contents

Dramatis Personae

Members of Green Pod

Dvarin Tkal – a Tvern An, the leader of Green Pod who requests that David be assigned to the pod. His name often appears in reverse order.
Gronorgh – a Gravgurdan of warrior caste, the pod's military specialist
Dai-Soln – a Taisiran, the pod's protocol expert
Shintikaisen – a Trelkairni, a generalist
Ael Ktea – a Human from Halcyon
Xtp – a Xttg
Red-shimmer Gold-streak – an Iridian, the pod's commerce expert
Enemwenu – an Alelliawulian, the pod's best computer expert
Fthofsis – a Fthsaisthf
David Asbury – a Human from Earth, linguistics specialist

Allies of Green Pod

Jva Uel – a Human from Halcyon, Ael's betrothed, an arts student, not diplomacy

Enemies of Green Pod

Prince Kvran – a Kzati
Sven Torstad – a Human from Earth
Ryan – a Human

Faculty of Shel Matkei Academy of Social Sciences

Chancellor Tal Hatlir – head of
Dean Haerkarn – Dean of the College of Xenopsychology

Supradoctor Ihsshiis Shisahrhs – teaches History/Diplomacy crossover course, very tough grader
Dr. Chikiki – teaches Cultural Parameters
Dr. Vekhtil – teaches Conflict Resolution
Dr. Mig Deluv Naktukh – one of Prince Kvran's professors
Dr. Dgan – teaches Cross-species Interaction
Dr. Eshkidzidzo – a professor in the college of arts, one of Jva's professors

InterStellar Commonwealth (member species and worlds)

Commonwealth worlds/stations
Epemthu, a Commonwealth world settled by dozens of species. Tolari Market is a Human-style Renaissance faire on this world.
Shel Maktei Station, an ISC station orbiting the same star as Epemthu. This station hosts Shel Maktei Academy.

Alelliawulian – Enemwenu's people

Chiurdoun – several members of this bear-like species make brief appearances
Shianchuir

Hiltar – a member species who molt

Hnng – a member species

Hopherl – the restaurant owner's people
Pherlat

Human – David's people
Earth/Luna

Mars
Halcyon
Gallaudet

Iridian – Red-shimmer Gold-streak's people

Meridab – a member species

Oezh – a member species, known for their love of gosip

Tal Chin – a member species, very tall

Talamikar Shelei – one of the founding species, extinct

Tilet Thel – one of the founding species

Traiqi – one of the founding species
Qitrivuq

Trelkairni – Dean Haerkarn's and Shintikaisen's people

Tvern An – Tkal's people
Tvern

Varktis – one of the founding species, Chancellor Tal Hatlir's people.
They have withdrawn from the Commonwealth.

Wkkho – the leader of IR2 Pod's people
Nkkhah

Xttg – Xtp's people

Fthsaisthf – Fthofsis's people, a candidate species for ISC membership

Non-Commonwealth worlds and species

Dwelek – extinct species that once ruled several of the founding species
of the ISC

Gravgurdan Stronghold

Gravgurdan — Gronorgh's people
    Gramurgh
Taisiran – Dai-Soln's people
    Taisirul

Kzati Empire
Kzati – Prince Kvran's people

One

An Uncomfortable Meeting

David caught himself tapping the arm of his chair. The receptionist glared at him as if he were damaging the silverwood. He stopped tapping.

Two years on this station. Two years at Shel Matkei Academy, and he had never landed in a dean's office, not once. But here he was, waiting for his appointment with Dean Haerkarn. Waiting made him nervous. This dean was known to both students and faculty for her punctuality. The Trelkairni, Dean Haerkarn's people, had a saying: *Shikairn guvonza,* "Good news won't wait."

The receptionist scowled. He was tapping again. He shoved the stylus up his sleeve. He couldn't really blame her. Silverwood was not cheap. And here David sat in a silverwood chair, in a reception with silverwood wainscoting. A sure sign of wealth and power. He felt so out of place here. And it wasn't just the waiting room. Waiting. How he hated waiting. Exactly how bad was this news?

He reached out, fingering the wood grain of the wainscoting. All those little bumps and grooves. The patterns were awfully regular, so the wood was probably cloned, but there was enough variation to show that it must have been grown, not copy-pressed, very expensive to have on a space station, and so much of it.

The receptionist shot him another dirty look.

Oh good grief! His finger wasn't going to damage the wood. David sat on his hands. What could be taking so long? What could he have done to earn him a visit with the dean of the College of Xenopsychology? David wasn't even a psych major; he was linguistics—well, more or less.

David was sweating. Anonymous was good. Being called into a dean's office was not.

Finally, the receptionist touched her ear bud, whispered a few words, and gave him a squint-eyed nod. "Student David Asbury, you may go in now. Dean Haerkarn will see you." She sounded disappointed.

David exhaled and levered himself up from the chair. He stepped forward, and the doors opened for him, rather faster than he wanted.

The dean stood at the end of the room, opposite the doorway, placing a realbook on one of the shelves that lined the walls of her spacious office. Her head reached slightly higher than the top of the bookcase—also silverwood.

She wore a sleeveless tunic of some silky material that hung nearly to her knees, but exposed her brawny arms and her shoulders, which were as broad as the shelf where she had just placed the book. Very conservative by Trelkairni standards. David tried to straighten his slightly rumpled and thoroughly worn jumpsuit.

She twitched an ear and motioned David to a functional chair by a study table at the opposite end of the room from the formal Trelkairni seating pit. David would have preferred the seating pit with its comfortable-looking cushions to the chair that he could tell was too tall for him. His feet would dangle like he was on a bar stool, or worse, in a highchair. But even so, it was a compromise. The chair would be too short for most Trelkairni, the females anyway. David mounted the chair with as much dignity as he could salvage. Dean Haerkarn took her seat at the opposite side of the table. "Student David Asbury, I have been reviewing your file—both as dean of the College of Xenopsychology and as one of three advisers for the Diplomatic Track. You are here on a diplomatic scholarship from the government of Earth."

David bobbed his head in the Trelkairni fashion.

"You also seem to be aware that your scholarship requires you to take four courses in the College of Political Sciences per year, at minimum. And that is exactly what you have done. Not more, not less."

David bobbed his head again, but more slowly this time.

She angled an ear at David. "You realize that you are now in your third year at Shel Matkei, and you still have not officially declared your major field of study nor your track for intent to graduate."

David bobbed his head again continuing to refrain from a verbal reply since Dean Haerkarn still had not signaled him to speak.

"So far your government has not complained, but they have inquired about your progress twice this last quarter. Usually, this is followed by a formal inquiry as to your intent and then formal review of your scholarship."

David's palms started to sweat. "Formal review"—code for *termination*. So this was it. He had ridden this scholarship as long as he could. Very quickly now, if he could find no other way to fund his education, he would have to give up his dream of quietly studying linguistics, declare himself a student in the College of Political Sciences and move into the Compound—the housing for Diplomacy Track. David sat in silence.

"If you are waiting for my permission to speak, I will not give it. I do not follow the ancient ways, and I do not accept men as inferiors. You will have to choose to speak for yourself."

"I…I'm sorry," David stammered.

"Don't apologize. Just accept. You should not apologize for trying to be polite and respecting the customs of my people. That I do not follow them is irrelevant. The gesture is appreciated. And I have never seen a Human male wait so long without speaking. Which, in a way, connects with another issue we need to discuss."

David was astonished at her tone. Trelkairni had a bewildering array of politeness levels, honorifics, disrespect markers and structures for marking social distance, but this seemed most like he would expect for "friendly to a woman of slightly lower status" to translate into Standard. Quite unorthodox. He was, after all, only a student, far younger and male. She *really* didn't follow the ancient ways.

"Your grades have been exemplary. The lowest on your transcript seems to be a 9.35 in Commonwealth History in Diplomatic Perspective, which you took with Supradoctor Ihsshiis Shisahrhs." She paused for half a beat. "Did you realize that is the highest grade he has awarded in twelve years?"

"No, I didn't. I was really disappointed with that grade," David replied.

"Don't be. It is a very respectable grade under any circumstances. However, the last student to achieve a similar grade from Supradoctor Ihsshiis was Chishaak of Shianchuir."

David's mouth fell open a little. Chishaak of Shianchuir was the most noted first-contact xenopologist in the Commonwealth!

"I see, too, that you have taken an excess load most quarters, usually to fit in more language or linguistics courses." She glanced sidelong at David who could barely resist squirming under her gaze. "I see that you took a 10.0 in Traiqi Grammar. I'm not sure I have ever seen a non-Traiqi do that before."

Of course, that meant she had checked the database quite thoroughly and was absolutely sure. David was not yet certain where this was leading, but he was quite positive he did not like the road.

"You have also taken a number of classes in the College of Xenopology: Comparative Cultures, Politeness Systems, Cultural Parameters—most xenopology majors wait till just before their field work to take that one."

David's fingers started tracing the contours of the chair arms. Where was this leading?

"You have been very bold in your coursework. You have chosen what you wanted to study, and you have taken the classes out of sequence when that fit you. You have chosen the most demanding professors and succeeded. But your non-academic life has been quite different. You have had a different roommate every quarter—randomly assigned. You have never chosen a roommate, and a roommate has never chosen you."

"I'm not sure what…" David trailed off.

"I'm a xenopsychologist, so when I detect an unusual pattern like this in a young Human male, it troubles me. After consulting my data files, it still troubles me."

David averted his eyes.

"I have spoken with six of your former roommates."

David swallowed hard.

Dean Haerkarn continued as if she had not noticed. "Three of them could not remember you, except that you were quiet. One remembered that you snore. One said that you get up very early and take very short showers. One said that you 'read a lot and mostly alien stuff.'"

"That would be Rajendra," David said without thinking.

She swiveled an ear at David. "That is correct. Of the other four, one has transferred. One has been expelled. And two have not responded. Can you tell me who the others are?"

David cleared his throat. "Um, Dodger said I snore. Chan said I take short showers. Vladimir transferred. Yoshii didn't respond because he always goes sunward to Epemthu during breaks. Aristotle didn't reply because he never checks his mail. Michael, Oluwole and Trevin don't remember me. And…Sven finally got caught at something."

"Right on all accounts." She harrumphed. "Seems like the students always know years before the admin," she muttered, as if to herself. "You seem to know your roommates much better than they know you. The same is true for your professors. Very few of them have any real memories of you, though they all remember your work."

David felt his throat tighten.

The dean angled her ears back. "I did not remember you myself, when your name was brought to my attention. When I pulled your identity file, your holo looked vaguely familiar, but I did not truly remember you until I pulled your course sheet and saw you had been in one of my classes. I retrieved the papers you wrote for me, and I immediately remembered your work. You, however, are still a mystery."

David cringed slightly as Dean Haerkarn rose to her full height of just over two meters and smiled in a way that reminded him of the warrior heritage of her people. Humans hadn't nicknamed the Trelkairni race "Amazons" for nothing. Right now, David had the uncomfortable sense that he had just become her quarry.

Dean Haerkarn walked across the room and retrieved a netbook from the shelf behind her desk. She accessed a file as she returned to her seat. "Apparently, you have not been quite so invisible to everyone at Shel Matkei," she said giving David another of those sidelong glances. "One of the pods in the Diplomatic Compound has requested you be assigned to them. Their linguist has been dismissed, and they requested you, by name, as the replacement."

David's jaw dropped. He was only third year! "I…I don't think I'm ready for that. Only fourth-year students are included in pods."

"Don't look so surprised. About now is when a diplomacy major would normally move into the Compound and begin competing to be noticed by one pod or another. I would guess that more than one pod has already noticed you as a potential recruit." She paused. "How well do you understand the way the pods function?"

David hadn't really paid much attention, because he hadn't planned on having to go that far with this farce. He'd had no intention of honoring the part of his scholarship that actually made him become a diplomat. He searched his brain for something—if not intelligent, at least not foolish—to answer the question. "I know they're the final project for diplomacy majors, a year-long simulation of some kind."

Dean Haerkarn frowned. "I thought as much. Pods function as governments in miniature within a simulated galaxy, as much like the real world as possible. Each pod tries to assemble a team with the skills to keep their simulated nation, planet, confederation—however your team chooses to view itself—functioning competitively. The core members of the team form a sort of cabinet or privy council or politburo, depending on the theory of government under which they currently function." She crossed her arms. "Occasionally, the computers throw random, disruptive events into the mix. A couple of decades back, the computer decided a star should go nova and take out the governing planet of a rather successful confederation, which threw economic relations among the remaining pods into chaos for several quarters. That eventually led to several revolutions, a couple of wars and assorted other unpleasantries. In the process, several new pods were created, and several long-established ones were demolished.

"Every now and again the computer decides that some obscure pod will make a startling advance in physics or technology that gives them the opportunity to rise dramatically among their peers…or to become the object of attack by stronger neighbors who wish to control that discovery."

David frowned. "That seems like an unfair advantage to hand out randomly."

The dean tilted her head to one side. "Some events in the galaxy are basically, or effectively, random. Why did the Dwelek discover transluminal flight before the Chiurdoun or the Traiqi or the Tilet Thel? All three of those races had all the pieces of the puzzle in front of them for decades before the Dwelek showed up and conquered them. Why did the Varktis and the Talamikar Shelei both make that same leap of logic that eluded the other three—under almost the same circumstances of development? Why did the Sheleian homestar go nova right in the middle of the Dwelek Wars? The computer attempts to simulate such random, unaccountable events. The pods are then graded on how they deal with these situations, as well as how they conduct their ordinary affairs of governance, commerce and diplomatic maneuvering."

David made another attempt to forestall the inevitable. "But I'm still only a third-year and—"

"You have enough hours to be classed as a fourth-year. I could change your classification right now, and you would only need to take one more diplomacy class—say, Conflict Resolution—to be on track."

"But that would be twenty-four class hours. I couldn't possibly do that *and* be responsible to a pod." The walls were closing in.

"Then there's the fact that refusing such an honor might be very disappointing to the Terran Diplomatic Corps Scholarship Fund." Again the feral smile. "But there is precedence for third-year students in pods."

Trapped! He had to accept, or he'd be in real danger of losing his scholarship right now—well before he could find another way to finance his education. This scholarship had seemed so wonderful when he received the award letter back at the Grey Street Orphanage. An orphan with no inheritance didn't have many options. A full scholarship to the most prestigious center of learning for the social sciences in all the Commonwealth was a dream, a fairy tale offer. But like the offers in fairy tales, this one had turned out to be more than he'd bargained for. Now he was going to have to keep his end of a bargain he didn't want to keep. Diplomacy meant dealing with people. David didn't like people. He liked languages. He liked words and etymologies and grammars and writing papers about them—not sitting around arguing over the wording of treaties that no one intended to honor.

"Okay. I'll declare my major, but can't I keep my third-year classification?"

"Done." Her smile instantly shifted from the smile of the huntress to one of genuine kindness. "I know this isn't what you really wanted, but if you try, I think you can enjoy this adventure."

Adventure. David winced at the word. That was the last thing he wanted.

Dean Haerkarn acted as if she hadn't seen David's reaction. "As soon as you are moved into your new quarters, I'll message you with a schedule of meetings. I'm going to be monitoring your progress. You have interested me."

Oh, great. The dean of the College of Xenopsychology was interested in him. He'd probably end up as a case study presented at some conference of xenoshrinks.

Dean Haerkarn handed him a datapad, pointing with an ear twitch. "Here is your new room assignment and door codes. You will find a small deposit in your account. It's a part of your scholarship that only becomes effective when you join a pod. Just place your thumb here to verify your declaration."

He took the offered datapad and placed his thumbprint appropriately.

"If you have any questions before our first appointment, message my secretary, and she will work you in."

The interview was over. David's world had gone nova. He took his leave and stumbled off down the hall as the station spun around him.

Two

Moving On

David swung the two bags containing his few possessions over his shoulder and started out for his new quarters. On the lift, he consulted his netbook again—LEVEL SEVEN, GREEN CORRIDOR, SUITE ONE, ROOM ONE. While he fumbled with the zipper on one of his bags, the lift stopped to let on a couple of Traiqi students who nodded vaguely in David's general direction before continuing their conversation. If they had suspected that David was following all their opinions about their professors, the cafeteria, and the quality of cloth on offer by some vendor on one of the mercantile levels, they might have been less vocal. They also made a comment or two about mammalian body odors, which made David squirm.

The lift doors opened, and a voice that teetered between a locust and a musical saw demanded, "All beings off the lift! Make way for His Royal Excellence, Kvran, Prince of the Line, Descant to the Throne Imperial of Kzati, Chief and Head of the Clade Secundus."

David scuttled out as quickly as possible and retreated to the side wall of the lobby. The prince—tall and trim with half-closed, cat-pupiled eyes and a forehead like something out of a Mayan painting—moved with his openly armed guards surrounding him. *Armed?* The two Traiqi began to argue their prior occupancy of the lift until the page?—herald?—the guy holding the lift door open with his foot, touched his sidearm and nodded to the guards. Even such staunch egalitarians as the Traiqi conceded in the face of that form of encouragement.

The Traiqi, grumbling animatedly, took up spaces near David while the royal party absconded with the lift. "Armed guards. Ridiculous. What? Does he think any Commonwealth citizen, any student in this university, *cares* enough about his royal title to kill him?"

The other Traiqi answered, "Well, none of *us* care enough. But there are other of his own people here. *They* might have cause enough. Can you imagine living under such arrogance?"

David couldn't help smirking. The Traiqi were about as un-royal as beings could get. Out of every thirteen legal adults, one was chosen, at random, to represent his or her group in a neighborhood assembly. From those, one individual was chosen to represent each neighborhood at a township assembly, and so on all the way up to the randomly selected Planetary Council Assembly.

The Planetary Council Assembly, comprising thirteen members, drawn from the Regional Assemblies, collectively served a three-year term as the executive ruling body of Qitrivuq—the Traiqi homeworld. David had heard their system described as *democracy*, as *communism*, as *republican*, and as *institutional anarchy*. None seemed very accurate, or completely wrong. Traiqi grammar class had included an astonishing number of, well…propaganda texts promoting their system of government was *not* an unfair description.

Whatever their system really was, the idea of eternal rule by a single family was about as foreign, and repugnant, to the Traiqi as anything imaginable.

David and the Traiqi students called another lift. David got off at level seven and jogged away down the hall fumbling in his bag for his netbook again to check his destination once more.

"Oof!" David hit the floor.

"Look where you go, Human!" roared the Gravgurdan David had run into. He was clearly warrior caste. No one else could be so huge. He stood there, arms crossed, looking like a carved block of mahogany. "You may injure yourself, and then your clan will want reparations. You look even more frail than most of your kind."

As David got his knees under him, he noticed the Gravgurdan's companion: a Taisiran male, about David's height, slightly higher than the

Gravgurdan's elbow. His vibrissae—appendages that looked like a moth's antennae, or fern fronds, that attached where a Human's eyebrows would be—arced from his forehead out over his narrow shoulders. "I-I'm sorry," David stammered. "I wasn't looking where I was going. *Ghramzh!*" He scrambled back to his feet, turning to the Taisiran with a slight bow, and said, *"Didzai."*

The Taisiran rustled his frond-like antennae. "Gronorgh, he greets you in your language and me in mine!" said the Taisiran, stowing the handset game he was carrying and palming the hilt of the ceremonial sword that all upper-class Taisiraniu wore.

"Yes, and not very well," Gronorgh rumbled. He seemed in a surly mood and Gravgurdan warriors weren't noted for friendliness in the best of moods. "His voice is so weak, it sounds like the wind whispering or insects chirping in the arboretum. Do not insult my language. If you cannot speak it with strength, do not defile it!"

David trembled inside.

"Gronorgh, don't be rude. He tries to be polite, and you return rudeness." Turning to David, the Taisiran introduced himself. He bowed, levering the sword out behind him with practiced grace. "I am called Dai-Soln. This," he gestured toward his behemoth companion and flickered his nictitating membranes over his obsidian eyes, "is Gronorgh. *We,*" he glared at Gronorgh, "are pleased to make your acquaintance."

"Hrgh," was Gronorgh's only comment.

"And I'm sure Gronorgh was not injured by you."

Gronorgh snarled with indignation. "*That* is absurd. I have other matters to attend to." He spun on his heel and left.

It truly was absurd. David probably didn't weigh as much as one of Gronorgh's legs—maybe not even one of his arms! Either of his massive hands was large enough to wrap all the way around David's neck—with room to spare. And the Gravgurdan home world had 1.4 times Earth's surface gravity!

Dai-Soln sighed and shuddered his fronds, nictitating a couple of times. "He's not always like that. I didn't receive your name in keeping."

"Oh, David. My name is David, for your keeping."

"I am pleased to meet you. And I will keep it well. May I help you with those bags?"

David had dropped both his bags when he had smacked into the rock-hard Gravgurdan. "No, I'm fine. Thank you."

"Did you just return from a trip?" Dai-Soln asked.

"No, I'm only changing rooms." David glanced at the time.

"Well, I won't delay you. *Dosail.*" And with that Dai-Soln levered his sword out of the way and turned to go, retrieving his game from his pocket, continuing down the corridor in the direction the Gravgurdan had gone.

"*Se dosail,*" David returned completing the Taisiran departure—elegant words for an elegant people. David walked around the corner and collapsed against the wall. His knees just wouldn't hold him. "I could have been killed!" He took a moment to pull himself together before continuing on his way. That Dai-Soln might be an interesting person to know, but as long as he was keeping company with that—with *any*—Gravgurdan warrior, David would stay clear. What if he bumped into Dai-Soln next time and hurt him? Gronorgh might pound him for hurting his friend. That, David would not survive. He took a deep breath to steady himself. "Okay, now I have to find Green 101."

David found the suite at the head of Green corridor, and entered the pass code. The doors admitted him to a large common room. Chairs and seating cushions and pillars clustered here and there between the doors leading to the dorms sharing this common, to make it comfortable. A long table, like a conference table or a communal dining table sat at the end near the cooking area. There was an entertainment center at the other.

The entertainment center was equipped for holovids and a dozen kinds of music storage from crystals to thread. It even had a tactile unit and an aromalizer along with several other devices that David didn't even recognize.

He peered across the counter into cooking area. It looked like something designed by a committee, to accommodate as many races as possible. No one would be completely happy with the compromise, but everyone would get something and most would get enough to satisfy their needs by improvising. Still, it was a lot better than the quarters for the first- and second-year students, which had nothing, dooming those students to the whims of the cafeteria.

He caught motion and a flash of color down low. Could it…? He leaned over the counter to see. Sure enough, it was, an Iridian. Iridians looked like rocks, about a meter long, like basalt or something—until they spoke. David loved to watch them talk.

This one was muttering to itself. Ripples and flashes and explosions of every color in the rainbow danced across its skin. What was it saying? *Yellow-spark, violet-wash.* Idiot? Idiots? Trees who walk? That was a form of the verb *to hide. Red-spark green-wave.* That meant food. Something about stupid walking trees hiding food. Her food? His food?

"Hello?"

The Iridian vibrated with incoherent color. Then its speech-synthesizing voder kicked in. "Oh, I did not see you up there. May your road be flat. I am Red-shimmer Gold-streak." Its voder spoke in one of those rich, creamy, electronic female voices that would sound ridiculous coming from a real woman, but seemed perfectly acceptable coming from a machine. This Iridian, then, must be female. Iridians were usually very careful about such things.

"May you never cross broken ground. I am David Asbury."

The voder on her back came alive with color, translating his sounds into her colors, while she colored like iridescent soap bubbles. Was that laughter? Maybe. David thought he remembered reading about that.

"Ah, such a shame you cannot color since you know our greetings. It would be nice to speak to someone regularly without this machine," Red-shimmer lamented. "Are you the new linguist?"

David nodded, before thinking how foreign that gesture must be to a being who didn't have a head as such. But she seemed to understand completely. "I am a trade specialist. We may be working together from time to time." She paused. "I know we just met, but there is rubble in my path."

She was testing him to see if he understood a basic cultural idiom and metaphor. David knew how to respond to this one. He'd read it many times. "Can I clear the path?"

Soap bubbles again. "Yes, and if I can clear for you, one day all roads will be smooth. One of the vertical students, like yourself, has seen fit to move my foodstuffs again. I have an elevator that I can bring over here to reach the counter tops and upper cabinets, but it is currently in my room, and…" She let the thought hang.

David finally caught on. "This path is easy to clear." He set his bags down and started opening cabinets. "What am I looking for?"

"Containers with red and orange labels, with small, preserved animals inside."

David had just picked up one of the gaudy-labeled jars when she got to the animal part. He turned the can over and it made a soft squelching sound. He wished he hadn't done that. David gave one or two more a gentle shake and found they all sounded liquidy. If these weren't produced on-station, if these were imported, they must cost a fortune. And if they *were* breeding and packing these things on-station, well, they *still* probably cost a fortune. He quickly pulled out all the like containers and passed them down to her, where she re-stored them on a bottom shelf.

David retrieved his bags with a wince. He hadn't fallen gracefully when he had run into that Gravgurdan. He excused himself and crossed the common room toward his new quarters. He entered his door code and thumbprint, said "open" for his voice print, then walked in. He looked around. One side of the room was clearly occupied; the other was his. He had a bed and a three-drawer chest. There were two closets.

David put down his bags and began unpacking. He opened the top drawer of his chest, stooped over his first bag and scooped out an armful of socks and underwear which he dumped in. He closed that drawer and opened the second. He scooped his shirts and pants out of the second bag and dumped them in the chest. He closed that drawer and opened the third. He dumped his two bags, one empty, the other half empty, in the bottom drawer. That finished moving. It was an easy task when everything a person owned fit in two bags.

As he shoved the bottom drawer home with his foot, an idea struck him. Dean Haerkarn had said something about a stipend and a deposit in his account, now that he was signed up for this pod thingy. So, he would finally have a little spending money. What was it Red-shimmer Gold-streak had said? A shame he couldn't color? But what if he could? David had seen a rack of coloform shirts, idiotic things like mood rings, but what if …? Could he program something like that to actually speak B-G-2-3, the Iridian language Red-shimmer Gold-streak used? He already understood some. But what if he could *color* it?

Enough of that. He looked around the room. What kind of roommate did they stick him with this time? He hoped this one wasn't into cruncher music like the last two. Or gore flicks! "Hmm. Lots of books…Standard, English, Terran, Dridzadi, Tvern El, current fiction, poetry, physics, biography, enigma verse. Keeps his required texts," he said aloud as he scanned the rack of book cubes sitting among the detritus scattered all over one side of the room: little silver Eiffel Tower, Navajo rug, Chinese dragon, Statue of Liberty, ebony giraffe, Tvern ceremonial bowl and knives, Malaysian kris, Iae wonderwheel, Iridian touching stones. "Wow, this guy's eclectic!"

"I try to be."

David spun around. A broad-chested Tvern An, with glittering gold eyes, extending a big, green-and-yellow-striped hand in welcome.

"I didn't hear you come in!" David apologized. He shook the offered hand and tried not to wince at the firmness of the grip.

"I hope I didn't startle you. I'm Tkal Dvarin."

"No…um…well, yes, you did, but…I hope you don't mind me looking at your things?" David was still recovering from the start. "I'm David Asbury."

"No, I don't mind at all. Are you ready to go get your stuff? I'll help you carry it over."

David glanced down at his feet. "I'm already moved in. I already put my stuff away."

"You're finished? You must have just chunked everything in the closet. Well, if you don't want to get into that right now… Where are you from?"

"Earth," David replied, assuming that was answer enough.

"Well, I know that. You're American aren't you?"

David blinked. He wasn't used to aliens knowing Earth geography. "Yes, I'm from Texas."

Tkal plunged ahead. "Texas? Wow, that's crystalline!"

"W-wait a minute," David stammered, switching out of Standard. "You're speaking English. Most aliens only bother to learn Terran. If that." Now David was even more interested.

"Oh, I've lived in New York for most of my life. You don't hear much Terran on the streets except in the touristy places. And Standard, well, people will *act* like they don't know a word of it sometimes. In fact, *I've* been known to pretend *I* don't understand it when some shopkeeper wanted to treat me like a tourist." Tkal grinned. "English is almost my first language!"

"Come on out to the common room," Tkal continued. "We're about to have a meeting and I want to introduce you to the leadership team."

"Maybe I could meet them some other time. I'm really—"

"Some other time?" Tkal laughed. "No, you need to meet the rest of the team now."

"Rest of the team?" David blushed a little. "Oh, are you on the team? I didn't mean to be rude or anything."

"Am I 'on the team'? Of course I'm 'on the team,'" he said making air quotes. "I'm the president." Tkal paused while David stared. "Don't look so surprised. You're on the team too!"

"What?!" David's voice cracked. "Don't say things like that!"

"Things like what? You're our new linguist, our new head linguist, and as such, you're on the team. You didn't realize that Green Room One on Green Corridor would be headquarters for Green Pod? Welcome to the top. You're a cabinet-level post. The guy you're replacing left a lot of unfinished business, and we need to get you up to speed really quick."

David just stood there blinking.

"Don't go fritzo on me. Come on!" Tkal clapped him on the back and guided him out to the common room before the shock could wear off.

Three

Meeting the Neighbors

"Let me introduce you," Tkal said, drawing David toward the center of the room. A Xttg rose from a pillar seat and came toward David, with second arms raised in greeting. David couldn't tell if the insectoid was male, female, or sterile.

"*Xqtt pg Xtp*," it clicked at David. Its voder, worn as a golden medallion around its neck, translated, "'I greet you as Xtp'." Ah, so it was a sterile. The "p" click at the end of its name gave that away.

"*Qqt. Xqtt pg* David," David replied, setting off a flurry of clicks and clacks which neither David nor the voder could hope to follow.

Tkal laughed. "I think its glad to meet you!"

The stream of clicks slowed considerably, and the voder began translating again, "I am sorry I have become so excited, but I have never been greeted by a round-mouth who speaks my own language so staccato! It is wonderful to hear." Xtp spread all four arms in the 'it-is-true-as-I-say' gesture.

About that time, an attractive Human walked into the common room from a dorm on the far side. She was about David's height, with long, jet-black hair and startling crystal-blue eyes. She wore a black jumpsuit with electric-blue piping around the high mandarin collar, the cuffs of the sleeves and the hems of the pants, down all the seams. She strode over and stuck out a hand. "You must be the new linguist. I'm Ael Ktea."

David accepted her hand and replied, "I'm David Asbury. Are you from Halcyon?"

"Sure am! What gave me away? The eyes, the accent or the name?" She laughed. Those were the three things Halcyans were most known for.

The Humans who had colonized Halcyon had genetically self-selected for black hair and blue eyes. Halcyans were also frequently parodied for their particular accent on Terran and Standard. As for their names—all feminine names began with two vowels, all masculine with two consonants, and the surname combined the names of the two parents.

"All three actually."

She laughed again. "Have you met Red-shimmer Gold-streak yet, David?" She flourished her hand in the direction of the Iridian near the entertainment center.

"Yes, actually. Just a few standards ago."

Red-shimmer Gold-streak levitated a few centimeters and drifted toward the gathering group. As she approached, David could see the scores of short tentacle hand-feet she was walking on.

The Iridian's body vibrated with color again. "I welcome you to this pod. May we serve well together," her voder hummed.

Tkal walked up and clapped David on the shoulder a little harder than David expected. "Come on and sit down. The others will be here soon."

Others? David was already overwhelmed. Too many people. Too much.

Just as David was about to take the indicated seat, the dorm door next to Tkal and David's hissed open and two more beings joined the group in the common room. One was an Alelliawulian—a hoofed, tripodal, cephalopoid alien. It curled its tentacular arms in greeting. It didn't look muscular enough to be an alpha gender nor tall and wiry enough to be a beta. Definitely not a petite and rotund epsilon. It might be a gamma or a delta, but probably a gamma gender. The second being through the door was a type that David had never seen before. It reminded him of a three-winged butterfly, only much larger.

"This is Enemwenu," said Tkal, indicating the cephalopoid. "Hii does a lot of our computer security work, among other things."

Hii, that pronoun confirmed David's guess; Enemwenu was gamma gender. "*Nawweme eniDavid, meluwimmu nnawi*," David said by way of introduction.

Enemwenu unfurled hii's tentacles in surprise and sucked hii's speaking mouth inward. Turning to Tkal, hii said, "I may have been wrong about this one. Already he is very different from Sven."

David's head snapped from Enemwenu to Tkal and back again. "Wait. Sven? Sven Torstensson? *He* was your linguist?"

Enemwenu rotated slowly to let more of hii's triple row of eyes look at David, then flexed two of hii's three knees, setting his head-body at an angle in a gesture of suspicion. "Cryptologist, actually. You knew this being?"

"Yes," said David quirking his mouth in disgust. "He was my roommate one term. He treated me like a disease." David relaxed his face. "I heard he got expelled. What did he do?"

Enemwenu straightened hii's body, flexed all three knees to squat-bow, then uncurled one tentacle toward Tkal, flexing the tip up and down in a forgiveness gesture. Tkal squatted slightly and extended his arm to Enemwenu, curling and uncurling two of his fingers in the best imitation of the gesture his humanoid anatomy could manage. Then both straightened and touched tentacles, or fingers, respectively, to their mouths.

"Did I miss something?" David asked not understanding why they were apologizing to each other.

"It's nothing," Tkal said.

"No, it isn't quite nothing," Enemwenu said and repeated the gesture to David.

David leaned slightly to the side, imitating one of Enemwenu's gestures.

"I opposed requesting you," hii explained. "Opposing it strongly, I wanted nothing to do with another Human, after our experience with Sven."

David quickly squatted somewhat lower than Enemwenu and repeated Tkal's attempt at the Alelliawulian gesture. He waited for Enemwenu to begin drawing hii's tentacle back before doing likewise, touching his mouth and straightening. Then he immediately went back into the squat and extended his hand in the curling gesture once more. "*Nawweme wo eniDavid, melleye na liye wannayye lo, mamennewammu ni yallalelunno.*"

"Are you and Sven truly clansmen?" Enemwenu asked.

"We are not of the same family, but we are both from Earth," David answered, holding the squat.

"And on this basis, you would ask forgiveness as if you had committed a great wrong?" asked Enemwenu still standing erect.

"For the act of one member of the clan, all bear the shame." David's legs began to cramp.

Enemwenu paused only a moment, as if considering, then bow-squatted and uncurled one tentacle, then the second, and repeated the curling gesture with both arms alternating to show a complete forgiving of a grudge-debt. Then both Human and Alelliawulian drew their respective appendages back to their mouths and stood up straight, David grimacing as he did so.

"You are very different. I thought all Humans were *individuals.*" Enemwenu said the word with something approaching disgust. "But you understand clan and clan-debt. We could be meal-sharers."

Just then, the door Ael had come through opened again. At first David thought Dean Haerkarn was entering the common room. Then he noticed that *this* Trelkairni's hair was braided in one of the most traditional styles. Her skin, much more on display than the dean would have approved, was more yellow than Dean Haerkarn's slightly pinkish brown. She covered the space from door to table in just a few strides. And she was at least two decades younger than the Trelkairni woman who had trapped him into this impossible situation. Why had he agreed to this?

Ael stepped forward. "David, this is my roommate Korgairn Shintikaisen. Shintikaisen, this is David… *Asbury?*"

David nodded while keeping his eyes averted.

"Our new linguist."

David just stood there, eyes still averted, head down and arms loose at his sides.

"Don't be so shy, David. She won't bite. Shinti's really nice. Don't let the two hundred four centimeters intimidate you."

David didn't respond.

Shintikaisen let out a laugh like a cross between a dog's bark and an eagle's screech. It chilled David to the bone. "Speak, boy. I will hear you."

"*Bikairn vi zimoku, si shiganal.*"

"Pretty words. Do you understand their meaning?"

"I said that I am honored that you would hear the words of a mere male like me," David embellished the plainer meaning of the Trelkairni phrase just a bit.

"David!" scolded Ael. "Stop debasing yourself. All members of this team are equals—male, female, sterile, gamma or mono."

"I'm just impressed he can choke the words out, knowing what they mean. Human males are so prideful."

"And Trelkairni females aren't?" Ael asked, her voice teetering between sarcasm and incredulity.

"You have a smart mouth Ael. If you were a male, I'd slap you."

"And you're a sexist. Jva has always been a perfect gentleman to you."

"A woman who speaks ill of another woman's boy is asking for a blade at her throat."

"Oh, like you're scared of me."

They both laughed. This was obviously part of a long-running banter between the two.

The outer door to the corridor hissed open. David turned to see who was entering, but froze midway. Ice formed in the pit of his stomach.

"What is *that* creature doing here?" thundered the Gravgurdan warrior from earlier.

David's eyes locked on the warrior's fists. Sweat beaded on his brow and the fabric under his arms grew wet.

Dai-Soln stepped from behind the Gravgurdan's shadow to see. His fronds swept back over his shoulders as his obsidian eyes darted around the room. He must have been trying to piece together *exactly* what was going on. Before everything blew up.

Shintikaisen huffed. "Lower your volume, Gronorgh. None of us here is deaf."

"Nor blind," added Red-shimmer Gold-streak, whose voder had just assaulted her with some very intense color to translate Gronorgh's shout.

Gronorgh brought his voice down to a low rumble, but still demanded, "I ask again, *what* is that creature doing here? It better not be the linguist."

"*He* is," said Tkal, striding forward. All the muscles along his jaw stood out in sharp relief and both his green and his yellow stripes darkened fiercely. "He is the best on this station, and I had to jump through all kinds of hoops to get him."

"Pah! It's too scrawny to make out-caste. And too timid to breathe. Ones like that foul the gene pool. It should have been *exposed* at birth."

David trembled on the inside. He fiercely hoped it was only on the inside, but he couldn't stop the sweating, and he knew there must be no color left in his already pallid skin. Gronorgh had used the Terran word for *exposed*, driving home the fact that Humans had once practiced the most abhorrent of Gravgurdan customs—disposing of weak babies like garbage.

David knew he had to say something, but his brain wasn't working right. All he could think about was how big Gronorgh was and how far on his bad side he had already managed to land. He took slow, careful breaths trying not to faint. He wanted to run for the door and never look back. But he couldn't. Doing that would mean giving up everything he had worked for, everything he wanted for the future. He had to find a way out of this, or around it, or through it. His brain was buzzing for an answer.

Dai-Soln stepped in between David and Gronorgh, facing the behemoth. He planted his feet like a fighter, or like a swordsman, and swept his fronds back along the side ridges of his head clamping them tightly down to meet between his shoulder blades. It was unmistakable. Even though he kept his hand well away from his sword, this was a fighting posture.

David's stomach knotted. The idea of someone no taller than David, and maybe not as heavy, facing off against Gronorgh? David was about to witness death. But Dai-Soln stood firm, not even flickering a nictitating membrane, as Gronorgh leaned in, towering over the Taisiran, staring him straight in the eyes. Gronorgh rumbled from so deep in his chest that David could feel it through the floor plates, as if the sound were coming from several levels downstation. He wanted to look away, but he was riveted, his eyes glued to the spectacle playing out in front of him.

Finally, the slight Taisiran spoke, his voice matching the flint in his black eyes. "Gronorgh, you are rude."

The rumble became a growl.

"You are rude, and your words are childish." Dai-Soln held his ground as the monster leaned in closer, breathing in his face. The Taisiran rose slightly on the odd bends of his legs bringing his face closer to Gronorgh's. "You are offensive. Such behavior is for the weak. I give you one word—apologize."

They stood like that, glaring eye-to-eye like some parody of a Greek statue of Achilles and Hector preparing to drive their blades through each other.

Finally, Gronorgh straightened. "You may be the tiniest warrior I know, but you stand well. And, you make your point. He must have his chance to fail."

Dai-Soln sort of snapped to his full height, now maybe five centimeters taller than David. He turned his head at an odd angle that would have given David a crick in his neck, and balled his three-fingered hand into a fist.

Gronorgh seemed confused for a moment, then heaved a sigh like a gust of wind in a cave, and stood as straight as a soldier at inspection with his massive chest thrust out before him and his jaw set like the spine of a mountain range. He raised his left hand as if taking an oath with the wrong hand and stood frozen.

Dai-Soln straightened his head and gave a sharp sort of backward nod, thrusting his chin out at Gronorgh.

Gronorgh spoke with something in his voice which David hadn't heard there before. Respect? Chagrin? Amusement? David didn't know him well enough to judge. "Dai-Soln, my friend, I have spoken when I should have ruled my tongue. I have crossed you for no reason. I accept your verdict."

Dai-Soln hauled back and smacked his fist into Gronorgh's upraised hand. The blow was enough to impress David, but had no visible, physical effect on Gronorgh. He looked down, however, at Dai-Soln and said, "*Folsain tholait,*" 'Forgive me friend', in Taisiran. Perhaps no one standing in the room understood except Dai-Soln and David, and David felt quite sure that Gronorgh would not have said it at all if he realized David would understand his words. David had seen this ritual only once before, on a video in Cultural Parameters. But he remembered the basic elements of the ritual, as presented in class, well enough to know that this version had not followed the tradition precisely. Gronorgh and Dai-Soln had acted out something that David suspected included bits of some similar ritual among the Taisirans. He was still pondering the implications of that when Dai-Soln levered his sword behind himself and took an odd, sliding step to the side leaving David directly facing Gronorgh.

Gronorgh stepped forward and squared himself in front of David. He pulled himself up to stand at attention as he had in front of Dai-Soln. And then he raised his hand.

David steeled himself against the panic. He was going to have to *hit* a Gravgurdan warrior who was more than three times his mass. The ritual required him to strike Gronorgh's hand with force enough to represent the offense he felt, but if he overdid it, then Gronorgh would have an offense of his own for which he could demand satisfaction. Of course, it didn't seem likely that David was capable of striking that hard. Still. David struggled to stand his ground.

"Student David," Gronorgh said, "I have spoken when I should have ruled my tongue. I have not given you sufficient opportunity to prove yourself for good or for ill, to succeed or to fail, to stand strong or to fall as a weakling. I have been… rude. I accept your verdict."

Something snapped inside David. He reached back into all his years at Grey Street, every time one of the bigger boys had bullied him—and they were all bigger—every jeer, every taunt, all the nights here at Shel Matkei in rooms with roommates who pretended he didn't exist, who sat with their friends and talked about him as if he weren't even in the room. He dredged it all up. All the pain. All the anger. All the hate. And he balled it all into his fist. He lifted his chin and glared into Gronorgh's eyes with a fire he had never allowed himself to feel, all the flames he had shoved down into his own soul and smothered as they burned him from the inside out. He took it all into his hand, and he slammed his fist into Gronorgh's hand so hard he jammed his own wrist. Tears sprang to his eyes, but he refused to let them spill. He hoped he hadn't broken anything.

Gronorgh looked down at him and blinked. "Short as you are, you stand well. Not so well as Dai-Soln, but better than I thought. And there is fire in you where I only expected water." He nodded, just short of a bow.

Respect? David wasn't sure, but he had survived the encounter.

Shintikaisen gave one of her bark-screeching laughs. "If the males are finished urinating on each other, perhaps we can start our meeting?"

Several of the pod laughed, including Gronorgh. David did not laugh. Neither, he noticed, did Tkal. David made his way to the table and took the seat Tkal pointed to.

"Okay," said Tkal as soon as everyone was seated. Well, not everyone. Fthofsis, the three-winged butterfly, sort of hovered above its chair, and Red-shimmer Gold-streak stood on a sort of elevator platform with a railing around it. "I call this meeting to order. We have a lot to discuss and we especially have to get David up to speed on where we stand as a pod and what we need from him."

Tkal launched into the business at hand. "Okay, we're three days from the start of the quarter, so we've got just that long to get our new linguist, David Asbury of Earth, up to speed on the history and workings of Green Pod." Tkal nodded to the Taisiran, "Dai-Soln, could you get us started with a *condensed* history of the pod?"

Dai-Soln nictitated, steepled his three-fingered hands on the table and nodded. Just as he inhaled to start speaking, Gronorgh grunted. Dai-Soln twisted his head at that odd angle again and waggled his fronds. "Gronorgh, I *did* hear the emphasis which Tkal laid upon the word *condensed*. I am capable of concision. We are taught such things." He turned his shoulder to Gronorgh and fixed David with his obsidian gaze, settling his fronds back into a neutral position. He hummed in a raspy sort of way. "Green Pod. We are the second-longest-running pod in the simulation, at present. Our current operation dates back twenty-five Standard years. Before that, we had a run of sixty-three years, interrupted by a five-year hiatus after a very foolish series of wars."

Gronorgh grunted again.

Dai-Soln sighed. "Yes, well that *is* irrelevant. Only the current run matters outside the pod."

David half raised his hand and sort of ducked his head.

Dai-Soln found another odd angle for his head and stopped blinking either set of eyelids.

Red-shimmer Gold-streak's voder purred, "What does this appendage lifting signify?"

Tkal cut in. "It means David wants to ask a question. It's more polite than interrupting since it gives the person talking the option of when to acknowledge the request."

"Ah? I don't remember Sven using this appendage lifting. And Ael does not do this."

Ael tapped the table. "We use this gesture on Halcyon. Different planet, different culture. Sven was from a different part of Earth. I'm not sure if they use that gesture or not."

"David," Tkal said, "Dai-Soln's posture, the head tilt and lack of blinking, means you have the floor."

David flushed to his collar bone. He knew that. Mistakes already. "Um, yeah, well, ah… What's a 'run'?"

"Basically, it's the length of time a pod has been in continuous existence and operation. It's not easy to draw the best into a pod year after year and stay on top. Right now we are the pod with the second-longest run. Only Aqua Pod has been in the game longer. It's been twenty-eight years since they were last reset. Three other pods that had been running even longer have failed during the past two terms, and Aqua may soon be gone."

"Are we pushing them out?" David queried.

"What? No. Actually, they are an ally, but they made some… unorthodox…economic and military decisions in the last quarter that did not pay off as they hoped. In fact, they lost quite badly. It is unlikely that their current team is up to the task of rebuilding."

Dai-Soln sighed, and went on. "Green Pod was doing quite well until two quarters ago. That's when Violet Pod began to suddenly rise in the standings. Their economy has tripled and their territory has doubled. By the start of last quarter, they had become a major power. By the *end* of last quarter, they were really the *only* major power."

"Thank you, Dai-Soln," said Tkal, who turned to Gronorgh, opened his mouth, paused, closed it again and turned to David. "Violet Pod has somehow found a code to use for their communications, internally and with their allies—a code that no one else has been able to break in two and a half quarters. Just like espionage is part of real-world politics, it goes on here too. We routinely code our internal communications and our communications with our allies."

"Not many of those left," rumbled Gronorgh.

"Indeed," Shintikaisen chipped in with her lip curled at Gronorgh who just rumbled even deeper in his chest.

Tkal ignored the interplay. "We have to change codes frequently—that's part of your job—because one pod or another breaks them pretty quickly. But this thing Violet Pod is using, no one's been able to crack it yet. It gives them a big advantage, being able to peer into everyone else's business from time to time while their own plans remain fully secure. And that's the other big part of your job, trying to break that code. Sven was a cryptologist, and he didn't get very far with it. I'm hoping having a linguist's perspective on this thing may give us the break we need. Other than that, you advise the team on linguistic, protocol, and cultural issues."

After that, the meeting progressed without any hint of the drama that had preceded it. It was, in fact, quite boring, at least when they were discussing other pod members' duties. When the focus came back to him and what he needed to do, it got overwhelming. It was David's task, as the head linguist, to break Violet Pod's impenetrable code and to get them back in a game they were swiftly losing, all while keeping up with an excess load of classes. So, no pressure. Perhaps he should rethink his class schedule.

The other interesting thing about the meeting—maybe *disconcerting* was more to the point—the other thing about the meeting was the way Tkal kept staring at him, when he wasn't actively engaged in the discussion, and cutting him odd sidelong glances when he was. It was really unnerving. So much so that David wasn't sure whether he was relieved when the meeting finally came to an end, or wished it would go on interminably so he didn't have to go back to the room he shared with Tkal. Maybe it was better when roommates didn't even realize you existed. This was new ground and he felt it sinking under his feet.

As soon as the meeting was over, the others broke into knots for further discussions. When Tkal was drawn into one of these knots, David bustled back to their shared dorm, hoping to grab his netbook and a couple of styluses and slip away to the library or the arboretum, or just about anywhere, before Tkal could disentangle himself.

He had just turned for the door when it whooshed open. Tkal, with his broad shoulders filling the doorway, blocked David's intended escape. David skidded to a halt just short of colliding with his second far-bigger-than-himself alien of the day. Tkal was actually only a little taller than David, but he was a lot more muscular. Of course, that wasn't saying much. Still, Tkal was pretty sturdy looking.

"Rushing out already?" Tkal said with a really odd smile plastered across his broad, striped face. "Decided to go get your stuff now?"

"I already did that. I told you before."

"Right. You did. Sorry." He looked at David with his head atilt and his eyes narrowed enough that the stripes radiating from their corners crinkled. "That thing out there. You and Gronorgh. Explanations?"

David shrugged to disguise his shudder.

"Come on. Gronorgh's a hot head, practically nuclear, but he doesn't usually go off like that the very first meeting, and he acted like he already knew you."

"I sort of, ah, bumped into him on the way over here this morning."

Tkal looked nonplussed.

"Literally. I ran face-first into him in a corridor on my way here and ended up flat on my backside." David grimaced.

Tkal laughed. "Your first day in a pod and you have a run-in with a Gravgurdan warrior. Literally!"

David didn't see the humor, even though the pun was interesting from a linguistic point of view, and as further evidence of Tkal's comfort in English. "I think I'm bruised in a dozen places after meeting him twice and he's hasn't even tried to hit me. This is such a bad idea. I should quit now."

Tkal looked horrified. "No way, David. We need you. All of Green Pod. And I need you. I have staked a lot on you being the one who can solve this thing so Green Pod can get back on top, where it was when I took the helm."

Before David could respond, Tkal continued. "That was really impressive out there. How you knew the whole ritual and all. You gained just a little respect from Gronorgh out there. I was scared you were in over your head when Dai-Soln started that whole thing. I could see the whole thing going nova. Smash! Right into the sun! But you pulled it out and got some space under you. Do you know every custom out there, or did you just draw all the luck cards? Anyway, I'm hungry and I'm out of food, and I bet you haven't eaten or bought anything yet, so let's head up to the cafeteria."

David had verbal whiplash from Tkal switching gears so fast. He just stood there.

"Food?" Tkal gestured to his mouth. "Come on, you need to eat, and so do I. And we need to talk. And all three can happen at the same time in the cafeteria."

David followed for no good reason, but then he didn't really have a good reason not to follow either. So two lifts and several corridors later, he found himself lined up at the cafeteria, just as if nothing in his life had changed in the last day.

Tkal took a tray and handed one to David. David flinched, thinking it was being thrown at him, before he realized it was just a gesture of friendship. He couldn't remember if he had ever walked into the cafeteria and not gotten his own tray from the stack.

The menu was as strange as ever, complete with all the colorful warning signs identifying who couldn't eat which foods. They were serving Earth food today—among other things—enchiladas with kimchi, mashed potatoes and gravy that looked like consommé, hummus and an egg roll, and red soda pop. David couldn't stand the sight of all that glopped onto one plate, so he accepted a bowl of some Verlairan dish called *traish*, and a glass of plain water. Tkal loaded his tray down with foods from five or six worlds, explaining something about dietary requirements and high metabolism when the server had balked at giving him his third entree.

Somehow or other David ended up with Tkal behind him, herding him to a table near the back of the room and into the seat nearest the wall. Tkal more or less blocked him in.

David set his tray down and cautiously skewered a chunk of what looked like a root vegetable. He eyed it suspiciously and gave it a sniff before popping it into his mouth. The texture was like a fairly well-done carrot or radish or something, but the flavor was like chicken.

Tkal looked up at the ceiling. He made a sort of "okay" gesture over his plate. Then he grabbed his utensil and started shoveling food into his mouth.

David was appalled at how fast Tkal was eating—and how much. He glanced down at his own bowl. He had eaten about three bites in the time Tkal had done some kind of ritual and eaten a quarter of everything on his tray.

Tkal finished swallowing what was in his mouth and took a deep breath. "Better." He looked at David. "One other thing I should mention. Some of the data you'll be looking at…well, it's kinda messy. The day Sven left, a nanoprion tore through our computer system and shredded terabytes."

David closed his eyes and let his shoulders sag. Even now Sven could make his life less pleasant.

Tkal took another break from shoveling in food. "So, about the punching thing with Gronorgh, did you already know that whole ritual or did you just absorb the whole thing while watching Dai-Soln—under those circumstances?"

David couldn't see how he was going to avoid discussing this with someone as persistent as Tkal, so he answered. "I had seen it once before, in a vid the professor showed in one of my classes last year."

"You saw a vid? Once? In a class. Last year. And that and watching Dai-Soln's improvised hybrid—while you must have been scared half to death—that was enough to get you through that?" He shook his head, Human style. "Amazing. You've got more steel in your spine than I would have had under the same conditions. Of course, I wouldn't have had any idea what was going on and would have completely botched the ritual."

Tkal started to launch into his next inquiry when a young Wkkho joined them at the table and introduced himself. He was joined in rapid succession by a Tal Chin, two Meridabs, and a Hiltar who was halfway through molt. Between the introductions and overlapping conversations, Tkal was never able to return to questioning David, and by the time David finished his lunch,

Tkal had been forced to retire from the table to get to a meeting on time. He shot David one final look of frustration as he left.

David finally relaxed and drifted out of the swirl of conversation the other students were keeping up. He smiled inwardly at having evaded Tkal's interrogation. He had survived this round.

Four

Finding a Path

"Well, what has our new linguist got to offer?" Gronorgh asked with a sneer.

Tkal set his jaw, and his yellow stripes darkened slightly. "I'd prefer for you to wait till I open the meeting before you start harassing the others. But since you've already brought it up, I guess we should start with David."

David felt two inches tall. "Um, well, I've only had time to look at the data, not really study it, so I can't really tell you anything new. I, ah, I'm sure there is some pattern to it. I can sense that much. It's not just random garbage thrown at you to make you waste your time. It *is* real communication, but it's very complex. That's all I can say right now."

No one spoke. David wished they'd look somewhere else.

"Well, that helps a lot. That solves almost everything." Gronorgh snorted.

"Shut up, Gronorgh," said Shintikaisen flattening her ears.

"You're telling me—"

"To shut up. We all knew he wouldn't have anything new for us in three days. Mother's name, you're a *kival.*"

"Would your words like to fight?"

Tkal's stripes faded. "Gronorgh, could we stay on task?" he said, in a clear attempt to regain control before the meeting went sour.

Dai-Soln rustled his fronds. "What *is* important is that he has already told us as much in three days as Sven did in three months."

"More really," Shintikaisen added, "since that *Sven* kept changing his mind. I don't think he ever said anything as solid as what this one has said.

All his words were quicksand and slipmud. I wondered about giving this job to another male, and another Human at that, but I'm willing to give this one my support, for now."

David shifted in his chair.

"That's very generous of you," Tkal said. The sarcasm seemed to be lost on her.

Dai-Soln caught David's eye. "Have you got any idea what kind of pattern is there?"

"No, I really don't know anything more right now. Tkal has given me several of Sven's attempts to go over and three or four of them look like he was on to something without realizing what he had. But I'll need time to figure out if there is really something there that he missed, or if they were actually dead ends."

"If you ask me, Sven," Gronorgh turned and spat, at which Shintikaisen nodded her approval and no one seemed to disapprove, "wasn't trying very hard to give us anything useful. I still think Kvran bought him."

"Well, we all have our suspicions regarding that. And other things about Sven," said Tkal.

David wondered exactly what Sven had done to get himself expelled. Now wasn't the time to ask, but he filed it away for later. Nothing would really surprise him after rooming with him for one quarter. Sven didn't have many boundaries.

David spent most of the meeting hunched down in his chair scanning through more of the data Tkal had given him. This data was like some ghost-filled ocean. Patterns seemed to swim in his peripheral vision, just out of focus, only to vanish as soon as he turned to look at them. Something in this data, but what? This puzzle would drive him nuts and haunt his dreams until he solved it. There was no way he could leave now. Leaving would mean giving up this data, admitting that a linguistic puzzle had stumped him and having to surrender this challenge to someone else. He was hooked.

"David!" Tkal snapped.

David jerked up straight in his chair and fumbled the datapad. "Sorry. Did I miss something?"

Tkal seemed to be trying to keep the smile off his face. "Red-shimmer Gold-streak has tried twice to get your answer to her question."

David's throat swelled and his ears burned. "I'm sorry. I…ah…got lost in the data."

Red-shimmer Gold-streak turned a non-verbal, swampy sort of non-color that her voder "translated" as static, or maybe it was a hiss. "I wished to ask your assistance for a meeting I have tomorrow with a trade representative from Aqua Pod. He is a Human and I wanted to ask advice on customs and language."

"Oh sure. Do you know his name?"

"His name?"

"Well, that might give me some idea which culture to advise you about."

"Oh, right. Let me access my voder's file so it can say the name." There was a slight pause. "Gan Waixiong."

"Well, his name is Chinese. If he's from one of the Chinese-speaking nations, I can give you information about the language, and if we can figure out which one, I can help more with the culture. But won't the negotiations happen in Standard?"

"He has an all-Human team, and I wish to be prepared if they plan to use a local language to obscure their communication."

"Do you have their names?"

"Wang Yuhua and Qiuju Li."

"Wow. You're right. All three are Chinese Humans. I'll help you find a reliable translator program. Actually, do you have any Human languages in your voder already?"

"I have Terran."

"Okay. Do you have any more information about where they are from or where they have lived?"

"No. That information is not in public records."

"Give me a standard," said David. He retrieved another netbook from the bag at his feet and typed a few rapid queries. "It looks like Gan Waixiong is from Guangzhou."

"How did you find that?" demanded Gronorgh. "Can you hack private files on students?"

"No. No need to. I'm searching public files for images he has posted himself, and there are several pictures from Guangzhou. Here's a paper where he mentions Guangzhou and Hong Kong as examples of commercial centers, and here's a message board rant about those egg rolls in the cafeteria last tenday, where he mentions his grandmother in Guangzhou."

"What was the second student's name again?"

"Wang Yuhua," someone repeated as David typed away.

"Hong Kong. She's from Hong Kong. And the third?"

"Qiuju Li."

"San Francisco. All three of these students could know at least Mandarin and Cantonese dialects of Chinese. And English. I'll look a little more and put together a suite of translation packets for your voder. You should be able to listen in on anything they think they're slipping by you." David looked up to find everyone staring at him. He squirmed under the gaze of so many eyes. "Did I do something wrong?"

Tkal closed his gaping jaw, then spoke. "Wrong? No—ah—no." He turned to Gronorgh. "Maybe we should have officially classed him as espionage instead of linguistics."

Gronorgh muttered something about erasing message board posts.

During the meeting, David ferreted out whatever clues he could find about the three students. Wang Yuhua had posted at least one message that was half in French. Qiuju Li had posted several times in Spanish, and Gan Waixiong had complained about some other Chinese student's Hakka sounding as rough as his mother's uncle's. David added those and had the translation packet ready to downburst to Red-shimmer Gold-streak's voder by the time Tkal adjourned the meeting. He hoped that working this fast would earn him some points with the pod. He needed to show he really could make a contribution, to try to get some breathing room to work on the code problem. If he didn't have anyone on his side, Gronorgh would grind him to dust with sneers and barbed comments.

"Red-shimmer Gold-streak, I have that translation packet ready for you if you want to downburst it now."

"What? Already? Are you sure?"

"Well, I'm sure the English, Spanish, and Mandarin applications are top quality, and I think the French, Cantonese, and Hakka applications should be adequate."

"Alright, I have my voder ready to receive."

David touched his screen and downbursted the suite to the voder. "It should initialize on its own."

"Yes, it is doing so now."

Tkal leaned over David's left shoulder, and soon most of the others gathered round. David felt claustrophobic. "Would you like to test it?" he asked Red-shimmer Gold-streak, trying to ignore the others.

"Yes, please."

"*Nǐ haǒ. Nǐ shì nǎge xīngqiú de shēngwù?*"

"I am well. I am from Iridia. Oh, wait, I have the reply mode still set to Standard."

"No, that's fine. You don't want to speak to them in Mandarin do you?"

"No, I suppose not. Its translation makes sense."

Tkal leaned in closer. "Let me try."

"You speak Mandarin?" asked David.

"*No, pero hablo español y quiero practicar un poquito.*" Tkal said, switching to Spanish.

"*¿Dónde estudiaste?*"

"*En los barrios riqueños.*"

"Amazing. I didn't know you spoke other Human languages."

Tkal beamed.

David turned back to Red-shimmer Gold-streak. "Did you follow that?"

"Yes, quite well."

"Well, you might want to check the library for some video in each of the languages to test it out. Maybe even look for topics you might be discussing, to make sure you're getting good translations."

Red-shimmer Gold-streak agreed and thanked him. She backed between the legs of the on-lookers and headed off.

Tkal grabbed David by the arm and said, rather louder than necessary, "David, come back to the room. I have something I need to show you."

David more than willingly let himself be dragged away from the contracting circle of podmates with far too many questions. Whatever Tkal wanted, he was only one person and the room would be quiet.

As soon as the door hissed shut behind them, Tkal flopped down on his bed so hard that he bounced several centimeters into the air a couple of times before coming to rest, smiling at the ceiling, with his big arms propped behind his head.

David stood waiting. "Well?"

"Well what?"

"You said you wanted to show me something."

"Oh, that? That was just so the others would let me drag you away. You looked like you needed to escape."

David stared. "Thanks." He sat down at his desk. "I really mean that. I was trying to figure out how to get away. How did you know?"

"I would have felt the same way if they were pushing in that close while I was trying to work, too."

That wasn't quite why David had wanted to flee, but it was close enough that it had the right effect—it got him some place safe. Strange. When had he started thinking of this room as "safe"?

Tkal flopped over onto his stomach. "Want to get something to eat?"

"Maybe later."

"I don't think I can wait till later. I'm starved."

"Are you always hungry?"

"High metabolism."

David sat down at his desk.

"Hey, don't get started on anything right now. I'm serious. I'm starving. Let's get some grub."

"*Grub?* Nobody says grub."

"I say grub. All the cool people say grub."

David gave him a look.

"Okay, well not all of them, but I'm cool and *I* say grub. I'm hungry. Let's go get something."

"Tkal…" David whined.

"Yes. You were going to say yes."

"You're obnoxious."

"And that's why everyone loves me." Mischief danced in his golden eyes.

David cringed, but it was really hard to stay annoyed with him. And even harder to say no. "I don't want to go back out there this soon."

"We'll just dash through on our way out."

David sighed. "Don't you have any—?"

"I'm almost out of everything, and I don't want to cook anyway."

"Already? You just bought food two days ago."

"High metabolism, okay?"

"All that food in two days?"

"I've been working out more. Being around Gronorgh makes me feel like I need it. You should come with me sometime."

"No, thanks. And I'm on a really tight budget. I've got food. I'll—"

"No. You need to get out. I need to eat. I've got money. You've got time. And I hate to eat alone." He paused just until David started to open his mouth. "Good. It's settled. Grab your jacket. The place we're going is cold."

A few standards later, they stood outside a Pherlatiz restaurant on a level of the station David had never visited before. It was a good thing Tkal had warned him to bring a jacket. Phernulo, the Hopherl homeworld, was one of the colder homeworlds, and the restaurant recreated that atmosphere. Summer temperatures in the temperate zone of Phernulo averaged between seven and twelve degrees Celsius, which was why Hopherlik usually wore insulated cold suits on station. Truth be told, station ambient temperature of twenty-six was a bit warm for David's comfort as well. He had adjusted, but for the Hopherlik living on the station compared to roasting in the Sahara for a Human.

"Have you ever tried Pherlatiz food before?"

"No, but this place looks expensive." David peered in at the décor. All the soft grays, powder blues and faded mauves gave David the impression of the inside of an ice cave.

"No way. Cheapest Pherlatiz food on the whole station. How do you feel about sour?"

"I love it."

"Good, because nearly everything on the menu is to some degree. If it's marked with a green circle, it's probably sour enough to make you pucker. Two circles will turn your tongue inside out. And they usually won't serve anything with three circles to a non-Hopherl. If you like spicy, look for the blue squares. And don't worry, the menu's intelligent. It will automatically flag anything not Human-consumable."

A Hopherl youth in a sleeveless tunic approached and waved them to a table. David wanted to jump out of his chair as soon as his bottom touched down. It felt like sitting on an ice cube!

"Quite soon," the youth muttered, and scurried off.

Tkal glanced up at David from his menu. "Sorry. Should have warned you about the chairs. At least you didn't jump up and knock yours over the first time like I did. They do warm up after a few standards. I promise."

David scanned the menu and noticed that the word *niphaz*, "chilled", appeared in the name of about half the dishes. Chilled soups, meats, fruits, even what sounded like chilled casseroles. No way he wanted that in this room. Just watching that youth walk around with his arms exposed, while he was freezing his own tush off in this chair, was making David wish he had a thicker jacket. What he wanted was hot chocolate or a steaming bowl of stew. He finally decided on a plate of lukewarm sliced meat with a green sauce, a bowl of soup barely warmer than his mouth and a room-temperature beverage—some kind of fruit juice.

The youth returned to take their orders. "The customers would choose?"

Tkal rattled off his choices, including some dessert that wasn't even on the menu. The youth nodded in a way that David assumed was meant to be grave, but just looked awkward. He wasn't sure if that was due to culture, biology, or inexperience. David read off his own choices, including his soup choice, which was marked with two circles and two squares.

"Perhaps the customer would prefer the soup half-strength," the youth balked, surprising David.

"No, full-strength please."

"The customer might enjoy the meal more if the soup were half-strength."

"This customer enjoys sour and spicy. Full-strength would be best."

"This soup is very strongly flavored and should be three circles in this one's opinion." He wrinkled the skin around one eye, the equivalent of raising an eyebrow which Hopherlik didn't have. "Not for the weak tongue. And you…"

Tkal stiffened. The waiter turned gray. He had seriously over stepped by using a pronoun to refer to his customer, and the look on Tkal's face made it obvious that the Tvern An knew Pherlatiz manners did not allow that. It was contemptuous.

Tkal knew how to be rude back. "If the servant doesn't know where the soup is, perhaps the owner can be of aid."

The Hopherl youth grabbed the menus and rushed back to the kitchen.

David drew on the table top with his finger. Without looking up, he asked, "Don't you think the threat to call the owner was a bit much?"

"He used a pronoun!"

"I know. But he's young. Younger than us. Maybe it was a mistake. This could be his first day."

"And maybe he thought he could get by with insulting you because you aren't Hopherl and wouldn't know what he was doing. Or maybe he thought you'd just take it, and I wouldn't know or get involved."

"I wish you hadn't."

"What? Known or gotten involved?"

"Both. Either. He may try to pull something now. It's easier to just take it."

"Is that what you always do? I mean I can kinda understand just taking it from Gronorgh. He intimidates everyone. But this scrawny Hopherl waiter with manners that would humiliate his mother?"

"He's bigger than me, too." Even Hopherl waiters.

"No way," said Tkal.

The youth returned with their drinks. David's was intensely red and tasted like barely ripe persimmon. "The customers' meats will arrive quickly," said the waiter as he backed away.

"You've scared him."

hired as a courtesy to a favorite sibling.

"Full-strength soup will arrive quickly. Should the bowl be larger?"

"No. Please no. After all that meat," David pled.

"Wait. This customer? Stand up."

David obeyed.

"This customer ate all that meat? The kitchen thought the big Tvern An ordered so much."

Tkal spoke up. "*Nem phazat.*"

"No customer?"

The cook rounded on his cowering nephew. "You force so much on a customer? Why? To embarrass the kitchen?" The cook had used a pronoun on his nephew—in front of the customers! He chased the nephew back to the kitchen shouting about washing dishes—by hand.

David's soup arrived by different hands, in a small cup with a handwritten note granting the customer seconds if desired and a free return visit, if such were possible. David took one sip and made a face. He was in heaven.

"Is it sour this time?"

"Enough to make me kiss my own uvula. And burns like molten lava."

"Too much?"

"No. Incredible."

"You're crazy."

"Yes."

The cook came out twice more to apologize or offer enhancements to the dishes. He forced on David a bottle of the crystallized Pherlatiz plant resin that provided the ultra-sour zing, and a box of the ground spice that produced the spicy kick. David assured him, repeatedly, that all was forgiven. Tkal refused to give similar assurance, but did finally say, "This friend seems satisfied," gesturing to David. At that, the cook relaxed somewhat, but refused payment, informing them that his nephew had "offered" to pay for the meal.

Outside the restaurant, David belched loud enough to cause an echo. "Oh, Tkal. I think I'm going to be sick."

Tkal grabbed David's right arm and pulled it across his shoulders, helping him to the elevator.

As the doors opened and Tkal helped him stumble inside, a ridiculous picture popped into David's head. "I feel like Cool Hand Luke."

"You mean the egg scene?" asked Tkal. At least someone had paid attention in Early Modern VidLit.

They both started laughing as the doors closed. Laughter turned out not to be a good idea for someone in David's condition. Not all the meat left the elevator when David and Tkal did.

Five

No Road Among the Stars

David left the session with Dean Haerkarn feeling as if he'd been mulched. This was impossible. Why did the universe hate him? How did he end up with a xenoshrink trying to poke around in his head?

There had to be a way to use the social script of the inferior male—don't speak until given permission, avert the eyes, all of that—there had to be a way to use that to his advantage in these sessions, even if Dean Haerkarn didn't "follow the ancient ways."

Her shuffling through his past and encouraging him to "explore his feelings" was like being stabbed with knives—long thin blades that went in one side of him and exited the other, then got pulled back out with a twist, leaving ragged, gaping holes that whistled when the wind blew. Okay, no wind on a space station, but same feeling.

Information. David needed more information. He fished a netbook out of his bag, called up a text on Trelkairni social customs, and read as he walked. He'd find a way out of this trap. Somehow.

Tkal entered the dark room. "Lights," he ordered. "Oh, David, what are you doing in here with the lights off?"

"Nothing."

"I really hate that answer. That's one Human quirk I've never understood."

"How about, 'I don't know'?" David snarked.

"Don't get snappy with me. All I wanted to know is why you were in here with the lights off."

"I was just being alone, thinking."

Tkal frowned. "You do too much of that."

"So?"

"It's not good for you. You need to come out and join the rest of us."

David picked up a netbook and started opening files. "I don't have time now."

"Yes, you do. We're having a culture exchange out in the common room. Bring a piece of literature and come share."

"I think I'll skip this one."

"You can't. You skipped the one last tenday. Besides we need you."

David quirked an eyebrow. "For a literature exchange? You know Human literature as well as I do. And besides, Ael can—"

Tkal hissed through his teeth. "To be part of the team. To join in and care what happens to the rest of us. I'm already presenting Tvern An lit. And Ael is supposed to give examples from Halcyon, not Earth. This team can't succeed without you."

"Ha!" David rolled over to face the wall. "But I'll do my part. I'll crack that code. Then the rest of you can win your game, and I can get on with my life."

"What life? You're sitting in the dark with a blanket over your head."

"I don't have a blanket over my head."

"Yes, you do. Every day. All day long. Come see if you can't learn to like a few of us enough to care. And besides, I bet you're dying to know what Fthsaisthf literature is like. Fthofsis is supposed to be giving us a taste of one of its favorite pieces, a real classic. It should form a nice contrast with whatever Gronorgh brings."

David couldn't help laughing at that.

"There, you see. Now you've got five standard minutes to be out there, with book in hand, or I come back in here and haul you out over my shoulder like a sack of grain."

David rolled back to face Tkal. "You wouldn't dare."

"Oh yes, I would. I'll do anything. I'm crazy. And…I got the muscle to do it." He hit a most muscular pose and growled.

He looked and sounded ridiculous, but he was right. He was strong enough to do it. And maybe crazy enough. David didn't want to risk it.

"Okay. I'll come to the stupid party."

"Great! And no Shakespeare!"

David harrumphed as Tkal sprinted back out of the room.

No Shakespeare, was it? He reached for another netbook and downloaded Hamlet. He scanned for the soliloquy and saved a tab on it.

Tkal looked up and smiled—an expression David read as somewhere between triumph and relief. David frowned. Tkal looked down for a second, drew in a breath, and plowed forward. "Since David hasn't been to one of our exchanges yet, I thought he should go first."

David sucked his teeth, shot Tkal a dirty look, and sat down. He pulled out his netbook, ran his finger across the screen, and started to read:

To be, or not to be, that is the question:

Whether 'tis nobler—

"Hold it!" Tkal shouted. "First of all, didn't I say no Shakespeare?"

"I'll read whatever I like. If you force me to come to this thing, you get Shakespeare."

"And second, you can't just start in the middle with a speech like that and not give any of the background. David, nobody will understand what's going on."

David was unconcerned.

Dai-Soln spoke up. "Some background would be nice. I have heard this name before, Shakespeare. He is very respected among your people, yes?"

David sighed. "Yes. Most consider him the best writer ever in my native language. He wrote almost seven hundred years ago and his plays—he wrote mostly plays to be acted out on stage—his plays are still regularly performed for large audiences. This is from one of his most famous plays, called *Hamlet*.

The main character is Hamlet who is prince of a country called Denmark. His father was king, but his uncle killed Hamlet's father, the king, and married Hamlet's mother, the queen."

"Shouldn't that make Hamlet king now?" asked Shintikaisen, twitching an ear.

"When kings had real power, that wasn't always so clear. And different cultures had different rules about who became king next. In the first act, the dead king's ghost appears to Hamlet and tells him that he was murdered.

"Wait," said Enemwenu. "What is a 'ghost'?"

"A ghost? Well, it's the spirit of a dead person that is still wandering among the living instead of going on to the afterlife, usually because of unfinished business, but sometimes just for mischief's sake. And no, I don't believe they are real, but you will find Humans who do."

"Ah. Many cultures have such beliefs, and almost all believe that part of us continues," Enemwenu responded.

"So, anyway," David said, "it is Hamlet's duty, as son, to avenge his father's death."

"Did the dead king have no clan brothers?" asked Gronorgh. "On Gramurgh, it is the duty of the clan brothers to avenge murder."

"Among us," said Shintikaisen, "that is a sister's duty, not a daughter's."

Enemwenu curled a tentacle around hii's left leg. "For us, the whole clan has a stake. Having a stake, we work collectively to see such wrongs righted."

David cleared his throat. "Yes, well. But he has no proof that his uncle is the murderer, and he isn't sure whether his mother helped or not, and killing a king is no small thing. Neither is killing your own mother or even your uncle. Hamlet goes mad, or at least pretends to go mad, while trying to decide whether to kill his mother and uncle, his king and queen, or... And this is where Act Three starts with Hamlet's most famous speech." He read:

> To be, or not to be, that is the question:
> Whether 'tis nobler...in the mind to suffer
> The slings and arrows of outrageous fortune,
> Or to take arms against a sea of troubles
> And by opposing end them. To die: to sleep.

No more; and by a sleep to say we end
The heartache and the thousand natural shocks
That flesh is heir to: 'tis a consummation
Devoutly to be wish'd. To die: to sleep.
To sleep? perchance to dream. Ay, there's the rub;
For in that sleep of death what dreams may come,
When we have shuffled off this mortal coil,
Must give us pause. There's the respect
That makes calamity of so long life;
For who would bear the whips and scorn of time,
Th' oppressor's wrong, the proud man's contumely,
The pangs of dispriz'd love, the law's delay,
The insolence of office, and the spurns
That patience merit of th' unworthy takes,
When he himself might his quietus make
With a bare bodkin? Who would fardels bear,
To grunt and sweat under a weary life,
But that the dread of something after death
The undiscover'd country from whose bourn
No traveller returns, puzzles the will,
And makes us rather bear those ills we have
Than fly to others we know not of?
Thus conscience does make cowards of us all,
And thus the native hue of resolution
Is sicklied o'er with the pale cast of thought,
And enterprises of great pitch and moment
With this regard their currents turn awry,
And lose the name of action.

"What sniveling cowardice!" Gronorgh roared. "You poison your children's minds with trash like this and then wonder why you are a weak race?"

Shintikaisen bark-laughed. "Oh, so you'd just take up the knife and plunge it into Mother's breath?"

In a flash, Gronorgh overturned the table and shoved Shintikaisen's chair over backward. She rolled with it and came up on her feet, in a ready stance, ears flat back. In a blur of motion, Dai-Soln stood between them, knives aimed at their throats. Where had those come from? Gronorgh was growling, and Shintikaisen was making a sound like air escaping through the nearly closed neck of a balloon. There was about to be blood. The others cleared away fast, all except for Tkal who stood right on the periphery. Any closer and he would be identified by both of them as a third (or maybe fourth) combatant. He seemed preternaturally calm. He nodded, and Dai-Soln took the initiative.

"Friends, there is a misunderstanding here. Allow me to explain so we may retake our seats."

Neither behemoth responded. Dai-Soln continued. "Shintikaisen, Gravgurdanûn do not do...the thing you suggested. It is the worst dishonor imaginable. The word is not even used except in the most blasphemous of curses. When you suggested..." He let the rest of the thought dangle. "Gronorgh, among the Trelkairni there are situations of honor which demand...that action, where it is the only option for recovering honor or shielding loved ones." He paused. "Gronorgh, you despise this Hamlet for considering such an action. Shintikaisen, you equally despise him for not swiftly completing it. There are two deeply conflicting honors here."

Slowly the two giants framing the tiny Taisiran relaxed and drew themselves upright. Shintikaisen spoke. "Perhaps...I did not understand how seriously you take this matter." Gronorgh nodded. "I know I did not understand your way. I thought us more alike than that."

They backed away from each other.

Shintikaisen looked down at Dai-Soln and twitched an ear to point at him. "But if you ever draw a weapon on me again...be prepared to use it."

David expected Gronorgh to defend Dai-Soln, but instead he leaned over the Taisiran and muttered, "You and I will settle this later."

Gronorgh and Shintikaisen righted the table and pulled their chairs back into place. No one else moved. Then Tkal nodded at Dai-Soln, and they started pulling their chairs back to the table. Gronorgh glared around at the rest of the room and snarled, "Well? What are the rest of you waiting for? An invitation? Sit down and get on with it! You," he ordered pointing at Fthofsis, "It's your turn. Read."

Fthofsis fluttered forward, backed off, sort of dithered to one side then the other and made a strange fluting sort of sound.

David's heart was still racing and he could feel the sweat on his hands. His breath came in shaky gasps, and his chest felt too tight. He could see that Fthofsis felt the same shakiness.

"Well?" Gronorgh rumbled.

"I…" Fthofsis's voder began. "I…I think David…I mean…I don't know if he was…"

"No, I'm through," David said, trying without total success to steady his voice.

"Are you? I mean, after that storm. No, the winds blow from the wrong quarter. Appreciation would be…at crosswinds."

"Asthenia!" Gronorgh roared. "No blood was spilled, not a single drop. Stop acting like you just witnessed death for the first time and get on with this fool exchange."

Tkal made a rattling sort of hiss and muttered something that sounded like *Shakespeare*. "I'll go next." The irritation in his voice was very clear. What wasn't so clear was where that irritation was directed. Fthofsis backed a bit farther from the group, fluttering higher than it usually would. Gronorgh shot Tkal the sort of look the Gravgurdanûn would describe with the phrase *yingmasîn pangśangîn*, "eyes like fists." David studied his shoes.

"I brought the story of Vgan and Dtinal." Tkal's voice already sounded much more like what the group were accustomed to hearing—calm, imperturbable—but still hadn't regained the spark of enthusiasm. "This tale is very old and comes from one of the southeastern empires that fell thousands of years ago."

The next morning David woke late. Somehow, he had forgotten to set his alarm and hadn't heard Tkal's. He skipped half his morning routine to catch up, all the while trying not to move his shoulder too much. Gronorgh had "accidentally" bumped him into a cabinet the night before when they had both ended up in the food prep at the same time. David wasn't sure he wanted to go back out there this morning, but if he wanted breakfast, he had no choice, so he scurried into the narrow room. As he poured a glass of juice and palmed some cookies, he heard Red-shimmer's voder out in the common room, coming from somewhere near the seating area. "So, did you ever get him to calm down enough to explain this *Hamlet* to him?"

Dai-Soln's voice answered, "Gronorgh does not do calm very well. Not when he is threatening my life for pulling a blade on him. Besides, I am not sure I understood well enough to explain it."

Red-shimmer's voder hissed. "True. It seems very complex. Ael spent half the night explaining to Shintikaisen and me."

Dai-Soln's fronds rustled. "And when I suggested that he should invite David over to explain…"

Oh, David wanted to finish eavesdropping this conversation, but he'd have to run to get to class now, as it was. He shoved the cookies into his pocket, snatched up his bag and bolted for the door—leaving Red-shimmer awash in jumbled color and Dai-Soln nictitating madly with his fronds aquiver.

Six

Trivial Matters

David had finished going through his messages. Three of the four projects he had farmed out to Green Pod's talent pool—students who were not diplomacy track, but who had useful skills and could use the problems generated by the diplomacy simulations for their own project grades—were already back, completed. The fourth was a cryptography problem he hadn't really expected back yet, but the pair of Chiurdoun textual analysts he had working on it were good enough that he wouldn't have been surprised if they had already finished a preliminary analysis, and *would* be surprised if they weren't finished by tomorrow evening. It felt strange, very strange, handing out work to other students, some of whom were in the year ahead of him. But then, everything felt strange now.

In the four tendays since his initial meeting with the dean, his whole world had been turned inside out. Some days, just thinking about it could almost trigger a panic attack.

He had a roommate who spoke to him and treated him like an equal. He had to face a surly Gravgurdan warrior at every turn, and had managed not to get himself pummeled to a pulp.

He was keeping up with a massive course load of really tough classes.

And the most infuriating data set in all of history rested in his lap, taunting him to solve it.

He stood and paced. There had to be a clue somewhere in all this. Something so obvious that he would have to get the word *idiot* tattooed across his forehead in letters six centimeters high once it finally occurred to him. It had to come soon, or everything he had now was going to come unraveled. Tkal's support and respect would evaporate like summer dew in Texas, if he just couldn't find the key to this code. And the others would be no more generous. They would probably give Gronorgh their blessing to crush him. He reached up to massage his bruised shoulder. Even if that didn't happen, it would ruin his GPA, and haunt him for the rest of his life. The one time succeeding really mattered, he was going to fail.

He pinched the bridge of his nose, rubbing his thumb and index finger in between the bone and his eyeballs. He couldn't let that happen. He couldn't. He *had* to figure this out.

Codes. He hadn't paid over-much attention to them until now. He regretted that. Every language was a code, and learning a new language, especially in a first contact situation, was a lot like code breaking in some ways. But there were also vast differences. Code breaking depended almost entirely on the brute strength of computers. First-contact linguistics required leaps of intuition and recognizing unexpected patterns. His intuition insisted that real language lay buried beneath the cipher. But the patterning was jumbled somehow. Disjointed. Fragmented in ways that had little or nothing to do with the *process* of encryption.

No. They were doing something to the text before it was ever subjected to whatever code they were using. But how were they mutilating…? Mutilating the text? Was that what they were doing? But if so, then there had to be a simple enough way to un-mutilate it once it was received and decrypted. Was it possible that he had one or more properly decrypted texts already in hand but just couldn't see it? No. No, he was sure that he would know when he had a proper decryption before him, no matter what they were doing to the text.

His whole life, the life he was almost enjoying—*would be* enjoying if he dared let his guard down—would come crashing down around him if he failed at this.

He still hadn't given the computer the right instructions, still hadn't given it the right trail to pursue, to get the result he needed, so he could do his part of the job. Maybe if he…

Enough! He slammed his hands down on the desk top, bit his lower lip to keep from yelping, then headed for the arboretum.

No more than a dozen paces into the common room, David stopped dead in his tracks. Enemwenu and Fthofsis were arguing. Not debating. Not discussing. They were flat-out arguing. Fthofsis accused Enemwenu of "fouling the air," and Enemwenu derided Fthofsis for being "uncooperative" and "individualistic." The argument seemed to be about that stupid game of Dai-Soln's.

"If only you had gone left like I told you!"

"I told you, I have already been left and you cannot get past the monster there!"

"No, no, NO! Your mistake was firing the torpedo too soon. I told you to wait!"

David couldn't even remember why he had come out to the common room in the first place. Now he wished he hadn't. He wanted to slink back to his room and seal the door, but—

"Ask David!" Fthofsis shouted through its voder.

David threw up his hands and started backing away.

Just then, Tkal entered from the corridor. His huge laugh filled the room. "Is this a stick up?" he boomed, scanning the ridiculous tableau.

David clamped his hands to his thighs.

Fthofsis and Enemwenu charged Tkal, shouting their recriminations at each other.

David turned and fled for the safety of the dorm room.

Ten standards later, Tkal entered, his golden eyes ablaze. "Gee, thanks for throwing me to the wolves! I just finally got them talking to each other with civil tongues…or whatever they have."

David tried to hide his smirk. "Alelliawulians have tongues, just not in their speaking mouths. Not sure about the Fthsaisthf."

"Har, har. You could have stayed and helped sort it out—at least clued me in that it was all about that game."

David turned back to his homework. "You're the ambassador in training. I'm just a linguist."

Tkal growled. David drew back.

"Oh, for Pete's sake. I'm not growling at you." Tkal paused. "Well, not exactly." He jabbed a finger at David. "You know, on second thought, I *am* growling at you."

David's eyebrows shot up.

"You just left me out there when you really could have helped. You're taking Conflict Resolution right now."

"I—"

"Well that was a conflict you could have helped resolute, er, resolve."

"Why would they listen to me if they didn't to you?"

"Not the point." Tkal threw his hands open. "And besides, you probably know Fthofsis and its culture better than anyone here, except *maybe* Enemwenu. And when it comes to the Alelliawulian, you have hii's body language down to the point where I heard hii telling Red-shimmer Gold-streak that conversing with you is almost like talking to a funny-shaped Alelliawulian."

"I just watch and listen."

"Don't interrupt. It's more than that. You have a way of getting inside other people's skin and seeing through their eyes."

David cringed.

"What? I read people, too. All of us do. That's part of why we're here. But I have to work at it, to try. Sometimes it's like you have to try *not* to."

"Oh, come on, you act like—"

"Like you've got a special gift? Like we need a top-tier linguist on the team?"

David rolled his eyes and turned his back on Tkal, only to find that Tkal had slipped around in front of him as fast as he had turned.

"Well, that is exactly why you are on this team, because I saw that in you and knew you were what this team needed."

David tapped his stylus on the chair arm and wouldn't look up. "Puh-leez."

"What? Are you calling me a liar? Or an idiot? Or a fool? Or blind? Or…"

David gripped the arms of the chair and leaned back, dropping the stylus.

"Breathe, dude! I'm not going to attack. Even if you do need someone to 'slap some sense into you,' as they say in Texas." Tkal started laughing and the tension broke.

David couldn't really find it in him to laugh, so he forced a sort of moan disguised as a chuckle that sounded more like a whimper.

"David, I'm just saying that you belong here—just as much as anyone else. Gronorgh can't do your job any more than you can do his. Shinti has her jobs. Enemwenu does computer security better than anyone else on team. We all have our jobs. Between all of us, the whole team, we got by in the interim, while we searched for someone to replace Sven. We survived. That's all. Even though you haven't broken Violet's code yet, we are still doing better than we were without you."

"Any linguist could do—"

"No, David. I looked at dozens of candidates. *You* are the man for this job. Like, the way you reworded my invitation to Diyangi Nahyama, the leader of Gray Pod. I had sent variations of that request four times. Twice while Sven was still here, and he didn't catch how my wording would seem insincere to a Hiyadi. You spotted it right off. Now we have a chance to make our case to Gray Pod, which is why I want you at my side for that meeting. I *don't* want to mess this up. I need your gift there to help me through the mine field without stepping on anything."

David drew a breath to answer, but Tkal plowed ahead. "And if Violet's code can be licked, you're the one to do it. I really believe that. But you've got to accept the idea that you are valuable to this team—even to yourself."

"Tkal."

"Don't interrupt."

"Tkal."

"David, I said—"

"Tkal! Stop. You're wanting too much from me. I'm not all this that you seem to delude yourself that I am. I'm just me. And that's not much."

Tkal bark-laughed, sounding like Shintikaisen. "Whatever. You are one stubborn dude. You really don't listen to what anyone says once you make up your mind."

"I know what I know."

"Whatever. I'm not going to argue any more tonight. But I need you at that meeting next tenday." Tkal put up a hand. "I was very careful to schedule the meeting for a time when you have no classes and no other reason to refuse to help."

David looked away.

"I learn quickly. If I'm going to get you to contribute, I'm going to have to *vta e tgiln dfal kdern e vi.*"

"Oh, so you have to 'Lead me in backwards like a *tgiln*? So, I'm what? A goat to be milked? A sheep to the slaughter?"

"No. More like a really small mule. You're too stubborn to go to your food!"

David threw his hands up. "Fine. Whatever. I'll be there. Downburst the info. I'll look it over and keep you from stepping more than waist high in a pile of—"

"David! You wouldn't really…?"

David sighed. "No. No I won't do that. I will do my best. I'll learn everything I can about the minefield of Hiyadi sociolinguistics by tomorrow, and I'll have you clued in, in time for the meeting and do everything I can to help you win."

Tkal shook his shoulders out. "You scared me. And we're not exactly trying to 'win' here. Gray Pod isn't an enemy. They're a potential ally, so it's as important for them to 'win' as it is for us. We need this alliance, and so do they, but it won't happen just because we both need it. Trivial matters can become big disagreements, and opportunities can slip through your fingers. Wait. The Hiyadi don't have fingers. Would that phrase be insulting? I don't know."

David sighed. "I don't either, but I'll find out."

"And I know you will." Tkal slapped him on the back. "By next tenday, you'll practically *be* Hiyadi when we walk into that meeting."

Tkal flopped onto his bed. "I didn't think to ask who Diyangi Nahyama is bringing with him to the meeting, but I know he's the only Hiyadi on team for Gray Pod, so there will be some other race in the mix as well."

David turned in his chair. "I'll find out now."

"How?"

David looked back over his shoulder. "I'll send Gray Pod a message about something." He tapped the desktop with his stylus. "Is Gray Pod providing the meeting space?"

"Yes."

"Did you discuss seating?"

Tkal reached for a rubber ball on his desk. "What? No. It's only the four of us."

"Hiyadi respect formality. And symbolism. I'll send a message to Gray Pod stating that we will require one bench with a green cushion and one green chair at the table."

"I'd be fine with a chair," Tkal said, bouncing the ball against the ceiling.

"No, you're Tvern An. You want to sit on a proper Tvern-style bench with a cushion."

Tkal squinted.

"Trust me. Be Tvern An, not Human. It will earn points. And the green is a must to represent our pod."

"Okay." He smirked. "Enemwenu said the same thing." He sent the ball zinging into the corner to ricochet a couple of times before flying back to his hand.

"So, you were arguing after you already…? Gah! Who's going in the pen backwards?"

"Call it revenge." Tkal's smile stopped just short of laughter. "So how does this tell us who the number two will be?"

David shook his head. "I'm not the leader of Green Pod. I'm the number two for this meeting."

"Of course. So Diyangi Nahyama won't answer a note from you. He'll have *his* Number Two do it. Thus, we don't look like idiots who forgot to ask, or just show up and get a surprise." He sat up and tossed the ball to David. "This is why we need you."

"Whatever."

Tkal clenched both fists at his sides making cords of muscle ripple in his forearms.

David set to work composing his message.

Eight days later, Tkal was clapping David on the back as they emerged from the meeting with a new trade treaty in hand. "We did it!"

"You did all the negotiating."

"David, can't you ever just be happy? And take a little pride in your work. This gets tedious after a while."

"I'm just being honest. Half the time I didn't even know what you were talking about. I don't know much about your side of things—all the trade concessions and boundary disputes and all that. But that's the real goal of all this diplomacy stuff. And most of it is well outside my skill set, and honestly, some of it is beyond what I even care about."

"Well, we need to work on some of that."

David pulled back.

Tkal smirked. "I'm not saying you have to be interested in everything or care about all of it, but we can't have you ignorant, can we? That could lead to you missing something important in some communiqué."

Tkal was right. David instantly shifted from prepping for arguing, to embarrassment. And curiosity.

"But that can wait till later. Right now, all I want to say is *good job*." Tkal gave David another hearty slap on the back.

David managed to brace for it just in time not to stumble.

"One thing I've gotta ask you, though. The thing with the knickknack on the table?"

"Oh that?"

"Yeah, the Imthiqoraqar was getting really antsy until you turned that thing. Then he just relaxed completely. One moment he's about to explode, and the next I thought he was going to curl up and take a nap. What was up?"

David twisted his mouth. "I don't know why beings set themselves up like that. That knickknack is a *ssiviqu*. It's used in formal situations, like the negotiations, to show respect. But symbols like that are tricky enough across cultures within a species. I can't imagine injecting something like that into a cross-species situation and expecting it to work out well."

"Why do I feel like 'oops!' is not quite sufficient to cover whatever I did?"

"Well Nivaq had set the *ssiviqu* 'facing west', relative to station rotation. West is neutral to all parties. When you admired it and complimented the workmanship, you set it back down facing 'north'—our side of the negotiations—with its back to the leader of Gray Pod."

"I dissed them?"

David raised his eyebrows and nodded. "Well, I don't think the Hiyadi had any more idea of the import of the *ssiviqu*'s position than you did, or he surely would have reacted. But Nivaq was sweating it. It took me longer to realize what was wrong than it should have. When I did, I turned it to face 'south'—their side—and left it that way just slightly longer than it had been turned our way, then turned it back 'west'. Disaster averted."

"You're sure?"

"Yes. Well, reasonably. That should have said, 'We are in a position of strength. So are you. Let us proceed as equal partners.' If they liked what you had to offer, the Imthiqoraqar should argue for our suitability as an ally."

Tkal inhaled sharply. "Well done, David." He looked slightly ill. "That was close, but you saved it. If he'd left offended or insulted, we'd have lost this, because the Hiyadi is only half convinced—enough for the trade treaty, not quite enough for the alliance. It could still go either way. If this alliance happens, it will be to *your* credit."

"All I did was—"

"Keep me from stepping on that land mine I was talking about. I can't keep up with all the political, economic, military and other governmental stuff—which is my job—*and* be an expert on all the cultural and linguistic stuff too. That's your job. You saved us. Green Pod has you to thank."

"If it happens."

"Whatever happens. Gray Pod's ill-will would have hurt us more than just failing to seal the alliance. They have a lot of influence still, even if they are struggling almost as much as we are."

"Why *is* that?"

"I don't *know*. That blasted code Violet Pod uses has been giving everyone fits for ages. It's a real boost to be able to read other teams' mail when they can't read yours. But I can't figure it out. Even with the code problem, this game was pretty even until just after Sven was expelled. I mean Violet Pod was stiff competition. Prince Kvran grew up at court, politics is the air he breathes. But Gray Pod, us, White Pod, UV2 Pod, Aqua Pod—we were all about the same level. It was a very multi-polar game."

"White Pod?"

"Yeah. They're gone. Folded a few tendays before finals last term. UV2 still exists, but they're a very minor player now. Gray Pod and us, we're on about the same level, but we're definitely second tier to Violet Pod now."

"So, I've been wanting to ask, but…"

Tkal quirked one of his imaginary eyebrows.

"How did Sven get himself expelled?"

"You know, even *I* haven't been able to find out. Not exactly. The official story is…" Tkal inhaled and switched over to the most ridiculously officious voice, "'Behavior unbecoming a student of Shel Matkei Academy, resulting in denial of right to matriculate.'"

"What does *that* mean? 'You've been so bad we don't want your name on our diploma'?"

"Exactly. It's more a result than a cause. But it had to be something to do with the simulation, and really serious to get that result. Serious enough to send him to prison in the real world."

"Or get him executed?"

"Or that." Tkal stared off into the distance. "I've tried to get something more, but no one in administration will say a word more than that. All we have is guesses and suppositions. But whatever he did, it hurt. We've been fighting for our existence as a pod ever since. And nothing we do seems to get us ahead."

"Could the nanoprion have had anything to do with it?"

"Oh believe you me, we've searched for anything left over from that. Enemwenu even wiped the system. Twice. Hii went over every file before restoring it—history files on the pod, homework, diaries, war games simulators, communications systems, entertainment files. Absolutely nothing turned up, at least nothing that could have anything to do with our string of disasters. The only benefit was having the computers run faster than ever after Enemwenu scrubbed out every little leech file and unneeded bit of code."

"So you don't know what he did, only that he didn't break the code, and probably *did* do something that hurt you badly."

Tkal frowned.

"What?"

"I just wish you'd you'd finally think of yourself as part of this pod."

"What? Because I said 'you'?"

"Yes. You're still counting yourself as an outsider, as disconnected, separate."

David rolled his eyes. "Sorry if my pronouns offend you."

Tkal sighed.

Neither of them spoke again till they were in the lift.

"I need you to prepare a report on this meeting, and another one on the current state of our coding and code breaking for the next meeting."

"When is it?"

"Day after tomorrow."

"I'll have it ready."

Seven

Hurdles and Pitfalls

Tkal adjourned the meeting.

David jumped up, shot Tkal a look that could kill, and made straight for their quarters.

Gronorgh crossed rippling, corded forearms like gnarled mahogany tree trunks over his massive chest and made that gravelly Gravgurdan laughter sound. "Looks like there's some fire mixed with his water after all. Beware lest you die in your sleep, Tkal." Then he laughed like an avalanche of ringing pebbles.

The door snapped shut behind David. He threw his netbook, shattering it against the wall.

The door snapped open as Tkal followed him into their quarters. "What was that?"

"What?" David rounded on Tkal.

"That temper fit?"

"I didn't ask to be here."

"No, I asked for you."

"And I should thank you for that?"

"Yeah, I think you should." Tkal flashed one of his smiles.

"You, you…"

"What?"

"Arrogant, motherless, *Fgaln ki vkirl!*"

The smile vanished from Tkal's face, and the glitter left his golden eyes.

"Hey, I may be many things, but I am *not* a…'a spawn of the Dark One.'"

David clenched and unclenched his hands a couple of times, then dropped his head. "Sorry."

"I don't know what this is about, but you need to cool it." Tkal stooped and picked up a fragment of David's netbook. "Dude, you've got a temper as bad as Gronorgh's. Thank the Eternal you're not as strong."

"And he's better at controlling his."

"He's also very good at provoking others. Right now, you're his favorite target. It used to be spread around a bit more evenly. Though Sven did get an extra helping."

"Not as much as he deserved, it seems."

"Don't be too harsh, David. Let Gronorgh do that."

"No, Tkal. Gronorgh's right! Sven knew something. A big something. I think he'd broken the code…or knew how to at the very least."

Tkal cocked his head and narrowed his eyes. "What makes you say that?"

"It's right here." David grabbed a fistful of printouts, and threw them on his bed. "Look." He riffled through the wad and pulled a page from the mess. "See?"

Tkal took the page and frowned at it. "Yeah, I remember that one. It's one of the dead ends."

David puffed his cheeks and blew out a puff of air. "It's the first of them. And it's the best of them. And he never went back to it."

"Why should he? …You mean…?"

"I mean this one leads to the answer, and Sven knew it!"

"You're saying he deliberately backed away?"

"I don't think he did. I think he found it."

"David, think about what you are saying."

"I have thought about it. *You* think about it. Look at the date stamp on that file again."

Tkal looked. "470:10:36. That's—"

"Just before things started to get really bad for you guys. About two tendays later is when the attacks on your shipping lanes got really intense."

"Well…"

"That's enough time for him to figure out the code alone…once he had the key to how it works."

Tkal blinked. "So, you can have it for us in two tendays?"

David swept the printouts from his bed, scattering them. "No."

Tkal wrinkled his brow in a very Human gesture. "But?"

"I don't know what he did to get this. It's the only one with no documentation. No notes."

"Sorry. I tried to copy as much as I could find, to save whatever I could salvage for you."

"I don't think you could have copied it. I think he destroyed it a long time before he uploaded that nanoprion. Probably right after he broke the code and took his results to Kvran."

"You've been listening to Gronorgh too much."

"You forget. I knew Sven, too. We were roommates my second quarter. He got a severe reprimand that semester for blackmailing a Traiqi student he caught cheating on an exam. It was all handled very quietly, but roommates hear things. He was on permanent probation after that. I kept my ear open from then on and watched him. He had other less-than-honest things he was involved in. I caught bits and pieces here and there."

"And you didn't turn him in?"

"And if he had covered his tracks well enough? I had to live with him. It was miserable enough when he thought I was an idiot. If he had thought I was on to him…well, he'd have found a way to make it look like it was me, or he and his friends would have…" David shivered.

"Yeah, you might be right, but David, you let him go free doing… whatever he was doing."

"He got caught eventually, didn't he?"

Tkal sighed. "So you think he broke the code and then went to Kvran. For what? Money?"

"That'd be my guess. Sven loved the stuff. He probably asked for a tidy sum to keep it under his hat, and got it. Then Kvran probably started paying him for info."

Tkal hissed. "Get Enemwenu in here."

David raised an eyebrow and started for the door.

"Wait. Get the others, too. The meeting is reconvened. I'll be right there."

David hurried out to regather everyone. He went first to the room next door, the one shared by Gronorgh and Dai-Soln. He palmed the door chime.

"Enter."

David stepped just far enough inside to keep the door from closing.

Dai-Soln's fronds stood out parallel to his shoulders. "Oh, David. What are you doing here? You never come to visit."

It was true. David had never been inside this room. He was only just barely inside now. "Wh-where is Gronorgh?"

"He went out, I think."

"Can you find him quick? Tkal's reconvened the meeting."

"What?"

"It's back on!" David shouted over his shoulder as he dashed back out to the common room.

Ten standard minutes later, everyone but Tkal had reassembled in the common room.

"So, where is he?" said both Gronorgh and Shintikaisen.

"You know what they say about great minds, but I'd've never suspected you two," said Tkal as he emerged from his dorm room with David's stack of printouts under his arm.

Gronorgh glared.

"What does that mean?" asked Shintikaisen.

"David will tell you later," he answered with a golden-eyed wink at David. "Okay, sorry to call you all back so fast, but I just had a very interesting talk with David."

Gronorgh leaned back, making the chair groan under his weight. "If this is going to be another one of your fairness and equality speeches…"

"Call me Johnny One Note. But no. This is far more interesting. It looks like David has proved you right Gronorgh, at least to my satisfaction."

Everyone sat up, leaned in, or assumed whatever their equivalent posture was.

"You have my attention." Gronorgh gave David a strange look which he couldn't interpret.

"David has found enough evidence to finally convince me that we've all been right in suspecting Sven of treachery."

Shintikaisen leaned in closer, angling an ear at David. "What has he got?"

"It's still not enough to go public with, or to take to the administration, but it *is* enough for me to authorize us to start pushing back. Hear David." He turned and gestured for David to stand. "Show them." And he handed over the huge stack of papers.

David spread them out randomly across the table.

"We've seen these before," Gronorgh rumbled, "and they still look like garbage."

David indulged a smile that had nothing to do with pleasure. "That's because they are. All of them. Except this one." David held up the copy he'd shown Tkal moments earlier.

Fthofsis hovered over David's shoulder. "It still looks incomprehensible to me," it said through its voder.

"Oh, it's not decoded correctly, but it's close. It's on the right track. And I have no idea how it was done."

"Well, *that's* helpful," said Gronorgh, and he slumped back in his chair.

"Actually it *is* helpful, Gronorgh. Hear him out. Go on David. Tell them what you told me."

"Well, the reason I don't know how this result was achieved is, it's the only one out of all of these *dozens*…" He scattered the papers even more, spilling them onto the floor, sending a few fluttering across the room. "The only one that doesn't have *any* documentation."

"We lost a lot of stuff in Sven's info dump. That nanoprion he programmed ate through scores of files," said Enemwenu, pulsing hii's head-body and going slightly off-color.

"It was a really nasty bit of malware, but stopped before we lost everything. Which we would have without your computer skills." Shintikaisen reassured hii.

David waved the printout. "But you didn't lose this to the nanoprion. This file is practically untouched, and it is the only one out of all of these, and dozens more, without even a fragment of documentation, not even a word.

"I don't think so. He's acting. But I guess you're right. He is bigger than you."

Tkal really could have left that last part off.

"He's going to pull something."

"How can you know that?"

"I just do." David twiddled his skewers.

When the youth returned with their meats and quickly retreated, David realized that he had ordered way too much. "You want part of this, Tkal. There's no way I can eat this much." Then he froze, remembering another random bit about Pherlatiz social customs: not eating everything on your plate was really insulting.

Tkal started to reach across with his skewer then froze. He looked David in the face. "Okay. You were right. He pulled something. I can't help you unless we both want to seriously insult the kitchen. You'll have to choke it all down, or not. How far do you want to take this?"

"It's already gone too far."

Tkal hissed.

"What? You're not mad at me for not wanting to start a fight about too much meat on my plate, are you?"

"No. That weasel was watching from the door to see if we flubbed this. David, if you can eat that at all…"

David looked at the mound of sliced meat on his plate. "I'll do my best." He moaned and started eating.

This had to be the worst meal ever. Well, except for that Thanksgiving when Ivan and Greg had been at the orphanage. Second worst meal. This was the second worst. He really hoped the waiter hadn't thought to… No, he couldn't let his mind go there. He could barely swallow after he thought of that. Fortunately, the meat on his plate right now was delicious, and that helped to banish the other thought.

David amazed himself by finishing the whole plate. He'd never eaten so much meat—maybe not so much of anything—in his life. He felt like he might be sick later, if his sides didn't split first, but he had gotten it all down.

Then the soup arrived.

David waited to groan until the door closed behind the waiter.

"Oh, come on. It isn't *that* much," said Tkal.

"Maybe for you. This is like a week's food for me."

"No wonder you're skinny. You should gain some weight after this."

David supposed that was meant to be encouraging, but the look on Tkal's face gave the lie to his jesting tone. He was genuinely worried.

David dipped his little ladle-like spoon into the soup and took a cautious sip. Nothing. *This* was two-circle sour and two-square spicy?

Tkal saw his face. "What?"

"Nothing."

"No. What?"

"It's just…they consider this sour and spicy? I've had tarter lemonade."

Tkal glanced toward the kitchen to be sure the waiter wasn't watching and slipped his spoon into David's bowl. He sipped. "That isn't even half-strength. Don't eat it. Just lay your spoon down across the bowl and leave it."

"But…?"

"Do it."

David really didn't want to eat the watery mess, so he did as Tkal said and waited for the youth to return with the desserts.

"Has the customer decided not to eat the soup?"

"The customer has not received the correct soup," Tkal said, standing up and taking charge of the situation. "Perhaps Standard is not well understood. *Nef shitai sigal phener tophaz.*"

The youth's eyes glazed over and sort of crossed. "Right away. Immediately." He scooped up David's bowl and rushed back to the kitchen.

The cook came out, carrying the same bowl, with the waiter following submissively behind. "The customer of this soup?"

"*Nem phezat,*" 'No customer', was Tkal's answer. "*Sem* Standard *nishizal phezan.*"

"Working here requires Standard. Standard is spoken and understood."

Tkal gestured at David. "But this friend ordered full-strength."

The cook eyed the waiter, retrieved a ladle from a pocket and tasted. He spit the soup back into the bowl, and began a stream of abuse and invective that David tried not to translate. It seemed the waiter was a nephew and only

And it's the best attempt of them all. It's still only a partial decode, but he was on the right track here. I just wish I knew what track he was on."

"So how does this help us prove anything?" Shintikaisen asked, twitching both ears.

Tkal stood and reached for the paper in David's hand. "It doesn't really…until you see what David saw. Look at it closely." He passed it to Enemwenu, who passed it on. It was passed from tentacle to hand around the table with varying degrees of confusion, interest, or disappointment, until it reached Dai-Soln.

He was just handing it off to Gronorgh when he snatched it back and nictitated several times. "The date stamp! This is about the time of the first big attacks on our shipping."

"Let me see that!" Gronorgh reached over and snatched the paper from Dai-Soln. The page tore in his grip. He let out a roar like a lion in the throes of fury. "That treacherous little piece of Human scum!"

Tkal frowned. "Yes, and it took another Human to find him out."

Gronorgh growled. "Perhaps." And he eyed David suspiciously.

Dai-Soln spread his fronds. "So what do we do now? What *can* we do?"

"That," said Tkal, "is what we need to decide. But I am declaring Violet Pod not just competition. From here on out, they are Enemy Number One."

Thinking about the problem and nothing else for the last hour and a half had given David a splitting headache. He headed to the common room to see if he had any painkillers. Three days had passed, and he still had nothing new on the code-breaking front. He went straight to his cabinet, grabbed a couple of pills, and opened the chiller for some juice. He didn't even notice that the common room was occupied, till after he had swallowed the pills and turned around.

Gronorgh sat back and propped his massive arms behind his head, stretching the leather of his jerkin across his chest with a creaking noise that gave David the willies. He seemed to be talking to Dai-Soln who had his head in that game of his.

When he gave up, David took the opportunity to slip in a question. "Um, Dai-Soln? Do you have those notes I asked about yesterday?"

No response. Only a muttered curse at the game.

"Dai-Soln!" Gronorgh practically shouted.

Dai-Soln fumbled the handset. "What? I'm in the middle of this game!"

David could sympathize. That shout had nearly given him a heart attack, and it wasn't even directed at him.

Gronorgh uncrossed his arms. "I have been speaking to you for several standards, and you did not hear me."

"Impossible. I would have heard you if you had said anything."

Red-shimmer Gold-streak rippled with color and her voder spoke, "No, Dai-Soln, he speaks truth. He has been speaking to you for some time. And I do not believe you ever noticed when David tried to ask you for your notes from some meeting."

"What?"

"Or when I asked you to assist me with retrieving my food stuffs from the upper cabinet."

"You did? Really?" Dai-Soln's fronds waggled in confusion. "I promise, I did not hear you."

"You've had your mind air-locked to that game for hours," Gronorgh rumbled.

"Not…hours? What time is it?" His fronds stiffened and obsidian eyes stared unblinking.

"Day cycle 6:00," Red-shimmer Gold-streak replied.

That set his fronds vibrating and rustling like autumn leaves. "Day cycle 6:00? I missed a class!"

Gronorgh and Red-shimmer Gold-streak exchanged a look.

Gronorgh started pontificating about irresponsibility and how ridiculous handset games were, but Dai-Soln leapt from the seating center, shoved the game into Gronorgh's hands, and dashed from the room at full tilt.

Gronorgh looked down at the game in his hand, up at the closed door, then back down at Red-shimmer Gold-streak. He shrugged. She turned black all over.

David just stood there.

Just then, the game came alive in Gronorgh's hand as the start-up screen invited him to start his adventure. He pulled back to throw the game down, but stopped. He turned his head toward the door and narrowed his eyes. He heaved a breath somewhere between a sigh and a huff of disgust, looked back down at the screen and followed the prompts.

Gronorgh glanced down at Red-shimmer Gold-streak, who was rippling colors in random non-patterns. "Well, I'm curious. If Dai-Soln finds this thing *that* interesting, there must be *something* to it."

Red-shimmer Gold-streak burbled a muddy almost-color that it's voder didn't bother trying to translate. She went back to composing on her netbook via the keyped under her hundreds of typing feet.

"Blackness of night and a gap in the floor!" Red-shimmer Gold-streak exclaimed through her voder as she pulsed with angry color.

Gronorgh glanced up from the game. "Isn't that pretty foul language for you people?"

Red-shimmer Gold-streak went muddy. "Sorry. My netbook just glitched and dumped a page and a half of this report."

Gronorgh laid the game aside and leaned down to look at the netbook where it lay on the floor in front of Red-shimmer Gold-streak. "It looks fine to me."

"Sure, it does now, but it just dumped my work. Now I have to type it all over, and Standard is such a pain to type at a reasonable speed."

Gronorgh stood and shrugged. He walked into the food prep area and pulled a handful of Dai-Soln's beetles from the chiller. He turned and walked back toward his room munching noisily. As he passed, he bumped David's shoulder hard enough to nearly unbalance him. "*Oops,*" he said in English, without looking up from Dai-Soln's game.

When Dai-Soln had learned that David was presenting a paper for a linguistics panel, he had decided that politeness, and curiosity, demanded that he attend and offer congratulations on the results. He very much hoped it would not be necessary to offer condolences. David was not a bad sort, just rather timid and unsure of himself. Gronorgh had mocked him as a "flickering candle." That wasn't such an inaccurate description. There was fire there, but it had not yet burst into full flame. David had been a great help to Dai-Soln. When completing the excessively complex make-up work Supradoctor Tal Hatlir had assigned him for missing class, David had supplied information that cut his search times in half. Dai-Soln should have taken care not to displease the chancellor of the academy, especially not when he was nearly three hundred years old and one of the few remaining members of one of the founding races. He took a seat about midway back in the lecture hall. He hoped it wouldn't be too boring.

Well over an hour later, just after David had completed his presentation, Dai-Soln left the symposium. He was somewhat in shock and nictitating erratically as he pondered. That was a David he had never seen before. That was no candle flickering in the wind; this David was a blazing inferno. David's paper had been a very technical discussion of some problem in the normal voder translation of some very specific type of pronoun construction—or rather the placement of that construction, and why David thought the voder programming regularly mistranslated this particular thingy in B-G-2-3, Red-shimmer's language. David's arguments had seemed well laid out and logical, at least to the extent that Dai-Soln could follow them—the paper was very technical and filled with linguistic jargon that flummoxed Dai-Soln. Who could have guessed how complicated linguistic terminology really could get? At times, it was like trying to follow a discussion of sub-photonic physics. But the structure of the argumentation had seemed sound. Who would expect anything less from David?

As soon as David had finished reading the paper, however, someone in the audience, a Chiurdoun who Dai-Soln knew from somewhere, had launched into denouncing the paper, top to bottom, attacking every part of it. David had fired back. And *fire* was the only word for it. He was like an atomic furnace burning to ash every word that came from his opponent's mouth. David confidently gave no quarter, none at all, to his foe. When one of the professors on the panel had supported a point made by the Chiurdoun, David had been just as vigorous in his defense of his position against that august personage. In the end, the panel had suggested that David rewrite the paper to include the clarification of several points, as had been done during the discussion, then submit the paper for peer review and publication.

Dai-Soln spread his fronds. He suddenly remembered where he had met the Chiurdoun. It was at the Taisiran Royal Court. They had spoken once or twice at business functions while the Chiurdoun's mother was negotiating a deal with the Court for a contract to supply voders. *Htezakh!* Perhaps it had not been wise for David to be so impassioned in his defense of his paper. Without knowing how or why, David had quite likely made a real-world enemy today. His paper could damage the very business that Chiurdoun stood to inherit.

Dai-Soln spotted Gronorgh at the end of the hall. "Gronorgh, I need to speak with you. Have you time?"

Eight

No Man Is an Island

"David, how long have we been meeting?" Dean Haerkarn asked.

"About six tendays."

"Six tendays. And in all that time you have yet to open up to me."

David tried to look utterly innocent. "What do you mean? I answer all your questions."

She held her ears immobile. "Yes, you answer my questions and not a word more."

David opened his mouth, then closed it as Dean Haerkarn continued.

"I was going over transcripts of our conversations, and I realized that there were dozens of places where I would have pressed you for more information if you had given me one word less in answer to my query." She stood and paced over to the book shelves. "You are very skilled at limiting what you reveal about yourself. Very skilled at reading your opponent—that is how you see me isn't it?—and giving her or him just enough to satisfy. And not a drop more."

"I—"

She angled an ear back at him. "Wait, I'm not finished. You know, that is a *very* useful skill to have as a diplomat. I'm beginning to think this really is a good field for you." She turned to face David. "But it is *not* a good relationship building strategy. I have rarely met one so young with walls so high. I have underestimated you." She raised a finger. "A very dangerous thing to do when one is at war. If you can make your opponent underestimate you, you have an instant advantage. Again, very useful for a diplomat, but potentially hurtful to friendships."

She ran a finger across the screen of her netbook. "You amaze me. I was checking on how you are dealing with your course load since it is extra heavy and can be quite a source of stress to any student. In the course of checking on you, I found that your grades are remaining quite high." She nodded approval. "So, I thought I would check your library activity to get an idea of whether you are overwhelming yourself to maintain this level of performance. Your use seemed extraordinarily high, and so I thought I had found the source of much of your stress…"

"No, no, I—"

"Let me finish. But I realized after just a quick look that only a minimum of your library activity had anything to do with your course work. You were finding ample time for leisure reading on an astounding variety of topics. You have a wide range of interests."

David sensed an opportunity to sidetrack the conversation. "Everything is interesting in small doses and many things in depth."

"Like me?"

"What?" His voice broke.

"You studied me."

"I don't…don't, ah…"

"Don't give me that. I have eyes even if I have no ears or nose."

David couldn't help but smile slightly at the Trelkairni idiom.

"Immediately following our first meeting, you downloaded a number of Trelkairni novels—several classics followed by several contemporary. You then read a sociological study on non-conformist Trelkairni and a couple of religious texts. Then two of our great philosophers and a study on the role of males in Trelkairni society with special focus on how that affects Trelkairni interaction with other races. You studied me and got a good idea of my cultural background, combined that with your own observations of our first few meetings and quickly figured out just how much information would be enough to avoid giving anything else away."

David crossed his slim arms and frowned till the corners of his mouth met his chin. "I didn't ask to be here."

"No, you didn't. But David, you *need* to be here. You need to learn to relate to other people. One of your writers said, *'No man is an island entire of itself.'* You are trying hard to prove that wrong, but you cannot because it is truth. You have been alone *far* too long. Your psyche was not meant to be alone, not entirely. You need others. You are going to crack if you do not learn to trust."

"I can request a different counselor. It's my right. And I can request these records be sealed. I know how strong the ethics are that govern your profession. You won't be able to communicate any of what you've learned, and I can just say that we had a 'personality conflict' and refuse to elaborate. It will probably take another counselor far longer to get as far as you have. Perhaps long enough for me to graduate before she or he really learns anything."

"Yes, David, that is your right. You can do that. *You* are in control of this situation. But is that what you *want* to do? Why don't you give me a chance to help you?

"Maybe I'm not convinced that this *is* helpful."

"What do you think *would* be helpful?

"How am I supposed to know? You're the stupid doctor!" David's face blanched even as the words left his mouth.

"Finally."

"I'm sorry. I'm sorry, I…"

"No. You finally displayed an honest emotion."

"No, I'm not. I said I'm sorry. I don't believe that, and I can't believe I said that."

"You're not?"

"No, I am *not* angry."

"I did not say you were angry. All I said was that you displayed an honest emotion. You labeled it 'anger.'"

David glared at her and quickly looked away.

"It's okay. You can be angry. You can even be angry at me. I am not indestructible, but I am very strong."

David snickered.

"And a sense of humor, too. David, I learned long ago that life is full of pain, but also full of joy. Sometimes it is easier to see the pain, to feel the pain. But the joy is there too. You just have to look harder to find it sometimes."

David's eyes started to hurt and his nose burned.

"Work with me, and I can help you find the joy in your life."

David didn't respond or look up.

"David?"

He nodded, still without looking up.

"Think about that today, and I'll see you tomorrow at day cycle 6:75, okay?"

David nodded, picked up his netbook and left the office without speaking to the receptionist.

It was late into the sleep cycle when David returned to their quarters, five hours later than Tkal was used to him showing up.

"Oh, there you are. I was starting to get worried about you."

"Sorry. Did I wake you up?"

"No. I just finished an analysis I've been working on. I'd like you to look at it tomorrow. I'm sure I'm missing something, but I'm not sure what it is. I've looked too long and only see the same thing every time. Fresh eyes, fresh perspective, you know."

"Sure."

David removed his shoes and socks, in silence, and placed his netbook on his shelf alongside the others. He started rummaging in his drawer and pulled out his pj's.

"How does pizza taste?" Tkal asked.

David turned and faced Tkal. "You've lived in New York your whole life and never had pizza?"

Tkal shrugged. "I can't eat it. Yeast. I have a potentially lethal reaction to yeast. Most of my people do. Some nasty protein in the cell walls that we can't deal with. Causes an outrageous allergic reaction."

"Well, if you've never eaten bread…"

"I've eaten matzoh," Tkal offered, trying to be helpful.

"What, those Jewish crackers? Not the same."

"So I've been told," he sighed. "I tried soda bread once or twice, but the medicine I have to take to negate any possible yeast in there leaves a funny aftertaste."

"Soda bread is different from pizza crust too. It's sweeter."

"Yeah, it seems like every kind of bread tastes different. I hate being left out."

"It suits me fine." David snarled.

"What? That I can't eat bread?"

"No, being left out."

"Can I ask you a question?"

"I'd rather you didn't."

"Why do you try so hard to be alone?"

"I said I didn't want you to."

"Well, you don't have to answer, but I still wonder. I suppose I could just make up my own answer and assume whatever I want like the others do. But I have this thing about the truth. I always prefer it to a lie."

David went to the shower room and changed into his pj's.

"Gronorgh thinks it's because you're weak." Getting no response, he continued, "Gronorgh thinks everything is because someone else is weak. But he's wrong."

"Well, I'm not exactly an athlete," David said, as he returned to their room, sort of shrinking back into his body.

"Gronorgh forgets that even his own people say there are twelve kinds of strength, and only six of those are even remotely physical."

David said nothing.

"Shintikaisen thinks you are cute. Kinda like a pet. Because you 'know your place as a male.'"

"Which means she takes my side when Gronorgh attacks in the meetings."

"But that only lowers you even more in his sight. You let others fight your battles."

"I don't want to fight anyone. I didn't ask to end up in a pod."

"But you're Diplomacy Track. This is the goal of the program."

"I was undeclared until you forced the issue. Then Dean Haerkarn trapped me into this."

"Trapped? But I looked through the public files of likely candidates. Yours said you are here on a scholarship from the Terran Diplomatic Corps. I asked for you three times before they agreed to review the possibility. I had to fight to get a third-year student assigned to a pod, search out precedents, give proof that your qualifications were as good or better than any fourth-year candidate, interview with all three advisers, *and* meet with the chancellor of the academy."

"You did all that?"

"Yes."

"So that's how I got stuck here."

"I don't understand."

"Just because I accepted the scholarship doesn't mean this is what I want to do. I took the stupid scholarship because I'm poor and didn't have a chance of paying for study at a place like this. I was still hoping to find some other way to pay for my studies when your request cut me off two quarters early. When Dean Haerkarn reeled me in, I had no choice but to accept, and declare my track or lose my funds. I got trapped into this." David pulled back the covers on his bed.

"What about your parents? Couldn't they help?"

David turned his back to Tkal and fluffed his pillow. "Have you ever heard me mention them? Ever?"

"Only in your sleep."

David went rigid. "They're dead. Okay? You satisfied? I don't have to *try* to be alone. I *am* alone. I have no family. No one. No parents, grandparents, aunts, uncles, or living cousins close enough to ship me off to. I grew up in an orphanage, and I took that stupid scholarship because it was my only way out. Well, if I had known it was going to land me here, I'd have turned it down and lived in government housing on minimum wage."

Tkal sat and stared at David for several heartbeats. "No you wouldn't."

"What?"

"You wouldn't have turned it down. Even if you knew you would end up here. You would have had to take the chance and see if there wasn't some way to avoid it. You couldn't have given up the opportunity to do what you love. You'd have been scared to death and still hated getting trapped in this, but you'd have tried it anyway."

David sighed, and his body unclenched. "I guess so."

"So, you're here now. And it's my fault." Tkal looked down at his feet. "What do we do now?"

"It's not your fault. You're right, I would have done it even if I knew this would happen. I guess I sort of did know. I just hoped it wouldn't."

"Well I'm not guilt-free. I did hunt you down and fight the system to get you dragged into this half a year early. You might have avoided the Compound if I hadn't meddled."

They sat in silence for a few moments.

"David, I had no idea. That sort of personal info isn't in the public files."

"It's okay. It all happened a very long time ago."

"So, what do we do now?" He repeated.

"It's late. We go to sleep." David rolled into his bed, pulled the covers over himself ,and waved off his light.

Tkal sat on the edge of his bed for the next two hours, just listening to his own thoughts and David's breathing, until David began to mutter in his sleep. He slipped into his shoes pulled a Tvern robe on over his head and slipped out of the room.

In the morning, David was just finishing getting ready when Tkal came stumbling into the room.

"I looked at that analysis you wanted me to look at. It looks fine to me," David said.

"Oh, thanks. I realized what was wrong with it about three hours after you went to bed. I'm glad it makes sense now."

"Three hours? Did you sleep?"

"Well…"

"Wait, what's all over your hands?"

Tkal quickly pulled his arms up into the big sleeves of his robe.

"Is that wax?"

"I have to get ready for class."

"Why is there wax all over your hands?"

No answer.

"Candles?"

No answer.

"All night?"

"What all night? I don't know what you're talking about."

"I'm talking about you holding burning candles all night. You were, weren't you? Why?"

"I needed to."

"What? Pray? That's the only thing Tvern An use candles for, isn't it? For religious rituals? You were praying all night?"

Tkal sighed. "Yes. But repentance is a private thing."

"Repentance? For what? Not last night, surely?"

Tkal looked away.

"I said it was okay. I don't blame you. You couldn't know. And it was going to happen to me soon anyway. I could have ended up somewhere worse."

"Worse than here with a Gravgurdan warrior who hates you just because you're the same race as the last guy who was…well, Sven was Sven."

"Yes. I could be in Violet Pod now."

Tkal shuddered.

"What?"

"Nothing. Some other time. I need to get a shower and some breakfast before I'm late for class."

David watched Tkal stumble into the shower room. He shook his head, pulled on his jacket, and left for his Transcultrural Literature class. Prayer. What a strange response. And all night. Was it that hard to be forgiven for a little thing like accidentally forcing someone into a corner when you thought you were doing them a favor? He'd have to do some more research into Tvern An beliefs if they were that important to Tkal.

Dean Haerkarn and John Donne were right; no man is an island, not even him. Everything people do affects every being around them, for good or bad.

What he had told Tkal had certainly affected him. There wasn't any way to be completely separate. But being part of *everything* terrified David. Maybe he could be a peninsula, just attached a little bit, and in ways of his own choosing.

Classes had not gone particularly well that day. Dr. Dgan had given them a pop quiz on social customs related to eating, and afterward had singled David out to explain Tvern An rituals. The Tvern An professor obviously expected deep insight from a student with a Tvern An roommate. David had remembered Tkal's gesture over his food that first day in the cafeteria and again at the restaurant. He'd seen it a hundred times since, but had left it a private thing between Tkal and his divinity. He knew it was a thankfulness ritual, a sort of prayer to the Eternal, but he had no idea if the gesture was the whole ritual. Tkal never spoke during the ritual, but the fact that he always looked up while doing it made David think there was more to it.

David had muddled through a description, and Dr. Dgan had prodded him into making some suppositions about significance and non-surface content. It was very intimidating. He didn't intend to get caught flat-footed again. He intended to learn more. Twice in one day he had felt the need for more understanding.

In Comparative Communication Systems class, another professor had zeroed in on David's experience meeting Gronorgh. The class had delved into non-primary communication modes: non-verbal for spoken languages, non-tinctural for Iridian languages like B-G-2-3, and non-manual for gestural languages. Somehow the discussion had drifted to variations in personal space among and within different species, and from there to Gravgurdan posturing and ritual intimidation. David's classmates had laughed at him at several points during his description, but the professor had been merciless, pushing him to continue the story against his will.

So, when he arrived back at his room to find another meeting scheduled for that night, he was less than thrilled. In fact, David had just decided to slip out of the room and skip the meeting when Tkal came barreling in.

"Great, I caught you time. I need you to give us a full update on the code situation at tonight's meeting. Can you have something put together by then? And not just the Violet Pod code, but any others that we're working on as well."

David sighed. "Yeah, sure."

"Great. I've got a presentation on establishing ties with Indigo Pod to give tonight and some of the trade concessions may not set well, so I hope you have some good news."

"Well, other than the Violet situation, everything is going well. We're reading most of the others' codes clearly, even IR4's new one. They just switched three days ago."

"Good."

Tkal had hurried back out and left David alone to prepare another presentation that was sure to draw snide remarks from Gronorgh. He was really tired of Gronorgh's mouth. If it were anyone else, David would have found someway to put an end to it. A couple of times, he had almost launched himself across the table for Gronorgh's throat before remembering that he couldn't even get his hands halfway around the Gravgurdan's massive neck. Gronorgh would have just swatted him out of the air with those hyper-fast, high-g reflexes and left his broken body quivering like jelly on the floor. So he swallowed what remained of his pride again and again, like forcing his own bile back down when his stomach insisted otherwise.

Sometimes David wondered what it must be like to be Tkal. Growing up as an alien on a world full of Humans had to have been strange and lonely. He would have always been an outsider, but somehow it didn't seem like it had touched him. Tkal seemed more attached to Earth than David felt, more in touch with the culture. Maybe Tkal was just one of those people who was never anything but at home. Maybe the difference was that he had grown up in a family and had parents who loved him. Still, school must have been miserable. There couldn't have been many other aliens, unless maybe he had gone to some kind of interplanetary school for the children of diplomats. But if so, how was he so connected to Human culture? The only thing he seemed to have missed out on was pizza. It was hard for David not to feel jealous. But Tkal was so nice, well at least when he wasn't driving David crazy with one of a thousand ways he had of being obnoxious. David could almost dare to think of him as a friend. Almost, but not quite.

No. No matter how much he wanted to believe that, the truth he had to face, and face squarely, was that he was still alone. He might not be an island, but that didn't mean he was connected in any meaningful way either. Being roommates wasn't the same as being friends. But it was close enough that David dreaded the day when Tkal would graduate and go off on the great adventure that awaited him in life, leaving David here to muddle on with whatever roommate he got stuck with. David had to admit that this was pretty good, while it lasted. But he also had to admit that it would end soon enough, and then his life would go back to the way it had been before. This was just a brief interlude before the tide came back in and cut him off once more. It was all well and good for Dean Haerkarn to dish out advice, but the universe didn't work that way. He couldn't just snap his fingers and change the geography of his life. He was meant to be alone and nothing could change that.

He threw together something resembling a presentation on Green Pod's code breaking and on the newest code they were about to implement for their own communications. He hoped it was enough to satisfy Tkal and not embarrass himself in front of the others, because it was all he had the will to prepare. He'd just wing the rest.

Nine

Sing Not, O Stars

David sat on his bed with his pillow propped behind him and his netbook braced on his knees. He had only meant to spend a few standards before dinner scanning files on Tvern An religious customs, but, as he tended to do, he had gotten lost in the labyrinth of research—following one trail after another down the dark and wending paths of knowledge, hunting his prey…what a Gravgurdan way to phrase the thought. When his netbook chimed and he glanced at the time, he realized he would have to run part of the way and make good connections with the lifts to get to his next class on time. Dinner would have to wait till very late, or maybe he'd just skip it and eat a bigger breakfast.

He snatched up his data crystal and a couple more netbooks, dumped everything in his bag and dashed for the door. He jogged across the common room and out to the corridor. He palmed for a lift and fidgeted while he waited for it to arrive. As soon as the doors opened, he slipped inside, ordered "level eleven" and retreated back into his thoughts.

There really was quite a bit more to that dinner ritual of Tkal's than he had realized. When a Tvern An looked up, he or she was talking silently to the Eternal. The gesture conveyed thanks and was the only part that was necessarily connected to the food. The conversation—and apparently the Tvern An did consider it a conversation, with the expectation that the Eternal would speak back in some way or other—the conversation with the Eternal could be about anything, but rarely was that something the food. David had been witness to dozens of these silent "conversations" between Tkal and his god. Tkal ate a lot, and frequently, and David had never noticed him skipping the ritual, so Tkal must be having conversations with this Eternal several times every day.

What did they talk about? What could anyone possibly find to say to a deity that frequently? And did Tkal, and all the other Tvern An followers of the Eternal, really think they were hearing the other side of this conversation?

It was baffling. Tkal was one of the most rational people he knew, or at least he had always thought so. Did he really hear voices five, six times a day? Wouldn't that make him clinically insane? No, Tkal might be many things, but there was no way he was insane. But how could he believe stuff like this, and take it seriously enough to spend most of the night in what David now realized must have been a repentance ritual? No, this was all very real and very important to Tkal.

Most of the non-Human races had religions they took more seriously than many Humans took theirs. Grey Street Orphanage hadn't included any religious instruction. When the topic came up in history or literature classes, it had usually been presented as a curiosity. There were Humans who took faith very seriously; David just hadn't met any of them. But here, Shintikaisen had her little shrine to the Mother in her room. Ael had mentioned Shintikaisen performing rituals in front of it—rituals that often included blood. The Gravgurdanûn never did anything by half measures, so they were deadly earnest about the Twelve. But David had always taken Gravgurdan devotion as being to ideals rather than actual gods—a way of refocusing themselves on the pursuit of strength and the perfecting of strength within themselves, rather than truly worshiping something external and living. Kind of like Platonic forms with a Gravgurdan twist. Alelliawulians had a very complex set of ritual observances and days set aside for particular practices, but they preferred to keep their religious lives very private from the eyes of aliens.

But this constant communication that Tkal practiced…

The lift doors opened and David dashed for class.

On his way back from Conflict Resolution—easily his least favorite class—all David could think about was his stomach rumbling. He guessed he'd have to get something to eat before bed. His body probably did need the food. He'd skipped lunch, and breakfast had been rushed. When he entered the suite, everyone in the common room, which was everyone in the pod, looked at him from where they were pulling chairs and pillars and such into the circle Tkal liked for—oh, no. Not another culture exchange. How could he have forgotten? But Tkal had warned him two days ago. Somehow it had slipped his mind until this very minute. If he'd remembered, he'd have gone to the library, or the arboretum, or the port, or *anywhere* but back to the common room. He wanted to melt through the deck and ooze out onto the floor below. Poetry. Tonight was poetry.

There was no escaping now, so David dropped his bag by the food prep and squatted down to retrieve a netbook. He hurriedly found a seat and started tapping away to find something he could read to the group. Tkal rolled his eyes.

This night it was Ael's turn to start. "I guess I should give some intro to this poem first. Well, no, on second thought I'll just read it and then answer any questions you guys have."

Shintikaisen coughed like a Human.

Ael threw her hands up and rolled her eyes in a ridiculously exaggerated pantomime. "If any of you *beings* have any questions. Better?" She squawked with hands up like the most animated circus barker of all time.

"You mock me?"

Ael made a face in reply. "Now if you will allow me to read?" She composed herself and waited a moment before releasing her inner actress in a soft voice filled with sadness that rose with volume and turned hard and bitter as she read:

Sing not joyfully, O stars,
For I will not sing with you.
Sing not joyfully,
For I was more than one, am less than two.

Sing not sadly, O stars,
I cannot bear the sound.
Sing not sadly.
Give not my heart another wound.

Sing not carefreely, O stars,
For if you do I die.
Sing not carefreely.
Let silence fill the sky.

Sing not, O stars, sing not.

Ael sat back and waited.

"Had she lost her favorite husband?" asked Shintikaisen.

"Or her birth parent, er, mother?" asked Enemwenu.

"Actually, the poet, Gze Oast, was a male," Ael answered. "He was engaged to a woman he had loved since childhood. The night after they celebrated their engagement, she was found drowned in the Pax River. She had fallen over the railing of a bridge when she slipped on the rain-slick cobblestones. The poet came to the place when he was called and saw the stars reflected in the river. He began composing this on the spot. Someone standing by wrote it down as he spoke it."

David had chill bumps.

Gronorgh looked uncomfortable. "Why do poets write so much about the things that absolutely cannot be controlled? The things that are utterly futile and no strength, none whatsoever, can change."

"Maybe because it's these emotions that overwhelm us to the point that they can't be expressed in normal language. If you can say anything at all to explain, it has to be in ritual or poetry."

Everyone stared at David. He wished he hadn't spoken, hadn't realized he was voicing his thoughts until it was too late.

Tkal cleared his throat. "Well, not all poetry is about death and tragedy. It can be about anything really. A lot of Tvern An poetry is about other things.

We are also very fond of concision. Humans have a form called *haiku* that is three lines of five, seven, and five syllables. This Tvern An form is called *kvar*, which just means 'three.' It's also three lines long, but only five, four, and five syllables, so a kvar is three syllables shorter than a haiku. It has to express a complete idea, and the first and second lines should have contrasting or complimentary images, with the third offering some kind of resolution of the scene set up in the first two. Here's one of my favorites. I'll read it in Tvern El first so you can see how short it is, because I just couldn't find or make a translation into Standard that was equally compact." He read:

> *Gen dernal ftilil*
> *Gtarn e kteln gvan*
> *Da tfel dferlnil da*

As he read. A translation in Standard scrolled across the other pod members' screens:

> WHISPERS IN THE DARK
> A CANDLE LIGHTS THE WAY
> TO NEW UNDERSTANDING

David cocked his head. "Candles sure have a lot of meanings in Tvern culture—understanding, the self, love, death, time, hope."

Tkal cocked his head. "Well, yeah, they *can* have all those meanings, but, well, I think death only applies when the candle is snuffed. Otherwise, I guess I'd say the candle represents life at the most basic level, and then all the other meanings branch from that core symbol. So, the understanding here is a spiritual kind of knowing, the kind of knowledge that brings life."

Shintikaisen tapped her nails against each other. "You make your religion sound almost happy—candles and knowledge and life. We have the Great Mother."

Tkal paused, "I must admit I find your Great Mother somewhat… uh…disturbing."

Shinti twitched an ear and shrugged. "That's okay. So do I. So do all of us. She is *not* a gentle mother. She is terrifying. We pray for her *not* to send us visions." She shivered. "Enough of that. I brought two poems and couldn't decide which to share, but I think I know now. I will read this one because it is less…well, no, it is more… Well, I do not need a reason. Hear." She read:

> If by my hand I slay
> My enemy
> Do I become
> The one I slay?
>
> If my hand plunge the knife
> Is my blood
> The price
> My children pay?

Tkal's face took on that not-quite-in-the-same-room-with-everyone-else look that David now knew meant that he was trying to weigh the benefits of saying something that could go very wrong. When Tkal sighed, David winced. Whatever it was, Tkal had decided to go for it.

Gronorgh was just finishing saying something about how a good warrior had to count the cost before entering battle, but once engaged must go all out and let nothing block him from obtaining his goal.

Tkal waited till Gronorgh was winding down, then cleared his throat and waited for Shinti to wave, giving him the floor. "Well, given the differences in cultural context, I think this is very much like the bit of *Hamlet* that David read a couple of tendays ago.

So, this was what Tkal had been weighing. How David wished he had decided to let it pass.

Gronorgh and Shintikaisen cut glances at each other. Tkal struck his chest with his fist, then held his palm out toward Gronorgh. "I'm sorry, Gronorgh, but use of this word will be necessary for open discourse. The muscles along Gronorgh's jaw bunched repeatedly in reply, and his mouth became a thin slit. Was that a nausea reaction?

Tkal looked back to the group. "The poet here is not considering suicide as such, but it seems likely that Trelkairni custom would demand it at some point if the speaker chooses to slay her enemy. Am I correct, Shintikaisen?"

Shintikaisen smiled in a way that looked *shivkhati*. Trelkairni linguists had been arguing about how to translate that word into Standard since Contact. Some said "sadness" was a sufficient translation. Others opted for "anger at the past." Still others liked "nostalgia with dread." Shintikaisen leaned forward. "The poet is recounting a historical event in this poem. And in fact, when the voice of this poem did choose to slay her enemy, she did 'become the one she slew,' or just as bad at least. After her daughters had paid much of the price for her choices, she did try to salvage the situation by...pardon Gronorgh."

He grunted.

"By slitting her own throat before the Council of Mothers. Shinti looked at a spot on the floor somewhat to the left and forward of her left foot. "The voice in the cycle is a good deal more heroic than the actual woman. Literature."

David gestured for the floor. Shinti waved.

"Yes, that is often true, but the job of a poem like this isn't really historical accuracy, is it? It's the transmission of cultural values, right? The teaching of what society expects. And I gather that this one has maintained a place in your culture for a very long time."

Shinti quirked her mouth like an auntie would at discovering her niece had been quite clever. "It has. This cycle has been mother to many deeds more worthy than those of the real Shivrakhatri."

"I'm curious what your other choice was."

"It is actually a better poem. Only kind of mournful and weepy. Typical male poet stuff."

There was plenty of eye rolling, tentacle curling, and going off color from the others, and an impressive grunt from Gronorgh.

Tkal's voice overflowed with ironies. "Well, go ahead and read it. We weepy males simply *have* to hear it now."

"Yes do," said Xtp through it's voder. "We non-male, non-females would very much like to meet this *typical* male you speak of."

Shintikaisen breathed in with a sucking noise to show her exasperation.

Ael giggled in uncharacteristically girly fashion, earning her a sharp look from Shinti. "I will read this in Skrivakhti, the original language, and let Xtp's voder translate as I read. We upgraded it last night with a program to handle this language." She cleared her throat and declaimed:

If you left this home, I would not cry.

If you left this place, I would not weep.

For there is no place for you here.

Yes, there is no home in my heart for your soul.

And tears do not run in a dry riverbed.

And streams do not flow on my face.

The sun does not shine at night.

Nor the moon shed its beams in the day.

There is no home for you in my heart.

None *shehaknichadal* thatit wanders…tears

David creased his forehead. "Wait, I don't understand the last line. And neither did the voder. It came out all garbled. Everything else was clear but then that line…something about a well that wanders or…"

"Ah! You caught it. The last line is completely ambiguous. It is either *Ge sehak ni-chad-al gime-u tivadanu,* 'None place your-soul-for that-it wanders,' or *Ge sehakni cha dalgime utiv a-danu,* 'None well for collect gather the-tears.'"

"And there is no way to be sure which the poet intended." Shinti continued. "At the time he wrote, they didn't use spaces between words. I believe he intended both. Two fitting messages in one line. It is what makes this poem a masterpiece. There are two traditions for writing the last line of this poem, either leaving it all run together as a single word so the reader may divvy it up how she chooses, or writing one of the choices but reading the other."

David got that over-enthused-scholar sound in his voice. "So it's…two complete and fitting messages at the same time. Brilliant."

Enemwenu curled both of hii's tentacles. "It is curious how many of our poems tonight deal with or depend on the mysteries of words. The words of stars, whispers of enlightenment, lines that can—perhaps must—be read more than one way. My own selection carries this theme as well. We are achieving *ullomalmwe,* the 'unconscious harmony,' an 'unplanned unity.' Here is my poem. It was written by Alewenu of Enewalo circa 5893, Alelliawulian calendar." Hii read:

> Ah, words, the vapors of spring in the nostrils of the poet
> Which having risen from the depths of the soul
> Come forth to perfume the humble thoughts of one
> And, thus having risen, find their rest within the bosom of one's friend
> There inspiring other vapors yet more pure
> Each breathing life into the next
> Until that dizzying Empyrean is reached
> Which issues forth from God alone
> And inspires the sacred song God put in each our selves.

Tkal frowned in thought. "I'm not sure I understand this poem. I'm looking at it from two sides. From one side, it says God put a song inside each of us and we can help each other find and sing that song. From the other, it seems almost as if it is saying…I don't know…that we can reach God by our own efforts? Maybe even become or even create God? It's very confusing to interpret. I can agree completely with it from the one angle, but from the other…"

David did *not* want to sit in on a discussion of theology, so he blurted out, "My poem talks about the boastful words on a statue, and the futility of those words." Without pause he launched into "Ozymandias."

> I met a traveller from an antique land
> Who said: "Two vast and trunkless legs of stone
> Stand in the desert. Near them on the sand,
> Half sunk, a shattered visage lies, whose frown
> And wrinkled lip and sneer of cold command
> Tell that its sculptor well those passions read
> Which yet survive, stamped on these lifeless things,
> The hand that mocked them and the heart that fed.
> And on the pedestal these words appear:
> 'My name is Ozymandias, King of Kings:

Look on my works, ye mighty, and despair!'
Nothing beside remains. Round the decay
Of that colossal wreck, boundless and bare,
The lone and level sands stretch far away".

"That was written by Percy Bysshe Shelley, AD 1818 on one of Earth's calendars.

Gronorgh sneered. "Is this meant to insult me? To devalue the Gravgurdan obsession with strength?"

"No, I—I, no, no, that's not what I…I only…"

"Guess again, Human. Our own poets have said the same thing a thousand times. A warrior should celebrate his strength *now* because time robs everyone of his glory. Muscles weaken. Minds fade. Eyes cloud. Ears dull. And after only a few years—who will remember your name? And that's if disease or an even stronger warrior or Chance doesn't cut you off before time even starts to grind you away. That is why we work so hard to accumulate all the strengths we can in the short years we have—hoping we can achieve enough that our names *will* go on for hundreds or even thousands of years. It is all but hopeless, but still we strive, for a few *will* succeed for that while."

David breathed in, teetered on the brink of indecision, then plunged ahead. "That is exactly what this poem is about, though it takes a more dismal view, something along the lines that even if you *do* achieve, time will destroy your name eventually. Another verse that expresses the same idea, only more humorously, is 'On the Vanity of Earthly Greatness'."

The tusks that clashed in might brawls
Of mastodons, are billiard balls.
The sword of Charlemagne the Just
Is ferric oxide, known as rust.
The grizzly bear whose potent hug
Was feared by all, is now a rug.
Great Caesar's dead and on the shelf,
And I don't feel so well myself!

Gronorgh sounded like an avalanche of gravel. "Little Human boy, if you understood those words as a Gravgurdan understands them, you could not hide in your shriveled self like you do. You would be forced to go out and *dare*, to *risk*, to *try* to be something. Your poets write the words, but you fail to feel them deeply enough to affect a change in yourself. The ability to *feel deeply* is one of the Twelve Strengths. You seem to lack this as much as the ability to lift or to endure pain. Humans are sad little people. One of *our* poets said…" and he read:

I wake at dawn, too weak to lift myself.
I force my will upon those far larger than me.
In morning light, I wrestle with the demon, Pain
Until the river of tears dries to desert sands.
And under heat of noon sun my skin darkens,
My muscles shine, and I make mockery of every riddle.
The God of Sweat extracts his due;
I work till none else can stand,
And then the fever comes, and emotion learns to roar.
With all the Canons memorized,
I kill one who would challenge for my mate.
A punch that cripples and one more that kills.
A wily foe learns my guile can lay him just as low,
When visions speak to me, and I twist all his plans to his own demise.
As night falls, in one last rage against time,
I create a monument to all I have been and all I have done,
But as the work takes form, my muscle fails.
I lose the fight. The weights no longer rise.
My mind slips and things forgot, are remembered by my foe.
Emotion pries itself from my grip and makes of me a fool.
Little pains bring tears, and a boy without three names
Overtakes me in the streets.
Then, before my work is done,
Death, who is mightier than us all, and all of us combined,

Comes and crushes the breath from my lungs
Leaving but a husk to wither beside, and with, the unfinished art.

"This, Human," Gronorgh continued, "this is the fate we all must both face and fight. If ever you realized this, you could make more of yourselves."

Dai-Soln stamped his foot and flicked his nictitating membranes. "I have a poem." He read:

Insight blazes like a lamp.
Knowledge gathers like "moths."
Wisdom illuminates all around.
But if the eye be blind what profit to the man?

Gronorgh opened his mouth, closed it, opened it again. "Are you agreeing with me or mocking me? Your poem could be taken either way."

Dai-Soln shook his fronds. "Ambiguity is the goal of this type of verse."

Gronorgh frowned. "This is not exactly an answer, small one."

Dai-Soln stroked his fronds back along the sides of his head. "No, I suppose it is not. What did Red-shimmer bring?"

Random bubbles of color popped all along Red-shimmer's skin— laughter. Then her voder hummed to life, "I did not prepare anything tonight. I knew this exchange would run long. I defer to Xtp."

Why hadn't David thought of that approach? David's stomach rumbled, reminding him that he still hadn't eaten dinner. And in David's experience with Qttx poetry, it was pretty difficult to make sense of—lots of biological and cultural references that weren't clear at all to non-Xttg. As much as he wanted to learn more about this style, he really was hungry and hoped this didn't take too long.

Xtp turned its voder off, spread its second arms in the welcome gesture and began:

jp gg npjk xj ccjx
kk dtt mmp cjxx gdmk
kk gg ckqx pg mn
xj cxdx mg ccd dd
ccx ggxd ktp nd xcld

No one was quite sure where to start, so everyone just waited for Xtp to give some direction to the discussion. It bowed its head and twisted it slightly to each side. "I have programmed my voder with a rather literal translation of this poem and will allow it to speak that now."

I sit myself inside the tree and speak with the star.

Do I and the moon see as fools under the darkness?

Shall I drink mercy with you or

Speak I lies before the egg and

Really lying to and with myself defile my sensory ridge with honey?

Yep, that was just about what David had thought it said. He hadn't quite caught that double preposition on the pronoun in the last line, to-with-myself, and the line with the moon in it hadn't been quite clear as to who was doing what with whom, but other than that... It was quite possible to understand every word of one of these poems and still have no idea what it was really talking about.

Shinti leaned in and tapped on her knee. As soon as Xtp looked her way, she nodded and spoke, "Before I even begin to ask for the meaning of this poem, I wish to know the form. I do not speak your language, but I only heard a string of sounds."

Xtp rasped in a way that served it as a sigh. "The structure is carefully defined. You must have five words in each line. The last word in the first line defines the sound pattern, and that pattern climbs through the next five lines. If this poem were longer, the last word of the fifth line would define the next pattern."

Shinti pursed her lips and flared her nostrils, "What?"

That earned more rasping from Xtp. The words *ccjx*, *cjxx*, *ckqx*, *cxdx* and *ccx* are alliterhymes. They start and end with the same sounds. They are the last, next to last, middle, second and first words in their lines. This is the pattern." It spread its first arms. "Will no one address the meaning? David?"

Oh fantastic. David would kill Xtp for this. Or go home on the next bargain freighter. Or both. "Well, I think most of us are probably a little confused by this poem. Some of the lines are pretty difficult for us aliens to understand." He frowned. "I think I understand the bit about drinking mercy, as long as it simply means choosing to show mercy. Maybe even when it is very difficult?"

Xtp waggled its head in joy. "It does mean this. It is a reference to the ceremony where two, who have cause to harm each other, instead drink together from the same vessel and choose to live in peace. It is a hard drink to drink. And it does not always set well on the stomach, but it is a very strong medicine which cures a great many diseases of the gut and the mouth parts and palps."

Tkal frowned Human-style. "This is the kind of cultural information that David was saying that we lack for really understanding this poem. Personally, I am baffled by the part about putting honey on your head!"

There were general postures of agreement all around the circle. Gronorgh extended his open palm. "And the part about lying to eggs? What does this signify? Are your people aware inside their eggs? Before hatching?"

"That's some kind of religious reference, I think." David bit his lip, hoping he hadn't just made a fool of himself.

Xtp rasped its second arms down its thighs. "Yes, the egg is a reference to the Promise To Be, one of the most important prophecies of our faith, one that will be completed very near the end of all things. To tell lies in the presence of a representation of the Egg is a very serious blasphemy."

"And the part about the honey?" Tkal prompted.

Our sensory ridges are very sensitive organs of perception, but they are not for tasting. Honey is very sweet, but it belongs in the mouth. If I put this good thing in the wrong place, it will damage my perception of truth. And if these words only seem sweet like honey, but are themselves sweetened lies, then I am deceived, and lose a part of my perception, and miss the taste…and I have done all this damage to myself."

Gronorgh rumbled. "Far too subtle. Truth should not be hidden under layers and layers of metaphor, but displayed openly like weapons or like the strength of one's arms."

Of course he would look at it that way. David's stomach rumbled loud enough that the entire group heard it. After that, Tkal wrapped the exchange up pretty quickly and dismissed. David was so hungry he could eat some of Dai-Soln's beetles or one of Xtp's dried roots!

Ten

Marking Time

David pulled the collar of his jacket up around his neck and made sure all the seals were tight before entering the level-four auditorium. He had no desire to spend the evening shivering. He took stock of the frigid room and found a comfortable cushion, all covered with gold embroidery, near the back. At the front of the room was a huge, ornate hourglass full of deep-violet sands. The sands appeared to have run two-thirds of their course, and the air was full of the heady perfume of incense and the dance of sacred music.

The atmosphere was charged with the expectation of awaiting a familiar and sacred event for the Hopherl—and the anticipation of the exotic for David and the other guests—at the Renewal of Covenant ceremony. The ceremony marked the Winter Solstice, the New Year on Phernulo, homeworld for the Hopherl. David waited quietly with the others for the start of the ceremony celebrating the beginning of longer days as a symbol of Hrelun's Covenant of Renewal—the promise of eternal life, between the Hopherl and their god.

He shoved his gloved hands into his jacket pockets and massaged the warmer packs stowed there till the chemicals mixed and heated up. The thermos of hot chocolate he drank before coming was already wearing off in this room where his breath curled away in tiny fog banks. The lights dimmed as the music became a whisper, like a dying wind, and the first chant began.

Three hours later, David left the Hopherl New Year ceremony, rubbing his cheeks to warm them, with the nagging feeling that he had just witnessed something important. He had enjoyed the complex beauty of the rituals and the opportunity to hear two more of Phernulo's living languages in use. The language used in the first two chants was especially different from Standard Pherlatiz. It allowed initial vowels and seemed to have tones. Though it wasn't really easy to tell in a chant, the brief spoken segment had definitely sounded tonal.

That was fascinating in its own right, but there was something more. There was something…something David couldn't quite put his finger on, but why did it feel so significant? His finger. He stopped dead in the corridor and stared down at his hands, rubbing each other to get the cold out. Of course. The priest had made all those grand gestures. And the dancers. They had used some of the same gestures, only more of them. And that singer, too. It hadn't been waving its arms, it had been *signing*. A fourth language had been happening all around him and he hadn't realized it till now. What had they signed and when? David whipped out his netbook and started writing descriptions of the gestures he could remember and the context of their use. Two-tenths of an hour later, he realized that he was sitting, sweating in his still sealed jacket, hunched over tailor-style, in the middle of a public corridor, scribing notes. He scrambled to his feet, opened his jacket, and started back towards his quarters with a list of about fifteen gestures he could remember well enough to describe. Could *this* be the key to the puzzle? It had to be. They were coding more than one language simultaneously. No wonder all they got was gibberish! And somehow a key to it all lay in this data he held in his hands. David looked back at his descriptions as he walked. They would serve as a memory tool, but they were gibberish as far as recording a text. He needed to find a resource fast. How did one record an unknown visual-gestural language? He sprinted straight for Green Room.

Tkal fumbled his netbook and nearly fell out of his chair as David burst into the room shouting, "Eureka!"

"You-who?"

"Eureka!"

"Eureka? Eureka! You found it? You've got the code?"

"I've got the code! Or at least I've figured out what it is—why we haven't been able to break it. It's layered. Two, maybe more, languages simultaneously."

Tkal's hope fell. "No, we tried that before. You know that. It didn't work. We've tried every combination of languages we could think of, in every pattern we could conceive. Just gibberish. All we get is gibberish no matter what we try," he sighed. "And Green Pod has sunken lower in the standings than we have been in the last thirty-five standard years." His shoulders sagged with the burden of failure.

"No, I'm not talking about any kind of sequence. I'm talking about simultaneous. Not taking turns. Both, or all, however many, at the same time."

"What? Can that be done?"

"I think so. I think I've just seen it. And I think I remember it happening on Earth, back before genetic engineering and nanotech eliminated deafness. Deaf people had visual-gestural languages, and hearing people who would translate for them. Some of those translators could speak the local dialect *and* the gestural language at the same time. They even had a special name for it."

"Wow, you're talking about *old* records. Can you access them from here? You'd need Old Earth Archaeological Archives. And you're talking about stuff from when? Back before the Purge Wars?"

"Yes, but there's an old colony world that went independent and mostly isolationist way back. It was settled entirely by Deaf people who saw the new gene and nanotechs as a threat to their language and culture. They'd probably have it in their historical files. Who knows? It could even still be in use. I mean, even if they engineered hearing out of their population, they might occasionally have hearing children born, maybe in numbers great enough that they evolved spoken language again and continued or reinvented the two-languages-at-the-same-time thing."

"What's the name of this planet?"

"I can't remember. It was a long time ago when I heard about it. Let me check the data base of Homo sapiens-populated worlds." David dropped his netbook on his desk with a clatter, and nearly tipped his chair over as he pulled it out to sit down and get at his terminal. Fifteen standard minutes later, part of that with Tkal standing over his shoulder making suggestions, helpful and otherwise, David pushed back from his desk. "There it is. Gallaudet is our planet. And the two languages thing was called *SimCom*. Apparently, those who tried to use it—signing ASL, one of the many Deaf languages, and speaking English simultaneously— usually produced distorted versions of both. So, you got lousy ASL and lousy English simultaneously. Not surprising really. Actually producing two languages at the same time must be unbelievably difficult. Grammars won't match. One language needs a whole phrase to express what the other expresses in a single word or sign, so timing wouldn't match. Prosody would get all messed up."

Tkal gave his best imitation of quirking an eyebrow, which involved wrinkling the skin near the corner of his eye. "Prosody?"

"Oh, the natural flow of rhythm in a language, how the stresses and timings and tones and stuff work together to tell you the difference between, 'Right,' meaning you agree, 'Right?' meaning you need clarification or reassurance, and 'Riiight,' meaning you don't believe a word of it. And it gets *really* complicated over a whole sentence. And no two languages will ever agree on the way all that stuff works. Stuff will get scrambled and distorted. It would take real skill to do it for rehearsed material, and doing it live—well it pushes the boundaries of what's possible. A quick glance shows that most of the comments about the practice are negative. But I still think this is what Violet Pod's codes are doing. Text doesn't have prosody, and a computer could take as long as necessary to adequately combine the messages and wouldn't need to worry about the lengths of messages not matching... Not matching?" David sprang from his chair. "THAT'S IT!"

Tkal jumped back. "Sheesh! Don't do that. I'm too young to die of shock. It'd be really crystalline if you really do have the answer. But how does the messages not being the same...? The ends of the messages. The computer may be shifting the shorter message to one end or the other, meaning that the head or the tail of the message may only be a single layer."

"Exactly!"

"Oh, David, if you're right…"

"I am." He sank back into his chair. "At least I hope I am."

"No, I think you've got it. How long?"

"I don't know. Codes can still be tricky. You know that. And now we'll be looking at tiny fragments of text, which lowers the chances of success." David stood again and started pacing. His terminal pinged. He dove for his chair and touched the icon on screen. "I have a prelim from Old Earth Archaeological Archives. OEAA believes they have the records I requested, but they need transfer protocols and access authorization."

"What will that mean?"

"I'll need to get permission from the academy to arrange a databurst reception and prove I have a legitimate academic reason to access the information. They don't want to waste time and resources on crackpots or curiosity seekers. They want their data treated seriously."

"Why can't you just access it directly like a normal library system?"

"Archive systems aren't interfaced with the stellarnet or even the web on Earth, to protect the data from hackers and malware and ghostfingers and nanoprions. The data has to be physically downloaded to a cleanroom device, then transferred to a stellarnet-capable device to avoid contamination of the closed-system archives."

"I'll request the permissions and provide the academic reason right now." Tkal spun in his chair, but found his wrist caught in David's hand before he could touch the screen.

"Wait! Stop!" David gasped and let go Tkal's wrist like he had grasped something hot. He threw up both hands in front of himself. "Sorry! Sorry! I'm so sorry!"

Tkal laughed. It was hilarious how easily passion over came David's shyness, and how terribly that always flustered him. "'Sokay. What's the problem? Why shouldn't we request the permission?"

David struggled to recompose himself. "It-it's not *us*. It's *you*. You shouldn't. Violet Pod may be watching this data. If you request it, they'll know we are on to them. If I request it, it could just be buried in my usual flurry of random searches and requests about everything."

"Hmmm. You're right, but I don't think you can request it, either. I don't think they would miss a request like that," He paused. "Is there another way to get the data?"

"Another way? Maybe. I might be able to go through Gallaudet archives, or…give me some time, and I'll see if there isn't an even more back-door route to the data."

Tkal smiled. David was good at devious when the problem was presented in the right way. "You know, David, I would never want you as an enemy."

David looked aghast.

"No seriously. You'd be a very dangerous enemy. You're smart, and your mind works in some really strange ways. And you aren't anywhere near as weak as everyone thinks you are."

David's ears were flaming. "I…I…you…what? I mean… wouldn't…"

"No. That's not what I mean, David. I mean I have a great deal of respect for you and your abilities. And I am very glad I recognized who and what you are before anybody else did. Green Pod would have been doomed if you had ended up on any other team. And if it had been Violet Pod that snatched you up, it would have been over for everyone."

"Oh, right, make fun of me."

"No, David. Look at me. I'm serious. I've never met anyone quite like you."

David searched his face.

"David, how much do you know about Tvern An culture?"

David blinked at the change of direction. "Well, quite a bit, I guess. It comes up often enough in various classes, and I have you for a roommate. And I've read."

"Yes, you've read quite a bit of Tvernish stuff since we've been roommies." Tkal paused, deciding whether to continue or not. Then the choice came clear, and he plunged ahead. "Have you read about the *fdinel* ceremony?"

"The blooding?"

"Yes. That's the one. Do you know about it?"

"Well yes. At least…I came across it in an old epic, *Tgernar and Fgerin*. It's some kind of old-fashioned treaty ceremony, right?"

Tkal nodded.

David studied him. "There's more to it than that, isn't there?"

"Yes. At the end of that scene in *Tgernar and Fgerin*, what happens?"

"They embrace each other by the forearms and call each other 'brothers.' Their fathers break down the doors and find them standing there dripping blood and declare the war ended. I didn't really understand that part. It seemed so abrupt, while the rest of the story was so well crafted."

"Ah." He paused. "You know that tale is historical."

"I think I read that somewhere, probably in the introduction or apparatus."

"That war was really bloody and had gone on for three generations. Tgernar and Fgerin were the heirs of their respective thrones. It would be their responsibility to carry the war into the fourth generation if neither of their fathers triumphed. If either did triumph, the other would become the winner's slave. But after Tgernar and Fgerin had met three times on the battlefield, their respect for each other had grown to the point where they decided to do the *fdinel*. When they called each other brother, they weren't just flipping words. In matter of law, tradition, and faith, they were, in truth and fact, brothers from that moment on. Actually, a *fdinel* brother can never be disowned, while a natural brother can be. The reason that their fathers ended the war right then, as soon as they saw the blood, is because neither could kill his own son, and both these young men were now their sons, and both equally heirs to each kingdom."

"I see. It makes much more sense now. But I—"

"Do *fdinel* with me."

David just stared at him, his face devoid of comprehension.

"David, I have no brother and no sister. I am the only child of my parents. When I marry, I have no *ktirn* to stand with me. Do *fdinel* with me and become my brother.

David's mouth moved like a fish taken from the water.

"David? Are you, okay?"

"I.. I…what is the ceremony?"

"Well, I've never done it before. Most Tvern An never do. It's really rare. I've never even seen one done except in movies, and we want to do it right, completely legally binding. But basically, it involves slitting our hands open and letting our blood mingle. That's another thing we'll have to check—make sure mixing our blood won't hurt either of us. And then there are certain symbolic herbs and stuff—we'll have to check those against your chemistry as well."

David just stood there.

"Think about it. Work on getting that information through whatever 'back door' you have in mind and get your notes ready for the meeting. We're almost late now."

Everyone except David was gathered at the table in the common room, and Tkal had already called the meeting to order when David slipped into his seat as unobtrusively as possible, which wasn't saying much. He sat fidgeting, dividing his attention between tapping away at his netbook and staring strangely at Tkal.

"What is wrong with him now?" asked Gronorgh, pointing at David. "He looks like a *ngifuezh*."

David knew that was a kind of food animal noted for its flavorful meat, high quality hair—and stupidity. He didn't react, but Dai-Soln did. He glanced at David, nictitating repeatedly, suspecting he would understand the import. The look on Dai-Soln's face was somewhere between shock and embarrassment. David seemed not to notice. He next glanced at Tkal. Tkal had clearly understood, and the fire in his eyes was unmistakable. "I have news to report," Dai-Soln interjected, trying to stop the argument before it started.

Tkal clenched his jaw, then turned and snapped at Dai-Soln. "Your report is out of sequence."

Several of the others, including Shintikaisen, stiffened at that, not accustomed to such sharp answers coming from Tkal.

Tkal took a deep breath. "But go ahead. We might as well hear it."

Dai-Soln made one of his half-nod, half-bow gestures, as if he had been addressed with the utmost respect and grace, and started in, relieved at a catastrophe averted, however briefly. "Our revenues are continuing to shrink. Trade is down another three percent. Orange Pod and Gray Pod have been hit especially hard. Orange Pod lost three more transports. I have an unconfirmed report that Orange Pod's leader is in negotiations with Violet Pod."

"I can now confirm that report," Gronorgh growled. "I had one of my agents trail the little sneak. He's been to Violet Pod three times, in person, this week. He has yet to inform us of his activity."

Tkal bowed his head. "How long till we lose them?"

"Tomorrow. Maybe the day after."

Shintikaisen whistled through her nose. "We could try to get something out of this. We could announce that we've discovered that Orange Pod has been secretly working for Violet Pod and passing them information all along. If we time it just right, just before they make their switch in allegiance public, they'll never be able to deny it effectively. And having Orange Pod as an ally will become a liability rather than an asset. We'll score a blow against both of them."

Tkal frowned. "Yeah, but at what cost. And what do we do when the losses continue? Say Gray Pod's been leaking too? And UV3? No, we've got to stick to the truth. It's the only thing we've got."

Shintikaisen looked disgusted. "It certainly has served us well."

"Tkal is right," said Gronorgh, looking like the words tasted bitter in his mouth. "There is no strength in lies. They are like ghosts."

Shinti whistled. "Well, those ghosts seem a good deal stronger than your soldiers at present."

Gronorgh's face turned purple, and veins could be seen up and down his neck. "If that little fool could break their code so we knew where they'd be, I could crush them in a week." His hand fairly trembled with rage as he leaned over the table and pointed at David with index finger and sixth finger—a gesture of utter contempt.

David looked like one of those ghosts.

Tkal's voice was like ice. "Gronorgh, sit down."

"You may be the leader of this ineffectual group, but you should be careful how you speak to me. Do not forget that the Gravgurdan Stronghold is *not* a part of your Commonwealth and many of its laws do not apply to me. And you are *not* classed as a child-race."

"Gronorgh, we all know that you are the strongest here, but this is not a kratocracy. And we also all know that *I* have the most power here. Sit down."

Gronorgh stood for just one defiant moment longer to remind everyone that no one, likely not all of them together, could force him to do anything he did not choose to do. "That does not change the truth of what I said. We are all being held hostage by *his* inability to break that code, if it is indeed a code."

"David," Tkal said turning to look at him with some relief among the stress on his face. "I think you should give your report now."

David paused, collecting himself. Then he looked at Tkal with something like a plea on his face. "Well, I—" His voice cracked and he cleared his throat. "I don't really have anything new to report. The code still isn't broken, and I can't tell any of you what Violet Pod is planning. The situation hasn't really changed since last meeting." He glanced at Tkal, despite his best effort not to, and saw the look of betrayal on his face. He tried hard to steel himself against that, and to do what he had decided had to be done, while he had been tapping away at his netbook throughout the meeting. "However, I do have several, ah, strange requests. Just some things I need from each of you." He paused. "For a new line of investigation," he added, throwing poor Tkal a bone.

"Great," Gronorgh's rumble was so deep that David could feel the vibration in his own chest. He tried very hard to avoid the glare he knew Gronorgh would be casting his way. Looking at him right now could melt all the courage it had taken to decide on this course. He would have to endure days more of the others' contempt. Okay, Gronorgh's contempt, and the others' questions. And things would not be easy for Tkal either, but it had to be like this.

David turned to Fthofsis, who was fluttering above the table over Enemwenu's…well *shoulder* certainly wasn't the right word…fluttering next to Enemwenu. "Fthofsis, if the breeze blows well for you, would this day be a good one for making new friends?"

Fthofsis whistled lightly, its analogue of laughter. "David, your words waft well. All days blow well for new friends. To whom should the breeze take me?"

"I have downloaded the information to your voder," David replied. "The breeze may not blow so smoothly to this one's door, but to connect will make streams in the air, bringing clouds in season."

Fthofsis whistled again at the delicate way David phrased his request. Then as its voder brought up the information for it to review, it stopped. "David, the breeze has blown smoothly between us, and the winds have made a stream for our path. But perhaps, this wind should blow for someone else. I do not know if the air will carry me this far. A storm could arise."

"I trust you," was all David's answer. Before anyone had a chance to ask what strange task he had given to the Fthsaisthf, he turned to Xtp, and speaking in as rapid-fire Qttx as he could manage, he asked, "*Could-you-please-download-any-materials-you-can-find-on-Hopherl-singing-styles?*"

Xtp clacked its mouth parts in confusion, while its voder translated, "Can you not find this information for yourself? Surely the database…"

"*No-please-make-the-query-as-if-it-is-for-your-own-research. You-were-at-the-New-Year-ceremony-today-weren't-you?*" David didn't even wait for the answer; he already knew. "*Try-to-make-it-look-like-a-research-paper-for-one-of-your-classes.*" Xtp was clearly confused, but tilted its head anyway.

Next, David turned to Shintikaisen, "Could you arrange to leak the fact that Orange Pod is leaving us, and make it look like an accident, like we didn't intend to leak the information…because it is damaging to our position?"

Tkal and Gronorgh both leaned forward over the table, ready to nix that request.

"We won't be accusing them of leaking information, just leaking the fact that we know they are leaving. It should still keep Violet Pod busy with damage control for several days, and it won't eliminate the possibility of recovering Orange Pod as an ally if we want them back later." Tkal and Gronorgh both leaned back somewhat, but neither looked convinced. "And maybe Gronorgh can use the confusion to do something military to strengthen our position for a while longer." Gronorgh tried to look confident that he could do exactly that. Tkal still had questions striped across his face, but he was holding back, trying to trust what David was doing.

Next, it was Ael's turn to be nonplussed. David said, "Ael, would you mind asking Jva to talk to some of his artist friends and find out how they document movement for their research? Stuff like dance, especially narrative dance. And if there is any relation to the documentation of gestural languages."

"Sure, but…"

"Thanks." Then, David turned to Enemwenu and continued his tidal wave of unfathomable requests. "The Alelliawulian New Year is next month, isn't it?"

"Yes," Enemwenu replied, a tentacle spiraled in question.

"Could you find me some instructional material on the rituals for the ceremony? The kind of stuff that would be needed to participate?"

"I could, but it is freely available in the database."

David twisted his arm in a way that looked almost painful and said, "Thank you."

Then, he turned to Red-shimmer and, opening his shirt, revealed a coloform undershirt. He took the electrodes from the coloform shirt and placed them at various spots on his head. He was concentrating so hard that sweat broke out across his brow, but soon the shirt was flashing ripples and waves of patterned color, and Red-shimmer was responding in kind. Several of the others were on the verge of demanding an explanation, or to be let in on the conversation, when David turned to Tkal.

"I only need one more thing. Could you get authorization for the computer time to rerun every one of Sven's decryption attempts…as well as all of my old ones? Back-to-back? I think I'm on to something here, but I need to have all that data rerun."

Tkal tried not to smile, but was only partly successful at turning it into a frown. "That's a lot of computer time. But if you really think it will help. We've got to get this cracked. I'll make it a priority." Tkal glanced around the table. "Did any one else have anything?"

A couple of items were presented, during which much of the attention was focused on surreptitious, puzzled looks in David's direction. These were, seemingly, completely lost on their target, as he was tapping away at his netbook, lost in some mental fog deeper than usual. Tkal adjourned the meeting. David pretended not to notice for several standard minutes and then rose from his seat and sort of wandered back to his room where Tkal was already waiting for him.

"That was either the most ridiculous waste of time I've ever witnessed, or absolutely negmag!"

"Is that the newest slang for brilliant? Negative magnitude?"

"Aw, man, you always have to kill it. You don't analyze slang, you go with it. I still don't know what you asked from Xtp or Red-shimmer—by the way where'd you learn to do that?—but I *think* you just arranged to get all the research materials you need to crack this code while sending Violet Pod off on several wild geese chases. Goose chases?" He shrugged. "Whatever! And no one else on the team can give the game away because they don't even know why they're getting this junk for you."

"That's what I hope I just did. We'll see."

"And the shirt?"

"Oh, that? I'd been saving up for it since my stipend kicked in."

"And you can use that thing to actually speak Red-shimmer's language? Is there any language you can't master?"

"Probably. There are some really weird brains out there, and senses I don't even have that could be used for communication. I probably couldn't learn some radar language. And there's bound to be a limit to how many I can store at once. I'm sure to start dumping languages to make room for new ones at some point, or else hit a brick wall and then there's just no more room in the wetware."

Tkal just laughed. He laughed until he was gasping for air.

David couldn't decide whether to join him or not.

Eleven

Whispers in the Dark

David found Jva in the common room with Ael. They were over in the corner by the entertainment center with their heads together. He needed to ask Jva if he could handle the room design for the summit meeting, but he hated to butt in. Clearly, they were…well, he didn't feel right about interrupting.

"We should tell David first; he's Human after all," Jva said none too quietly.

"I don't see…" Ael started, *sotto voce*. "Well, it shouldn't make a difference, but I guess it sorta does." She glanced over at David, then looked away, as if she was trying not to look like she was doing so. "Okay, you're right. It does matter. But then we have to tell our roommates. Shinti would kill me otherwise."

"She's such a romantic," Jva teased.

"Well, she is, actually. After her fashion."

"Like a caveman with a club."

Ael laughed.

David was trying hard to pretend like he wasn't hearing any of this conversation. He felt like a lowdown snoop. His own privacy was very important to him, after all.

"David, stop playing oblivious and come over here," Ael called.

David could feel himself turning ten shades of red.

Ael and Jva clasped hands and stood. Facing him, they bowed. "David Asbury," they spoke together, "we have the joy of giving you knowledge that we are now sworn."

David just stared.

"We just sent notice to our parents," said Jva.

David stood there.

Ael pulled one eyebrow down, the other up, as the corner of her mouth frowned. "Well, say something."

"You're, you're engaged? Just now? But I thought you already were."

Jva chuckled and encircled Ael's waist, drawing her closer to him. "We were. Now we're betrothed."

Ael smiled. "We like to keep things complicated on Halcyon. It's a four-step process before marriage. This is the fourth." She looked into Jva's eyes. "Next is the wedding."

"As soon as our parents schedule the event."

Ael looked at David. "This stage is our parents' responsibility."

Jva smirked. "You know what my father will say."

Ael laughed. "Jva, my son, you're much better—"

"At this than I am," Jva completed. "Mother will do much of it, but I will still have plenty to do."

David shuffled his feet. "Well, ah, congratulations to you both." He paused and opened his mouth, only to close it, then, "I was going to…but, well, you sound very busy, I…"

"You were going to ask one of us something?"

"Never mind. I don't want to add…"

"David, spit it out!" said Ael.

"It's just that I have this project that, well, Jva, it's only that I thought, but now…"

Jva leaned forward. "What kind of project?"

"Oh, there's this summit coming up that Green Pod will be hosting. All the other pods, who agree to come, will be there, and we need someone to design the room and stuff, but…"

Ael squeezed Jva's hand. "Beloved," she smiled, obviously trying out the new title, "this could be exactly what you've been looking for."

Jva twisted his mouth. "I don't have an Integration Project yet, and I have to complete it this term. As Ael keeps reminding me."

"Integration Project?"

Jva waved his arms as if taking in the whole universe. "Yeah. Multidisciplinary, multicultural, multi-what-have-you."

"Oh," David replied. "Well, this has plenty of multi. We need room layout, décor, art, music, food, placement of speaker space, cultural representation for a dozen or so species. There are biologies, cultures, religions, personal preferences, taboos and necessities involved here and it all needs to come off in a way pleasing to all and offensive to none."

Jva started pacing back and forth, nearly stepping on Ael's toe. "Perfect! I'll need to bring in subbies and consults."

"Use all the subordinates you need, contract whatever you like, but we can't advertise this until next tenday. That only gives you three tendays from public notice to live event."

"Three tendays? Ouch! But I can do it. And if it goes well enough, this could be my capstone project. I could write a paper on this to satisfy even Dr. Eshkidzidzo!"

David frowned in thought. "We should probably get Dai-Soln's advice on the Kzati. His people have a lot of contact with them, and they're both monarchies."

David and Jva had cornered Dai-Soln in the common room, and filled him in while stepping all over each other's words. It would have been far more efficient if just one of them had tried to explain, but Jva was excited about the project and filled with romantic notions, while David actually knew what they needed from Dai-Soln.

The Taisiran leaned against Xtp's seating pillar and shuddered his fronds. "I don't think you quite realize what a royal court can be like. I'm sure it's quite civilized and refined and a lovely show when it's only a historic relic left over just for nostalgia's sake. But in a real court—one where a monarch holds real power—just under that beautiful surface things get ugly. Really ugly."

David plopped down on a cushion and tried not to smile.

Dai-Soln glanced at him and immediately seemed to have the situation pegged. He turned all his attention to Jva. "I've spent a bit of time at our court. I have to from time to time. I'm actually in the succession."

Dai-Soln flicked his fronds in response to David's gasp. "Well down the succession, mind you. Someone would have to bomb the capital while court was in session, and I off planet, before the throne came to me. There are forty-some others ahead of me. We're a subsidiary line of a subsidiary line. Strictly third tier. But still, there are duties." He pulled a beetle out of a pocket and munched. "That's part of why I'm here—to prepare to fulfill those duties. But just the little time I've spent at court has shown me, graphically, how dangerous and very unpleasant, and uncivilized, such a place can be. A whisper in the dark can bring enlightenment, like in Tkal's poem, and with it, ascendancy…or it can lead you into a trap to ruin a career—or cost a life."

Jva frowned and poked another of the sitting cushions with the toe of his boot. "So, I can expect plenty of snide comments?" Jva asked. "Maybe even deliberate bad reviews meant to hurt my grade?"

Dai-Soln's obsidian eyes looked bemused. "That's quite possible. But this is much more important to Prince Kvran than mere grades." He sighed at Jva's nonplussed look. "Kvran is higher, much higher, in the Kzati hierarchy, and they play by an even more ruthless set of rules. It's rumored that Kvran owes his current fourth-in-line position to his father's decision to dispose of the youngest son of the previous Emperor's first wife, his own half-brother, along with the man's entire family, just before disease took him. Oh, officially, it was an accident during a vacation, but…"

Jva spluttered.

David was intrigued. This was the being with whom he was locked in a mental fencing match. No wonder the code was so devilish. This gave him a better measure of the next move in the game, once the code was truly cracked. This was well past knight to queen's rook.

Dai-Soln turned unnictitating, obsidian eyes on the two Human faces, avidly searching expressions. He nodded, inhaled and continued. "That, and an unfortunate string of miscarriages, which have kept the Crown Prince from producing a son, has left only two females between Kvran and the Crown

Prince. Large and powerful elements in Kzati society dislike the idea of a reigning Empress."

Jva made a face. "That can't be…really? How does a government function with all that infighting going on?"

Dai-Soln shook out his fronds. "It's more complex than that, even. Emperor Fedol and Kvran's father, Prince Tving, were both sons of the previous emperor, Tzefan, but from different mothers. Emperor Fedol was second child from the first wife, a mere duchess whom Tzefan wedded when *his* elder brother was to inherit the throne. Tving was eldest child of the second wife, a Princess of the Line. And the families of the two mothers are from competing political parties. Interest groups? Factions? I'm not sure what the best term would be." Dai-Soln spread his fronds to wave away Jva's attempt at asking a question.

"Anyway, there are powerful elements within the Kzati Empire who would not hesitate to remove a Daughter of the Throne, a Daughter of the Crown, or even the Crown Prince himself, if they thought they could get by with it, in order to get Kvran on the Imperial Throne as an ally beholden to their cause. These elements likely view Prince Kvran's time here at the academy as a test of his fitness to rule the empire."

He settled his fronds along the sides of his head. "There are opposing elements, at least equally powerful, who would love to see Kvran dead to ensure the ascension of the current Crown Prince, and thus secure their own cause. But with only two living grandsons of Emperor Tzefan—but three granddaughters and one great-granddaughter—both sides fear losing all males of this line and having to go to some distant—and I do mean distant—cousin to become the Throne. Since only a daughter, and not her children, is counted as Line, you have to go back something like five or six emperors to trace out a line with an eligible male descendant in this generation. A system like theirs is very effective at pruning male lines."

Jva scrunched his eyes closed and shook his head at an angle.

Dai-Soln settled his shoulders. "I don't expect you to understand or remember all that. It's not your line of study. But David needs to."

David rolled his eyes.

Dai-Soln sighed. "Kvran is an arrogant *sid khaln*. He will find something to criticize no matter what any of us do." He frowned. "We do want to get all the niceties right, though. Kvran could rule the Kzati Empire someday, and *will* be, already is, very important in the hierarchy. It wouldn't be good for any of our future careers to offend him completely, or unnecessarily."

After class, David had grabbed some chili-and-lime chips from his pantry and dashed back to his room to check on the results of the most recent decode attempt. He sat staring at the printout in his hand. This was it. The last five words were in perfectly clear Traiqi: *eftruezhme qaindi em neqwehlti somaizh,* "after-the-attack remainders they-are for-benefiting orange." Orange pod's linguist was a Traiqi named Qafenti Hozhatru Kaidam Deazidiq. This was a true decode. Now the question became, how to peel away the layers of the other text smothering the rest of the message?

David squeezed his eyes shut and pinched the bridge of his nose. He leaned back in his chair, catching his feet on the underside of the desk to keep from falling. "I wasn't the first to get this far. Sven got here too. What did Sven find? What two or three words? What phrase had he seen? A formula greeting? An honorific title in a closing? A color word, like caught my eye?"

What would the decode mean to Sven? Respect? Reprieve? Apologies from Gronorgh? No. He didn't want that by the time he had gotten this far. He'd suffered Gronorgh long enough. It was a wonder Sven hadn't just exploded under Gronorgh's insults. Sven's personality…he didn't want respect. These were just a bunch of aliens, and a Human girl who was stupid enough to choose Jva when she could have had the magnificent Sven. He wanted revenge. But how would he work it? There had to be a way to make money out of this. Sven had blackmailed more students than the administration ever realized. Blackmail would be a natural groove for his mind to fall into. Kvran might pay to keep the code undeciphered. Kvran would *definitely* pay for that. But why wouldn't he have gone ahead and changed the code again anyway? On the off chance that Sven had left more clues behind than he thought. David would have. Tkal would have. Gronorgh would have. Red-shimmer,

Shinti, Ael, Enemwenu, Dai-Soln, Xtp—any of them would have. Fthofsis might not. No, even it was versed enough in the devious, in cat and mouse— or rather wind and leaf—to jump first thing to change the code as soon as anyone had broken it. So why wouldn't Kvran? Kvran was smart. Kvran grew up at court, in an environment where his own relatives were as likely to do him in as enemy agents. Why wouldn't that kind of hyper-intelligent paranoia instantly order a new code? Wait. Maybe this *was* the new code that David had just cracked. Maybe this decode wouldn't work on the older stuff from before Sven's decode. He'd have to test that soon.

Right now, it was the inside of Sven's head he needed to figure out. Sven would go to Kvran and…what? Offer to keep quiet? Definitely. Show Kvran how to fix whatever flaw had allowed Sven to break the code? Yes. He'd made a little side cash blackmailing students, but this? With this in hand, he'd believe he had money enough to…what? Get a private fortune started? No. Not that much. Sven had a trust fund, but couldn't get at most of the money for a couple of years yet. That was it. He didn't want enough to start a life, just enough to live a little wild until his own money was released.

Kvran had that kind of money. He had to. He was a prince. Fifth in line for the Imperial Throne of the Kzati Empire. Or was it fourth? Anyway, he was rich beyond anything David could dream. Sven would have known how to get a reasonable idea of just how much Kvran would have at his disposal. From that he'd know how much to ask for. Sven would go in knowing he was making a reasonable demand.

Or would Sven want more? Sven's family weren't diplomats; they were big business. Shipping? Transport? Or was it electronics? Something like that. David wished he had paid more attention that night Sven had been boasting about it all to that girl. But it had been so nauseating, he had done his best to tune it out. And succeeded too well, it seemed.

Sven had probably already done something else that was about to catch up with him. He might have taken this opportunity to score big for his family business just before he got himself expelled. Maybe the expulsion *wasn't* for what he had done to Green Pod. Maybe he did what he did to Green Pod to smooth his way *after* he got caught for whatever he had already done. Maybe it was both.

Whichever, Sven would have taken his data to Kvran, or at least to Violet Pod, and made his offer. Kvran would have…countered. There was no way a Prince of the Line would let a weasel like Sven dictate terms to *him*, even if they were perfectly reasonable terms. No, he'd counter with something else. Something…what? A trap. He'd counter with something to trap Sven. Some way to make sure he had something more, something else, that would do more damage to Sven than it would to Kvran if Sven ever let slip what had happened. But what would that be?

Well, what did they know or suspect Sven had done? One, he had broken the code without telling anyone in Green Pod. Two, he had sold that information to Kvran. Three, he had left that nasty program behind in the computers to destroy data and throw Green Pod into confusion for weeks. Still not enough. Four, they suspected that he had done something else that was still in operation, that was still making their plans and data vulnerable to Violet Pod. Was that enough? It would be for some. It wouldn't be for Gronorgh. He wouldn't leave an enemy with that much freedom. Neither would Shinti. If Tkal chose to play that game, he'd play it better than that. Even David wouldn't let it go there if he had a way to tie it up better. But what? Of course. There had to be some way to get Sven to do something that would produce an immediate benefit to his family's corporation, but would leave Sven at Kvran's mercy if such a real-world crime became known. Something that seemed innocent enough, but in the hands of the right lawyer or government committee could destroy a company and send a lot of people to prison. Kvran would know just how to play games like that.

So Sven cracked the code. He went to Kvran with a blackmail offer. Kvran countered with something that looked even better, but included Sven doing just a couple of things for Kvran first—a bit of sabotage, which Sven would relish, and something…else. Something that he ate up without realizing, until it was too late, that he'd swallowed poison. Maybe he didn't know yet. Maybe Sven still thought he'd won. But either way, Kvran now owned Sven, and sooner or later Sven would have to pay up, doing whatever Kvran demanded. And Sven would do it. David wondered where Sven was now. Probably at Daddy's corporate HQ in some overly cushy office, in charge of something he wasn't qualified for. Except by blood.

And what about Tkal? What would he do now? Well, they'd all be excited about this—even Gronorgh—though the first words out of *his* mouth would be either complaint that it had taken so long or a demand to know how much longer this final bit would take. David couldn't really fault him on either, but the *way* Gronorgh would do it would be as demeaning as possible.

Actually, the more important question was what to do about Tkal. *Fdinel.* He'd asked David to slit his hand open and drink some awful mix of…stuff…as part of a bizarre, barbaric ritual that would make them brothers of a sort. David had researched the ceremony thoroughly. It was weird. But alien ceremonies tended to be weird.

Actually, ceremonies, period, tended to be weird, if you stepped back and looked at them objectively. Wearing silly clothes and waiting in a long line to receive a piece of paper after someone mispronounces your entire name, even the parts you never willingly use, so you can move the tassel hanging from your hat before you throw it in the air—all to show that you have finished a stage of your education. Getting drunk and doing really stupid things you will later regret on the night before you marry, so you have a hangover for the important day. Weddings. Now those had silly ceremonies. And funerals. And birthdays, especially the fortieth.

Why shouldn't this ceremony be just as strange? But did performing this ceremony, doing *fdinel,* did that really make them brothers? According to Tvern An law, yes. According to their cultural traditions, yes. According to Tkal's religion, yes. And there was no way to undo a *fdinel.* If you chose someone as brother or sister in this ceremony, Tvern An law treated you as biologically related, and your families after you, forever.

You became automatic godparents of a sort to each other's children, and you owed a portion of your estate to the other's children at your death. You had to help each other bury parents and spouses and, God forbid, children. And you were responsible for helping educate each other's kids.

Why? Why would Tkal want to make such a lopsided bargain—one *so* binding. Maybe this was just Tkal's blind optimism. After all, Tkal had continued to believe all sorts of ridiculous things about who and what David was.

Tkal's family had wealth and power. David had no family and was attending school on government charity. Tkal would marry, have children. He and his wife would eventually be assigned as ambassadors to some world or other. They would probably both inherit substantially. They'd—

David would take whatever job the Terran Diplomatic Corps offered him, hopefully as a junior linguist on a first-contact team. But if he ended up in a back room in some dark basement analyzing alien transmissions—pretty much what he was doing right here for Green Pod—he'd take that too. It would be a job. He'd never be rich, but he wouldn't starve on a government salary. He wouldn't mind marrying someday, but who would want him? And the thought of children was terrifying. All the children he'd known were at Grey Street. Well, that wasn't true. He had known children before that, but they were vague memories. But if David *did* have kids, Tkal would have a duty to help educate them. And how would David discharge that part of his duty? English lessons over the stellarnet?

No. It was just too much to contemplate. David needed a snack. He needed a break. There were cinnamon candies in his cupboard out in the food prep. Really intense ones. He pushed away from his desk and blanked his terminal.

When he reached the prep, he almost tripped over Red-shimmer Gold-streak backing out of the bottom cabinet where she stowed her stores of, well, David couldn't help thinking of her food as canned rodents, though it was nothing of the sort. They chatted for a moment about homework and the strange odor of cinnamon, while Red-shimmer got her elevator in place so she could reach the cook top to properly sear her dinner. Then David excused himself and dashed back to his room.

Red-shimmer rippled with color like the surface of a soap bubble when David returned wearing the coloform shirt. Laughter. *Violet wash, silver spark, tangerine stripe, indigo spray, yellow stripe, aqua ripple*—"Ah, conversation for real!"

David smiled, then strained to activate the shirt. *Indigo spray, yellow stripe, yellow wash, aqua ripple*—"One hopes for real." David paused. "Does your voder make you feel…alone?"

Red-shimmer put the bit of meat she was reaching for back on the floor tray. She let her skin go muddy green-gray-brown for a moment, then scuttled around where her broadest side was facing David squarely, so her words would be exceptionally clear. *Fuchsia wash.* That was what she called him.—"David, we are all of us here outsiders. All of us. Xtp is a sterile who wants to do something of galactic importance when it should be training as a nursery worker. Enemwenu is from a broken family and grew up without hii's bond parent; hii's prospects for marriage and family are slim. Fthofsis is the first of its kind to be educated off world. Dai-Soln is a prince who just wants to be Dai-Soln. Shintikaisen has come to think of males as people, and she thinks Gronorgh is cute."

David gulped.

"Tell me you hadn't noticed."

"I thought it was just my imagination."

"No, it is real. And then there is Gronorgh who had to fight, literally fight, for the right to come here—three of his clan brothers and his own biological father. He sees a value in learning here that they did not. Ael is a diplomat-in-training who will wed an artist. Tkal thinks like a Human, and you do not. We are all outsiders, all of us strange and strangers. But Green-stripe Yellow-stripe, Tkal, you can trust him. He is the sort who will not betray. How he will survive as a diplomat, I do not know."

Why had she said that? How could she know where half his thoughts had been for days? "Who do you trust, Red-shimmer?"

"Me? I think I trust all of us…in one way or another."

David watched soap bubble laughter.

"Yes, Fuchsia-wash, even Gronorgh. He is rude, self-important, obnoxious, intimidating. But he is also competent. He guards his honor. And he wants to do good, no, excellent work."

"I guess you're right. You can trust Gronorgh to be Gronorgh."

"More than that, even, I think." She paused. "I trust Tkal very much. Ael has brains, integrity. Actually, *you* are the most difficult to—"

David's shirt became completely incoherent.

"Calm, my friend. I *do* trust you. Only, you are so closed. You are difficult to know. Difficult to predict." She paused again, longer than before. "I will quote Gronorgh. He cannot understand my speech, and I trust you not to repeat."

David slit his eyes and nodded, then colored, "I speak to him as little as possible and tell him even less." That earned a very few soap bubble swirls.

Red-shimmer colored, "I was speaking to Gronorgh about trade issues, and when I mentioned needing your valuable input for cultural understanding, he…well, he exploded, as he does. 'Who is David? I can't tell. One standard he is Alelliawulian, twisting tentacles he doesn't even have. The next, he is Iridian, actually speaking through that stupid shirt. Then he tries to be Gravgurdan. How can I trust a shapeshifter? How can anyone know a being who doesn't have his own shape?'" She paused. "He overstates, but we all face this in relating to you. Which you will I meet next time?"

David sat down, stunned. Was this what Tkal meant? Was he really such a weirdo? But this was just who he'd always been. Nothing special. Rather nondescript. Boring.

"David? I do not mean offense." She waited for a reply that wasn't forthcoming. "Have I hurt you?"

"No, I'm just…confused. I'm so ordinary. So boring."

Soap bubbles appeared, only to be replaced by mud. "You really believe that?"

"Yes."

"This is confusing. Somewhat. You see everyone else so clearly, but when you look at yourself, you are blind."

David made several attempts, but couldn't get the shirt to work again. He got up and walked away, his feet autopiloting him to the arboretum.

Twelve

Negotiating

David entered his room, after spending far too much time discussing how to translate Qttx poetry with Xtp, to find Tkal in the middle of a call with another pod leader. "We don't *want* to be allied with Violet Pod. IR2 Pod has a long tradition of independent neutrality. Besides which, we find their tactics abhorrent. But however abhorrent those tactics may be, they are quite effective, and they have us backed into a corner." The Wkkho who led IR2 Pod snorted in disgust and continued. "If you could offer us a way out of this corner, we would take it. While Green Pod was strong, and Green Pod or its allies surrounded us on three sides, and we were at peace, we prospered. We prospered and flourished economically. Our economy is now in trouble. Trouble which we can only solve by allying with Violet Pod. Violet Pod and its allies now surround us on three sides. Violet Pod and its allies now refuse to trade with us, or to allow us passage through their space, unless we ally with them. There was a time when Green Pod could guarantee the safety of the shipping lanes, but that time seems to be past. You cannot provide reliable security for our transports. You cannot guarantee us a monopoly. We have no choice. If you do not offer us some reasonable alternative within one tenday, we will be forced to abandon our long tradition of neutrality and ally with Violet Pod."

Tkal sighed, "Can't you wait until after the summit?"

"No. We need to clarify our position before then. We must go into the summit knowing where, and with whom, we stand."

"Very well. You will have our answer within nine days."

The transmission ended. Tkal slumped in the chair, letting his head loll so far back that he must've gotten an upside-down view of the opposite wall.

David sighed, "I'm trying, Tkal."

"I know you are. And we'll have it soon. That last little bit has to come. But there is more. Even without that code, we should be more effective than we have been." He slammed his hands against the desk edge and went sliding across the room, dragging his feet to stop the chair just inches before it slammed his face into the shelving.

David squawked in reverse.

Tkal sat bolt upright. "What?"

"Your face, you nearly smashed it into the shelves."

"Nah. I knew what I was doing. Anyway, Violet Pod's good, but they're not *that* good. At least not that much better than we are. They didn't just suddenly become mega-geniuses. They don't even have any new people on team. Until halfway last term, they were just annoying competition, stiff competition, but no more so than four or five other pods. Then, all of a sudden, they're just sweeping everyone away, and we're just barely holding on by our fingernails. It's like they know everything everyone else is doing, but we can't get a line on anything they're cooking because of that motherless code of theirs."

"When did you become a Trelkairni? I thought only Shintikaisen swore like that."

"Ha. Well, it seemed appropriate in this case, since we *don't* know where it came from."

Tkal stared at the ceiling. "There has to be something we're missing." He slumped back down in the chair like he might ooze out of it, fished Dai-Soln's handset game out of his pocket, and started playing.

Several standards later, David activated his terminal to do some work for Selected Case Studies in Diplomatic History. He wasn't exactly behind on the project, but he had no intention of getting there. Supradoctor Ihsshiis did not cut anyone slack. And David was determined to snag a record grade for this class, even if it killed him.

Tkal looked up from the game. "David, you really should give this game a try. It's fun."

"I'm not good at those things."

"This one's easy. You'll love it."

"Gee. Thanks."

"That's not what I meant, and you know it."

"I've got work to do for Case Studies."

"You're two weeks ahead."

"Ten days. And…hey! Are you keeping tabs on me?"

"Don't need to. You're always working ahead."

David sighed in disgust.

"Come on. Try it out for five standards. If you don't like it, just give it back, and I'll never say another word."

David arched an eyebrow.

"About games. I'll never say another word about games."

The eyebrow again.

"Okay. *This* game. Sheesh. When did I get to room with a dean?"

"Oh, for heaven's sake, hand it here so I can satisfy you and get back to work." David pushed back from his desk and snatched the game from Tkal. The screen was blank. "How do you start this thing?"

"It's biometric. It has to register you first. After that, it knows who is holding it and tailors the game to you."

David looked at Tkal as if to say, *And this is a good thing?*

"It's fine. It won't bite you. It makes the game personalized. It figures out what parts of the game you like best and shifts the play in that direction. It'll probably have you reading clues in hieroglyphs in half an hour."

"Hmph!"

"What do you want to bet?"

"Shut up. The screen just came up. Now what do I do?"

"Just follow the prompts for a couple of standards, and then you'll just sorta know what to do next."

David wasn't buying it, but if it was the only way to get Tkal to let him work in peace… "Hey, this is sorta—"

"See!" Tkal leaned in to get a glimpse of what was happening in the game. "Hey. What the…?" Tkal had stepped away and hunched over David's terminal. David was about to ask him what kind of brain fever had possessed him when Tkal whipped around and snatched the game from his hand.

"Hey!" David exclaimed, rubbing his wrist.

Tkal had already dashed over to his desk and was scrunched over staring at his terminal. He straightened and dashed out the door so fast it had barely opened wide enough for him to squeeze through the crack by the time he was gone.

David was left baffled.

Ten standards later, Dai-Soln rang the door chime. David let him in. Dai-Soln peered around the room, obsidian eyes unblinking, like he was checking for monsters. "Has Tkal been acting…strange?"

"I'll say. He made me try that game of yours. Just insisted. Then—"

"Snatched it from you and ran off without a word?"

"Yes. How did you…? You too?"

Dai-Soln spread his fronds.

"I have no idea." And David truly didn't.

Tkal opened the meeting by tapping something on his netbook, so a message appeared on each of their screens.

Violet Pod requests a summit with the leader of Green Pod to discuss the terms of the future interactions between our two pods, as prelude to the upcoming summit, so named. Time— SY471:09:35, day cycle 10:75. Place—level three conference room.

The message was terse and haughty. It would have been recognizable as Prince Kvran's words even if it hadn't carried his student ID ghoststamped to the message.

Enemwenu was first to speak. "This is supposed to mean what?"

"Terms? Of our future interactions?" asked Dai-Soln.

Ael threw her netbook on the table with a clatter. "He thinks we will surrender? Ally with him? Let him dictate terms? And what's this summit? He's holding one of his own to compete with ours?"

Tkal frowned. "Judging by his tone, I'd say he hopes to *preempt* ours. This looks to be just Violet and us. He's probably hoping to get us to capitulate before the summit even happens."

Fthofsis fluttered down to just above the table. "This message translates with a bad wind. This is not the mistake of my voder, is it? He truly blows a wind this sour?" Fthofsis fluttered sort of sideways until it was at an odd oblique angle to David and Tkal. "Is it true that the Human language English says the wind is broken when it smells bad?"

Tkal looked puzzled. David felt himself turning red.

"I think he has broken the wind in this message," said Fthofsis.

"*Fart!*" Tkal bellowed. "Kvran *farted!*"

David and Tkal laughed till the others were sure they had gone insane. Several searched translation databases, only to be assured that the two of them really were nuts. Meanwhile, Tkal gasped, and David clutched his sides and whimpered between gales of laughter.

There was no salvaging the meeting after that.

So, David's big surprise, his first, partial decode of a current transmission from Violet Pod to its allies, did not get revealed during the meeting. It actually got revealed a few hours later, as a printout handed to Tkal in private. Tkal immediately called a secret planning meeting in their dorm room—just David, Tkal, Dai-Soln, and Gronorgh.

The next day, Tkal, Gronorgh, Dai-Soln, and David walked into the conference room one level up from their quarters. David and Gronorgh were missing classes to be at this thing. As they approached the table, four of the five beings seated at the other end rose and bowed slightly. Prince Kvran, however, could have been a statue for all the acknowledgment he gave them. He just sat there with his cat-slit eyes half closed; his high, back-slanting forehead polished to a shine; and his fingertips resting on the table top as if he were about to play a piano concerto. Not a very diplomatic greeting. They had been led to believe this would be a meeting of equals, four-on-four.

Tkal sat at once. Gronorgh gave a low rumble. Dai-Soln twitched his fronds. Only David gave a sort of clumsy bow. This had all been decided beforehand.

Prince Kvran sat like stone. The Hopherl, the Madrindalan, and the Tal Chin gave their versions of snarls, while the Human looked at David with something like pity on his face. David wasn't buying that. Ryan had been friends with Sven at one time, and David was pretty sure he had helped Sven set up a couple of blackmail victims.

All through the meeting, Kvran only spoke to Green Pod through his subordinates. Tkal should have been furious at the slight, and with the repeated offers of "reasonable" terms for Green Pod to surrender to Violet. But Tkal seemed unnaturally calm, like he knew something no one else at the table knew. That made David uneasy. Tkal was up to something he hadn't let the rest of them in on.

As soon as the negotiations were concluded, while Tkal and the others began gathering their netbooks and recorders, Ryan approached David. He stuck out his hand. As soon as David took it, Ryan gently tugged him over toward the wall. David followed. "I'm Ryan."

"David."

"I know." He nodded toward the others. "They always make you dance the nicey-nice? You get to bow and be polite while they put on the strong guy act?"

David shrugged.

"It can't be easy for you. Gravgurdans aren't exactly known for being warm and fuzzy."

"This one can't stand me," David confessed.

Ryan grimaced. "Sorry dude."

David looked at his shoes and shuffled his feet.

"You ever think of ways to get back at them?"

David let a nasty smile play across his lips.

"Ever follow through?"

The smile vanished as David blanked his face.

"Yeah. I don't think I'd have the guts either. Not when there was any chance of a hulk like that Gravgurdan catching me at mixing itching powder into his protein shakes."

David couldn't help laughing, but quickly tried to disguise it as a cough. Ryan reached over and patted him on the back.

"Thanks," David whispered.

"No problem," Ryan replied. "I've got your back. Humans gotta stick together. But I hear that Halcyon hottie on your team is a real cold one."

David twisted his mouth. "She only notices Jva." He tried to sound resentful. It was easier than he expected. But he couldn't help wondering... That comment sounded so much like something Sven would say. But Ryan hadn't...

Ryan appeared to hesitate, though David was pretty sure he was acting out a prepared script. "You know, my group really aren't so bad. I mean, yeah, Prince Kvran is pretty distant, but he *is* a prince, fourth in line to the throne. He could end up ruling twenty-six planets. And either way, it sure can't hurt actually knowing someone that important. It's pretty cool, actually. And the others treat me as an equal. I've got a good bit of respect. It isn't the same as being back home with our own kind, but I think I've got it a lot better than you do."

David quirked his mouth and shook his head. "I almost said I wish I could trade places with you, but I wouldn't wish Gronorgh on anyone."

Ryan glanced over David's shoulder at the Gravgurdan and shook himself like he felt a chill. "No, I don't think I'd want to do that."

Ryan's eyes stared off into space.

David had almost decided the conversation was over and was starting to sidle off to where his group was nearly ready to leave, when Ryan came back to the present and fixed David with a very earnest gaze. "You know, I bet I could get you in with this bunch if you wanted to transfer."

"Transferring isn't that easy. I'm on a scholarship and...well, it would be complicated. Maybe impossible."

Ryan looked disappointed. "Maybe just as good. You wouldn't want that warrior coming after you."

David shuddered.

"Still, I might be able to hook you up a bit, so to speak. You know, get you in good with the team here for when Green Pod goes down. I hear you're a good linguist, I mean *really* good. Someone like you could fit in well here. I bet Prince Kvran would take you in, when the time comes, if you showed some interest. I mean, I used to be in Yellow Pod, but I found a place at the top here when we got absorbed."

David looked nervous and glanced back over his shoulder at his teammates.

Ryan took the cue. "Don't say anything now. You better get back to your leaders before they get suspicious. Think about what I said and let me know." Ryan slipped away back to his pod, and David slunk back to his, where Gronorgh was scowling, and both Tkal and Dai-Soln were looking annoyed and impatient. David slid into formation behind the others and followed them out the door with only a single glance behind, where Ryan stood with his back to him chatting with the Hopherl.

No one spoke till they entered the elevator. Gronorgh took a tiny detector, about the size of a button, out of his jerkin pocket and waved it over each of them in turn. As he swiped it down David's back, it lit up. Tkal did his just-pretend-I-have-an-eyebrow-to-quirk gesture, and David nodded. Gronorgh clenched his fist and pumped it overhead, narrowly missing the ceiling. It was scary how big his biceps were when he did that. Dai-Soln did that teeth baring-thing that was neither quite a smile nor quite a snarl, but something in between. David wanted to act like he was holding an Oscar, but only Tkal would have any chance of understanding the gesture, and if he did, might start laughing, which would spoil everything. The others would just think he was weird, and he *would* look like a dork doing it.

Dai-Soln started their preplanned conversation. David made a couple of feeble attempts at contributing which the others ignored. Gronorgh slipped in a couple of derogatory comments about Humans, which were ostensibly directed at Ryan, but could equally apply to David. No one contradicted him.

Dai-Soln referred obliquely to the fact that Green Pod was still suffering from a lack of information due to not being able to break that blasted code, and Tkal joined him in a thinly veiled discourse on how one team member's failure affected everyone else. David sighed in appropriate places, but otherwise remained silent. Once they got back to the pod, David removed his clothes and threw them in the laundry chute. Then he showered and changed into fresh, unbugged clothes.

Tkal, Gronorgh, and Dai-Soln were waiting for him when he emerged fresh and clean. "So?" Tkal asked.

"He tried to recruit me. I didn't say yes, because I'm too intimidated by Gronorgh. He bought that."

Gronorgh looked pleased. Dai-Soln wiggled his fronds in a gesture equivalent to rolling his eyes.

"Careful, small one," Gronorgh rumbled.

More frond waggling.

David plunged ahead before he could get caught laughing at Gronorgh. "He made it clear that, if I play my cards right, there could be a place for me in Violet Pod when Green Pod gets absorbed. Their linguist can't be happy with that."

"He probably suggested it," Dai-Soln supplied. "He graduates this term."

Tkal clenched his beefy hands into fists and tensed his arms, pressing his fists into his thighs. "Gah! That makes me... Ah! I just want to put my fist through a wall. Or better yet, Kvran's face." Tkal's fists flashed up, the left arching up just ahead of the right arching down and out, in a display that would have left the Kzati prince sprawled on the floor and, most likely, bloody.

Gronorgh smiled. Dai-Soln looked a bit taken aback.

Tkal caught Dai-Soln's look. "I wouldn't actually do it. But it felt good to think about it."

Dai-Soln did the wheezing thing that served him as laughter, but David thought it sounded a bit forced.

"I just don't like *vultures*." Tkal had used the English word and Gronorgh and Dai-Soln both had questions plastered on their faces.

"It's a kind of bird," David explained. "They're very big carrion eaters. They circle overhead waiting for things to die so they can swoop in and tear the carcass apart."

"Ah," said Dai-Soln. "An appropriate image. Unpleasant. But appropriate. I don't think we have anything quite like that at home."

"We do," said Gronorgh. "Vile things. They carry disease and are used as a symbol for Theshilfikh, the demon of weakness. *Vulture*, I'll have to remember the word. What do they look like?"

"Very ugly," David answered.

"Very," Tkal agreed.

David pulled up an image for Gronorgh.

Gronorgh looked at it with a start. "Asthenia! It looks like it's been locked in a twelve-day kiss with Theshilfikh. That thing will haunt my sleep!"

Dai-Soln took the netbook and looked at the image. Astonishment played across his features. He looked at David.

"Yes," David said. "It's real."

Tkal looked over David's shoulder as he retrieved the netbook from Dai-Soln. "Yeah, they're ugly. I hate knowing they're just circling out there, waiting to pick apart and devour our team. I hate that they went for David first."

"Well, we kind of set them up for that," David reminded him.

"Yeah, well, they didn't have to take the bait. Or to swoop in so fast."

"You named them *vultures*," Gronorgh said. "These things go for the weakest one."

Tkal glared at him. "They may think that's what they're doing, but they clearly don't know who they're messing with."

David was at least as stunned as Gronorgh. Dai-Soln eyed David narrowly though half-closed nictitating membranes, until a strange sort of smile-like expression spread across his features.

Tkal's stripes intensified dramatically as he looked Gronorgh in the face. "You underestimate him as much as they do. You should know better by now."

That was coming dangerously close to challenging Gronorgh's intelligence, which was not safe and not true. Gronorgh was intelligent, very intelligent, or he would never have been at Shel Matkei, but his prejudices did blind him to certain things. David was just as happy to leave the warrior unenlightened. His life was hard enough when Gronorgh thought him a joke. If he decided David were a threat… Well, David preferred not to follow that line of thought.

He decided it was time to redirect the conversation.

"How long do you think they'll wait before they send Ryan back after me? Or do you think I should try to contact him?"

Tkal looked from face to face, his stripes fading back to their normal hues. "What do you think? I vote having David play it completely passive."

Gronorgh nodded. "It seems more believable, more in character, to me."

Tkal glared at him.

Dai-Soln twisted his mouth in an expression David wasn't used to or sure how to read. "More to the point, I think it is what *they* will expect. If David tries to contact them, they could be scared off."

David nodded. "I agree. Ryan seemed to think I'm pretty much abused by the group. I don't think I would have the courage to go seeking an opportunity to betray my pod if I were as downtrodden as he seemed to suggest I was. He really seemed to think I would be completely starved for contact with another Human—especially since Ael is…unavailable. And, that just a bit of pity was all it would take to win me over. Gronorgh is right. Passive."

Tkal gave David one of those looks he hated, golden eyes sparking like flint. Now he was going to have to dodge another one of Tkal's attempts to convince him to stand up to Gronorgh and start acting like he was as valuable a member of the team as Tkal wanted him to think he was.

"Okay, we'll give it half a tenday and if nothing happens by then, we'll discuss how to proceed from there."

Gronorgh and Dai-Soln rose and headed for the door. David waited till the door opened, then darted and slipped out between them. "David!" Tkal shouted. But by the time Tkal made it to the common room the door to the corridor was already closing, covering David's escape to the arboretum. Tkal would guess that was where he was headed, but he wouldn't follow him there. For some reason, he treated the arboretum as off-limits whenever David fled there. For that, David was thankful. He needed a willow tree all to himself.

Thirteen

And 'Neath the Willow Tree He Sat

David relaxed as the arboretum airlock cycled through and hissed closed behind him. He breathed in the scent of soil and water, of green growing things, of sap and sand and bark and bloom and he could feel the tension of the last hours drain from him, seeping into the cracks between the cobblestones beneath his feet. He wandered aimlessly through the plantings from world after world, knowing that sooner or later his feet would carry him around to the big willow tree in the middle of the Earth section. They always did. He strolled from bed to bed touching leaves—waxy, woody, rough, smooth, cool, or warm—inhaling fragrances familiar and foreign.

Sooner than he expected, he found himself sitting under the cool umbrella of his willow tree. He really did think of it that way, as his, even though he had nothing to do with the tree other than enjoying its shade as a sanctuary. The Saint Augustine grass that grew beneath its branches made a soft, cool carpet to lie on while he let his mind wander and unwind.

He tucked his hands behind his head and stared up into the branches as they rustled, swaying gently this way and that in the aircycler-induced breeze. It was almost like being on Earth, except there were no clouds above, only the plasteel and geodesic piping forming the dome between him and the vacuum of space.

When he noticed a patch of pale, iridescent blue dodging among the branches, he scrambled up onto his knees. Fthofsis drifted down to flutter at eye level for David where he knelt on the grass.

"Have the winds blown us together?"

"So it would seem," David answered.

"Perhaps you would prefer the winds breathe another course."

"No, it's fine Fthofsis. I was just startled."

"I would not wish to blow a foul wind on your day. I get much pleasure from the way the wind plays in the branches of this tree."

"Yeah, me too," David sighed.

"This plant, it is from your world?"

"Yes," David answered.

"Then perhaps I should leave it to you."

"No, stay," David replied. "I wouldn't want to refuse this tree to anyone who finds joy in it. It's called a *willow*. It's a symbol of sadness and tears."

"Sadness? Tears? But why? It is so beautiful and so fun. The breezes dance among the branches like children at play."

David got a mental image of dozens of tiny iridescent blue, green, lavender and yellow Fthsaisthfith fluttering in and out among the branches of his tree. It was a beautiful picture.

For several moments David knelt and Fthofsis fluttered in front of him. David closed his eyes and tilted his head back. He inhaled deeply and then scrambled to his feet much less gracefully than he felt the moment called for. He reached out and gathered branches in to himself, then stepped through the curtain of slender leaves and whip-like branches, letting them spill behind him as he walked through, arms spread wide. David wished he could dance, but even if he possessed the skill, he would have been too embarrassed to do it where anyone could see him.

Fthofsis swam through the branches darting gracefully this way and that among them emerging with a sort of spinning twist.

David sighed again. "I wish I could do that."

"What?" asked Fthofsis.

"Fly," David answered. "I think it's a dream every Human has—the desire to fly through the air, gliding wherever you want."

"How strange. You are all the wrong shape for flying. Why do you wish for that when walking will take you wherever you need to go?"

"It won't take you into the clouds."

"You cannot walk through fog?" Fthofsis asked, even its voder sounding baffled.

"Ah! Don't ruin a dream," David cried.

Fthofsis fluttered in agitation.

David found himself sighing again. "Yes, I know fog is really a cloud come down to the ground, and no, I don't find fog pleasant. And it isn't the slightest problem to walk through. But nobody thinks of fog as a cloud. Or of cloud as a fog. Clouds are beautiful, fluffy, soft, and dry—the stuff of dreams and full of light. Fog is a sticky, damp mess that closes in around you and turns everything gray."

"But this is totally irrational," Fthofsis said, its voder voice trembling as if it were on the verge of hysteria. Surely the machine was over-translating something in Fthofsis's grammar, because, while his body language seemed confused, it didn't seem hysterical.

"Yes, but I did say it's a dream, something buried deep in our subconscious that isn't subject to rational thought, or at least is destroyed by it."

Fthofsis said, "Ah," which was followed by a burst of static that drowned out its whisper-soft words.

David's bugged his eyes at the unexpected sound.

"My voder did not translate that, did it?"

"No," David answered. "All I got was a burst of noise."

Fthofsis switched off its voder and said "*Sifisthaif*," then switched the machine back on. "This word is very difficult to translate. I do not know a word for it in Standard, and it seems my voder does not either. And there are entire books of philosophy trying to explain the idea and define it and how it does what it does in the soul of the dreamer. I cannot explain."

David smiled. "I think you just did. Walk with me?"

"Now *that* is something *my* people cannot do," Fthofsis teased.

"Share my wind?" David asked.

"It is a wind as good as any," it replied. "Why do you think all beings wish to do things that they cannot, things for which their bodies were never designed? You wish to fly. My people wish to swim. And a fish, it would wish to walk on land."

"So true," David replied.

David strolled along the path with Fthofsis float-fluttering along at his elbow. They stopped to smell the roses. David inhaled the intoxicating scent deep into his lungs, letting it suffuse throughout his body, clearing his head and warming his toes. Fthofsis inhaled and hissed something its voder translated as a really ugly obscenity.

"Please, let us follow the breeze elsewhere before I become sick."

David couldn't believe how repulsive Fthofsis found roses. *Roses.* But he did hurry on, because his friend's distress was quite obvious. "You clearly don't agree with Shakespeare."

"Again Shakespeare? What words did he blow to this stream?"

"A rose by any other name would smell as sweet."

David was sure Fthofsis shivered. "No, I would not agree with him. Roses are vile."

The gardens didn't have any plants from Fthsaisthf yet, so they just wandered from planting to planting looking at the placards explaining or warning. One bed was full of leafy green plants bearing the most vibrantly variegated red, orange, and yellow fruits. The sign said they were called *firefruits,* and warned, in bold text, in a dozen different languages, in addition to Standard, that touching the fruit could be quite painful, causing a burning sensation that could last for hours, and if the skin of the fruit were broken, actual blistering of the flesh could occur.

Fthofsis trilled a light whistle. "I suspect that fruit would not be so dangerous to me.

"How so?" David asked.

"My exocovering of silica-chitin is not damaged by many of the chemicals that are so harmful to skin-covered beings like most of you."

"Oh. You could be right. I don't know much about chemistry."

"I am not an expert either, so I am not sure enough of that supposition to test it out. Besides, if I transferred some of the oils to you and caused harm, the winds would blow very cold in my heart."

David wasn't sure how to respond to that, so he was glad that Fthofsis just drifted on, leading the way. Finally, they came back round to the willow.

There David took his leave of Fthofsis, and headed back to the airlock. He watched with a wistful smile through the window as the lock cycled him back out to the corridor, while Fthofsis returned to drifting in and out among the willow branches.

As he walked the corridor back to the lifts and rode down to the academy levels of the station, his mind kept returning again and again to the same thought. If he could share the arboretum with Fthofsis, why not with Tkal? It was time to build another bridge between this peninsula and the mainland.

David ran into Tkal coming out of the library. "Tkal, can I talk to you for a bit?"

Tkal looked a bit surprised. "Sure, David. What's up?"

"Nothing really. I was just talking to Fthofsis, and it made me think. Well, I think everyone knows that the arboretum is where I go to be alone."

"Yeah. Everyone knows that. And we all respect that. Even Gronorgh doesn't intrude on your time there." He squinted at David. "Does he?"

"No. Never. But it also happens to be where Fthofsis goes. And we run into each other from time to time. And talk."

Tkal looked both puzzled and disappointed. "Well, I can't really do anything about that."

"Oh, no, that's not what I meant. It's as much Fthofsis's space as mine. But I was just kind of thinking. See, I don't... Well, I haven't really had friends before. Not growing up in the orphanage. Not since I came here either. I never had brothers or sisters, or any of that. And even if I did, I never had anything to share with anyone."

"What are you talking about? How many times have I told you, or at least tried to tell you, how much you have to offer?"

"Let's not have this argument again, okay?"

"Fine. What did you want to talk about?"

"I just thought that since I'm already sharing the arboretum with Fthofsis, you might as well feel free to look for me there."

"What? No. I wouldn't intrude on your quiet like that."

"Well, you're kinda like the family I don't have. And family butts in everywhere."

"I can't really respond from experience, not about brothers or sisters, but parents do. And aunts and uncles, and grandparents. Cousins don't hold back from saying anything and everything either." Tkal twisted his mouth. "I've visited Tvern several times, for several months each time. Most of my cousins have felt free, at one time or another, to tell me exactly how un-Tvern An I am. And suggest ways of improving that deficiency."

David forced a little laugh, and stared at his shifting feet.

"What? You agree with them?"

David's head popped up. "No. What? No. Not that. I just…I didn't know what to say. I, uh…well, you do have a lot of Human mannerisms and stuff that must seem strange to them, since they expect you to be just like them, but you've lived a very different life from them. That doesn't mean you're deficient, or 'un-Tvern An.' Whatever that means."

"Yeah. Right. It just means I'm me. I know I straddle two worlds. My face means I will never be Human. That and the problems with bread and stuff. And I am still Tvern An in biology, and there's enough of the culture in me from growing up in my parents' home, and hosting functions to show off our culture, and hosting trade delegations from the homeworld, and cultural exchange groups, and students, and… You wouldn't believe the Tvern An who have been in and out of my home growing up. Diplomats, artists, business leaders, scientists, educators—people other Tvern An, including my cousins, could only dream of meeting. People that I've had dinner with, and bumped into in the hall, and gotten glasses of *kfital* juice for. But I haven't known regular Tvern An—classmates and bullies and waiters and trash collectors and tailors and cops and barbers."

"Tkal! Tvern An don't have hair! How can you have barbers?"

"Well see, we don't even have a word for that job because it's such a outworldly concept. But I've grown up in a world where barbers are normal. But I don't know the kinds of normal everyday Tvern An that all Tvern An know, so I am weird. I'll never be Human, because I'm not. But I'll never be quite completely Tvern An either, because I've spent too much of my early life away from that world and its ways. I stand between worlds. I'm comfortable with that."

"You know," David said, "we're more alike than I would have ever thought. I don't stand between worlds. I kinda don't even have ones to be between. I'm Human inside and out, yet I find my place when I'm with non-Humans. I'm more at home—don't laugh!—I'm more at home in a pod with a Tvern An, an Amazon, an ogre, a talking rock, two bugs, a hoofed octopus and a three-winged butterfly than I ever was on Earth."

Tkal smiled and did his ersatz-eyebrow quirk. "You forgot the pretty Human female who's engaged to an *artiste*. And the Taisirans aren't bugs."

"Well, the Xttg aren't technically, either. But the Taisirans *do* have antennae, or vibrissae, or fronds, or…whatever they are."

Tkal's face sobered. "So, what is it about the arboretum that you like so much?"

"The willow tree."

"Ah! By the rivers of Babylon."

David knit his brow. "What?"

"By the rivers of Babylon, there we sat down, yea, we wept, when we remembered Zion. We hanged our harps on the willows in the midst thereof."

"You're quoting something. What?"

Tkal looked surprised. "The book of Psalms."

"In the Bible? You mean you've read it?"

"You haven't?"

"No. Of course not. Religion wasn't encouraged at the orphanage. It was state run. Besides, all those ideas are so old-fashioned."

Tkal frowned deeply. "I've never been able to understand the Human attitude to religion. It's like your people are stuck in their teenage rebellion. Most races pass through a period like this, but it usually passes quickly—long before spaceflight."

"Yeah, Dr. Chikiki got real pontifical about that in Cultural Parameters. I can't see that it's any business of other races if we do or don't take religion seriously."

Tkal ducked his head. "Sorry."

"No. I didn't mean you. You're an Earther. You're entitled to an opinion."

Tkal twisted his mouth and looked at David without really raising his head. "You still don't know where I go to be alone, do you?"

"Well, no, but I didn't try to find out. It's too much like snooping."

"But you know where half the others go."

"Well, some of them talk. And some of them tell…" David waited, but it seemed like Tkal was waiting too. "What? You want me to guess?"

"No," Tkal sighed. "I just hoped you'd ask, so it wouldn't be so awkward to tell you that my alone place is a little *gtarn kder* three levels up from the campus."

"A 'candle room'? That's what? A…a chapel?" David's voice cracked.

"Yes." Tkal frowned. "I knew you'd—"

"I didn't mean anything rude. I'm just surprised. You go to, to what? Pray? Meditate? Watch candles burn?"

"A little of all that and more, other." He paused. "I could show you where."

"Maybe some other time."

"Oh."

"I just don't know what to do in sacred spaces."

"You went to the Hopherl New Year."

"That was just in Auditorium Three. And there were dozens of outsiders there. We just sat and watched." David looked at his feet and breathed out. "You're right. I'm being silly. It's not like the room will bite me. No one's going to chase me out screaming 'heretic,' or…"

"No! Of course not!"

"I won't accidentally defile the place and ruin some priest's week? Or…"

"David, no. It's just a candle room. It's for private devotional use. There is no priest. It's just a quiet place to be quiet before the Eternal and listen."

"This is very important to you, isn't it?"

"Very."

"Then I guess I really should see it. To understand. To try to…see why."

The candle room was smaller than David expected. Somehow, despite Tkal's insistence, David was braced for a Gothic cathedral, not a room barely larger than the dorm they shared, with unpainted metal walls covered only by narrow, woven—maybe hand-woven?—textiles in simple geometric designs, with yellow and green predominating, and a few simple benches with cushions stitched in the same geometrics. There was something like an altar at the far end of the room and a rack of unlit candles by the entrance. Nothing more. No sculpture. No writing. No sacred books. No priests. No room for a choir. Just an altar, a few benches, the wall hangings, and the candle rack.

David glanced down. He had questions, many questions, that he wanted to ask—some of them not exactly polite. But he just couldn't bring himself to ask things like, "Do you really hear voices when you pray?" or, "How can you rationally believe this Eternal thing actually exists?" He wanted to ask. But he was pretty sure that if he did, both questions would come out sounding like "Are you nuts?" since that was what he really wanted to know. Was Tkal crazy? Was a lunatic asking him to become his brother? Or was there something this big, this important, that David had just missed? Did it really matter? Well, yes, it did. But it also didn't. If Tkal was crazy, it was a very good crazy. He really wanted to be brothers. To have a family again.

That would mean that when Tkal left next term for his practicum, they would still be connected, would stay in touch. Yes. He wanted that. A lot. And it would be fun to be best man at Tkal's wedding someday and shout for him. And to have Tkal stand as best man at his own—provided he ever found anyone. Most people did, eventually, whether it lasted or not.

It was time to redraw the map. No more islands. No more peninsulae. Time to risk joining society. Even if that meant becoming brothers with a green-and-yellow-striped alien who used more English slang in five standard minutes than David did in five months.

"I'll do it."

"What?"

"The *fdinel*. I'll do it."

Tkal stood staring for several beats. Then his fist was in the air pumping to a "Yesss!" so drawn out that David couldn't help thinking of reptiles.

To avoid anything more boisterously demonstrative, David stuck out his hand. It took all of his self-control, and holding his breath till his ears popped, not to yelp from the grip Tkal used to return the handshake.

"Okay, well, I'll need to tell you all about the ceremony, about all the things that go into the chalice and the exchange of garments, and—"

"I already know."

"What?"

"I already know. I looked it all up. I had to know what was in the ceremony first. Before I decided. I mean…"

"You mean you were you. You were careful and researched and made sure you knew what you were getting into. My parents are always encouraging me to be more like that. You'll like my parents. *They'll* like you. I'll introduce you next time they come for a visit, but that might not be till I graduate. They probably won't waste five standards before they start encouraging me to be more like you— careful and checking all the angles."

"Maybe they won't like the idea of you having a Human brother."

"Dude, they're the ambassadors to Earth. They like Earth and Humans. They raised me there and encouraged me to fit in with the culture as much as biology allowed. No, they'll like you. Besides, I already told them all about you in my letters. They think you're cool."

"Uh, yeah, sure." David felt his ears burn and suddenly knew why Red-shimmer's name for him was Fuchsia-wash.

Tkal frowned. "I *really* hate to say this, but I don't see how we can fit it in before the summit."

David looked away and nodded. "No. Neither one of us has time to even breath before that's over."

Tkal sighed, then brightened as he launched back into planning mode. "We don't absolutely need witnesses for the ceremony. This oath is just between you and me, and the scars serve as the public witness. But it's considered advisable to have one. We could, well, would you want to invite the pod to watch? I dunno, as a cultural experience? Or have a Tvern An…'authority' present just to be extra careful…what with this being cross-species and all?"

David thought about it. He wouldn't mind having Fthofsis, or Red-shimmer. Actually, he'd be more or less okay with any of them except Gronorgh. But there wasn't any way to shut him out and let the others in without having a *really* dissed Gravgurdan to deal with. "I don't know. Maybe not."

"Gronorgh?"

"Gronorgh." David paused. He knew what Tkal meant when he had said "authority." He meant a priest. But maybe a lawyer would do.

Fourteen

How to Sing When the Music Stops

David left class in a fog of thoughts that had nothing to do with *Conflict Resolution*. The summit, Tkal, the *fdinel*, dinner, grocery shopping, the arboretum, how to phrase that dispatch Tkal wanted him to send to Aqua Pod—all of that and more had a place in the swirl of thoughts howling through his head. He rounded the corner and yelped as he stumbled to a stop, just short of running into Ryan. It was excessively obvious that Ryan was waiting for David. There wasn't even an attempt at surprise on Ryan's face.

"Do you have time to talk?" Ryan asked, but he didn't take time to let David answer. He just grabbed him by the biceps and steered him into an unoccupied classroom.

David wanted to yank his arm back. Who did this jerk think he was anyway? But this was the role he was supposed to play, so he bit his tongue and tried to look somewhere between frightened and curious, rather than furious.

Ryan seemed to buy it. "Calm down, buddy. I'm not going to pound you. I've got some good news, sport. I talked to the prince. He's looked at your file, and he's interested. We have a linguist spot opening at the end of this quarter, and I've convinced him that you've got what we're looking for."

"What?" David stammered. "I thought you were just joking, before, back at the meeting. You mean he'd really want me? I could be working for a prince? On a team with no Gravgurdans at all."

"Sure could," Ryan beamed. "I thought you'd be excited."

"Yeah, but I still don't see how I can get away from Green Pod, not with my skin intact."

"Well, I wouldn't worry too much about that, champ. I don't really think there will be a Green Pod to worry about much longer. Tkal's in way over his head. Prince Kvran has the inside track and way more experience at this. I'd be surprised if they make it into the next quarter." He eyeballed David through slit lids. "How much do they let you in on the actual operations of Green Pod."

David hung his head. "Not all that much. It's not really my strength, and well, they don't listen to much I say, since I haven't been able to break your pod's code. That's the one thing that might have made my life bearable over there. But I couldn't do it, so I'm worthless to them."

Ryan sneered at him. "No chance of that happening from the outside. But I bet you could do some real good work from the inside. And from what I've heard, you're doing a pretty good job of frustrating everybody else's codes. The other pod's linguists, or code specialists, all hate you."

"What?" That one genuinely surprised David. No acting required this time.

"IR4 Pod's linguist was crazzing about having to change his codes three times in the last two weeks because of you, bro. Nobody likes having to work that hard. That's the kind of thing the prince likes to see. He can totally use someone like you."

Use. Yeah, that was exactly what he wanted David for, to use him. Tkal looked at him and saw a person, a friend, maybe even a brother. Prince Kvran saw a useful tool. David decided that he wanted this conversation to end quickly, but he wasn't sure how to do that and stay in character for this role.

"You don't have to give me a straight out answer just now, but are you interested?"

"Interested? Yes. But Gronorgh… even Tkal…"

"Don't worry about that. Like I said, Green's going down before the end of term. Then Prince Kvran will snatch you up and give you a place with us. No sir, chief, just keep your head down, and we'll do all the planning. All you have to do is say you want in, and I'll make it happen. Like you said, you aren't any good at this stuff, but I've got it covered."

Did Ryan not realize now insulting—? No, of course he didn't. That burned it. If this charade accomplished nothing else, David was going to find a way to make Ryan rue the day he underestimated David Asbury. He'd called him every obnoxious thing in the book except *big guy*.

Ryan didn't wait for an actual answer. "Catch ya later, big guy." He just turned and left, humming so off-key that David couldn't guess what song it was supposed to be.

David clenched his jaws and murmured, "You'll pay for that one." That verbal slap would come back to haunt the little creep. Even if he was half again David's size. David turned and spat, startling himself by using one of Gronorgh's gestures.

He hadn't intended to return to his room for another couple of hours. He'd actually been on his way to buy food and a few other necessaries when Ryan had ambushed him, but now that would have to wait. Or would it? What if Violet Pod had someone tailing him to see what he did next? Ryan might even have bugged him again. No, he probably should go shopping, maybe even hang out at the arboretum, and *then* go shopping before he headed back. Wait. There was another one of those stupid culture exchanges tonight. There wouldn't be time for that much playacting. No, David would have to just go buy his food and hurry back.

Fortunately, he'd already prepared for the exchange tonight. This time it was music.

So he'd be okay even if he had to haggle a little longer than usual over the chili peppers or the lemons.

He might have argued his way out of this one if Tkal hadn't fought dirty. He'd sent Enemwenu to remind-invite-cajole him.

Tortilla chips sounded good. And several kinds of canned vegetables were discounted.

The Alelliawulian had wheedled about wanting to hear some Earth music other than Sven's cruncher trash. David couldn't blame him.

Freeze dried meat, or dehydrated. Neither one was very good, but the freeze dried was cheaper.

It only took a minute or two before David realized that Enemwenu's body language had been saying more than hii's words. Hii seemed partly angry, partly offended, partly hurt by the memory of the stuff Sven had subjected their ears to. David couldn't understand why anyone liked cruncher music, but Enemwenu's reaction was more extreme than it ought to be.

"Why does this music bother you so?" he had asked Enemwenu.

Hii had turned an alarming color and twined hii's tentacles in ways that expressed grief. "It is difficult for me, even now."

David had been puzzled and had plowed ahead with a clumsiness he now regretted. "I know that music is awful, but why did it bother you so much. I just tune it out as much as possible."

"It is the words," hii had answered.

"That's the worst part for sure. Why does anyone want to listen to 'songs' about family violence and murder?"

"You do not understand." Enemwenu had shuddered in obvious distress. "I have seen this. My own bond parent…was murdered before my eyes when I was young."

David had gasped. What could he say? He'd really messed up this time. "I'm so sorry. I lost my parents when I was…" That wasn't the right thing to say.

Enemwenu nod-bowed. "So we are both orphans."

"What? You only lost one par—" David would have bitten his own tongue off if he could have unsaid those words.

"Hii was my bond parent. The gamma who gave birth to me. It is…damaging."

A sweet potato? Maybe he could do something with that.

David knew he'd messed up. He had studied some of that back in Cultural Parameters. The bond parent was the same-sex parent of an Alelliawulian, the one responsible for teaching the child the appropriate gender role. Coming from an incomplete or broken family unit made it more difficult to find a marriage group, but for the child who lost the bond parent, it was nearly impossible to marry. For the highly social Alelliawulians, Enemwenu had suffered a blow about as great as could be—forced individuality, no unity to enter. David had apologized till his thighs cramped and then had done the only thing he could think of. He'd put together as varied a sampling of Earth music as he could. And none of it was even remotely like cruncher music.

Chocolate! He grabbed one of the bars and threw it into his bag, no matter if it cost five times what it would back home.

Now, as he finished paying for his purchases and headed back to Green Pod, David still felt the guilt searing him hours later as he finished paying for his purchases and headed back to Green Pod.

"Whose turn is it next?" asked Red-shimmer Gold-streak.

"I think it's David's turn," said Ael.

"Great," Gronorgh growled.

David looked down at his hands.

Tkal sighed. "Come on, David. What did you bring?"

David puffed his cheeks out and fished in his pocket for his crystal. "Enemwenu told me that Sven only played one kind of music at these things, so I put together something different." He paused unsure whether to go on or not.

"Different is good," said Enemwenu, who was curling and uncurling hii's tentacles, clearly trying to make it obvious that all was forgiven.

"Well, I didn't really know what to bring, and I had too much time to think about it during a boring lecture."

Ael piped in, "You had Dr. Vekhtil today. Boring is a given with that old windbag."

Fthofsis whistled up and down it's odd scale.

David frowned. "Even by its usual standard, this was dull."

Shinti swore.

"Anyway," said David, attempting to get back on topic. "So, I think I may have gone overboard."

Gronorgh frowned. Enemwenu curled a tentacle. Shintikaisen cocked her head at an odd angle and leaned forward. Tkal crossed his arms and leaned back in his chair with an obnoxious smile on his face, as if he knew what David would do.

David tried to ignore him.

Fthsaisthf fluttered down nearer the others. "I for one, would like a fuller breeze of what winds blow in Earth music. Sven gave us only one stale draft again and again. You could have my time if you need it."

David looked aghast. "Oh no. I don't want to take up anyone else's time."

"I give it freely. You do not take. The breeze blows cool between us."

"Okay, well, I don't like the kind of stuff Sven listened to. My taste is really weird. I like old stuff and well…odd stuff. And most Humans don't, at least most my age don't, well, I just. It's just that…"

"David stop apologizing for liking what you like, and let us hear what you brought to represent Earth," said Tkal.

David went hot in the face and stepped over to the console. He inserted his crystal and adjusted the volume and playback controls. The "Winter" movement from Vivaldi's *Four Seasons* filled the room. Soon Enemwenu's tentacles were dancing in the air and Dai-Soln looked like he was in a trance. The others sat quietly, some more interested than others. The piece finished and David paused the machine. "I can just sit down now if you don't like it."

Dai-Soln seemed to start awake and nictitated several times to regain his focus or re-moisten obsidian eyes dried from lack of blinking. "No, please, no. That was beautiful. In fact, I could get lost in that to the point that it might be dangerous to listen too much."

"Oh, please," Gronorgh snarled, earning a glare from Dai-Soln. "What is that music for?"

"For?" David asked. "For listening? It's supposed to be a musical description of winter."

"Winter?" asked Shintikaisen, twitching an ear. "How is that supposed to be winter? It sounded like herds of *sikatavi* migrating across the plains!"

Enemwenu's head-body darkened. "It sounded like a mating dance to me."

Gronorgh made a sound somewhere between a cough and choking. "Play your next piece, Human."

David willingly obliged, and Bach's Toccata and Fugue in D-minor filled the room with all the violence of a truly grand pipe organ under the hands of a master. The first phrase set Dai-Soln's fronds at straight angles and stiff as broom handles. A phrase or two more and they were quivering in some rhythm that had nothing to do with the time signature. He looked, to David, like he was in pain. Shintikaisen and Gronorgh were both sitting forward, listening with intensity, and Fthofsis was hovering farther and farther from the sound projectors.

When the piece ended, Dai-Soln vibrated his fronds to the point that they rustled like dry leaves, then clapped them back alongside his head. "That was…"

"Painful," Fthofsis finished. "It hurt at both ends of the scale. The high notes felt like thorns and the low notes felt like my organs were going to liquefy. Please, never play that again."

"I thought it was awe-inspiring," Shintikaisen interjected. "A song like that could—"

"Inspire battle," Gronorgh interrupted. "Can Humans really hear notes that low?"

"That piece goes really low into our hearing range, to the point that some of the lowest notes really are more felt than heard, but yes, we hear them."

Tkal mimed a shiver, not a Tvern reaction. "Every time I hear that thing, it makes my hair stand on end."

Shintikaisen laughed. "Tkal, you don't have hair."

"Well, that's the English phrase. The Tvern phrase is, *dkarln kta ki dvil kdern,* 'My blood runs backwards.' It's the same idea."

"What does that piece represent?"

"Nothing. It doesn't tell a story like the last piece. It's just beautiful, or not, according to your taste."

Next, David queued up a recording of "Ey, Ukhnyem"—'The Song of the Volga Boatmen,' featuring Pavel Murometz, the best basso profundo the Russian tradition had produced in two or three centuries, depending on the expert you cared to quote. David had provided a quick-and-dirty translation of the lyrics for each of his podmates in their own languages so they could follow along. When the song was over there was silence for a moment.

Shintikaisen broke it. "He sounds large, like a Gravgurdan."

Gronorgh frowned and shifted his weight on the couch.

Shintikaisen pulled her bottom lip in behind her top teeth, the Trelkairni equivalent of a smirk. "That voice really is a Human?"

"Yes," David answered. "Voices that deep are rare, but the Russians have a tradition of using the very deepest voices in their music. Everyone else writes operas with tenors singing the male leads. The Russians like basses."

Gronorgh frowned. "This is from an opera? Those strange singing dramas?"

"No," David replied. "I was just explaining the Russian thing for low male voices. Actually, this is a work song. It was used by men pulling boats up and down the Volga river to keep their efforts synchronized."

Dai-Soln waggled his fronds. "These men sang while pulling boats?"

"They must have been very small boats—for a single fisherman—or very many Humans," Gronorgh sneered.

David looked down.

"Humans are stronger than you credit," Tkal frowned. "These were cargo boats hauling freight up and down the river. Commerce depends on getting as much freight in one load as possible, to keep profits as high as possible. The men worked in gangs, but again, as few as possible, to keep costs down and profits up. Humans can handle quite a lot when pressed by need."

Gronorgh made that gravelly sound. "By Tvern An standards, perhaps." He sneered and looked away.

Tkal closed his eyes and exhaled through his teeth.

David fumbled for the controller and got the next piece started before the argument could proceed. The hollow wail of a Navajo flute echoed through time and space. David had managed to find an ancient recording of the master, R. Carlos Nakai—a recording from before the Purge Wars. The mournful freedom, the quietly echoing joy of the desert filled the air giving David chill bumps, as it always did. He sighed as it ended and awaited.

Fthofsis fluttered down in front of David's face. "Now I know why we are friends. Your people, some of them, they blow our own songs. This is ancient, you say?"

"Yes, from long before we met aliens."

"*Hhaaah,*" it whisper-sighed with no translation. "May I play my selection so you may see how much of the same air breathes in them?"

"Please," said David, offering the controller to the butterfly, without thinking how ill-suited the device was for Fthsaisthf anatomy.

Fthofsis, ignoring the proffered controller, fluttered and glided over to the entertainment unit. Soon the air was filled with a sound that was so very different from, and yet so very similar to, the Nakai piece. Notes like a piccolo pretending to be an Andean zampoña or a clarinet speaking the tongue of the Chinese dizi mixed with sounds like wooden wind chimes and clear crystal bells, to produce something so indescribably alien that no Human of any tribe could have composed it, and yet so like the Nakai that somehow a Human would believe it really was Navajo music. The alienness was eerie, the similarity even more so.

A fifth of an hour and enough restated opinions to make a filibuster later, half the group was convinced that the two pieces were nothing alike while the other half were just as convinced that the first half must not be processing the same auditory input, which was absolutely true, given that they each had different hearing ranges. Finally, someone suggested that David play his next piece so that they could get to bed before time to go to classes the next morning, so he queued up "Zavilo Se Horo," sung by a modern Bulgarian all women's folk ensemble. Most of the group wore expressions varying from puzzlement to distaste. But Shintikaisen smiled, and Ael tried not to laugh at her roommate.

When it ended, Gronorgh started the discussion by "fouling the wind," as Fthofsis would have said. "I thought we would have one music night without a Trelkairni treat."

Shintikaisen made that air-escaping-from-a-balloon noise.

Ael jumped in. "It does sound a lot like some of those nursery songs you played for me once, doesn't it, Shinti?"

The Trelkairni woman shifted her shoulders and leaned back against the wall, fluffing the cushion behind her. "Yes, quite a bit. It especially puts me in mind of 'Kisto Ech Tivakhti.' That one is one of the didactics. It's a mother teaching her daughter how to deal with men and put them in their place when they get too full of themselves, preferably without striking their mouths, but it's all told with great humor."

No one seemed to know quite what to say to that. But Gornorgh narrowed his eyes, showing that he hadn't missed the point.

David queued up "Scotland the Brave," and amused himself watching the expressions on his audiences' faces—at least those who had faces. Xtp seemed to enjoy it most.

"Ah! These people must love their home very much to write such music for it."

"Oh they, we, do. You will find families five, six, even seven hundred years removed from Scotland, not even living on Earth anymore, who use this music to remain connected to Scotland. They say if you have even a drop of Scottish blood, the pipes will sing in your blood. And if not? Well, then you will look like Ael and Tkal do." David broke into choking laughter.

"Then I must be one of your Scottishes, because it sings in *my* blood," said Xtp with great solemnity. "If you will have me."

"*Bein a Scots isnae jist aboot bluid alane, bit whit's in yer hert.*"

Tkal studied David's face. "David?"

David only smiled till the corners of his mouth hid in his cheeks. He had managed to find and adapt a really good holorecord of the *Texas Skies* American Culture Day festival winner from six years back—widely agreed to be one of the best synchronized musical fireworks displays ever.

Music burst out of the speakers along with holographic fireworks—a medley of John Philip Sousa marches, and other American patriotic and cultural tunes, in perfect coordination with the colors exploding overhead all around the room. Awestruck eyes and gaping mouths matched quivering tentacles, and clenched fists. Red-shimmer Gold-streak vibrated in the middle of the floor, patterns like the fireworks dancing across her skin.

Tkal recovered speech first. "Oh, man, David! If you'd just given me a downburst of what you had planned, I'd've brought popcorn, or…or hotdogs!"

David's eyes widened.

"Mine without a bun, okay? Man, that was crystalline, negmag, ultra supernova!"

Red-shimmer reengaged her voder. "David," it quavered, "that was…it was…how do I explain? You know about these beings, angels? This was the singing of angels in the sky, in the air, shimmering down, not words, but meanings deeper than words. This is…can I have a copy of this? I wish to send this to my family—to my mother and father. Oh, my aunt will…This may be too much for her. Her health is not good, but oh, how she would love this! She used to have visions of shooting stars. We call them angel songs in our language. This was a hundred thousand angel songs all at once. A symphony of heaven." Her voder became incoherent, and finally, either she switched it off or it gave up.

Gronorgh unclenched his fists and spread his fingers like one trying to work out a cramp. "That was…impressive. I doubt I am enjoying the same parts as Red-shimmer, but…such explosions mixed in with the music, both mangling and making it, at the same time. To stand near those explosions…would it make a Human's ears bleed?"

"I suppose so. Yes. If you were close enough, it would probably deafen you."

Gronorgh sighed, "Then standing a bit farther back, I could feel those explosions slamming me in the chest."

"Yes it's quite a concussion."

"Someday I will visit your world just for this." He frowned. "Then I will leave before I have to eat any of your food."

Fifteen

A Morsel to Feast Upon

The summit was coming off better than David had expected. Jva and his artist friends had really come through. Everything worked together harmoniously. And so far, no one seemed to be offended by the placement of their cultural or pod symbols. Even Prince Kvran, who had arrived a quarter hour late, had not made any snide remarks about anything—at least not any that had filtered back to David yet. That had to be a first. Of course, the real test would come halfway through the second hour when Jva had scheduled a suite of Kzati tunes and some kind of incense injected into the aircyclers. His Highness was *sure* to find something lacking in the execution of that part. Jva had been willing to risk the ding to his grade, and David, Tkal, and Enemwenu had all agreed that leaving out a Kzati emphasis at some point in the evening simply wasn't workable.

The food was arranged artistically according to the sensibilities of two dozen races. The overall effect made David feel like he was damaging a work of art every time he sampled some delicacy, and yet each morsel someone removed seemed to simply change, but not destroy the arrangement. No mean trick, that!

David could see Ryan following His Highness Prince Kvran around like a puppy, or a toady…or worse. Every now and then, he would catch one or the other of them watching him. Maybe today would be even more interesting than planned.

David went about his duties as part of the hosting pod, making various fellow diplomacy students, members of other pods, feel at ease. He stayed busy trying to make sure he could smooth over the ruffled sensibilities of a Hnng offended by the sound of a Trelkairni war screecher, or a Wkkho who was repulsed by the scent of Tvern An desserts, or to distract the Lrahran while the Chiurdoun danced—though how they could find dancing bears offensive, rather than amusing, escaped David.

Tkal stopped by a couple of times to compliment his work, and to suggest more guests in need of attention. Dai-Soln came by to ask him for help calming a Hiyadi who was rather grumpy this early in the evening—not a dusk person. David was in his element, or at least found the challenge interesting. This was something he could do, a way he really could contribute to the team's success. And somewhere along the way, that had started to matter. He didn't have much to offer, but little things like this, he really could do.

Everything seemed calm for the moment, so David took the opportunity to join Dai-Soln and Red-shimmer at the food arrangements. He selected a plate and piled on a number of morsels, mostly recognizably Human foods, but also a few exotics he was certain were compatible with his biochemistry. Jva's team had avoided anything really spicy—even on the Hopherl menu— but the buffet still proffered plenty of tasty treats.

Red-shimmer glided closer to David and colored a couple of patterns before her voder kicked in. "Your choice to have Jva design this evening was wise. It is working out very well, and saved the rest of us much stress."

Dai-Soln twitched his fronds in agreement and bared his teeth in that grimace-like smile of his that showed joy, but looked like pain. So David was totally unprepared for what next came out of that mouth—the pastry, which fell with a half-chewed *splat* back onto Dai-Soln's plate.

"D'ulgh!" he exclaimed nictitating furiously. "Only a Human could ruin such a simple dessert so completely."

David jerked back as if slapped. Words were still wrestling for control of his tongue—whether to apologize or attack—when Red-shimmer caught his eye, flashing *Fuchsia-wash* over and over, with her voder silenced. He looked down and quickly saw her flash, "The Human from…the other group is behind you."

Other group? Violet Pod! She'd avoided the color word. Ryan. Ryan had walked up. Quick thinking on Dai-Soln's part. Even quicker on Red-shimmer's. David might have dressed Dai-Soln down if not for her warning. Now he just hung his head as Dai-Soln tabled his plate and stalked off at more than his usual height.

"Not a very pleasant creature, is he?"

David started and gasped, as if he hadn't know anyone was behind him. He spun around. "You startled…Who? Dai-Soln? No. Well, he's better than some." He tried to glance around for Red-shimmer down low, while Ryan scanned up high, probably looking for Gronorgh. Red-shimmer was no where to be seen. She seemed to have slipped away. But where to? Under the table? Or just lost in a forest of legs and skirts and robes?

"Yes, well, say…where is the ignorant oaf? No, never mind."

Ryan wouldn't have dismissed that line of thought half so quickly if he'd had any idea what Gronorgh was up to at that very moment. He put an arm around David's shoulder. Obviously, he meant it to convince David that he was his friend, looking out for him, his comrade on the lookout for a fellow Human. But he spoiled the effect when he couldn't resist a little posturing, too firm a grip, flexing a bit, puffing out his chest to prove he was alpha male here. "I told you I'd find a way for you to get in with us. Prince Kvran wanted me to ask you to come speak to him. He's giving you an audience."

David managed not to smile, but something must have shown on his face.

"Don't worry, squirt, he *wants* to meet you. He's serious about wanting you on his team. He wants it all settled before you're officially available."

"But why me?" David didn't even try to keep the curiosity and disbelief out of his voice.

"The Prince knows quality when he sees it. He had an…interest in Green Pod's last linguist before…'certain things' happened. He saw something of value in me when my pod collapsed."

Something? A certain amoral *je ne sais quoi*? Birds of a feather? It was getting exponentially harder to keep the revulsion off his face. David tried to look nervous, ill at ease, unsure of himself. Ryan ate it up.

"Dude. I'll be right there to help you. Prince Kvran thinks you're ready to sit at the table with the big guys. Come on, you can do this!"

The more Ryan tried to be…what? Helpful? Solicitous? Whatever. The more he tried, the more it tasted smarmy, smug and condescending. Oh well, David would have the last laugh tonight.

His Highness Prince Kvran was dressed in some kind of stiff fabric, covered in what looked to be actual gold brocade. It reminded David of a cross between a kimono and something Louis the XVI would have worn. He made a gesture twisting his hand, palm up, with the first two fingers more or less extended and the third curled back across the palm. He was allowing David to approach his royal person in a standing posture. But he should remain to the left and behind, next to the royal servant. David found himself in sudden sympathy with those Traiqi in the elevator, back at the beginning of term.

"Ryan has informed you of the position soon to open in Violet Pod. My linguist," he pursed his lips to point at the Tal Chin standing on the far side of the room talking to the leaders of Orange Pod and Silver Pod, "he tells me that you are one of the best students in the year below him."

David held his tongue, since he hadn't been given leave to speak.

Kvran gestured slightly and his servant reached forward to hand His Highness a drink. He'd brought his own glass? Goblet, actually. That certainly wasn't one of the glasses from the buffet.

The Prince wet his lips and swirled his drink. "He also tells me that unlike so many of you linguists who only study languages to get at the structure, you actually speak quite a number." He paused and angled his head. "Do you speak the Imperial Tongue?"

"No, Your Highness. I can read a bit, but I have never had the opportunity to speak him." What an affectation. Every other language got the Kzati version of *it*. The Imperial Tongue was *he*—with the inflection for noble rank. "I can learn him if he is needed for the job." And without much effort. David told the truth about not speaking Kzati, but he could read, write, and understand moderately well.

Kvran returned the goblet to his servant's care and flicked invisible dust from his sleeve. "He is a subtle tongue."

Subtle indeed. Baroque and choked with strained metaphors and snobbish references to Classical Literature, History, and Art. The language itself was not particularly complex. Except for the honorifics. Those really did get arcane. After a few more exchanges in the same vein, Kvran dismissed him, seeming to think that there was simply no way David could say no to the possibility of working for his august personage. David hadn't actually agreed to *anything*, but Kvran seemed to think it a done deal. David went back to tending his duties for Green Pod until it was time for him to do his bit.

Backstage David fidgeted uncontrollably. Why had he let Jva talk him into this? This wasn't art. It was rehearsed madness. There was no way he could make it through this without an aneurysm. David was not a performer. He wasn't a speaker. He wasn't going to survive this. He couldn't breathe.

"David!" Jva's voice had edge enough to cut through David's adrenaline fog. "Breathe! Slow down. You're hyperventilating. You'll make yourself pass out. I've seen it before. Stage artists get so worked up they pass out sometimes."

"Maybe I should."

"Should what?"

"Pass out!"

"No way. You go on in two standards. You can't do that to me. You're going onstage, on cue, and you're going to be perfect. People will be talking about this for months."

David started hyperventilating again.

Jva spun him around and held him by the shoulders, supporting him like a rag doll. He went eye-to-eye with David. "Listen to me. You've got this. This is language. This is your thing. Nobody. *Nobody* can do this better than you. You can collapse afterward, go into hysterics, pass out...or celebrate afterward. Right now, you're going onstage to do amazing things with language and ensure my grade."

David nodded when Jva shook him.

"Good. Now give me your shirt and get out there."

David peeled off his best shirt, revealing the coloform shirt he'd been wearing underneath all night. He breathed deeply and steadily. All the way in. All the way out. "Right. I got this. Yeah. The new version. Kvran's gonna croak."

Jva gasped and soto-hissed after him. "Wait! Kvran? What?" Jva grasped for him and came up with nothing but air. "David!"

But David was on stage. It was in motion. No stopping now. David ran the changes through his mind and glanced back. Now Jva was hyperventilating. He blocked that from his mind and stepped to his mark. He stooped and rolled out his keyboard mat. He straightened and stood for a moment. This was it…

Tkal watched David slip onto the stage and take his mark. What was that mat he was unrolling? Had he added another language? If so, he must have taken one out or he'd run over. AC#G, that's what it had to be. But why wouldn't he just whistle that? Tkal had heard him do it before. And why was he just standing there like he was in a trance? David couldn't have forgotten the words. He and Xtp had worked on translating that poem for a week. Tkal had been wakened in the middle of the night by David muttering the thing, in language after language, in his sleep.

And then David looked up, with that stare he got when he was looking at one thing but seeing something else, something in his own head—looking right through the audience to his own little world. David breathed in and started. The shirt started coloring as David danced over the mat, scattering tones, half tones, and quarter tones, with his feet while his mouth clicked Qttx, and his hands were— Was that the sign language the Hopherl used in their rituals? What was David doing? Reciting four translations of the poem at the same time? Impressive! Fascinating! Unbeli—Oh no! It was *Violet's code!* Oh, Eternal, no! David was—Kvran! Where was Kvran? There! His Highness was standing near the opposite wall, barely even noticing. The Tal Chin, Zang Nul, Violet's linguist…there. Mouth hanging open, muttering. What? Translating one or more of the languages? Matching it to the Standard words projected overhead? Maybe he wouldn't… He got it. He was headed straight for Kvran.

And there was Gronorgh, standing near the door arms crossed over his chest, leaning against the wall, sneering. How could someone that big move so silently? Never mind, it was done, Gronorgh wouldn't be standing there like that unless the attack had gone to plan.

And Kvran was in motion. He took a couple of steps toward David, turned and scanned the crowd for Tkal. But just as his eyes lit on Tkal and flamed into supernovas, his gaze slipped to Gronorgh. He figured that out too. A couple of quick gestures and his guards, who had been practicing being unobtrusive, appeared in phalanx around him, and spirited him from the room, past Gronorgh, who might have been furniture for all the notice he got.

David was finishing his performance as Tkal reached the stage. David skipped one more run up and down the scale, his shirt ablaze with a final burst of color while a final avalanche of clicks poured from his mouth and his hands came to rest across his chest. He took a shuddering breath and nearly collapsed. Tkal dashed on stage and helped him backstage.

"David? Why did you…? Are you okay?"

David's color was not good, and he was covered in sweat. He started trembling. "Jva, come help me!"

"Tkal, I can't! I have to go out there and…explain? Get the next set started? Something. Here comes Dai-Soln." And with that, he fled onstage.

"Tkal, did you—? Is David okay?"

"I'm not sure. Dai-Soln, can you get his other arm? Help me get him out of here."

"Did he just…?"

"Yes. Whatever you were going to ask, yes. He just did it."

Dai-Soln didn't speak again till they had David in a lift. "He just stood up there and recited that poem in four languages simultaneously, using his mouth, hands, feet, and skin. In front of Kvran."

"That pretty well covers it."

"Did you…?"

"No. Last I knew this was still a sequential recitation. I hope he hasn't fried his brain. Have you ever heard of anyone doing that before?"

"No. But I'd never heard about that two-languages thing, SimCom, until he explained it as part of how he broke the code. Maybe Humans are wired for this?"

"Not any of the ones I've ever known. And David doesn't look like he was either." Tkal and Dai-Soln studied David's sagging features in the mirror-polished walls of the lift.

Dai-Soln looked at Tkal. "He really doesn't look well."

David muttered something that sounded like "Ithing'mmgonnbarf."

"No David! Hold it in!"

The lift doors opened, and Tkal and Dai-Soln carry-drag-led David down the corridor to Green Room as fast as they could.

Tkal got David laid down on his bed and turned to Dai-Soln. "I *have* to get back there. You do too. But he can't be alone. Who?"

Dai-Soln vibrated his fronds. "I don't know. Go. I'll get someone here and rejoin you as fast as possible."

Tkal walked toward the door. He turned back. "David, are you alright? Do you need a doctor?"

"Just a headache. Splitting headache. Oh! Moving. Can't barf. My head will explode if I do. Go! I'm okay."

Tkal creased his brow and frowned like he was the one in pain.

"Go. I…go."

Tkal went, but not without wavering again in the doorway.

Dai-Soln felt David's forehead.

"What are you doing?"

"Um, actually, I am not sure, but Humans always do this in vids."

David started to laugh, but it ended as a gasp. "I don't have a fever. Go. I'll be okay soon."

"No. I told Tkal I would find someone to stay with you first. Red-shimmer? No. She will be busier than any of us, working the room to re-establish trade with lost partners. Ael? No. Xtp? Maybe." Dai-Soln sent a message and waited. David moaned. Dai-Soln looked down. David was asleep.

Sixteen

Brotherhood

David couldn't concentrate on his classes. He had only the vaguest notion of what any of his professors had said today. His mind was simply elsewhere.

Family. He was going to have a family again. Okay, so they were aliens, and he'd never even met his new brother's parents yet, but… Well, he was getting ahead of himself again. The ceremony hadn't happened yet. There was still time for Tkal to back out. No. Tkal wouldn't do that. Not Tkal. No way he could be that cruel. Some people he'd known, yes, but not Tkal.

All the details were supposed to be set. Everything arranged. But David kept running lists and details through his head. Over and over, in spiraling loops and eddying swirls. He was sure that something had been overlooked— or would be. The conference room was reserved and paid for. The stuff for the ceremony? Tkal had all of the cups and doodads and juices and syrups and pastes that went in them. Tkal had the robes for David. David was still waiting for… He checked the time reflexively. It was only day cycle 4:80. The tailor had said Tkal's suit wouldn't be ready until 5:75. Almost a standard hour to wait for that. Maybe he really should have gone with green or yellow to match Tkal's stripes. Too late for that now.

"Waiting stinks."

Two or three classmates gave him strange stares. David flushed to realize that he'd said that out loud.

He spent most of the rest of the class glancing at the time. How could time move so slowly? Curse Einstein and Relativity!

As soon as class released, David dashed for the tailor's shop to get the suit, which had required some re-cutting to accommodate Tkal's non-human anatomy, but not a whole lot. He was early. He was told to wait until 5:75. Then suddenly the suit was not only ready, but hanging, bagged, and on the wall behind the clerk the entire time David had been waiting! David snarled and glanced it over. He wished it could have been nicer. He paid, then zipped for the lifts.

He had to get back to the dorm, clean up, and change. Oh, and food. He ought to eat. Bland. Something bland. Who knew how all the weird stuff they had to drink would set on his stomach. Bread. Bread would— No. He'd been fasting bread for a week just to be on the safe side for Tkal. What was he thinking? He wasn't thinking. At least not straight. Something else. Bananas? Chips? He didn't have any fruit. Chips would do. Before he cleaned up. Couldn't get grease on his clothes.

He was rattling apart inside his own brain!

Calm. He needed to calm down.

Besides, they had decided not to tell the rest of the pod until afterward, so… If he was this frazzled, someone would notice and ask.

Calm.

David got on the lift and practiced breathing till he reached his floor. He tried to walk like a normal person, but surely he was shaking so bad…

Family. He was going to have a family again. Not since Aunt Katherine died. But now.

This was…exhausting. He had to calm down, or he'd make a fool of himself during the ceremony. Or die of an aneurysm before it even started. Oh, God! He couldn't remember the Tvern El words!

David took a deep breath. A very deep breath. "Okay. This is ridiculous. I'm not eight years old anymore." He squared his shoulders and tried to walk with some dignity. He couldn't decide whether to carry the garment bag over his shoulder or over his arm and kept switching as he walked. So much for dignity. Halfway down the corridor to Green Room, he met Jva going the other way.

"Hey!" Jva called out. "Been shopping?"

David tried to turn as he went past to keep the bag as much out of sight as possible. But Jva was quick and tall. He darted out one hand and caught a handful of the bag. "Come on. Let's have a look!"

"No, Jva."

"Fabrini?"

David bristled at Jva's frown. No doubt he bought his clothes somewhere nicer.

Oblivious, Jva kept talking. "I didn't think you went for suits! Function over form for you normally."

David glared at him.

"Sorry. I didn't mean anything. You just don't usually go in for show. Fabrini—well, his work is…distinctive."

"It's not—"

"Um, David? Not to be a critic, but, art is my specialty after all. And ah, that color…isn't going to work well for you. I don't know how much you spent, but—"

"Jva!" David sighed. "Thank you. I'll take that into consideration."

Jva blinked. "Um, yeah. Okay. I'll be on my way then. I have a class. Can't be late."

David turned and paced the rest of the way to Green Room. The door opened, and David was relieved to find the common room empty. He'd expected to find Ael and Shinti sitting somewhere in the room, discussing Jva's visit. But instead, he got to slip quietly into his room. Something had finally worked out today.

He showered and changed into the T-shirt and light pants he'd wear under the Tvern robes, which he'd put on once they got to the ceremony. He continued checking the time every few standards. Argh! Time could move so slowly.

Just then, Tkal came in. He looked frazzled. "Pop quiz in Treaty Writing." He threw his bag on his bed, and reached into his closet, nearly knocking the door off its track. "Nearly fried my brain." He dashed into the bathroom. "Didn't think I'd ever finish in time to get here!" He shouted through the closed door, "Thought I'd have to go straight to the ceremony!" Moments later, he re-emerged, dressed very much like David. There were distinct advantages to not having hair to wash and dry. Tkal quickly slathered on the waxy cream he sometimes applied to his skin, rubbing his hands together and running them over his scalp and neck and face and up his forearms. "Ah! My eye!" he yelled. "I got this junk in my eye! It burns like fire!"

David got Tkal a towel, and soon enough everything was put to rights, even if one golden eye had a red ring around it. The two of them hoisted garment bags over their shoulders, Tkal's holding a suit, David's a robe, and they headed for the conference room.

Lined up in a double row on the table stood twelve small, ornate cups like saki glasses—six on Tkal's side, six on David's. Each pair of cups bore designs different from all the others. Tkal had explained the designs beforehand, how they were symbolic representations of the contents of each cup. Tkal wore the Human-style suit. Not a very good one, but it was the best David could afford, and at least it fit him. David had tried to choose a color that wouldn't clash with Tkal's stripes and had settled on a light cream, which might not have been the best choice, considering the off shade Tkal was presenting at that moment. Tkal's off coloration made David really glad he had decided against trying to match a tie to Tkal's stripes. Instead he had gone with a dark purple, which was rather too garish, but Tkal had loved it and at least it didn't clash with his faded stripes.

David was dressed in heavy Tvern ceremonial robes. He was sweating under the thick fabrics and brocade. Tkal had gotten them cut down twice to better fit David's slight frame. He seemed not to comprehend how much slighter of build David was than himself.

The cups were ordered in a specific way according to contrasting tastes. The first cup contained the bluish *tganil* nectar, which was so astonishingly bitter that David had almost retched the first time he tasted it—just a drop on the tip of his tongue. It was paired with the second cup, which was filled with amber *fgilal* oil that tasted a lot like the hot chili oil used in Chinese cooking. The third cup held a dollop of yellowish *vgir* paste, intensely sour, but something David rather enjoyed. It was paired with the fourth, containing the sticky-sweet, violet *ktiral* juice. The fifth cup contained sea water from the town of Kgarln where Tgernar and Fgerin had become brothers, at the site of Gvar's death by betrayal, at the hand of his own son. It paired with the sixth, filled with milky-white *tinarn* root sap, which was about as bland as anything imaginable. Tkal described it as "nutritious enough to live on, but so boring you'd rather starve."

Between the rows of cups lay two Tvern knives. The blades were housed in sheathes of filigree. Each had a row of alternating green and yellow jewels near the top, as was tradition, but Tkal had modified these by having a row of some pale peachy stone—David supposed a topaz—added above the green and yellow on one sheath and below on the other. The blades within were etched with intricate patterns. On first sight, David had asked Tkal if they weren't too pretty to actually use, but Tkal had assured him that while the jeweled sheaths could be damaged, the blades would stand up to any use. They could kill through light armor, cut through *vger*-hide cords in a single swipe, or even be used as a lever against huge weights without damage. David knew they would slice paper cleanly and precisely. The knives framed the final object on the table, a chalice or goblet forged from a bluish metal that felt cold to the touch.

David faced Tkal across the table and waited.

Tkal reached for the first cup. He raised it to David.

"I pledge in this nectar of the *tganil* flower, which is my heartache…"

David likewise lifted his first cup to Tkal.

"Gvarln ta fge tganil e, e kfi kti ki gen…"

They each sipped from their own cup. David had to struggle not to gag on the stuff; it tasted like baker's chocolate mixed with bile. It was hard to imagine a more vile-tasting drink. Each of them poured what remained into the goblet.

Tkal raised the second cup.

"…in this oil of the *fgilal* seed, which is my joy…"

David copied.

"…fge fgilal e, e tvil kti ki gen…"

Tkal saluted him with the third cup.

"…through this *vgir* paste, which is my disappointment…"

David did likewise.

"…fge vgir e, e ftan kti ki gen…"

David reached for the fourth cup and raised it to Tkal.

"…fge ktiral e, e finirl kti ki gan…"

Tkal likewise lifted his cup to David.

"…through this *ktiral* juice, which is all my dreams…

David raised the fifth cup.

"…fge dveln el fan Kgarln ki tdar e Gvar kdi e, fge dveln e…"

Tkal copied.

"…with this water from the sea at Kgarln, place of Gvar's death, with that water…"

David saluted Tkal with the sixth cup.

"…vkerl tinarn e, e el vgar denerl kti ki va kfiln…"

Tkal did likewise.

"…in spite of the milk of the *tinarn* root, which is the worst of all our enemies…"

They added the remainder of this to the goblet where all the other cups swirled together.

Tkal bowed to David.

"…for all that—I am, now and forever, your friend, even your brother."

David bowed to Tkal.

"…fvil vde da dtarln ta kgir ar ki, va il tkel ar ki."

Tkal and David each reached for the knife on the side of the table opposite themselves.

"This pledge, I seal with this my blood."

"Gvarln e ta fge ginal e kti ki e ta dkarln e."

Each sliced his own hand and let three drops of his own blood fall into the goblet. They then exchanged knives.

"I take this knife in hand."

"Ta fdinel e fge kdar kvel."

"Gvarln e ta fge ginal e ar ki e ta dkarln e."

"This pledge I seal with this, your blood."

Three more drops from each hand, Human and Tvern An. Tkal raised the goblet and swirled the contents, smearing the stem and foot with his blood in the process. He then handed the goblet to David who inhaled deeply. The smell was intoxicating, quite literally. David felt dizzy as he swirled the goblet and handed it back to Tkal who took it, now smeared with David's blood as well, and drank from the goblet. Then he inhaled the aroma and handed the goblet back to David, who had to drink the goblet dry. Tkal had left him more than his fair share. It was delicious, like liquid gold running down his throat. Commingled, the sticky sweetness, the tongue-drying saltiness, the oily fire, the bland milk, the bitter gall, and the mouth-puckering sour all balanced each other perfectly, but the Tvern An said it was the blood of true brothers that transformed this drink into something that would linger on the tongue forever. David hoped it was true. He never wanted this taste to fade. He upended the goblet for the last drop, then set it on the table.

"Our blood commingled, we are now one, brothers inseparable. We are *fdinel.*"

"Ginal kte ki va kginrl, da kti kginrl, tkel tarln. Fdinel kti."

Together they chanted:

"Da ginal kti ki kti gvarln.

Ktal ktin ktal gdal kti fgan ki fdan.

Dtarln ginal kti ki kti gvarln.

Now we pledge our blood.

Neither sorrow nor joy will part us.

Forever we pledge our blood."

David's lightheadedness was surely due to the drink. He had family. For the first time since he was eight years old, he had family.

Seventeen

Getting There Can Be Half the Fun

David and Tkal stood in the station's arboretum, six levels above most of Shel Matkei Academy, eight above their dorm suite. David was glad of the break between quarters. As much as he enjoyed studying, even he needed breaks.

"Have you ever been to Tolari Market on Epemthu?" Tkal asked, his golden eyes sparking with mischief as the yellow and green stripes crinkled at the corners of his eyes.

"No," David answered warily, knowing that look. "I haven't been off station since I arrived."

Tkal's jacket creaked as he crossed his arms. "Not at all? For three years? How do you stand it?" He shrugged and looked astonished.

David shifted his feet uneasily. "I come here to the arboretum a lot…and look at the stars. Sometimes it helps. Sometimes it makes it worse. The stars are cold and lonely tonight." He stared out at the unwinking stars trying to think of a safe topic. "I miss Venus."

"Yeah, that's an amazing sister planet you have. When I spent the summer on Tvern a couple of years, I would look at the sky and see Tgern, our smallest moon, and think how much it looked like Venus. You've never been to Tolari Market."

David shook his head.

"Ya wanna go?" His green and yellow stripes intensified with the excitement of a hatching plot.

"It's too expensive." David had drained his stipend account for the suit.

"Yeah, but you wanna?"

"Sure, I'd like to see it…"

"Let's go!"

"What?"

"Let's go. Right now. The last shuttle leaves in twenty-five standards. We can catch it if we run."

"I don't have any money."

"I do. Come on! What are brothers for?"

David hesitated.

"Come on!" Tkal grabbed David's arm too tightly for comfort and hauled him out of the arboretum, down the corridor. David might have tried to resist if he'd had time to think, but it would have been useless anyway. Tkal was much stronger, and his big hand wrapped all the way around David's arm. Tkal bustled David into the lift. "Level one," he commanded, and the lift rushed downward.

"I don't have any clothes or a toothbrush or—"

"We'll buy it when we get there. Come on, we'll miss the shuttle!"

David chased Tkal down the corridor at full tilt wondering why his feet were following. "Tkal," he gasped. "This is crazy!"

"I know! Isn't it fun?"

It *was* fun and David's feet kept following.

When they reached the ticket counter, Tkal wasn't even winded, but David was gasping for air.

"Two, please." Tkal smiled

The ticket agent turned a bland face to greet him. "I'm sorry, sir. We're full."

"Are you sure?" Tkal said in his most charming tone.

She looked at him with one eyebrow raised. "I'm sure. You'll have to wait till tomorrow."

"Let's go, Tkal." David started to walk off.

One of the stewards, an unpleasant looking man with a hard jaw line, a doughy complexion, and pig-like eyes, whispered to the ticket agent, "Have you found anyone yet? We're two stewards down! We'll get an ore loader of complaints."

"David, wait!" Tkal called. He turned back to the ticket agent. "Are you sure you've got no seats available?"

"I told you sir, no seats available. You'll have to wait till morning. The next flight is at day cycle 01:00."

"So, you've got a full-to-capacity shuttle load of tired, cranky passengers and you're down two stewards?"

She nodded with a plastered-on smile of exasperation.

"How about us?" Tkal said, indicating himself and David.

David gaped at Tkal, awed at his gall.

"Here we are ready to help you if you'll take us down."

She raised an eyebrow at the steward who shrugged. "Okay, follow him. I know this violates a dozen regulations, but I don't want the complaints. If you can pull this off quietly, go for it." She closed the counter down as David and Tkal followed the steward.

The steward led them back to a small room David would never have known existed if not for this adventure. He handed them each a uniform and told them, "Put these on double quick. We launch in eight standard minutes, and you have to be in uniform, on board, and strapped in." Tkal and David pulled off trousers and pulled on trousers, pulled off shirts and put on shirts, pulled off shoes and pulled on shoes, and buttoned up jackets. David's uniform was a bit baggy and Tkal's a bit snug, but they worked. And David and Tkal made it into their seats just as the pilot sealed the hatches and announced take off.

"Did I ever tell you this is how my parents died? On a shuttle ride, on vacation." David confided to Tkal.

Before Tkal could respond, the head steward, sitting in the seat directly across from David hissed, "I'll pitch you out the airlock if you say another word like that on this flight!"

David ducked his head. "Sorry."

"We have a phobic in 16A. You're here to make sure the passengers enjoy their flight, not cause a panic."

"Sorry."

"You better be!"

Tkal broke in, "My brother said he's sorry. What are our duties?"

The steward's face couldn't decide whether to show confusion or to glare. "You'll be serving rows sixteen through thirty. Kenea and I have one through fifteen and Takko'let and Razhat have rows thirty-one through forty-five. They're loading their carts now. Get to yours."

Tkal and David quickly began loading the ready-made, pre-heated or chilled meals into their cart, trays at a time. There were three choices: a main selection edible to Humans and twenty-five other races, a second choice poisonous to twenty of those races but edible to six who couldn't eat the first choice, and third a tray of *chikatze* for the Eikarian seated in 17B. This was a budget flight. On a luxury flight, all passengers would have been served meals from their own homeworlds.

David and Tkal had their cart loaded by the time the other teams had theirs loaded, and waited for the next hissed instruction from the head steward. At his signal, they wheeled their cart up to row sixteen and started dispensing meals.

Passenger 16A, a thin, elderly Human, glanced up at David as he passed her meal to her. "How long is this flight, son?"

David looked into her worried gray eyes. "Not long, ma'am. Will you be staying long on Epemthu?"

"About six months. I'm visiting my son and daughter-in-law. I have a new grandbaby."

David smiled, handed a meal to 16B and started to turn to 16C and 16D on the other side of the aisle.

"Son?" She looked up at him, searching his face, "Am I safe here? I've never been in space before."

David realized that she must have spent the months on the trip out in cryo, instead of awake. This was the first part of her journey that was real to her. "Well, ma'am, this is where I live and work, and I'm none the worse for it. And you've come a long way from Earth yourself. When did you leave?"

"Just after the New Year."

"See. It's nearly March now back on Earth. You've been in space for almost two months, and not one bad thing has happened to you."

She smiled. "Thank you. Thank you for calming a silly old woman."

"Not silly at all. Quite natural the first time. But you'll be with your grandbaby tomorrow morning."

She reached up and patted his hand just like his Aunt Katherine had done when he was a little boy.

David quickly served 16C and 16D. He nearly forgot to give 17B the *chikatze*, but remembered just in time. He and Tkal finished with their rows and stowed their cart just as the head steward and his partner finished their rows.

The head steward waited till the third team had stowed their cart as well. "Okay, we go back out in twenty-five standards to collect the trays and offer more beverages." He stared at David. "That was good work out there, what you did with 16A. You sure you haven't done this before?"

"No, I'm just a student. And she's not really phobic. Just a little scared."

"Maybe now, but she rated a twelve at boarding on Earth. Almost didn't get to board. Had to go through counseling first and then straight into cryo, no option of awake time for phobes who rate as high as her. But as long as the trip out here from Earth takes, I'd almost rather sleep it in cryo myself. Anyway, you calmed her right down. If you'd said the wrong thing we might be sedating her again. Good work."

Tkal smiled one of his I-told-you-so smiles and went back to his seat.

"What?" David turned to follow Tkal. "What?"

Tkal just sat there sphinx-like. He really could be frustrating.

The bus from the shuttle port let Tkal and David off near the square, just as Tolari Market was waking with the rising sun. They had arrived on the day of the jousting tournaments. Garish gonfalons of the merchant guilds fluttered in the crisp morning breeze. Pennants of the Tolari Council streamed overhead. Already, the sounds of horns and pipes lilted through the air. David took a deep breath and inhaled the rich aroma of baking bread. Tolari Market was half active marketplace and half tourist faire. Soon it would burst into the full buzz of activity.

Tkal wore a satin pirate shirt he had bought as soon as they arrived. The yellow of the shirt exactly matched the yellow stripes of his skin. He had complimented the shirt with a green sash tied around his waist. The sash was about a half shade off from his complexion between the stripes. With the slightly military-looking pants he was wearing, all he needed was a tricorn hat to complete the picture. He rubbed his hands together and patted his can't-pinch-an-inch waist. "Let's get some breakfast. I know a place that sells soda bread—no yeast to poison me—and they have really good *mija* sausage."

"Mija sausage?"

"It tastes a lot like American breakfast sausage, but it's made from a local animal. It's supposed to be a lot healthier than pork."

David more or less agreed, and Tkal led the way down the market street to a stall that flew both the red-and-gold gonfalon of the butcher's guild and the green-and-gold of the baker's guild. "The husband's a butcher and the wife's a baker, so everything they sell here is as fresh as can be, and this early in the morning you get the first batch." He broke off his extolling of breakfast when he looked at David. "What are you smirking about?"

"You look like Long John Silver in that outfit."

"Only with debonair green-and-yellow stripes," Tkal laughed, and David laughed with him. "Just call me Yellow Stripe the Pirate! Uh, wait, that doesn't have quite the right ring to it."

"No, a cowardly pirate doesn't sound too good." David struggled to control his smile at Tkal's expression of disgust. Tkal hated it when one of his clever remarks failed to come out clever.

"Well, then, just call me Tkal the Magnificent, and you can be my side kick. We'll think of a name for you after we eat!" Tkal pushed aside the curtain covering the doorway of the stall and a glorious symphony of breakfast smells swirled out. David followed him inside eagerly.

"Hello, Tkal. Back for more mija sausage?" asked the burly butcher.

"And some soda bread, and a bowl of siga berries with sweet cream."

David raised his eyebrows at Tkal.

"Don't worry. No yeast."

The eyebrows again.

"I took my pills just after we landed, and I have my injector, just in case." He patted the pocket where he had stowed his emergency injector pen, and turned from David as if to end that conversation. "How is the business?" he asked the baker, who had stuck her head out from the kitchen.

"We're doing well. This season has started off better than last. The tourists are coming in droves." The baker smiled which deepened the lines around her mouth and eyes. She looked like she smiled a lot. "And what will your friend have?"

"I'll have the same, but without the sweet cream," David said.

"He'll take the cream, too," Tkal contradicted. "And a glass of grapefruit juice if you have it," he added.

"No. No cream. And water will be fine."

"Which will it be?" asked the smiling baker. Her husband could be heard chuckling from the kitchen where he had retreated to start the sausage cooking.

"I'm buying, so cream and juice," Tkal said.

The baker winked at David. "Just give up, hon. You can't win when Tkal wants to be generous. He won't be denied the pleasure." She disappeared into the kitchen.

"Tkal, I said no cream."

"I know, but you love it."

"How do you know? What if I don't like cream?"

"With as much of that fake stuff as you put in your coffee? And the way you ate those strawberry shortcakes that day at lunch?"

"Do you have to notice *everything*? I feel guilty freeloading on this trip."

"We're brothers. You need to start acting like it. I invited you. Remember? Don't worry. I won't suggest anything I don't want to pay for. I just got downloads of money from home, and my chit is burning a hole in my pocket."

The baker returned from the kitchen with two sizzling plates of mija sausage and a steaming loaf of round bread. The smell was almost intoxicating this close. David tore off a hunk of the bread and buttered it. The butter vanished into the dense bread turning it a golden yellow. David closed his eyes. "Mmm…This is wonderful!" His fork made haste for the sausage. "Oh, this is delicious."

The baker smiled. "Glad you like it, son."

"Tell your friends," yelled the butcher from the kitchen. An instant later, he was coming through the doors with two chilled bowls of siga berries and cream.

The baker placed the drinks on the table and stood over by her husband, who put his arm around her shoulder. They stood for a moment watching their happy customers. "Well, I have to get the rolls in," said the baker and disappeared back into the kitchen.

"Call us if you need anything," said the butcher as he joined his wife.

Tkal and David finished their breakfast, quite satisfied. Tkal tipped generously. No wonder the couple liked him so. "So where do you want to go now?"

"What? Gee, I don't know. You're the one who's been here before. I'd like to just wander around a while, I guess."

They started walking.

"Do you know why they chose such a medieval style for this place?"

"Tourism."

"Really? That's it?"

"It got *you* here didn't it?"

David gave Tkal a sidelong look.

"Okay, so it got me to get you here. Unwillingly. Kicking and screaming the whole way." He waited as David glared. "So you could have the time of your life." He added, just as David stared to smirk. "It's fairly accurate to the time period, if not to any particular place. From what I've been told."

"I don't know. It seems a lot more colorful than history class made it sound."

"Yeah. I thought the same thing. But it's still fun. You need some new clothes."

"Oh, no. If you think I'm going to wear something like you've got on, you're crazy."

"Don't be so dusty! Have some fun. How 'bout something like *that* guy's wearing?"

David followed Tkal's gesture to a tallish man wearing lederhosen and an outrageous hat with a huge plume in it. "You're crazy! No way."

"Okay, how 'bout that guy in the skirt?"

"It's a kilt."

"It's a skirt. And it looks a lot sillier to me."

"Well, it's a very old tradition. But I'm not wearing a kilt either."

"Okay, let's just stop in this tailor's shop and see if there's anything you *will* wear."

David tried to stop and argue, but Tkal had already entered the shop so he had no choice but to follow him in or stand in the street like a fool. A little bell sounded as he entered the shop, though David couldn't identify where the bell might be.

Seconds later, the tailor popped her head through a door opening from a back room. "Can I help you? Ah, brought a friend with you, Tkal?"

"Yes, we're looking for something—"

"Sedate."

"Fun," Tkal said, ignoring David's interruption.

"Tkal!" David whispered fiercely.

"But my brother doesn't quite share my idea of fun."

The tailor quirked an eyebrow at that, but didn't ask. "Ah, I see." She turned her back to open what had looked like a shelf of books and started pulling pattern holos.

"Does everyone here know you by name?"

"No, not everyone. But remembering names is good for business."

The tailor turned around. "Here, something like this might be to your liking." She popped a holo cube into the projector on the counter which beeped a couple of times and flashed an orangish light. "Oops. Forgot to scan you. Step over here, sweetie."

David stepped to the side of the counter as indicated.

The tailor took out a laser wand and scanned him from the front, from the back, along his arms, and down his sides. She aimed the wand at the projector to download his measurements, which almost instantly produced a thirty-centimeter holo of David wearing the most outrageous outfit.

"*What* is that?" David blurted.

"It's a tabard." She looked hurt. "It was worn by minor court functionaries, pages, and such. You're about the right age." Her tone said her choices weren't often met so. "How about this?" she asked more cheerily. "It's an Italian count, fourteenth century."

"Do you have anything with, ah, fewer colors?"

"I see what you mean about your friend's taste being different from yours." Tkal shrugged.

"Tkal there can't get enough color." She turned and eyed Tkal. "Say, I didn't sell you *that* outfit."

"Impulse buy. Off the rack."

"Ah." She didn't look impressed. "Well, I hope you got a good price. That sash clashes with your stripes. You should have come to me."

"You're the second person to tell me that." Tkal made a face at David.

The tailor smiled. "Ah, so this one has his own style *and* an eye for color. Well, sweetie, don't get out much do you? Kinda pale. Nice eyes. Kinda gray in this light. You should let your hair grow out. How do you feel about velvet?"

"Er…"

"No. You're more comfortable with linens and wools. How's this? English middle-class shopkeeper." She pressed something on the wand and the holo produced David in the new costume.

"Hmm. Not bad. The top half is interesting but knee britches and hose?"

"Mm." Her brow creased, and she brushed a wisp of hair back up into her bun. "Ah! This one. Well-to-do peasant from Zagreb."

"That's nice. I could wear that. How much?"

"Never discuss price after a sale. It's bad luck."

"After? What?"

"Tkal just transferred the credits."

"What?" David whirled to face Tkal.

"You're a Zagrebian peasant for the rest of the day. Deal with it. Where's Zagreb?"

"Croatia. You can't just buy it without even asking me. How do you even know if I like it?"

"You said it was nice. She thinks it's you. *And* you know where Zagreb is. You were destined to wear that today." Tkal laughed.

David sulked.

"Come back in an hour and it'll be ready."

By noon the town square was as full as David's stomach. Tkal had remembered another restaurant that served an early lunch in portions meant for far larger men than David, but somehow, to Tkal's amazement, and David's too truth-be-told, David had polished it all off. He was no longer sure that had been such a good idea. He had already let his Zagreb peasant's belt out, twice. He tried to take his mind off the difficulty of breathing with such a full stomach and focus on the hubbub in the square. He listened as the town crier read off a list of scheduled events: archery, bobbing for apples, candy tastings, dances, educating, falconry, glass making, hawking, imbibing, jesting, knitting, lumberjacking, minstrelsy, needlework, organ playing, piping, quoits, races, swordplay, trothing, udder milking, versifying, wrestling, yodeling and zookeeping. It promised to be a full and interesting day. David was finally starting to enjoy himself, even if the costume itched in the noon sun. He tugged at his belt again.

"I told you not to eat so much."

"Liar. You were daring me to finish it."

"Well, you shoulda known better after last time."

David threw up his hands and made a noise somewhere between a shout, a gag, and a cough.

"Man, don't hurt yourself! We need you able to talk when we get back to school." Tkal dissolved into laughter.

David tried to glare at him, but when Tkal laughed, it was very difficult not to laugh with him. "I think I'm going to go watch the jesting and the minstrels. What about you?" he asked by way of changing the subject.

"Well, I want to catch the swordplay demonstrations. They're crystalline! And the smithing demos are brutal gnashing!"

"You use too much slang, Tkal."

"Well, you don't use enough. It's *your* native language. Have some fun with it."

"I prefer to respect my language by not torturing it."

"Oh, alright. Don't go all dusty on me. So, you want to see the jesting. Just don't forget the jousting. You wouldn't want to miss the jousting for the jesting."

David laughed.

"Seriously. I know how caught up you can get in something like that, and the jesting is one of the few events that doesn't completely shut down for the tournament."

"They close everything down for the jousting?"

"It's spectacular. The locals don't want to miss it either, so just about everything closes. The whole town and all the visitors will be there, except for a few die hards. Mostly the ones who are too drunk to get up from the ale benches, and some of the jesters."

"Okay, I promise I won't lose track of time."

They parted ways, running into each other at random intervals throughout the early afternoon, exchanging excited bits of news and next destinations. Finally, David found himself at the jesting contest. He laughed so hard that his sides ached as much as his belly had earlier in the day. Suddenly he looked up, and there was Tkal gesturing impatiently. He glanced at the time. He was already ten standards late. "Sorry." He rushed over to Tkal. "I lost track of time."

"Yeah, well I knew you would, so I built in a cushion. We'll still be on time, but we won't get good seats."

David grimaced and followed quickly through the sparse crowd, all headed the same direction. Tkal was right about everyone attending the joust. When they entered the field, the stands were almost full. Tkal and David managed to find seats together, about halfway up at the far end of the field from the trumpeters. Only a few standards after they arrived, the fanfare sounded, and the "Duke" and "Duchess" arrived with their entourage. There was a long-winded speech and some largess. Then the first two champions rode onto the field in their dazzlingly polished armor. They were two very big men, but dwarfed by their massive mounts. David had never seen such horses, even in the movies, which was the only place he had ever seen a horse before. The Duchess held out her handkerchief to one of the champions, the one seated on the gray horse. He rode over, accepted the handkerchief, inhaled theatrically of its perfume and then had his squire attach the cloth to the hilt of his lance. This done, he rode back to his place on the field, the end nearest Tkal and David.

After a few tense moments, as the horses champed their bits and pawed the ground, the Duke rose and gave a signal. Like lightening, horses and riders hurtled toward each other. David winced in sympathetic pain as the more distant rider was shoved off the back end of his horse and slammed into the ground with bone-rattling force. Tkal sprang to his feet, cheering like a man who had money on the outcome. David was just about to ask him if that were the case when the monks came running out to help the unhorsed knight off the field, on a stretcher they obviously found rather much to bear. The knight was no small man, and that armor had to weigh a lot.

By the time the monks had cleared the field, the second pair were ready to charge each other. One after another, the knights were unhorsed though not all as thoroughly and quickly as the first. Soon the Duchess's champion returned to the field to unseat a second doomed knight. After several more appearances, the champion was eventually called out for the final joust against another knight even larger than himself, seated on a brown horse of unbelievable size. David would have needed a stepladder to mount it. The knight rode back to the royal box and received the Duchess's blown kiss and a promise of fabulous reward from the Duke should he bring the victor's pennant to his lady. The knight bowed as deeply as David thought possible while wearing so much steel armor and seated on a giant horse.

Returning to his place on the field, the knight sat erect, waiting. At the signal, he and the other knight charged each other with frightening ferocity. At the end of the charge, both men's lances were shattered, but both had managed to keep their mounts. Three charges and as many lances later, the duel finally ended when the knight on the brown horse slipped his lance under the champion's shield and lifted him clear of his horse, depositing him uncerimoniously on his backside. The way he flailed his arms around, David was glad the visor stayed down and muffled his words. He had no doubt they were not for general consumption.

Tkal was now cheering for the winner as fiercely as he had for the former champion just a moment before. David stared at him, speechless at how quickly Tkal could switch gears. The Duchess accepted a token from the new champion and the Duke accepted his homage. Whatever disappointment the Duchess might have felt about her champion's failure was quite overcome by the time she rose and called one and all to the dance. The stands quickly emptied as the musicians set up.

Tkal grabbed David by the arm and started to haul him down to the field with everyone else. This time David resisted. "Come on," said Tkal. "The dance is about to start. You want to find a partner."

"No, Tkal. You want to find a partner. I want to sit here."

"Don't be a stick. Come on. You'll have fun. It's not hard. You don't even have to try."

"I'm not going to try. I'm going to sit here and watch."

"David." Tkal snorted a huge breath out his nostrils, making him look more like a dragon than usual. He opened his mouth once, twice, then crossed his arms. "Fine. Suit yourself. But you'll regret it tomorrow. There's no getting today back." Tkal stalked out to the field. He shrugged his shoulders in that way he had that said, "I'm not going to let it bother me now, but it's not over." Then he joined the nearest group. He danced for half an hour or more. David was still obstinate when Tkal came back to try once more to get David to join in. He didn't try a third time.

It looked like Tkal and everyone else was having a good time. David almost gave in and tried one of the dances. Almost but not quite. He had had more fun that day than he could remember having since he was a small boy. But that wasn't enough to get him out on that field with everyone else. On the ride back to the station, he wished it had been. Tkal said something about not being able to get that day back. The whole return trip went sour.

Eighteen

An Ill Wind

David sat bolt upright. His alarm hadn't gone off. He'd had a dream, a nightmare of sorts, but it was already slipping away. He couldn't remember what had been so terrible, what had shocked him right out of his sleep, out of breath like he'd been fighting for his life. He unclenched his fists and tried to relax his arms, shoulders, and chest.

Something was still wrong. He listened to the darkness. Nothing but his own breathing as he struggled to calm himself. Nothing? He listened more closely, holding his breath. The blood rushing in his ears and the chill of evaporating sweat was distracting, but the room sounded wrong. That was it. There was no sound but what came from him.

He waved the lights on. Tkal's bed was empty. The sheets and blanket were tucked with military precision. No one had been in or on that bed.

David snatched his netbook from the desk. Night cycle 8:00. Only two standards before day cycle started, and with it the new term. All night? David touched his terminal to look for messages from Tkal. Nothing. He checked Tkal's public calendar. Nothing. A physical note? Just the sort of joke Tkal might play, but nothing. First day. Tkal had the second half of Applications of Force: The Diplomacy of Disparity starting at day cycle 2:00. He wouldn't skip a class like that. He checked the syllabus. A major paper was due today and there was an in-class exam. What a welcome back from the break. Maybe Tkal had gone somewhere quiet to pull an all-nighter. Those two-term classes could be killer.

David dressed and ran his fingers through his hair. He went out to the common room and made himself some breakfast—an egg and a slice of toast.

"It's no wonder you're so tiny," rumbled a voice right behind his ear. "Even for a Human. You don't eat anything."

David managed not to jump this time, but he had lost several breakfasts over the last months to Gronorgh's morning sneak attacks. It was disconcerting how silently Gronorgh could move. Monsters his size ought to make noise, and lots of it. He tried to act as if nothing had happened.

"Tkal never came back last night," David said. "His bed is untouched. Did you see or hear him last night?"

"Is the *mouse* talking to me? This is a special morning," Gronorgh growled. It was a sort of laughter, a sign of amusement for the Gravgurdan, but David couldn't help equating it with angry dogs or lions on the prowl. It made his skin crawl.

Again, David tried to act like he wasn't unnerved, but he knew Gronorgh could see through his false bravado. "He said he had something very important to discuss with…someone, but wouldn't say who. I think he was going to meet with Prince Kvran, but I'm not sure."

Suddenly Gronorgh was paying attention to David's words instead of how long it would take to get some embarrassing reaction out of David. "What makes you think that? Tkal would not go to meet that weasel without telling us. He would want backup for one thing."

"I didn't say I was sure that's where he was going. I just said I thought that might be where he was going."

"But he did not return last night?" Gronorgh narrowed his eyes.

"No," said David, sorry now that he had mentioned it before he knew more.

"I will ask him why not when I see him in class for the exam. Maybe you snore." He growled again, crumpled the can that had held his first protein shake, grabbed a second and his bag with his netbooks and stuff in it, and jogged from the room to take his exam and harass Tkal.

David wished he hadn't said anything.

Two hours later, Gronorgh returned with an expression on his face that David hadn't seen before and didn't like. "He did not show."

"Tkal?"

"No, the Kratarch of Gramurgh. Of course, Tkal. He skipped the exam, and it did not appear he had submitted the paper either. Tkal is never late with work. He just failed the class. There is no way to pass without those two grades."

"But…"

"Shut up and sit down, David."

David did as he was told, as much because he wasn't used to Gronorgh using his name as because he was too scared to contradict the behemoth when he was this agitated.

"Now tell me exactly what happened from the standard you returned to the station after your little trip."

David had been going over that very ground for the last two hours so it was easy to recite every detail for Gronorgh.

"And that is everything? You did not go anywhere else? Do anything else?"

"No."

"And you do not remember anything else he said?"

"He didn't say anything else. That's every word of our conversation after we got back. Tkal was mad at me about the dancing at the fair and not joining in. He wasn't exactly in his usual talkative mood."

"I do not see evidence in what you have told me to make me think he was going to talk to Kvran."

"Well, I did say that he didn't say that, that it was just my idea."

"Humans! You make no sense at the best of times, but you are completely useless when a problem comes up."

David couldn't agree more. That was exactly how he felt. Completely useless.

Enemwenu burst through the door from the corridor. "Dean Haerkarn is coming here."

"What?" asked both David and Gronorgh.

"She is looking for you, David. She said you have not answered any of the messages she left on your terminal."

David jumped up and dashed for his room.

"Where are you going?" demanded Gronorgh.

"I've been out here the whole time! What if Tkal sent a message while I was waiting out here?"

He disappeared into his room only to reappear moments later, even more upset. "Nothing."

"So you haven't heard from him either?" It was Dean Haerkarn standing in the middle of the food prep area.

"No. I haven't seen him since we parted after docking at night cycle 2:00. His bed is unused. He missed a class, a paper, and an exam."

"That I know. That is when *I* was alerted."

David repeated his non-helpful information about returning from Tolari Market on Epemthu, Tkal being miffed about David not joining in, and his cryptic statement about having something important to discuss with someone but refusing to say who it was. Then he talked about waking up and finding Tkal had never returned, and his conversation with Gronorgh.

"So none of you has seen him since last night?" she twitched her ears from student to student.

"Actually, I don't think any of us but David has seen him since mid-afternoon day before yesterday," Gronorgh rumbled and shot David a dark look.

"Pod leaders with near-perfect grades do not just suddenly decide to fail a class by not showing for a critical class meeting, in their last quarter, with employment offers already on file. Can none of you"—by this time the entire pod had gathered—"tell me anything more?"

She waited while the pod members muttered, flashed, or twitched their various apologies and excuses.

David had the feeling that he had somehow betrayed the only friend he had.

"Station policy says that it is still too early to officially declare Student Dvarin Tkal missing."

David felt odd hearing Tkal's name in the correct Tvern El ordering, with family name first. He was so accustomed to hearing Tkal order it English-style that it made it sound like a stranger's name.

"But I would ask you, do you think this is normal behavior for your pod leader?"

All agreed it was not.

"Then I am authorizing you to begin searching for him unofficially, and I will do likewise."

David had been searching for a little over two hours. He went first to every place that made sense for a student with a make-or-break exam coming up—the library, cafes, quiet, out-of-the-way spots Tkal had mentioned. Then he tried places Tkal might choose to blow off steam—amusement centers, theaters, the recreation fields on level two. He went in the gym and asked around, even as out of place and uncomfortable as he felt there. He even went by the candle room, where, not only did he wait a few standards, he lit a candle, having no idea if that's how it worked or not.

Now he was just wandering corridors in a more-or-less systematic way, asking anyone he saw if they had seen any Tvern An males recently and tracking down any leads he got. Bits of his dream started coming back. A hand reaching for him in the darkness, calling his name. A bloated face floating in water, a face he should know, but couldn't place. A horrible voice calling his name. He shuddered.

He hoped someone else was having more luck than he was. He pulled out his netbook and called Enemwenu, Fthofsis, and Red-shimmer Gold-streak. None of them had found anything useful. Shintikaisen and Ael were tracking a Madrindiu who had been seen talking to a Tvern An male very early that morning. Xtp had just confirmed that one particular report was not Tkal and was resuming the search.

David called Dai-Soln, hoping he would have news. Dai-Soln had found almost nothing, but suggested that maybe Gronorgh might have had more luck. David hated having to call the monster who made his life miserable, asking for help, but Gronorgh was out searching like the rest of them. He placed the call.

"What?" That passed for a civil greeting from the Gravgurdan.

"Um."

"Did you find him?" Gronorgh demanded.

"No, I was—"

"Then stop wasting time and keep looking." Gronorgh terminated the call.

If David hadn't been on the verge of boiling over. He had no time for Gronorgh's behavior. David caught himself as he drew back to smash his netbook to a million pieces against the wall. All he felt was the sting of Gronorgh's disdain, and a wish to vomit hot lava all over his ugly face.

He stormed down corridor after corridor, demanding they answer his questions. He came to a Y-shaped split in the corridor on a level of the station he didn't think he had ever visited before. He randomly chose a direction and started down that branch. This level was mostly occupied by the physical plant and was fairly noisy with various machines providing water, air, light, and gravity, and processing the wastes produced by the station and its inhabitants. Between the noise and his foul mood, he almost missed the sound. It was like a strangled gasp. David turned around and went back to the Y. He took the other branch which turned a corner just up ahead.

David rounded the corner, and there he was. Lying on the floor, reaching for him with one hand, looking like he'd been stung by a thousand bees, and all the wrong colors. "David, help!" The voice was so hoarse he could barely understand him. David whipped out his netbook and signaled for help, then ran and pulled the emergency response lever at the end of the hall. When he dropped to his knees at Tkal's side, Tkal was no longer conscious. Tkal's emergency injector was on the floor. David picked it up. It was spent.

The emergency medtechs arrived to find David cradling Tkal's bruised and bleeding head and trying to see if he was still breathing. They rushed to work, in all their cold efficiency. They efficiented David off to the side and cut him off from Tkal as they worked. The EMTs lifted Tkal onto a medsled and ran scanners over him as they zipped down the hall at a pace David couldn't match. He barely made it to the elevator in time to slip through the doors, still grasping the injector. He was clutching his side and gasping for breath so badly he couldn't even respond when they asked if he was also injured.

David finally gasped out a reply and somehow made them understand that he was Tkal's legal next of kin. Either that or they decided he was in shock and needed a psychiatrist as much as Tkal needed a medic. He caught snatches of words he couldn't really register, but sounded bad—*acute subdural hematoma, cardiac arrythmia, anaphylaxis, embolism.* Doctor talk. It was never good when they used doctor talk. Were all those things wrong with Tkal, or were they just guessing so the doctors could be ready for anything? One of them pressed a bandage to the back of Tkal's skull while the other put a tube down Tkal's throat and forced air into his lungs. Had he stopped breathing? The lift doors opened and the EMTs shoved the medsled into a waiting cart. They all jumped in and the driver tore off at full tilt. Did they have to drive so fast in a public corridor? Tkal couldn't be that bad. He couldn't. All he needed was his emergency injector to stop the allergic reaction. But he'd already used it. It was empty. Why wasn't it working?

He held the injector out to the EMTs. "He's gonna be okay, right? He used his injector. That means everything will be okay, right?"

One of them took it. They looked at each other, but said nothing.

Why hadn't Tkal told him it was *this* serious, *this* bad? Suddenly Tkal started thrashing around, writhing.

One of the EMTs shouted, "He's seizing!"

As they pulled into the hospital, Tkal went limp.

They shoved David aside into a waiting room as they disappeared with Tkal through a door marked SURGERY. Oh, God.

Nineteen

Death Walks Among Us

Gronorgh paced in front of the view window, stopping to glare at David and Tkal in the treatment room. "Why is he still in there?" Gronorgh turned away from the window and gave the palms up question gesture.

No one answered.

He turned back to stare at the incomprehensible red lights on the vital signs monitors. "Why doesn't he come out and tell us what's going on? The doctors said he could only stay ten standard minutes. He's been in there twenty."

Still no one replied. Several of the pod actively avoided meeting his eyes.

"I want to know what's happening!" Gronorgh demanded.

"Elder brother," said Dai-Soln addressing him in the most formal manner, "we all want to know what is happening, but only David is listed as family."

"I still don't see what Tkal sees in him. Why choose that weakling as a blood-brother?"

"You have me as a friend," Dai-Soln reminded him. "Remember, *Khuv gronmas hhasléuphatsaqqg hhogzhôn,* 'not all strength is in the arms.'"

"Yes, but you *do* have other kinds of strength."

"This is very inappropriate. They are brothers now. That is all that matters. David will come out when Tkal is through talking to him."

"Rather when he is through sitting vigil." The doctor's voice cut through the mounting tension giving everyone a start. "Your friend is dying."

Red-shimmer's skin exploded into an eruption of colors that her voder "translated" as a squeal of static. Xtp twitched and clacked its mouth parts rhythmically. Ael gasped and covered her face with her hands. Shintikaisen, ears flattened, began to sway and mutter-chant, "Ul, ul, ul, liliul, ul." Dai-Soln sat down hard, almost missing the seat. Gronorgh put his fist through the wall, "No!" Everyone jumped again. "Why can't you do something?" Gronorgh advanced on the doctor who blanched noticeably but, to his credit, did not bolt for the door.

"Your friend went into anaphylactic shock—a life-threatening reaction to an allergen—usually a food or insect venom. Food is much more likely here on the station."

"But how?" asked Dai-Soln. "He always kept his medicine with him."

"It looks like he used it, but he also had a subdural hematoma—blood pooling inside the skull, pressing on the brain—probably caused by a blow to the back of his head. If he used his injector, that may have worsened the bleeding. It may also have caused the heart attack and series of strokes he suffered. His heart and lungs are severely damaged, but it's the brain that's irreparable. Between the pressure from the intracranial bleeding and the damage caused by the strokes... We relieved the pressure and stopped any further bleeding."

Gronorgh growled. "You're saying...what? He's already gone?"

"I'm saying there is nothing more we can do. He's shutting down."

"Murder? This is murder!" Shintikaisen's eyes flashed and she bared her teeth. She let go a war screech to curdle the blood of the most fearsome demon, then resumed her cries of "Ul, ul, ul, liliul, ul!" Only louder.

Xttp's voder started in, "But if he ate bread?"

"We don't know what triggered it, but this level of anaphyaxsis in a Tvern An? Yes, yeast is a good possibility. It's one of the things they'll check for when..." The doctor stopped talking, his attention fully directed to the monitors. One by one, the lights were going out. "When they do the autopsy. He's dead."

They all watched as David threw himself across Tkal's lifeless body. They watched as the burly nurses pried him away from Tkal. And they watched as those same nurses carried their helpless teammate from the room.

"Please, take your friend to his quarters. There is nothing more he can do here." The doctor turned and left. The orderlies blackened the glass.

Ael, tears streaming down her face, joined Dai-Soln, and they each took one of David's arms, receiving him from the nurses. They led him out the door. Ael started sobbing when she saw Jva waiting for her outside. He took her place supporting David and put his other arm out to comfort Ael. He questioned Dai-Soln with his eyes. Dai-Soln nodded, but no one spoke.

Dai-Soln and Fthofsis kept vigil outside David's room all night after consulting Dean Haerkarn. Shintikaisen spent the night ululating before her shrine. Red-shimmer turned off her voder and bubbled color in incoherent patterns even in her sleep. Xtp began inscribing a *xj* stone, recording Tkal's deeds. Ael and Jva spent the night in the arboretum under the willow, crying and comforting each other.

Gronorgh stayed in the gym all night and reported several pieces of heavy equipment broken the next morning. He had trouble moving the next day when he returned with news of the autopsy. "They said he must have been restrained for three to four hours and beaten repeatedly—a fist with four fingers and a thumb. He had bruises on his arms and legs where he tried to break the restraints, and they found some bits of leather between his teeth. He was smashed in the back of the head with a blunt object and then injected with yeast proteins—a very concentrated dose of just the part Tvern An are allergic to. It was a Human-designed implement used to inject him. He used his medicine, and that made everything worse. He was probably dead anyway, but the medicine made it faster and absolutely certain. At least that's what I got out of it."

"Have the results already been released?" Dai-Soln asked.

"No, I threatened to break the techie's neck. He told me everything."

"You didn't hurt him?"

"I didn't touch him. I am terrifying." Gronorgh sounded weary rather than terrifying.

Dai-Soln's fronds drooped. "So, it really is murder."

"So it seems. And it looks like a Human did it. I'm going to sleep. I must." Gronorgh slumped to his room.

Dai-Soln flashed his nictitating membranes and flared his nostrils, trying to stay awake. If he had been Human, he would have yawned.

Fthofsis drifted down to where Dai-Soln sat. "Sleef Soln. Soon others here. I see for Thafith," it whispered without its voder.

Dai-Soln wagged his head in agreement and very slowly blinked his nictitating membranes. "You're right. Xtp or Ael will be here soon, and Red-shimmer should awaken soon. Watch Thafith…uh, David, carefully." Dai-Soln rose and stumbled off to his room, unsuccessfully attempting to keep his sword out of his way. Gronorgh was already snoring soundly.

Five standard minutes later, the main door chimed. Fthofsis hissed something to the computer and the door opened for Dean Haerkarn and Chancellor Tal Hatlir. Fthofsis swam quickly through the air to where it had left its voder the day before. It didn't want to be limited to the Standard words its speech organs could produce, not while speaking to two of the most important people at Shel Matkei. It clasped the coin-sized box to its "under side" and began speaking. "Welcome, honoreds-of-wisdom. Do you come for the mourning? I have learned many ways to mourn this night."

"Yes, Fthofsis—to mourn and to see the living," Tal Hatlir replied. "Dean Haerkarn, check on him. I will speak to the others." Tal Hatlir felt a great heaviness in his livers. He had seen so much suffering and waste in his two hundred and eighty-two years. It never stopped, and it was always so hard to find meaning in it all. He felt very alone as he sat down on a large cushion in the sitting area and motioned Fthofsis to join him. These interviews would take a long time. "Come, consider with me," he said motioning again to Fthofsis who finally drifted down toward where Chancellor Tal Hatlir was sitting. "Tell me what you know," he said in a voice that had been gentled by his long life.

After ringing twice with no answer, Brolkat Haerkarn released the door code and entered David's room. It took a moment for her eyes to adjust to the darkness. She found David wrapped in Tvern robes, sitting on his bed, facing the wall. She pulled the chair from the desk up alongside the bed and sat down, even though the chair was much too low for her. After five standards she spoke. "Have you slept?"

"No."

She waited.

"I see his face when I shut my eyes. Not his real face. I see that face now. But if I close my eyes, I see that awful, bloated face in the hospital. They killed him. Why?" David started sobbing.

"We don't know yet. Have you been here all night?

"Yes, I don't want to see his empty bed. I keep thinking he's in it. But it's too quiet." David pulled his knees up close to his chest. "I feel very lonely and empty and alone."

"Maybe you should spend a few nights in someone else's room. Tell me more about your feelings."

David just stared at the wall. "I feel hollow. I don't know what I feel. I feel so lonely. Oh, Tkal!"

"You haven't had many friends have you?"

"No. Tkal was my first friend. He was the first person since my aunt died that didn't think I was useless or stupid or weird or want something. He really liked me. I don't know why." He drew a shuddering breath. "He liked me enough to be my brother. I never had a brother before. He was the only family I've had since I was eight years old."

"And now he's gone too."

Tears flowed down David's face.

"Just like your Aunt Katherine."

David sobbed.

"Just like your parents."

David screamed, "It's not fair! He was good! Why did they kill him?"

"David, life is not fair, but we survive as long as we can and do as much good as we can while we live. Do you believe in a divinity?"

"No. I don't know. Tkal did. He asked me to read his holy book, but I never got around to it."

"Tkal did much good while he was here."

"But he could have done so much more. If…if.." David started sobbing again.

"If he had not been killed," Dean Haerkarn finished for him.

"Yes." David turned from the wall and looked at her for the first time. "Why?"

"David, that is a question that each of our races has been asking since the beginning of our histories. And still the question has to find a new answer each time it is asked. I cannot tell you. Tkal may know now, but I do not. And you will have to search long for your answer. Do not give up."

"Who did it?"

"We do not know yet. But we suspect it was a Human. The injector was a Human design. The yeast was just proteins, but it still may be possible to tell if it came from here on the station. We have been checking records of yeast purchases. But there is so much bought and sold on this station. It will take time to check every sale of yeast, and it may not have been bought. It could have been cultured from a food product or even from the air." She paused. "Security on this station is quite good at what they do. It may take time, but they *will* get to the bottom."

David wasn't very responsive after that, but Dean Haerkarn just continued to talk to him. He had no idea what she said. All he could remember, when he woke, was that she talked for a long time and the sound was soothing.

By the time Dean Haerkarn returned to the common room, Chancellor Tal Hatlir was finishing up his interview with a rather bleary-eyed Gronorgh.

"You understand, of course, that the technician has filed a complaint."

Gronorgh gave a sharp nod.

"I fully understand why you did it, and I am sure your podmates welcomed the information. And you showed great restraint by the standards of your culture. But this is not Gramurgh, and a second such complaint would…create difficulties."

Another nod, even sharper.

"Good. Well. Thank you for your time. I will give these recordings to station security. I am sure they will have further questions, not only for you, but for all of your podmates as well. Shel Matkei is autonomous in many matters, but this crime happened outside the campus levels, and we do not have the resources to investigate this at any rate. If you wish Commonwealth or Gravgurdan counsel to be present when you meet with station personnel, the Academy will cover the cost. Otherwise, I consider the matter closed for Shel Matkei purposes.

Twenty

Let the Dead Bury the Dead

David led the coffin into the dark, empty atrium. Three days already and he was wearing the yellow robes of mourning. David could barely feel his own body. He seemed to be floating free. None of this seemed real. Behind him, the attendants carried the coffin sideways, opposite of the Human tradition. Following the coffin in single file, the other members of the pod took their seats on the cold floor. The pallbearers placed the coffin in the center of the room. Tears welled in David's eyes as he pierced the silence with the tiny cymbals on his thumb and index finger. Nineteen times: once for each year of Tkal's life in Tvern years.

"*Geln arln. Geln kti vfarnil vde kti ki vfarn e. Vde kti ki kgirn e ka dan irn.* 'Come together. Let us mourn our loss. For our *kgirn* has left us.'" David paused as the mourners filed in and took their seats on the floor in radiating files. The porters closed the doors, plunging the room into darkness. The silence and darkness stretched on. Then slowly, sobs and other soft sounds of mourning, began to punctuate the silence. The strike of flint and a flash of light. The volatile oils in the cauldron of life ignited.

David stood in the circle of light with his hands stretched out over the flames he had ignited. "A flame in the dark. A life begins." He withdrew a candle from his robes and lit it from the cauldron. "It shines in the darkness, bringing hope. Tkal was born in the year 6385 of the Tvern An calendar, on the fifteenth day of the great moon Gvel, the eleventh day of the lesser moon Vferln, the third day of the least moon Tgern while Gtarl sat on the throne.

Dvarin Tkal, the beloved and only child of their Excellencies Dvarin Dgan son of Dvarin Kgaln, and of Dfal Kgarel daughter of Dfal Kdalin, ambassadors of Tvern to Earth, has crossed to the Shadowlands, having the grass green underfoot, yet early in the spring. He never tasted the fruits of summer, never harvested in the autumn, never felt the sting of winter gales. He was taken from the arms of his *varln*, his 'family and friends,' the circle of those who knew him and whom he knew, by a cruel hand, a hand which has committed the most grievous of all sins which one sentient may commit against another. May that hand stand in the judgment of the Lord of Time, The Everlasting, The Eternal, He Who was before the past and Who will be when the future is but a memory."

David threw bitter herbs into the cauldron and the vapors brought tears to his eyes again. Or were the tears there already? "Bitter is our sorrow. Cold are our tears. And empty, our hearts. Tkal was my only family, my *tdaln vkirl*—my 'brother of choosing'. There are not two friends like him to be found in one lifetime. Few will ever find one. I wear his scar on my hand till the day when I, too, cross beyond time.

"Tkal, your mother cries out for your voice. Your father searches for your face. My eyes grow weak from looking for you. You will not be found in this world again, for you have gone before us to wait for us. You will not wait long. We will not wait long. For life is but a vapor in the morning that vanishes away—a fragrance on the wind, which is soon past. A cauldron whose light flames and is snuffed."

David threw *valn* blossoms into the flames, releasing their sandalwood-like aroma. "The love of The Eternal is everlasting. The grace of the Everlasting is eternal. No love can out shine His, no peace compare. In His arms Tkal now rests. In His house Tkal yet lives. Tkal was a lantern who showed hope to all who came near. He held his lamp in his palm. I have known Tkal for less than one year, but he transformed my darkness. He offered the candle of friendship and dispelled the night of aloneness." David snuffed Tkal's candle.

The haunting strains of "Gtalan Fvarln," 'The Hymns of Death', began to drift from behind a screen that stood along one wall. David had managed to find an actual Tvern An septet to play the sacred song of hope and mourning all mixed together. Tears and sounds of mourning blended with the music as the flower bearers entered with *dan* blossoms—two for each mourner. The small white blossoms looked very fragile, but they were the first blossoms to appear in the spring and would bloom again in the fall, till the first snows hid them. They were a potent symbol of life to Tkal's people. Each of the mourners arose in their own time and approached the cauldron carrying a flower in each hand. Each mourner, in turn, would throw the blossom in their right palm, representing Tkal, into the flames and whisper a word of remembrance, committing him to the Hands. Most returned to their seats on the floor still holding the second blossom in their left hand. The self-blossom could only be cast into the flames by those who shared Tkal's faith in The Eternal.

David accepted his two blossoms from the flower bearer and sat quietly while the other mourners approached and cast their flowers into the flames. He watched the flowers swim in and out of focus as each tear welled up and fell on the tissue-paper-thin petals. Finally, the last of the mourners shuffled back to their seats. David rose and stepped in front of the cauldron. He held his right hand out to the flames and whispered a promise to Tkal. He let fall the flower and watched as it vanished in the flames. Then he stretched out his left hand to . . . He couldn't do it. It wasn't true. He was supposed to drop the second flower into the flames, affirming his faith in The Eternal, but he didn't believe. He couldn't believe. He gently placed his self-blossom on the ground in front of the cauldron. "I'm sorry Tkal," he whispered so low he could barely even hear himself.

He stretched his hands out over the flames. "His flame has gone out. His life here has ended. And this world is a darker place for his loss." David lowered his hands to snuff the flames and seared his palms on the hot rim of the cauldron. The room was plunged into darkness and silence.

David left the ceremony while the lights were still out, having memorized the number of steps to the hallway, and made his way to the arboretum. There the willow hid him within the umbrella of its branches. A sad melody from "Gtalan Fvarln" played in his head, and he began to half-whistle, half-hum the melody as tears rolled down his face. The sunlights were off for night cycle, and it would be hours before they came back on, hours before anyone but an occasional nocturnal like the Hiyadi would be visiting the arboretum. David was alone. As he always had been. But now it felt more real. Like the after taste of burnt coffee—bitter and lingering. David's humming turned to sobbing, and the stars swam in his eyes, as his tears turned everything into a ruined watercolor. The aircyclers started an artificial breeze—just enough to chill David.

When he woke, there was dew on his clothes and hair. He would be late for class again today. He followed the path to the airlock and cycled through to the corridor. Dai-Soln was standing there.

"There you are. We thought you might be here. You spent the whole night in the arboretum?"

"I can't sleep in that room. It's too full of Tkal."

"David, please do not be angry with me."

David looked into the Taisiran's face and knew that he had done something he should be angry about, but he simply didn't have the strength to care. He just stared blankly.

"David, I am worried for you. I went to Dean Haerkarn. She is waiting for you in your room." He paused, as if waiting for an outburst. When it didn't come, he went on. "I am supposed to find you and bring you to her. Please, come with me."

David just stood there. Dai-Soln grasped him round the biceps and began half dragging, half guiding David through the corridors back to Green Pod. At the door to David's room, he palmed the chime and Dean Haerkarn opened the door. She nodded at him, and he released David into her care. She placed a hand on David's shoulder, and as she guided him to a chair, the door slid shut. "David where did you sleep?"

"Arboretum."

She wheezed. "I suggested another student's room."

She waited a long time before she spoke. "David, what will you do next?"

"I don't know. I miss him so much." He kicked his desk.

"He was a good friend to you, wasn't he?"

"He was my only friend. And my family."

"You were young when you lost your family, weren't you?"

"Six. I was six when my parents died. They went on vacation to Tycho City on Luna. The shuttle decompressed. Everyone died. I was an only child."

"How did that make you feel?"

"Alone. And scared. Betrayed."

"Is that when you went to Grey Street Orphanage?"

"No, that's when I went to live with my father's aunt, my Aunt Katherine."

"Was she kind to you?"

"Yes, but she was old. She never had children of her own. I had just stopped having nightmares about my parents every night when she died. I found her in the living room."

"How old were you then?"

"I was eight. That's when I went to the orphanage. Aunt Katherine was my only family. My mother didn't have any aunts or uncles or cousins, and Aunt Katherine was my father's only relative on Earth. Some cousin was living on one of the colonies."

"Did you ever try to find this cousin? Did the authorities?"

"I don't know his name. Her name? I don't know. Earth policy is against sending children off-world to relatives more distant than parents' siblings."

"So you were placed in the orphanage because there was no one else living."

"Yeah." There was a long silence. "Why did it happen?

"I don't know, David."

Nobody knew why. It just happened. It always *just happened.* But not this time. This time there must be an answer. A real answer. Every question had to have an answer, right? Didn't it? What if there *was* no answer? What if it really was all meaningless? What if no one really cared? But someone *did* care. *He* cared.

"I care."

"What?" asked Dean Haerkarn.

"There has to be an answer." The tears flowed. "How? How could it happen?"

She let him cry, because she didn't have an answer for him.

He clenched and unclenched his jaw. "Death can't be the Supreme Master."

"It isn't."

"How can you know? How can I know? How can anyone but the dead know? And they can't tell us. We can't see, can't hear, can't feel, can't love them."

"You mean they can't love us. That's what you're afraid of."

"Yes, I guess. If he's gone, then I'm all alone again. Mother. Father. Aunt Katherine. All gone. Now Tkal. I have no one."

"But David, surely you realize that you have something that most people only dream of."

"Don't tell me how fortunate I am to be at Shel Matkei and how intelligent I am. It's not worth snot."

She sighed. "You're right. It's not. There are hundreds of students here. They are wealthy, powerful. Many will have fame. Some will rule. They are the elite. You are not among them. In this galaxy there are beings far older, wiser and smarter than you. Though not many your age. But even here at Shel Matkei, you are not the best. There are better. You have lost much. But you must first have much before you can lose it. Most of these students will never know your loss, because they will never know what you had. Friends like Tkal are very rare. Far more rare than we ever dare to guess, until they are gone. And then we know. Instantly, we know that never in this lifetime will there be another like that one."

"You lost one too?

"Almost. What I lost was a deception. A lie. But I think the pain was just as real. I believed. I believed with all my heart that she was my heartfriend. And she was, until she sold me to the Great Mother. Now you know why I am a heretic. She sold me to try to buy her own soul from the Goddess. But you had the real thing. That is why you have to live. You have to, to honor

Tkal. By dying now, you betray him. He believed in you and trusted you. You have to do this for your friendship, to prove to yourself that it was real. To prove that Tkal didn't believe a lie."

"That's not fair."

"No. But it is true. Many truths are not fair."

"Did I kill Tkal, just by letting him be my family? Am I…?"

"Cursed? No, David, *that's* not fair. And it's a lie. You were eight when your aunt died. You could not save her. Your parents were off world when they died. And Tkal was halfway across the station."

"The last thing we did was argue."

"That can't be changed. Friends often argue. It is unfortunate to have that unresolved. But—"

"If I hadn't made him mad, maybe he would have told me more. Maybe he would have taken me with him. Maybe—"

"David."

He stopped and just breathed.

"The past is past. Now we have to find ways to deal with what has happened and return to the present, to living life, and to honoring Tkal's memory. What would Tkal want you to do? Waste away mourning? Or would he want you to live your life as fully as he was living his?"

"I didn't dance. I should have danced. Tkal danced."

"Then you know what Tkal would want."

She though it was a metaphor. How could David ever make up for doing everything wrong on that last day?

Twenty-One

Choices of Consequence

David was the last to arrive, and Gronorgh was already calling the meeting to order before David entered the common room. He barely made it to his chair before Gronorgh launched into his agenda.

"We must formally choose a new leader for the pod. The rules of this pod were set up as a democracy, so we are required to vote to choose that leader—foolish as such a method may be—so the floor is open for nominations."

Everyone looked around at each other.

Finally, Shintikaisen tapped the table with her three longest fingers. "I believe we could benefit from female leadership. I nominate myself."

Gronorgh curled his lip. "Is there a second?"

Ael tapped the table in the same way Shintikaisen had. Roommates picked up each other's habits. "Seconded," she said.

"Xtp raised its second left arm for attention. "I would like to nominate Enemwenu for the post."

Again Gronorgh curled his lip, but he followed procedure and asked, "Is there a second?"

David cleared his throat, raised his hand and said, "Second."

Gronorgh glared at him but said nothing.

Fthofsis made a wheezing-whistley sort of sound and then spoke into its voder. "I nominate Gronorgh."

Gronorgh did not sneer this time. Instead, he looked like he was already in control. "Is there a second?"

Dai-Soln gave the second, and cocked his head at Red-shimmer while spreading his fronds slightly.

Gronorgh barreled ahead as if he already held the reigns. "If there are no other—"

Red-shimmer got her voder to make a grating noise, something she had recently programmed it to do to express disgust or frustration. "I nominate David."

Gronorgh didn't even try to suppress his laughter. "Will anyone second that?" he managed and resumed his gravelly laughter.

Enemwenu turned a very dark shade and slapped hii's tentacle on the table. "I second."

Gronorgh sobered. "You can't be serious." He paused. When Enemwenu did not move, he continued. "You are a contender and you second another's nomination?"

"I did not ask to be nominated," Enemwenu said. "And I do not like to see members, valuable members, of this team derided." Hii slapped the table again.

Gronorgh straightened to his full height. He stared at Enemwenu, and then at David. David gaped at Enemwenu.

Gronorgh shrugged his massive shoulders. "Are there any more nominations?" he rumbled. None were forthcoming, so Gronorgh barreled ahead. "Nominations are closed. We have four nominees: Shintikaisen, Enemwenu, David, and Gronorgh. Each of the nominees should make their case for why they should be chosen. Shintikaisen will go first, then Enemwenu, then David, and I will go last."

"Stop. Who decided that order?" asked Shintikaisen. "You? Why should it be that order and not another?"

"Yes, I chose the order. I even put myself last."

"So you can rebut everyone else? Last is the strongest position."

Gronorgh rumbled ominously, but said nothing. His ploy was so transparent that denying it would only make him look weaker than Shintikaisen's correct accusation already had. It was a dangerous move, trying to set the order to give himself the advantage, while trying to look like he was being humble or some such foolishness, and it had already cost him. "Then who should choose? You?"

"I would be more fair than you, but I believe we should let the computer randomly order us."

There was a general consent to that suggestion, but the question of who should feed the names into the computer and how to choose the randomizing seed took up the better part of twenty standard minutes. Finally, it was decided to call three representatives from Green Pod's talent pool and have them do the honors. After further discussion and arguing, they agreed on Jva, Nwkkhu, and Hla'leetnal'tsalts who arrived in less than ten standards. The three of them fed in the names of the nominees. Jva turned to the group seated at the table. "Your names are entered. May we have your numbers so the computer may randomize your order?"

Shintikaisen called out, "Three. That is the number of my sisters," and smiled at Ael and Red-shimmer Gold-streak.

Gronorgh growled. "Twelve, because a leader needs all twelve kinds of strength."

Enemwenu chose next. "I choose five, because all good things come in fives."

David glanced around. "Um, forty-two. For obscure cultural reasons."

The computer instantly returned the list, and Jva read it off with Nwkkhu and Hla'leetnal'tsalts as witnesses. "The order is as follows: Shintikaisen, Gronorgh, Enemwenu, David."

Shintikaisen and Gronorgh both sulked. Neither looked at all pleased with the random slots they were assigned, but to object now would look far too petty. It would be a sign of weakness that neither could afford to display when both would be trying to sell themselves as the strongest leader.

The meeting adjourned for fifty standard minutes, half an hour, to give the nominees time to prepare statements and organize their arguments. When they regathered in the common room, the conference table had been pushed to one side, and turned into an impromptu stage set up by the small audience—the remaining members of the Pod proper and a dozen or so of the talent pool—that had assembled. David was aghast. The thought of having to perform in front of an audience, to speak in public and make a case for why he should lead this pod… This wasn't going to work. He couldn't do this. He could kill Red-shimmer and Enemwenu for putting him through this charade. The only thing keeping him from bolting for the door was the fact that the others looked as unsettled by this development as he felt. Even Gronorgh. Of course, he also wanted to hear what the others had to say, so he could decide which one to choose. He was pretty sure he would vote for Enemwenu when it came time, but Shintikaisen might be stubborn enough to keep Gronorgh in line, and she had been nice to him…after her fashion.

But Shinti's speech was a rambling raft-load of nonsense that boiled down to, "Vote for me because I would make a great leader so you should vote for me because voting for me would be great and then I would be leader." After fifteen standards of that, David was just glad when she sat down. Even the barb at the end, to the effect that anything was better than choosing Gronorgh, did nothing to stop David from hoping Gronorgh's speech was better. If everyone's speech were this bad, David had to face the possibility of getting some votes—if he didn't hang himself to end the tedium first.

Gronorgh stood with a sneer playing across his mouth. He gained the podium in three ground-devouring strides. He pulled himself up to his full height for maximum intimidation and sort of flexed all over to remind the audience, just in case they had forgotten, just how big and strong and intimidating and leader-ly he truly was. "Thank you, Shintikaisen, for that *truly* inspired speech. I am sure you have helped many of us clarify our choice."

Shintikaisen gave new meaning to the proverb "If looks could kill." The look in her eyes at that moment would have frightened her fearsome Goddess. David hoped there wouldn't be a fist fight before the debate was over. He scanned the audience and could see a number of faces, including Dai-Soln's, which mirrored at least some of his own thoughts. David forced himself to redirect his attention to Gronorgh's speech as the juggernaut plunged ahead.

"Green Pod has a long and successful history at Shel Matkei Academy. We are one of the oldest pods in existence and have seen many years atop the leader board. Green Pod has graduated an impressive list of interstellar political powers—ambassadors, envoys, cabinet members, privy councilors, rulers, and law makers and revolutionaries—both within and without the Commonwealth. It is a glorious history and the reason I strove to join *this* pod rather than any other. But that history has been tarnished. In the past year, Green Pod has stumbled and lost its way. We have been brought near the brink of collapse. It has taken all my skill as a military commander to keep us afloat while the leadership of this pod debated the niceties of 'evidence' and 'proof,' knowing full well who the parties responsible for our ill fortune have been. Some of the contenders for this office would likely continue to tie the hands of the military, perpetuating the failed policies of our past, weak leadership."

David bristled. His speech was rapidly reforming in his mind. He would not simply announce his withdrawal and throw his support to Enemwenu. He would make a thorough defense of Tkal's leadership first, ripping Gronorgh's speech apart line by line. So what if it got him killed later?

"This pod deserves a return to glory, and I can lead us there. We know who our enemies are, and we should attack them with full force, cripple their ability to prey on our shipping and the shipping of our allies and friends. Tkal did not allow this, and his fear of conflict, his desire to appease and play peacemaker, have led us to this low ebb in the history of Green Pod."

Now, David was shaking. It was all he could do not to interrupt. But he managed to bite his tongue. Finally, Gronorgh's self-aggrandizing harangue wound to a close.

"We need resolve, vision and will. We need someone who is not afraid to act, someone who sees things clearly, and is willing to fight, and keep fighting, until our enemies are destroyed. Tkal's policies of appeasement have failed. His wait-and-see philosophy has brought us this close to failure, and then his final actions, whatever they may have been, led to his death, leaving us without a leader. It is time to choose strength over weakness, clarity over babble, experience over ineptitude. Thank you."

Silence.

Gronorgh looked confused. That *fliuhlang* obviously thought he had been inspiring. As he retook his seat, his confused countenance began to transmute to anger.

Enemwenu took the podium, spiraling hii's tentacles upward and then forward to the audience and finally outward to the sides. "I have only a few brief remarks. Firstly, I do not believe that the future of Green Pod will be well served by attacking everyone who gets in our way. Secondly, I do not believe that the characterization of Tkal previously presented is at all fair—"

"If Tkal had had any sense, he would have taken backup to his 'meeting' with whoever he was supposedly seeing."

"Excuse me, Gronorgh, but you do not currently have the floor. This is my time. You have already presented your case. Despite the difficulty of the times, Tkal was a good leader."

"Tkal was a fool who got himself killed being an idiot."

David lost control of his tongue. "*Qlamzlekyê!*"

"What?" roared Gronorgh. "You challenge my honor?"

David stood, trembling with rage. "What honor? You have none! You attack the dead! An enemy who cannot fight back!"

Dai-Soln was at David's elbow. "David, sit down. You do not want to do this. Avert your eyes and sit. David!"

David realized what was happening and did as Dai-Soln said.

Quickly, before anyone else had a chance to say anything, Dai-Soln turned to Enemwenu. "Please continue your speech."

"Gladly," returned the Alelliawulian.

Dai-Soln stood hunched over, whispering in David's ear as Enemwenu resumed.

"I did not ask to be nominated. I believe my nomination was a reaction against certain statements made weighing the relative value of male or female leadership. I do not believe that leadership has anything to do with gender, whether male, female, sterile, mono, or gamma. Leadership has to do with qualities of the heart and the mind that may be present or absent in any of the possible genders of sentient species. I believe that two very poor examples have been set here today, and I do not wish to be led by either of them. I believe that there is need for a single alternative candidate and so I move that my name be withdrawn from the ballot and that you vote for David."

"You would have us led by someone even weaker than that Tvern An imbecile who couldn't even see his own death around the corner?"

"Hurzhayav!"

Dai-Soln clutched at David's arm. David turned and shoved him aside.

"Ggîzhsibrakzhaghadh ghemêsklev jenzh?"

"David!" Dai-Soln screeched. "He isn't a pervert!"

Gronorgh stood and glared down at David. "I have not seen my mother since I was weaned!"

"Kidzamas dd'ahhoghsiuhliuviuqqg shtikhj'ê jegh!"

"I stand, and you call me a kidza on two feet?" He flexed his hands and made the cords of muscle in his forearms ripple like steel ropes.

"Nghawghnêyê, shisit'ezhsh'ch'uerhoevdh ddîghdhav."

"You mock me as one who fights the dead? You mock my strength?"

"David, stop!" Jva yelled from the front of the retreating audience.

Gronorgh leaned in, overshadowing David with his massive chest.

"Hgodmas drang tlahhahatszhaghqqg shéuvrôtblîng phwé."

Red-shimmer Gold-streak had tuned her voder to translate Gravgaln. "David! It is unwise to insinuate that the size of his chest is only to compensate for a weak mind!"

Dai-Soln was gesturing frantically at Jva. Jva entered Gronorgh's striking zone long enough to grab David by one arm while Dai-Soln grabbed the other. Together they hauled David halfway across the room.

Shintikaisen and Enemwenu darted between them and Gronorgh. "Gronorgh, please. He is very angry, perhaps insane, but he is a child. Please stand down. To kill him would be murder. You would dishonor your family!" Shintikaisen was the only one big enough to require any physical respect from the Gravgurdan warrior.

"Family?" David screeched. "Family? His own father would strike his face and call him coward!"

Gronorgh started forward. Shintikaisen planted both hands against his chest and pushed, but it was only enough to slow him. "Gronorgh! Think of your children! They will be dishonored before they are even born!"

"Children? He'll never have children! Who would mate with scum like him?"

Gronorgh shoved Shintikaisen roughly, tumbling her over Enemwenu. Her warrior reflexes gave her the agility to catch Gronorgh by the leg as she rolled, and nearly pulled him to the ground before he regained his balance.

"Even if he *lived* downtown!"

Gronorgh roared. "Back down, you idiot! You approach the line of no return! I will kill you! With these hands!" He spread his powerful fingers making his hands as big as possible—hands that could crush any part of David.

"Do strong hands mask blind eyes?"

Gronorgh growled, eyes blazing.

"Does the toothless *ghrurrdanggh* growl, hoping to frighten its prey to death?"

Gronorgh was vibrating, and still David wouldn't stop hurling insults.

Dai-Soln clamped his hand over David's mouth, gagging him, then bellowed in agony. "He bit me!"

"How did you escape being *exposed?*" David screamed, jabbing index and pinkie at Gronorgh. "Kill yourself!"

Dai-Soln and Shintikaisen gasped. The room fell silent. Even Gronorgh froze. Then he roared like a caged lion, threatening the ceiling with his clenched fists. Dai-Soln yelled at Jva, "Move him! *Now!*" And together they hauled David off his feet, across the common room, and back to his dorm, locking the door behind themselves.

Twenty-Two

Life Is a Challenge

"Do you realize what you've done!" Jva shouted in David's face.

"Give him some room, Jva," said Dai-Soln in his calming, peacemaker voice. He helped David to a chair, then stood aside levering his sword up and down.

"Yes, well not completely," David confessed. "I really lost my head out there." The gravity of what he had just done was only beginning to dawn on David. He unclenched his fists and tried to move his stiff neck.

"How much do you weigh, David?" Jva got in David's face and repeated the question. "How much do you weigh?

"About sixty-two kilos. Why?"

"How tall are you?"

"About a hundred seventy centimeters. Why? Oh, God!"

"Yes, it's time to pray. Pray hard. You're a hundred seventy centimeters and weigh sixty-two kilos, if that, and you just challenged a two-hundred-twenty centimeter, two-hundred-fifty kilo Gravgurdan warrior, who is strong enough to qualify for high level government, to a duel! You say you lost your head? Well, not yet, but we won't be able to find it with a molecular scanner after he crushes it! What came over you?"

"Jva, be quiet!" Dai-Soln ordered. "Sit down and think."

Jva just glared at Dai-Soln, who had gone back to levering his sword. "David, you've got to get out of here. If you need money, I can lend it to you. Just get on the next shuttle to wherever it's going, and *don't* look back. You could go to my parents on Halcyon. They would put you up for a while. I'll tell them to expect you." Jva started for the com.

"No, don't. I can't."

Jva spun back, mouth agape. "What do you mean? Of course you can! They'll understand."

"No. It's a matter of honor."

"What are you talking—"

"Jva, he's right," said Dai-Soln.

"Whose honor? He's gonna be dead!"

David waved his hand no. "Mine and Gronorgh's. And the pod's."

Jva placed a hand on David's shoulder. "Look, David, I'm pretty strong. I could kill you if I had to, but I wouldn't even dream of challenging a Gravgurdan. Even if I could find one half my size!"

"Jva, sit down," said Dai-Soln, raising his voice just a little and removing his hand from his hilt to gesture emphatically at a chair. Tkal's chair.

Jva continued standing. "Dai-Soln, I know you're friends with Gronorgh out there, but can't you see what David's gotten himself into! He's gonna die!"

"That is a distinct possibility," David said, stopping Jva's tirade. "How many challenge words did I throw out there? It must have been nearly a dozen." David wiped his sweaty palms on his pants and concentrated on breathing normally.

Dai-Soln looked at him, obsidian eyes barely nictitating, fronds drooping. "I counted thirteen. That's an unlucky number for your people, isn't it?"

"Yes, but I'm not superstitious."

"How can you be sitting here so calm! You're talking about unlucky numbers while death is waiting outside the door!" Jva was shouting loud enough to be heard outside.

David exhaled. "Jva, you'd think you were the one who has to fight him. Please sit down and be quiet. You're making me nervous."

Jva looked at David, blinked and sat down.

"So, I exceeded the perfect number by one. If he ignores a challenge… The thirteenth insult dishonors his great-grandchildren if unanswered, doesn't it?" David didn't look to Dai-Soln for an answer. He already knew it was so.

The door chime rang. David started. Dai-Soln gave him a brief look of encouragement. Jva jumped for the door lock. "Jva, let Dai-Soln open the door. It's only a messenger. There's a ritual to these things." Jva stepped aside, uncomprehending, and stared at David.

Dai-Soln opened the door. Enemwenu stood outside, hii's tentacles raised in greeting. Dai-Soln signed a greeting in return. "I come news-bringing. This news I tell: Gronorgh offers you right of choice. Do you accept this offer?"

David nodded, adding an Alelliawulian gesture of assent, or as close as he could get with his hands, and said, "I receive your words. Receiving, I accept," while signing his thanks. "And my thanks to you, Dai-Soln. Attend to your duties."

Dai-Soln palmed the hilt of his sword and bowed deeply to David. He turned crisply and followed Enemwenu out. Ael stepped through the door, into the room.

"What was that all about?" Jva asked. "I think something really important just happened, but I don't have a clue what."

Ael answered, "It was important, Beloved. Gronorgh has given choice of time, place, and conditions of the duel to David. Dai-Soln's plea worked. By coming in here, he forced Gronorgh to take a moment to cool off and think. He has offered David the only slack he can. Now Dai-Soln is committed as Gronorgh's second."

"He gets to choose the contest?" Jva sounded excited. "Now we've got something to work with. How long can you wait before this is supposed to happen?"

"Three days," David answered.

"Only three days!" Jva's voice cracked.

"But David—" Ael began.

"Three days," David affirmed, stopping her and setting his jaw.

"He's right, Jva, three days. He knows his xeno-customs."

"Okay. Three days. That doesn't give us much time to work with." He turned to David. "What weapons are you most familiar with?"

David knew Jva was trying to help, but couldn't stop himself from sighing. "None of them. I've never used a weapon."

"Never? Well, I could teach you to use a Takazi laser pistol. They're really easy to operate. I learned when I was eight. Ael was probably eight or nine. They're not powerful, but they work from a distance, so he can't just slap your head off."

"Jva," Ael stopped him, "weapons are not permitted, except for knives, and that's considered vulgar and low caste."

"No weapons?" Jva looked ready to despair. "You mean he has to fight him unarmed? It's impossible. He hasn't got a chance of winning. Or living." Jva sat down hard. He looked at David. "You've decided to join Tkal, haven't you? One death wasn't enough? We were afraid of this."

Ael touched Jva's arm. "Come, Beloved. There is nothing more we can do right now."

He stood and entwined his arm with hers. She laid her free hand on his chest, and he covered it with his own. "Oh, Beloved," he said, as they started toward the door. It felt like a second funeral. When the door opened, Shintikaisen was waiting outside. She bent down and Ael whispered something in her back-angled ear as she passed the couple on their way out.

"So, you've decided to join Tkal in death's arms. She is not a graceful mistress and does not reunite old friends."

David did not respond.

"You know this is foolish."

Of course, it was foolish. It was also irrevocable.

She twitched an ear at him. "Tkal would be furious with you."

"You may be right, but there's nothing I can do about it now. There's no way out for either of us."

"Do you know this for sure? Have you studied the *Canons of Challenge* thoroughly?"

"Well, no, I haven't studied it like the clerics do."

"All I'm saying is try. David, there is very little honor in this situation. Tkal was dishonorably poisoned, and his assassin is still at large. Gronorgh has dishonored the memory of his fallen leader. You have cast dishonor on children not yet born, and he will gain very little by killing you. He will have answered the charge, but still owe an honor-debt with no one to absolve him. He has given Right of Choice to you. Now, only you can salvage *anything* from this situation. You have to try." Shintikaisen bent down to David's height, aiming both ears at him. "Try to find a way to live. Don't just surrender. That honors no one. You must try!"

"You're right, but how? All he would have to do is fall on me, and I would be crushed to death."

She flattened her ears. "David, I have no answers. I only know you must try. I do not know how you can do it." Shintikaisen shut her eyes and sat still. "You hold all or part of many honors in your hands. Your own, Tkal's, Gronorgh's. Now Dai-Soln's. Some of mine. Some of Enemwenu's. Much of Green Pod's. Even some of the Academy's. It is a heavy load for…"

Someone as small as him? A male? A timid fool? David did not ask, and Shintikaisen had the grace not to finish her thought.

"How long have I been in here?" David asked after a while.

"Sixteen standard minutes," she replied. Traikarniag had an uncanny sense of time.

David did a quick calculation on his netbook. "That's almost exactly twelve Gravgurdan minutes. It's time to go out.

"Do you wish me to follow?" Shintikaisen offered.

"Thank you, but, no."

"Then I will leave now. I await you outside." She rose and left.

David waited about half a standard more, then made his way to the door. He swayed as he reached for the lock. He braced himself against the door. So, this was what it felt like to know you were dying. David pulled himself back upright and opened the door.

He stepped out into the common room where the whole pod, and most of the visitors, were waiting. They all stared at him. Gronorgh stood towering over everyone else, his face like a storm cloud. David faced him and bowed formally. Gronorgh struck his chest with his fist, and David copied the gesture, if somewhat clumsily.

This was just like a scene in that novel he had read, only the combatants in that story had been evenly matched.

"I give you three days at this hour," David said.

Why was he standing here?

"I will see your honor in the gymnasium," he continued.

How did this happen?

"I will give you means later."

Oh, God, help! He desperately hoped Tkal's Eternal was listening.

"Agreed. In three days, we meet in the gymnasium to test our honor," Gronorgh answered.

"To test our honor," David completed the formula.

Gronorgh saluted him with supine fist, turned on his heel and left the suite.

David turned without acknowledging his audience and retreated into his haunted quarters. All his memories of Tkal waited for him there, in their now half-empty room.

※

Brolkat Haerkarn entered Chancellor Tal Hatlir's spartan office, keeping her ears carefully neutral, and waited for him to motion her to a seat.

"I suppose you've already heard about Green Pod?"

"Yes, about an hour ago. I was checking the public bulletin boards for confirmation and details when your message arrived. It looks to be true, not just a rumor."

"Yes, I gather the same. This David Asbury, he's the one you meet with isn't he? The one the murdered student requested be assigned to Green Pod."

"Yes."

"And do we know why the Gravgurdan challenged him? There doesn't seem to be much honor in that."

"From what I've gathered so far, it looks as if the Human made the challenge."

"You assured me that he wasn't suicidal."

Her ears twitched. "I did not believe that he was...but now...I'm not sure."

"You're not sure? You mean that he could be using the Gravgurdan as a means of suicide?"

Her ears swept back. "I do not believe so, but I will not be sure till I meet with him again. He is a very…complex…individual. He was very close to the murdered student."

"Yes, I remember, they were roommates."

"Yes, and I believe the Tvern An's death testament named the Human as kin. He is the one who led the funeral ceremony."

"Yes, I recall. Quite a credible job he did with it. He's quite small. Why in all the moons would a boy that size challenge a Gravgurdan?"

She brought her ears back to neutral. "I believe that the Gravgurdan may have said some derogatory things about the murdered student, or at least things the Human boy took as derogatory."

"And that was enough for him to issue a challenge? I would think the difference in size would be intimidating enough to forestall any such urges…no matter how angry he was. Just disagreeing with one of them takes a good deal of courage."

"I have very few facts as yet. But this boy is unusual, as I have said. He has an incredible mind and a very fine feeling for other cultures. He seems to effortlessly slip into other modes of thought and function within the norms of other cultures. The very first time I called him in, to speak with him about his scholarship and the request for him to be assigned to Green Pod, he was playing the role of a subordinate Trelkairni male. He had all the body postures down and answered by gesture only until I informed him that I do not follow the old customs. He has also proved very adept at not telling me any more than necessary in our sessions and manipulating the direction of my inquiries, and yet there are times when it almost feels more like I'm meeting with a Trelkairni student than a Human."

"So, you're saying that he may have gotten caught up in the moment and, taking on the role of a Gravgurdan, reacted as if he were one?"

"It is possible. I simply do not know yet. It is also possible that he wants to die and has chosen a truly cruel way of doing that."

"This is reprehensible."

Her ears flattened. "Various cultures—"

"I'm not finished," Chancellor Tal Hatlir continued. "The mere idea of students killing one another in honor duels is repulsive enough, but to have this happen among fellow members of a diplomacy pod is nigh unthinkable. What sort of diplomats will any of them make if this is how they deal with things?"

"Any of them?"

"Yes, any of them. I consider the entire pod complicit in this, as well as Jva Uakt and a half-dozen others. There will be a formal inquiry into these events as soon as the barbarism is over."

Brolkat pursed her lips.

"Oh, yes, I'm letting it proceed. I don't have any legal option to stop it. But that doesn't mean that there will not be consequences for everyone involved." He paused and took a deep breath. "Provided David lives."

"Chancellor," Brolkat interjected, "from what I have gathered about the events so far, David has acted in accordance with Gravgurdan law and custom."

Chancellor Tal Hatlir took a deep breath as if preparing to launch back into his speech, then paused and gestured for her to continue.

"I am not saying his initial act was wise or thought out or anything short of suicidal," she winced somewhat at the word. "But since then, even in the heat of that moment, he has acted within the accepted ways of Gronorgh's culture. You cannot condemn the Gravgurdan for what his culture is, nor can you fault David's behavior in respect to that culture. Is that not what a diplomat is required to do?"

The chancellor flared his ear holes. "It is. But this situation should never have occurred."

"Agreed. But it has occurred, and from what I have gathered, the two boys have managed to sculpt a scenario which has the potential to allow the outcome to be salvaged. Again, is this not what a diplomat is required to do?"

"It is. But this sets a dangerous precedent for other students."

She clicked her nails. "I am not so sure. Wait till they see just how much suffering is involved. It could prove to be a deterrent."

David was reading as fast as his eyes could take in the information, which was rather fast. When reading for pleasure, he liked to go slow and savor the experience, but this reading was not for pleasure. This was to save his life, and meetings with Dean Haerkarn had taken up too much of his time.

First, he had read through tomes of Commonwealth law—practically every mention of duels and death challenges. It was quite clear that this Gravgurdan legal custom fell within the Non-Interference Directives—clause XII, paragraph three, subparagraph eight to be precise. The fact that he was a non-Gravgurdan did not protect him. After all it was he, not Gronorgh, who had issued the challenge in the first place. Commonwealth law would not and could not protect him.

Second, he had turned to Earth law briefly, but the treaty accepting the Non-Interference Directives clearly placed this matter outside the jurisdiction of any Earth court or arbitration. Similarly, Shel Matkei Station regulations were of no assistance. Personal injury law and criminal violence codes clearly exempted formal challenges carried out within the legal system of any race.

Finally, David turned to Gravgurdan law. There was no provision for release from a challenge as harsh as the one he had made. No provision was made for aliens at this level of challenge. The law stated,

> IT IS STATED AND ASSUMED THAT ANY BEING, GRAVGURDAN OR ALIEN OF WHATEVER SEX OR AGE, BEING COMPETENT TO CONSTRUCT A *CHIGHARRVE* CHALLENGE, IS AWARE OF THE CONSEQUENCES OF SAID CHALLENGE AND WILLING TO ACCEPT THE CONSEQUENCES OF MAKING SUCH A CHALLENGE; THEREFORE NO PROVISION IS MADE FOR THE REVOCATION OF SUCH A CHALLENGE OR FOR REVIEW OF THE VALIDITY OF SUCH A CHALLENGE.

A footnote to the legal text read: FOR FURTHER DISCUSSION REFER TO *CANONS OF CHALLENGE* AS AMENDED STANDARD 12 AFTER CONTACT. This was what David was currently reading.

"Have you found anything yet?" asked Shintikaisen as she barged in.

"No," David sighed as he pushed away from the terminal. "There doesn't seem to be any way out of this. I'm reading through the *Canons of Challenge* now to see if there's any kind of challenge that doesn't end with me dead."

"That does not seem likely," Shintikaisen said matter-of-factly, but not unkindly.

"No, it doesn't," David admitted. "It's terrifying reading these canons. I mean, we had dueling on Earth, but in our ancient traditions, you just got shot with a metal pellet or pierced through with a sword. You might live, and if you didn't, death would at least be fairly quick."

"The Gravgurdanûn do not think like that," stated Shintikaisen, ears carefully neautral.

"No, they don't. So far, I've learned that stabbing with *kitsa* knives—thin, six-centimeter blades—until one of the combatants bleeds to death, is a vulgar form, acceptable only to the lowest castes. A popular form with a certain set of the higher castes is the placing of weights on the chest until one of the combatants is crushed to death."

Shintikaisen jumped in, "Or barehanded combat to the death. Or drawing and quartering. I've been looking over the Canons myself, and while I find a number of the tales and descriptions exciting, I can't see you being able to survive any of the options given."

"Don't be so encouraging. You might get my hopes up."

"Well, you might be able to get really lucky with the *kitsa* blades. He probably has three or four times as much blood in him as you, but at least you're not absolutely doomed like you would be in most of the options."

"That's what Enemwenu said, too. But I don't want either one of us dead."

"The only way to do *that* is to force him to surrender. Since you made the challenge, you cannot surrender. Oh, you can beg and plead, but the one who makes the challenge has to win or die. And Gronorgh would have to be in unbearable agony before he could surrender without sacrificing the honor of his entire family for three generations. If he did that, he wouldn't live out the week. His own family would end him. He is not going to do that."

"Unbearable agony. That's the key, but I'll be dead before he even knows he ought to feel pain." David laughed like a hangman, like his own hangman. Then his expression changed so abruptly that Shintikaisen took a step back, ears flattened. "Shintikaisen, come back later. I have work to do," he ordered and whirled back to the terminal.

"I'll return in a pair of hours," she muttered and left.

David's only response was furious tapping at the data terminal.

Shintikaisen tried to keep her ears neutral, remembering that look on David's face. She had been quite taken aback when David had addressed her in her own language, in the register of one-speaking-to-her-equals. He had never addressed her in that register before. It was scandalous, but it meant he had not given up yet. That thought pleased her enough that she did not even mind the rudeness of a scrawny male addressing her as an equal. Well not quite. She'd let it pass.

She glanced at the time, then at Ael. "It has been two hours. I suppose I should go back in there."

"You don't act like you want to."

"You should have seen the look on his face."

If Ael didn't know better she could have sworn Shintikaisen's ears shuddered.

"It was like he was possessed by the Mother. I would never have known him. There was blood in his eyes. Like a warrior in a Mother-possessed frenzy. Much too bright. I have only seen eyes like that once, and the most bloody murder followed."

"What? Who killed who?" Ael asked.

"My aunt," Shinti replied. "She killed my cousin, after she found out that my cousin had put her newest husband to use the night before the wedding. Nilgara deserved to die for husband stealing, but I have never seen so much blood, even at a sacrifice. Mother! It was awful."

"And David looked like that?"

"Exactly."

"I find that hard to—"

"Believe it."

"You shouldn't have left him alone."

"I did as he said."

Ael was just trying to decide how to respond when the common room door chimed. "Who could—?"

Dai-Soln dashed across the room and opened the door.

Three Gravgurdan warriors, each almost as large as Gronorgh, stood outside. One wore ceremonial leathers of some sort. Dai-Soln had a brief, and very quiet exchange with the one who seemed to be of the lowest rank and then bowed them all three in.

Ael cast a confused look at Shintikaisen, who shrugged and stood to greet the visitors. Before she could say anything, Dean Haerkarn and Chancellor Tal Hatlir entered, and almost simultaneously the doors to all the other rooms opened, pouring forth every member of the pod except Gronorgh. There were exchanged glances and whispers. "Did you get the text, too?" from one. "You too?" from another. The commotion brought onlookers from adjoining commons.

When David appeared, a strange hush fell over the room. He looked very pale. His face shimmered with sweat, and his breathing seemed irregular. But his eyes still had that preternatural brightness that had so unsettled Shintikaisen. Once he reached the center of the room, he stopped and faced toward Gronorgh's room. The crowd parted, cutting a wide path with David at one end and Gronorgh's door at the other. No one wanted to be in the middle of this, but everyone wanted to see.

David steeled himself as well as he could. "Gronorgh!" he called out. "Gronorgh, come out!"

Gronorgh emerged from his room in answer to the ritual call.

The circles of sweat under David's arms were visible to everyone. "I have come to challenge you to means, you *hurrzha!*" It wasn't easy to call Gronorgh a *hurrzha* to his face, even if it was part of the ritual. It was like calling him a pig or a dog. To do so *calmly?* Well…

"You have chosen the means, *shidza?*"

"Yes, I choose to go outside the Canons."

Gronorgh cocked his head to one side and sort of half blinked. He looked up at the group of Gravgurdan warriors in the crowd and recognized the leathers of a lawyer. "Is this with precedence?" he asked. The lawyer nodded solemnly.

David proceeded. "Yes, there is precedence—two hundred thirty-seven examples in the last six hundred Gramurgh years. Eleven of which were later added to the Canons."

"Voice your challenge. These others," he gestured with his dinner-plate-sized hand, "must judge its worthiness."

"I challenge you to the eating of firefruits." David stood, still staring up at Gronorgh who was staring down at him, while the other Gravgurdanûn conferred briefly among themselves.

Finally, the one in the leather robes raised his voice and spoke. "It is strange, but it is acceptable. It should be excruciating for both of you. This mix of capsaicinoids, shogaols, mustard oil, and sulfenic acids should result in intense pain in the mouth and throat, agony in the nose, and such burning in the eyes that both of you will be blinded by your own tears. If the contest goes on long enough, other compounds should cause blistering of the lips and esophagus, possible vomiting, and/or damage to the stomach lining. If the two of you are able to endure so much, you should achieve fatal toxicity at approximately the same time since these fruits are more toxic to us, but Gronorgh's greater mass will help him compensate." The lawyer paused for the audience to absorb his description, then continued. "Yes, this is acceptable. It will be *horribly* painful and has the potential for death. It will prove your honor or leave you dead."

Gronorgh looked discomfited, but rumbled, "I accept your challenge."

There were sighs of relief from several of David's podmates and slight nods of approval from the other Gravgurdanûn. David had done it. He had found a way to satisfy the honor challenge that had the potential to actually bring honor to the victor, not just clear the debt. And there was a possibility that he could survive. Firefruits were incredibly potent, significantly hotter than the habanero peppers Amarilla had sometimes cooked in the chili back at the orphanage, but they didn't stop there. They added the unpleasantness of horseradish, super-concentrated ginger, and really harsh onions. Plus, they were lethally toxic in sufficient quantities. By David's calculations, fifteen or sixteen would kill him and fourteen or fifteen would do the same for Gronorgh. But the thought of enduring enough pain to eat that many was unimaginable. No matter the outcome, winner and loser alike would suffer great pain, and anyone alive at the end would be quite ill.

David jabbed his chin at Gronorgh by way of recognition, turned on his heel, and marched back to his and Tkal's—back to his room. He had to remember that Tkal was no longer here. Tears welled up in David's eyes, and he slumped against the door as soon as it closed behind him.

Almost immediately the door chimed. David jumped and yelped. He was trembling from the adrenaline shot when he palmed the door. It was Dean Haerkarn and Chancellor Tal Hatlir. After standing staring like an idiot for several heart beats, he came to and stepped aside for them to enter. The chancellor was first to speak.

"Well, that was quite a performance." The disapproval fairly dripped from his words.

David hung his head.

"Look up!"

David did as commanded. Supradoctor Chancellor Tal Hatlir commanded respect from everyone. His age would have been enough for that. But his status as one of the few Varktis still in Commonwealth space, a rare representative of one of the founding races, gave him an aura of awe.

"What? You thought the administration would look kindly on this barbarity being perpetrated on the station? Duels of honor. Pah!"

David started to open his mouth. There was nothing he could say to contradict the president's assessment. He was just plain right.

Twenty-Three

Trial by Fire

The gymnasium had proven too small to accommodate the crowds wanting to gawk at the spectacle, so Zhegrangkht, the Gravgurdan lawyer, along with the two other witnesses, had arranged with the challengers and the Academy administration to move the proceedings to Auditorium Four. And a good thing they had, because the room was full. Most of the Gravgurdan student body had come, but the number of Gravgurdan faces in the audience far exceeded the number the student body could account for. It looked like Gravgurdanûn from parts of the station not connected to the academy had come, drawn by the novelty of an extra-canonical duel. There was also a large number of Human students, as would be expected, all the members of the pod, most of the talent pool, representatives of allied pods, and a variety of onlookers. Few of the onlookers had any real idea of how or why this duel had come about. It was just the most entertaining event to come along in a long time.

David and Gronorgh were seated at small tables facing each other across the stage, separated by about double the distance of their combined reaches, so that if David and Gronorgh both reached for each other as far as they could without leaving their chairs, their arms would cover about half the distance between them. David sat with his head bowed, as if in prayer or a trance, but to his podmates the tension in his body was obvious. Gronorgh would have been more comfortable with a staring match, using his size to intimidate David before the match even began, but he had to make do with glaring into space. Either that or staring at the top of David's head and watching the fury vibrate through the tense lines of David's shoulders, neck, and arms. It actually unnerved Gronorgh, so he mostly glared into space.

The lawyer came forward walking between the two tables, his shoulders so wide that his robes nearly brushed the tables as he passed between them. Silence fell over the auditorium. "This honor duel has been convened in accordance with the laws and traditions of the Gravgurdan people as codified in the *Canons of Challenge*. The challenge was issued and carried out by the Human, David Ethan Asbury, son of Ethan Neal Asbury, son of Neal Crawford Asbury, of the clan Texas, of the planet Earth, against Gronorgh, son of Kveldrragh, son of Vreldhemveng of the clan Brolvang of the planet Gramurgh. Gronorgh has as his second Dai-Soln, son of Ka-Soln, son of Hte-Soln of the clan royal of the planet Taisurul. David has, against all council of law and wisdom, refused a second.

"As the challenger, certain extra burdens fall to David. First, he may not submit; he must triumph or die. Second, if his powers of will fail him, and he is unable or unwilling to constrain himself to continue, it becomes the duty of Kvikhtrraghneghal." He indicated the Gravgurdan warrior standing by David's table. "It becomes Kvikhtrraghneghal's duty to force David to continue until he dies or Gronorgh submits."

The Gravgurdan crossed his arms over his impossibly broad chest, as if to show he had the physical ability to enforce anyone's compliance with anything.

An uneasy murmur rippled through the audience as many of the gathered realized for the first time what it truly was that they had come to witness.

"Beings," the lawyer continued, "be assured, the challenge, issued *by the Human* is the most serious that can be issued under Gravgurdan law."

He waited for that to sink in, then continued. "The Human made the challenge. The Gravgurdan gave the Human Right of Choice. And the Human chose this hour as the time and the gymnasium as the place. He and the Gravgurdan both agreed to the change of location to this auditorium to accommodate the great numbers of you," he gestured expansively, "who wished to witness this matter. The choice of means was delayed while the Human studied the Canons to learn of his options, and he has most boldly chosen to go outside Canon. The contest of this duel is the eating of firefruits."

Someone, a Human judging by the vernacular employed, uttered a profanity.

"This panel," the lawyer gestured to himself and the two standing warriors, "has determined this to be a sufficient contest. According to medical information and experiential testimony from both races, this should be excruciatingly painful and the toxins in the fruits should become lethal to the challenger at fifteen or sixteen fruits, and to the challenged at fourteen or fifteen. According to the Principle of Overkill as enshrined in the Canons, each combatant will be supplied with twenty fruits—more than sufficient to kill."

At this, the gardener from the arboretum came forward carrying a large shallow metal bowl filled with the red, yellow, and orange variegated fruits. He wore protective gloves and an apron of some kind of rubberized material, goggles, and a filtering mask over his nose and mouth. He held the bowl out in front of himself as the two warriors stepped forward. Donning gloves they had worn tucked under their belts, they retrieved from the tables the ceremonial bowls engraved with geometrics that would have reminded David of Ancient Greek pottery if he had been paying attention to such details.

The two witnesses began choosing fruits, alternating between the two of them, until each of them held twenty fruits in his bowl. They strode forward in unison and placed the bowls in front of the combatants. The combatants looked at their bowls and nodded. The witnesses crossed to the opposite tables and examined the bowls to be sure everything was satisfactory and equal. They bowed their agreement to each other, to the lawyer, and to the combatants. Then, Dai-Soln confirmed the same to his satisfaction and likewise bowed to the judge, then to David, and lastly to Gronorgh.

"The Human does not have a second. Does he wish to examine his combatant's bowl?" the lawyer intoned with almost ridiculous solemnity.

David used the Gravgurdan gesture to sign no.

"Then the contest may proceed."

David and Gronorgh rose. Faced each other. Turned and bowed to the witnesses. To Dai-Soln. To the lawyer. They faced each other again, and at the lawyer's signal, they sat.

"You must chew each fruit ten times before swallowing."

David and Gronorgh each took their first fruit in hand and awaited the signal to begin. David finally met Gronorgh's eyes. The lawyer glanced from Gronorgh to David, preparing to signal the start of the contest, but took half a step back when he saw the steel and flames in David's eyes. Quickly, he recovered his composure, and raising his hand, palm up, in front of his chest, paused only a moment before flipping it palm down.

David and Gronorgh each popped their first fruit into their mouths. Instantly David's face turned bright red, and sweat and tears streamed down his face. Gronorgh's face flamed just as red, despite his much darker complexion. Gronorgh gripped the edges of the table so hard he broke the corner off and hurled the chunk across the stage. David's tongue was seared as every nerve fired at the assault of the chemical flame. Eight, nine, ten times he chewed, releasing more and more of the agonizing oils and gasses that assaulted his mouth, nose and eyes. Finally the witness tapped his table, the agreed signal that he could now swallow the poison and allow it to begin ravaging his stomach where more of the toxins would enter his blood stream. He fumbled blindly for his second fruit and, at the tap, began to chew.

At the end of the third fruit, Gronorgh let loose a stream of profanity that would be impossible to translate.

"Shut up you clanless *pfishazh*!" David screamed. "Eat your bile and lies!"

Gronorgh rumbled from deep in his chest, but both witnesses were tapping the tables signaling the combatants to eat their fourth fruits.

Just as David was trying to swallow, a commotion broke out in the audience. It seemed that enough of the sulfenic acid—onion gas—had been released into the air by David and Gronorgh's chewing and gasping that a Hnng in the first row went into respiratory arrest as its gill-filters swelled in reaction, blocking its airways. The paramedics, on hand to deal with the aftermath of the cruelty to which David and Gronorgh were subjecting themselves, had to rush to its aid, and a second squad was called to come and stand by, ready to assist the combatants.

By the time David and Gronorgh both swallowed their seventh of the virulent little fruits, several more observers required minor attention for irritation to delicate membranes in eyes, breathing systems, or external eardrums.

Both the witnesses had been forced, long before, to don breathing masks, regardless of the indignity to their prides, just so they could continue to visually witness the combatants' progress.

On stage, the combination of oils and gasses escaping into the air was overwhelming.

All cheering had ceased as the true horror of what was being endured began to really register, while the number of observers suffering ill effects slowly mounted.

Gronorgh roared in agony after swallowing the ninth fruit.

David's breathing became a strange rasping noise.

Something like a whimper escaped Gronorgh at the signal to begin the next fruit.

David's lips had swollen to the point where he almost had to crush the fruit just to get it past the oozing sores and into his mouth. Blisters were forming and popping on his tongue, and the skin on the roof of his mouth was hanging in shreds.

By the end of his twelfth fruit, David could see again, through the swollen slits of his eyes, as his body ran out of tears. He could see the mucus running down Gronorgh's face and the yellowish color his mahogany skin was turning. Gronorgh's breath was coming in great shuddering gasps, and he trembled as the poisons took effect.

The tap came, and both reached for the thirteenth fruit. David felt like his teeth were coming lose as the bleeding from his gums got worse and worse. He could feel himself running out of mucus to flush the vapors from his nose. When that happened, his nose would swell shut. His eyes had already gone dry.

Gronorgh roared like a wounded beast in fury and rage.

The signal for the fourteenth fruit.

David chewed five, six, seven times. He could hear gagging and worse noises coming from Gronorgh. Eight. Nine. Ten. Swallow.

Gronorgh bellowed and retched, expelling the unswallowed fruit and more. "No! I give. I was wrong! I will not die so that I may refuse to say I was wrong. I besmirched another warrior's honor, and I deserve this. Stop!"

David took the fifteenth fruit in hand and shoved it into his mouth. Gronorgh's eyes had just gone dry. "No!" he roared. He tried to launch himself at David to stop this madness, but the toxins had already started to paralyze him, and he collapsed across the table, which shattered under his bulk.

Kvikhtrraghneghal grabbed David's convulsing body and tried to shove his gloved finger into David's mouth to retrieve the unnecessary fruit, but David bit him. The paramedics rushed forward and tried to pry David's mouth open, while Kvikhtrraghneghal pinned his thrashing arms and legs, but quickly abandoned that course of action. David was strapped to a gurney and whizzed out the doors and down the corridors to the nearest medical facility right behind Gronorgh. Somewhere along the way the pain shoved him into oblivion.

Twenty-Four

Healing

David lay in the bed with the monitors all around him beeping in rhythm with his life signs. His stomach had been pumped and as much of the poison purged from his body as was possible, but it would take some time for it to heal. His tongue and esophagus were badly burned, and his intestines were also affected. Some of the toxins had been absorbed into his blood, leaving his muscles aching and his head throbbing. The doctors said the damage to his liver was reversible, and they would be able to take the tubes out of his bronchi the next day.

The door chimed. David pressed a button on the room control pad to open it. A tall Tvern An strode in. He was about six centimeters taller than Tkal, but otherwise… Tears welled up in David's eyes as he recognized Tkal's father.

"Hello, David, I am Dvarin Dgan, Tkal's father."

Tears streamed down David's cheeks and burned like rivers of fire in the still-unhealed burns around his mouth.

"I have heard what happened. My son was…my son was blessed to know you. I…" His voice caught, and he was unable to continue. His green stripes blanched toward yellow and his whole face had an emotional oily sheen. He reached for David's left hand. "I received the record of the memorial service. I understand you organized it. It was worthy in every detail. You have honored my son greatly. May I see your scar?"

David brought his right hand across to show Ambassador Dvarin.

"Yes, this is the scar of my son's chosen brother—his *tdaln vkirl*. From my son's letters, I do not think he had explained this to you completely. I will return in three days, when my wife arrives, and we will share the *ktiln*—the remembering for Tkal—only the three of us. Sleep now. And heal." Tkal's father turned and left slowly, as though his legs were partially paralyzed. Or he carried a great weight.

David sobbed softly, till he began to choke on the tubes and the medics rushed in to sedate him.

About lunch time the next day, the doctors removed the tubes. "Okay, David. Can you say your name?"

David cleared his throat gingerly. "Ah!" he gasped, wincing at the pain, which, of course, hurt the skin on his face. The pain was terrible. He tried again, more gently, "Dafit Asspery." Oh, how his vocal chords hurt! "David Asbury," he forced out. His voice sounded odd in his own ears, like a stranger speaking through his mouth. It sounded deeper and raspy. The med-tech explained that it was normal before the final regen treatment. David wanted to ask questions, but medicated sleep took him only moments after one of the nurses injected him.

When he woke, he was alone. He reached over to the bedside table, opened the top drawer and pulled out a mirror. There was still some poorly matched synth-skin around his mouth, and it still hurt to move his angry red tongue. He knew the swelling and pain in his tongue would go away in about an hour. He'd been through so many of these treatments, he'd lost count. He started to test his voice. His first hesitant attempt resulted in a coughing fit that scratched like sandpaper in his throat.

David tried again. "Tkal, I'll find him. I'll find the one who did this to you."

About two hours later, after the doctors had come and gone again and the med tech had changed the synth-skin around his mouth, the door chime rang. David pressed the button to open the door and Dai-Soln walked in.

"David, you are awake this time. I have been waiting to see you, but you have rarely been conscious these yesterdays. The techs have kept you sedated most of the time, to facilitate your healing. I understand that they will release you the next day of tomorrow."

David simply nodded. Speaking was too painful.

"We have voted while you and Gornorgh slept. I witnessed Gronorgh's vote yesterday. I will witness yours now."

"I fote for Enemwenu," David whispered.

"You know that hii wished to withdraw."

"Yes, but we never took the vote," David croaked.

"True. Your vote has been witnessed. Congratulations, Mr. President."

"What?!" David shrieked and instantly started a coughing fit, followed by tears of pain. He trembled with the effort not to cough and to hold back the cry of pain that would start the cycle again.

Dai-Soln looked horrified at what his words had caused, but was helpless to do anything constructive. Finally, he poured David a glass of water.

David took a sip and gestured his thanks. This time his voice came as a tiny whisper, barely audible above the life signs monitor, "What?"

"The council has chosen you with six votes. That is a two-thirds majority on an open ballot."

"Why?"

"I think you can answer that yourself, so I will not. However, I should tell you that we have captured another Violet Pod transmission, and your decipherment of the code seems to be correct. It still looks like there may be a set of keys rather than just the one, but we have good data now, and your linguistics group thinks they may have cracked a second key. Gornorgh is like a caged animal, waiting to be released so he can plan counter strikes. There will be plenty of information for you to review when you return."

"I can't. I'm not even sure I want to stay here."

Dai-Soln stared from cold, obsidian eyes. "You will stay."

"What makes you so sure?"

He levered his sword out. "First, we need you, and you understand duty."

David tried to lie and say he didn't care about duty, but the words wouldn't come to his lips.

"And second, you have an agenda." Dai-Soln paused and nictitated. "Do you know, yet, who did it?"

"No. But I will."

"I do not doubt that. None of us do. Ask for our help, and we will have hands," Dai-Soln said, using one of those delightfully ambiguous Taisiran idioms which could mean "we will help you" or "we will go to war" depending on the context.

David smiled, not even minding the pain. "Thank you."

After Dai-Soln left, David lay in his bed considering what he should do. In the end, he decided Dai-Soln was right. He would stay because he had an agenda.

One of the pod, Dai-Soln he suspected, had seen to it that the Tvern ceremonial robes which Tkal had given him were delivered to his bed before he checked out. David was relieved to be free of the hospital. He had not seen Gronorgh yet. As he was being released, he asked and learned that the Gravgurdan had been released several hours before him. He let his feet carry him where he had to go. This wasn't going to be a pleasant task, but it was absolutely necessary, and it was best to get it out of the way before he met with Tkal's parents. On the way, he met up with Jva and Enemwenu headed back to the pod. He didn't want to talk to them right now, but he didn't want to be rude and couldn't think of a polite way to tell them to go away, and then it was too late. There was Gronorgh standing at the end of the corridor with Dai-Soln. This was the moment he was dreading. He wasn't at all sure how this would play out. Gronorgh could not be happy. His pride had to be mortally wounded and he must have lost a lot of status, being defeated by a Human who wouldn't even make a decent outcaste.

He glanced to his left and right. Jva and Enemwenu were still there. He wasn't sure if that made this better or worse. There was no avoiding this, but David didn't know how to proceed.

Gronorgh took the initiative. There was none of his usual swagger in his step as he approached, head down. It was unsettling seeing him like this. He stopped several meters from David. He brought his fist to his chest like a centurion saluting Caesar. Then he knelt like a knight awaiting his dubbing.

"*Hhoghsidrangqoelzhaghaqdhav*, I salute you."

David didn't know this ceremony. He was lost.

Jva broke in, "*Hhogh*? That's *foot* right? Did he just call you a foot?"

"It means 'the one being heavy with the foot down toward me', but I don't understand the context." He looked to Dai-Soln.

"It is short for *T'oqdhavmas hhoeghsidrangqoelzhaghaq murglorj'ô*."

"'The victor stands with his foot on my neck'? No. Gronorgh, I am not proud of what I did. I am beginning to hate myself for it."

"You must not, *Hhoeghsidrangqoelzhaghaqdhav*. You achieved a fair and honorable victory. Some would have thought me strong. Some would have thought you unwise to challenge."

Jva squirmed noticeably at that.

"Okay, I do not hate myself."

Gronorgh let his breath out.

David realized he had just avoided some disaster. Could he have lowered Gronorgh's status even further, or damaged him in some other way, by despising the victory he had won? He looked again to Dai-Soln. "I need help here. If you know this ceremony, please advise me. I think I almost stepped on a land mine there."

Dai-Soln gave a very formal bow, brushing his fronds against the floor before drawing up to his full height. "This ceremony is only required when both parties survive the combat. It establishes the shape of the future relationship between victor and vanquished. The defeated kneels before the victor to learn how deeply the victor despises his weakness. You have the opportunity to inflict a wide range of indignities upon your victim, and the vanquished must eat his shame. He is never allowed to avenge anything done to him in this ceremony, and any attempt to do so can be punished by the cruelest legal custom. You could castrate him if you wished, and he would have to remain still and let you do it."

David nearly gagged at the thought.

"Stand up, Gronorgh. You are free."

"No, David!" Dai-Soln gasped. "If you do nothing, then he is unabsolved. You must choose something."

David looked at Gronorgh kneeling there. Even kneeling, he was as tall as David. "What would be the minimum acceptable indignity?" he asked Gronorgh.

"You could choke me out," Gronorgh volunteered.

"Ha! You overestimate me by a couple of magnitudes. Your neck is like a steel column. I could squeeze until *I* passed out and have no effect."

Gronorgh sighed. "It is easier than you think. There is a blood vessel that runs here," he said, drawing a line down his neck. "Your arm is very thin and the radius bone is very sharp. If you grasp like this," he said, gesturing the hold, "and pull back with your weight, you can do it. I will relax the muscles as much as possible. And I will lean forward so I will not fall on you."

"No, Gronorgh, I don't think it will work. I'm Human. Do my customs count for nothing in this ritual?"

"Hrngh." Gronorgh made a face that looked amazingly like a Human frown. "You are the victor. You control the ceremony. A Human indignity would be appropriate. It would demonstrate your control, and it would mark me as the only Gravgurdan to lose to a Human."

Dai-Soln nodded.

David ran through all the ugly things he had been subjected to back at Grey Street—licking Sergio's shoe, being tied to a chair and left there all night on the balcony stripped to his boxers, eating pudding that every boy in his room had spit in, and here at Shel Matkei there had been the shunning, the non-recognition of him as a person. And then Gronorgh's insults and sneers. David decided. He cleared his throat as loudly as he could, a choice that cost him, as he nearly gagged from the pain. He mastered the reflex to yelp, and spit directly in Gronorgh's face.

Gronorgh looked astounded. He just knelt there with his eyes unblinking and his mouth hanging open. "Is…is this fluid poisonous?" he asked, the tension audible in his voice.

Jva laughed, then struggled to disguise it as a coughing fit.

David considered. "I hope not. It certainly is not to us. It is a combination of digestive fluids and mucus. It's considered filthy and disgusting, but it isn't at all dangerous."

David turned to Dai-Soln, "How long should he stay there?"

"As long as you wish—standard minutes, hours, days—how much vengeance do you wish?"

"Stand, Gronorgh, and eat your shame."

Gronorgh continued to kneel. "There is one more thing, *Hhoeghsidrangqoelzhaghaqdhav…*"

"What?"

"You should now call me *Murglorj'ô.*"

"'On your neck'? Must I? It's so…" he sighed. The whole point of this was to demean. Of course he had to. "*Murglorj'ô*, you may stand now and eat your shame."

Gronorgh sighed and stood. He still towered over David, but he seemed much smaller.

"Will you consent to walk with the one beneath your foot?"

This was really bothering David, but it was important to Gronorgh. "Yes, I will walk with you."

They left the others there in the corridor and wandered for some time before Gronorgh spoke again. "*Hhoeghsidrangqoelzhaghaqdhav—*"

"Please stop calling me that."

"I cannot."

"It makes me feel awful. Like a monster."

"A monster? You don't act like one who feels like a monster. You act like one who feels likes a *mouse*. A monster would be walking with his chest thrust out, daring everyone who passed to fight him, leading me by a chain, not walking at my side. A monster would be roaring with the pride of his accomplishment. A monster would be bold and basking in his unbelievable victory. No, you are acting like a *mouse*."

"Gronorgh…"

"You must not call me that. You must use *Murglorj'ô* now. You are the victor. I am the vanquished. This is what I accepted when I surrendered."

"If I had known…"

"Once the challenge was made and accepted, this was the only possible result. This or death. I knew that. And I was prepared to see you die. I just wasn't prepared for *that* much pain. I don't see how anyone could be. I never realized it was possible to hurt that much. The fire was in my mouth and up my nose and in my eyes, and it just kept spreading and intensifying. I…lost control of certain functions. Half the time I couldn't even see. I just heard the taps on the tables and knew that you had managed to swallow another one. And then we were at the limit, and I realized that I fear death. I didn't know that before. I tried to put that last fruit in my mouth, the one that should kill me, and I just couldn't do it. I wanted to live. And then I couldn't even keep the ones I had swallowed down, which hurt even more." He inhaled. "And I had been wrong the whole time. I am very stubborn, but not a fool. I would rather live with the shame of losing to the most excruciating pain, than die to continue speaking a lie. And then you tried to eat another one." Gornorgh stopped walking. He didn't look at David. He just stood gazing off down the corridor at something that wasn't there. "Why did you do that?"

"Because I *did* want to die."

Gronorgh flinched at that and looked nauseated.

"I had made you call your words a lie. It was finished. I just wanted to…"

"You took that brother thing very seriously, didn't you?"

"Yes."

"Good. Such things should never be taken lightly. Do you still want to…that?"

"No."

"Good, because there is something much better you can do. You can find the one who killed Tkal. I will help you."

"Thank you. I will need your help."

"*Hhoeghsidrangqoelzhaghaqdhav—*"

"I asked you stop calling me that."

"I must. And you must call me—"

"Why?"

"I lost the challenge."

"And so…?"

"So this is who I am to you now."

"But I don't want to call you that. It is demeaning."

"That's the point. That's why a Gravgurdan should not submit. Submitting carries a heavy price. But I knew that. Death was a weightier price, this time, *Hhoeghsidrangqoelzhaghaqdhav*."

"But I don't want to do this. And I won't."

"Then you will further shame me in front of other Gravgurdanûn. They will think that I lied to you and did not complete the ceremony."

"What about a compromise?"

Gornorgh looked down at him. "Compromise?"

"I will try very hard to be as insulting as necessary in front of other Gravgurdanûn, if you will let me go on calling you Gronorgh among the pod or when we speak privately."

"*Hhoeghsidrangqoelzhaghaqdhav*—"

"And that has to stop too." The look of shock on Gronorgh's face made David hasten to add, "With the same conditions. You can call me that…name…when other Gravgurdanûn are around, but only then. Only so you can save face. I don't want this, but it looks like I am stuck."

"*Hhoegh*—" he inhaled and started over. "You have the heart of a warrior. You proved that in the duel. But you do not have the mind of a warrior, and this worries me."

"Why?"

"See. If you had the mind of a warrior, you would not need to ask that question."

David just stood there waiting for an answer.

"I will shield you as much as I can, but our schedules are very different, and none of our classes match."

"Shield me? From what?"

There was a pause. "David," he breathed out, accepting the inevitable name, "I believe I spent more time conscious in the hospital than you did, so I have had more time to think about this. You will face many challenges."

"Yes, well, I said I'm done trying to…you know. I said I'm after the killer now. I'm going to live, and I'm going to succeed for Tkal. And for myself."

Gronorgh shook his head. "No, you do not understand. There will be many challenges from males, challenges to fight."

"But why—?"

"Some will be Gravgurdanûn who cannot believe that one of us could ever be defeated by one of you—at anything."

David was appalled, but couldn't believe that any Gravgurdan would stoop to challenge him to a duel.

Gronorgh seemed to read his thoughts. "They will not be death challenges like you issued, but other lesser challenges, probably to eat more of those fruits. You should be able to turn many of those aside, I will teach you some ways that will work and satisfy the foolish."

David sighed.

"But I am more concerned about the Humans who will challenge you."

"What? We don't have a living tradition of duels."

"Don't you? It just isn't governed by any written or acknowledged codes. I understand you have a tradition called *bullying* and one called *hazing* and some of what I read about the *barroom brawl* sounds like an unregulated from of duel. In most cases, it seems the fights are initiated by the bigger male, and winning is accompanied by excessive bragging, or continued physical assaults on the weaker male over long periods of time. It sounds a lot like school, before we are casted. Can you not see Human males wishing to tell others that they *beat up* the only Human who has ever defeated a Gravgurdan in a duel?"

David was horrified. Of course there would be idiots like that. Jerks who would convince themselves that bloodying him was equivalent to fighting a Gravgurdan for themselves. He reached out and steadied himself against the wall.

"But it's illegal. And when did you learn so many English words? They'll face assault charges, even if I don't file. Human laws will apply, so will Commonwealth laws."

"And will that stop all of them? Can you not think of some who would take the risk?"

David could. Easily. Some of his past roommates even.

"Are you prepared for this?"

David couldn't even answer.

"I do not want to insult you. I only say this because you are so small. Even for your own kind. Take Jva for instance. He is not very big by my standards, and I have seen Human males here at Shel Matkei who are much larger than him, but he is much bigger than you. Could you fight him?"

David got an image of himself trying to fend off a real attack from Jva. "No way."

"Perhaps I am overreacting."

David thought about that. "No. I hate to say it, but you could be right. There are guys who think like you said. I already have a whole list in my mind, a list of ones I'm going to try to avoid till this dies down."

"That may be a while. You are famous now. You may have to face news services."

David recoiled.

"Do you remember how many beings were there? And not only from the academy, but station personnel and Epemthis and travelers just passing through. This may come up from time to time for years, maybe the rest of your life."

David stopped in his tracks.

"It will become less and less frequent. And if the news services do not pay attention, it could die out completely a year or two after you leave here."

David's mind raced like a hamster on a wheel.

"Let me help you."

"How?"

"You must learn to fight, and you must gain weight and strength."

"That will take years!"

"Yes, but you need those things anyway. Please do not be offended, but you are too weak. Even other Human males do not take you seriously. It will affect your career. You need strength and confidence. You already have fire. You just need to learn how to use it when you aren't trying to…uh…hurt…uh… yourself."

David started walking again, with Gronorgh at his side. A Gravgurdan warrior only slightly smaller than Gronorgh passed them going the opposite way. He looked at Gronorgh like he was sizing him up. "That one…"

"Yes, I saw. I will have to fight him in the next few days."

David looked worried.

"Do you doubt my strength?" Gronorgh rumbled and flexed.

"No, you're bigger than him."

"Not by much, but yes, I am, and I know I am stronger. He is barely a 1.4 and I'm a 1.2. He is a fool to challenge me, but he just arrived and probably thinks that I have gotten soft living on this station with such low gravity for so long."

"That would be the only explanation for losing to a Human." David realized that Gronorgh would probably be fighting a lot to claw his way back up to respectability.

"As I said, he is a fool. I knew that before today."

"You will take him. And the next. And the next."

"I only hope for some time to rest between. Even the strongest warrior can be worn down to the point where he loses to an unworthy opponent. Please think about what I said."

"I will, Gronorgh. Now I must go. I have an appointment."

Gronorgh nodded gravely. "Yes. Honor him well." He muttered something just below David's full hearing that sounded like an oath for a fallen comrade and turned back the way they had come.

David touched the chime, and the door slid open without a pause. He straightened his robes. He hadn't felt right about wearing them, but knew, on some level, that he had to. Now, as he stepped into the glare of dozens of Tvern candles, like the ones in Tkal's candle room, he was glad he had. No other garments would have been right in this room, among the hypnotically dancing shadows. Ambassador Dvarin came forward, the flickering light dancing across his strong features. As he reached David, a Tvern woman emerged from behind a curtain, dressed in the same ceremonial robes that David and Ambassador Dvarin were wearing.

The ambassador, touched David on the forehead, "David, my son, this is my wife, your mother, Ambassador Dfal Kgarel."

She tilted her head to the left and then the right in greeting. She then took his hands in her own and turned them palm up, exposing his scar. She touched her forehead to each of his palms. Then she stepped aside so that her husband could take David's hands and repeat the same ritual before tracing the scar with his pinkie finger.

"David, I told you in the hospital that I did not believe that Tkal had fully explained all the implications of what he did when he made you his brother. Now we will explain." He gestured for David to sit on one of the three cushions arranged in a careful triangle in the center of the floor. The two ambassadors sat on the remaining cushions. "You see, when he chose you as his brother, he actually adopted you into his family. By Tvern An legal custom, you are now our son as well as Tkal's brother. We have the same legal duty to you that we had to Tkal."

David took a shuddering breath. His chest felt very tight. "Then I freely absolve you. I would not have accepted if I had realized that Tkal's gesture bound others than himself. I have no right to lay claim upon you."

Tkal's mother gasped. "No, you misunderstand. We do not wish to be *absolved*." She said the word as if it tasted bad. "We rejoice that we have you to share our grief, that we may lighten each other's burden. And that, in the future, we may share our joys. Please." She glanced at her husband with something like fear in her eyes, "If you will have us, we are proud to be your parents. If our son chose you for his brother, we choose you for our son. Tkal was wise in many things. He would not choose a brother foolishly."

David was weeping. "I am not worthy. You don't even know me. I have even less to give you than I had to give Tkal."

Tkal's father spoke. "Tkal thought you worthy, and Tkal was wise, as my wife—" At this she glanced sharply at him, but he made a fluttering motion with his hand and she acquiesced. "As my wife has said, he would not have chosen you unless you were worthy in his eyes."

David wanted to deny that he had any worth at all, but doing so would be to name Tkal a poor judge of character, maybe even a fool, and that he could not do.

"As for knowing you, we are learning even now, but the man who led the memorial for Tkal is a man of great understanding, a kind and loving spirit, with deep respect, and one who honored Tkal greatly." He paused and looked to his wife.

"As a mother," she said, "all that…my husband…says is true, but I must add that I have read and re-read Tkal's letters. Tkal was never a sad boy, but he was lonely. He had many friends; he was skilled at that. But a new joy entered his letters after he suggested you become his brother. And his last letter, on the day you did *fdinel*… You gave him more than you realize." She paused. "A mother's heart rejoices when her son's heart rejoices. You have already given a gift to me—one of great price."

David could say nothing.

"Please do not *absolve* us. We do not ask to be absolved. We ask to take up our place in the pact Tkal made with you."

David could not speak. His throat was so nearly swollen shut that there was no room for the words to get through. So, he nodded and reached out his hands, palms up to show the scar. He let the tears flow as his new parents again touched their foreheads to his palms and then passed his hands across each other so they could touch his other hand as well.

Together they said, "Our son David," but David could barely hear over the blood rushing in his ears.

They spent the next several hours recalling all their joyous memories of Tkal, and sad ones too.

Kgarel recalled the first time she had taken Tkal home to Tvern for a visit and all his wonder at seeing so many Tvern An in one place, and the foods he tried until he had made himself quite ill, and his many, many questions. Dgan had told of his pride as he watched Tkal grow into a strong son and his joy when Tkal had been accepted to Shel Matkei, announcing his plan to follow in his parents' footsteps as a diplomat. David told them of the day at Tolari Market. Eventually, all the candles burned out, and they sat in total darkness for a time, contemplating their sadness and their joy and saying very private good byes. At the end, David felt as if all that was inside him had been washed. He still hurt, but the pain was transmuted into something else. Something other than the searing coal that it had been. It was a pain he could live with, one he could let go someday. There was more to healing than just the body.

Twenty-Five

Unblazed Paths on a Moonless Night

David woke from his nap. For the last two days, it seemed like all he could do was sleep. The doctors said his body was well enough to return to his normal schedule. But any time he didn't have a class or have one or more of the pod members in the room asking questions about this or that (but mostly when the first meeting would be)—any time he had quiet, he fell asleep. Somehow, he had pulled himself together sufficiently to call a meeting—one he still wasn't ready for, but he had managed to prepare a little. And he'd awakened with enough time to run his fingers through his hair, grab his netbooks, and find a seat at the table before he was late. Not an auspicious start.

He opened the meeting. "Okay. So. I don't know why you all did this, but I'll try to make a go of it." His new voice still sounded so strange. I am not Tkal, and I don't have his skills. Tkal was a generalist. I am a specialist. Most of us still here are specialists. Together we cover *most* of the skill sets we need to complete this mission, but there are holes." David took a shuddering breath. "Where does Tkal's…absence…hurt us most?"

Enemwenu knotted a tentacle on the tabletop, and waited for David's nod. "Tkal was the cooperation broker. He insured that we continued to work as a team, even when individualities were strong. He did not force conformity, but he created ways to cooperate despite differences."

Gronorgh thumped the table. David nodded. "Tkal pushed us. He knew our strengths and leaned heavily on those, but did not hesitate to give uncomfortable assignments that forced us to gain new strengths. I have the most tactical training, so he left that mostly in my grasp, but wouldn't hesitate to force me into a situation where I must deal with economics or culture or insulted prides, if it was convenient to do so."

Shintikaisen did the three-fingered tap. "Organization of group effort was one of his strengths. He insured we did not 'step on each other's toes' as he said. He made sure we worked efficiently, did not duplicate effort."

"So we need to look for a generalist with strong managerial skills?"

Ael frowned at David. Shinti leaned back and crossed her arms. Xtp rubbed its second arms down its legs making cricket sounds. Gronorgh grunted. Fthofsis, Red-shimmer, and Enemwenu were silent. Dai-Soln looked at the ceiling and waggled his fronds.

"What? Am I that boring?"

Dai-Soln fixed him with an obsidian stare.

"Dai-Soln?"

"David. Is it not too soon for this?"

"No. It has to be done, and quickly. Tkal told me how all of you had to struggle to make up the extra work caused when Sven was dismissed. And he was only the linguist, not the leader of the team. No, we need another being in here and fast. If we don't move fast, no one will be able or willing to transfer in until next term. Exams will not be made easier by waiting. Catching up with Violet Pod will not be helped by being one member short as an empty gesture. No. We honor Tkal best by completing his work as fully as possible, and he very much wanted to see Green Pod back on top."

"You are sure this is what you want? A new person in the pod? A new roommate in Tkal's bed?"

David could feel his throat swelling. He tried without complete success to steady his voice. "It is what must be."

Each of the others settled into postures and/or gestures of resignation or acceptance. David had never dreamed this would be such a hard sell. It was especially odd for Gronorgh to be this sentimental. His respect for Tkal's leadership had always seemed rather grudging, and his speech before the election… Well, Gronorgh had proven to be far more complex than David had realized. Still, Gronorgh was a serious pragmatist. Time to call on that. "Gronorgh. Is this not the most logical course? A warrior fights best with all his limbs engaged, does he not?"

"He does."

Why did that sound so reluctant? "Well, we are missing a leg. We need someone who can bring the kind of balance Tkal did." Why was everyone trying not to meet his eyes?

David assigned everyone to make lists of five candidates to fill the gap, and include a short argument for each candidate, to be submitted to him before next meeting. David would sort those lists and organize them for discussion at the next meeting. All the other items on the agenda seemed to be rubber-stamped or tabled or ill-prepared. It was a very disappointing first meeting.

As soon as David dismissed the meeting, everyone seemed to scatter into small clusters. Probably to plan a coup. No doubt they already regretted the sentimentality of their ridiculous vote, almost as much as David himself. What had possessed them? Gronorgh and Dai-Soln had their heads together, and Gronorgh was gesturing with far more animation than he had shown at any time during the meeting. David gathered up his netbooks and other junk, shoved it all in his bag, and with one final glance over his shoulder, retreated to his room. A very disappointing meeting indeed. He just hoped the coup was quick. And bloodless.

A short time later, the door chimed. David called "Enter," and the door slid open.

"Oh, Dai-Soln, what's—"

"Why, David?"

"Why what?"

"The meeting. Why are you doing this? You promised. You said—"

"Wait a standard minute. Promised? Promised what? And what did *I* do wrong in the meeting? You were all acting crazy. Not looking at me. Halfhearted presentations at best."

"You promised to stay."

"Stay? Of course I'm staying. What are you talking—?" And then it clicked. "You thought… *All* of you thought that because my first agenda item was… You thought I was *leaving*?"

Dai-Soln's fronds stiffened. Then he clamped them across his head and down his neck. "You weren't replacing Tkal so you could…?"

"No!" David held his hands out in helpless confusion. "Whatever gave you that idea?"

"You were very close to him. You… Why else would you move so quickly to replace him?"

"It was—*is*—the right thing to do, for the pod to have a chance."

"We had been…" Dai-Soln trailed off.

"You had been what? And which of you is *we?*"

Dai-Soln's fronds rustled against each other behind his neck.

"So, it was all of you. What were you doing?"

"You… Please don't be angry."

"The last time you said that to me, you led me into this room to meet with Dean Haerkarn."

"We had been meeting to discuss how to make you accept this, how long we could possible hold out to let you grieve, before we must force the issue. We were also… We thought it likely you would refuse to have someone else in Tkal's…well, to share the space of these memories. We even discussed the possibility of losing you if we forced the issue."

David felt sick. "This is not easy for me. I don't *want* to do this. I don't want anyone else in here. I don't want someone else trying to fill up the hole left by Tkal's murder. I don't want to talk about this, discuss it, argue it, vote on it. But it *has* to be done, and it has to happen soon, for the sake of the pod."

"We could wait a bit. Fill the post at midterm."

"No. It needs to be now. I may not have the nerve later."

Dai-Soln shook out his fronds, palmed the hilt of his sword and bowed himself out of the room.

David felt something and reached up. How had his face gotten wet?

Once Dai-Soln convinced the others that David had no intention of leaving, David was flooded with lists of potential candidates for the tenth member of the pod. Some were not workable in David's opinion—too specialized, too contentious, to likely to be…over-enthusiastic. But there were still quite a number of reasonable candidates, and several really good ones: a Traiqi, another Trelkairni, a Wkkho, two or three others.

Were any of them significantly better than the others? Were any of them worse? David didn't know any of them well enough to tell. Well, one meeting with that Imthiqorakar was enough to tell David he couldn't room with him, probably couldn't even work with him. Why had Xtp put that jerk on its list anyway? *He argues forcefully and has been connected to at least three different pods.* That was supposed to be a plus? Well, maybe. But that hardly made up for his obvious deficiencies. Red-shimmer had included a Human on her list, a highly qualified Human, but David didn't think it wise to try to bring a third Human on team. He also really didn't want another Gravgurdan, even if both Ael and Shintikaisen had included her.

Actually, that could be a nasty joke at Gronorgh's expense. David could just imagine how uncomfortable Gronorgh would be living in the same suite with a female of his species. Gravgurdanûn males and females didn't even live in the same sections of their cities, except during mating season. Surely Ael knew that. Shintikaisen *definitely* knew. Were they testing to see if he would do this to Gronorgh? Well, would he? No. There was no way he would go out of his way to humiliate Gronorgh *or* this Vikhalgh, for whom the snide comments about "living downtown" would be just as vicious. But could he bring it up as a possibility, just to see Gronorgh squirm? Maybe just put her way down the list with a notation: Female Gravgurdan. It might be fun. But what if Shinti pushed to make her a serious candidate, to bring her up for debate? Well, she sort of had to go on the list somewhere. She did have a fair number of the skills David was looking for. Still it would *never* work. If she had any sense, she'd turn it down, even if the position were offered to her. Okay, so put her on the list about where her skills would place her anyway, and then point out the cultural impediment as tactfully as possible and move on. If they got that far down the list. David grabbed fists full of his own hair and pulled. How had he become an HR director? This was horrible!

Mercifully the door chimed. It was Dai-Soln. "Are you busy? I can come back."

"No, please. I'm working on these lists. I'm ready to pull my hair out trying to sort them."

"Does that help? Does hair inhibit thought?"

David was about to answer when he realized Dai-Soln was making a joke.

"Well what qualities are *you* looking for?"

"That's part of the problem. I only have the vaguest notion. We need to replace Tkal's skill sets. Add new skills if we can. Find a personality that will fit in without…"

"Do you have a short list?"

"Yes. Well, sort of. I keep changing my mind."

"Just pick some of the better ones and put them on your short list. Put the rest on a second- or third-tier list, and then set the rest of us to hash it out. Tkal often sat back for discussions like this—who to bring on team, who to accept into the talent pool. Oh, except when he wanted you. Then he argued, strongly. Oh, and he usually kept names, and sometimes even species, off the lists, identifying candidates by number so we had to argue on the merits of skills and talents, grade sheets." He waggled his fronds. "You may wish to do things differently."

Differently. David was going to botch this so bad.

Red-shimmer Gold-streak sat in the middle of David's room. "I miss our conversations, David."

He sighed. "I'm sorry, Red-shimmer. I'm just… There's been so much… I'm not dealing with all this very well. Tkal, the challenge, ya'll voting me leader, my classes, Tkal's parents, the funeral, the hospital, not sleeping, sleeping too much, Dean Haerkarn, these blasted meetings. And station security isn't doing *anything*."

Red-shimmer Gold-streak sort of wobbled on her pedi-graspers. "It does appear that station security is not making much progress in finding Tkal's killer."

David huffed and started pacing, punctuating his accusations with random wild gestures. "They're looking in the wrong places. They're looking at us, at enemies of his parents, at the possibility of some random crime—a mugging or someone who just hates Tvern An. They seem to be purposely looking everywhere *but* at Prince Kvran and Violet Pod."

"Have you said anything?"

David stopped mid-pace. "Have I said anything?" He threw his arms wide. *"Have I said anything?* I've practically shouted myself hoarse. But it's like they shove their fingers in their ears and start singing 'LALALALALA' real loud to drown me out."

"Yes, well, some of them do seem to be a bit—"

"A bit? A bit vacant? A bit empty-headed? Ha! If you listen *real* hard, you can hear the tornadoes in their heads!" He spun his chair and sat down with a thud.

Red-shimmer bounced up and down on her pedi-graspers. "David, that might be more than a little over-colored. And I was going to say, 'unwilling to look in that direction.' I am afraid this is real-world politics in play here. No one wants to offend Prince Kvran, grandson of the sitting Emperor of the Kzati."

David slapped his desktop. "I know he did it, or rather ordered it. He wouldn't actually dirty his delicate little hands. I just can't prove it."

Red-shimmer went muddy. "Neither can station security, and they will not do anything until they are very sure they *can* prove it. No one is willing to offend an entire empire."

"Well, I am. And I *will* prove it. Somehow."

She drifted closer to David's knee. "Be careful David. This is no game. This is real. Kvran has probably killed before."

David narrowed his eyes and looked at her sidewise. "Dai-Soln asked you to say that."

"Yes, he did. He is concerned. I am concerned. We all are. Gronorgh…has lost color. Dai-Soln has no doubt that Kvran has killed more than once, and I have no reason to doubt Dai-Soln. The prince he describes would not think twice about arranging something for someone as…unconnected…as you."

"Do you really think that matters to me? My life in exchange for the truth would be a fair deal in my mind."

She backed away. "You will find no agreement on that thought. David, you have become…monochrome. There is no variety in your color any more. And I think the color I am seeing is…hate. This is not the man that Tkal called brother, or I called friend. You are in a dangerous place, and I am frightened for you. Tkal would know how to force you to see yourself. I am not sure you are hearing my words, or seeing my colors."

David tuned Red-shimmer out after that, and just auto-piloted the conversation until she gave up and left.

David wasn't sure he could face another day of debates about who to bring on team. He'd almost lost it at the first day's meeting. That day, the debate had gone in so many directions, and been so unfocused, that David had decided to only allow two candidates to be considered at a time for the second day's arguments. The second day, he'd come even closer to losing it. Three days of this was all he could take. The pod needed a tenth member. If they didn't choose someone today, he'd see if he could go to the administration and just get someone assigned. That would not go over well, but David had to put an end to this.

He'd started the "discussion" on day two by putting forth the Hiyadi and the Wkkho. Half of the others preferred the Hiyadi and half preferred the Wkkho. Some strong arguments were made against both candidates. So David had tabled them and turned the debate to the Traiqi and the Trelkairni. *That* had nearly come to blows when Gronorgh and Shintikaisen ended up on opposite sides of the debate. No surprise there, but the *heat* of the argument was something David hadn't been ready for. Dai-Soln had sided with Shintikaisen, and Ael had sided with Gronorgh. David still couldn't figure that one out. But he had forced a motion to table *that* pair as well. David had brought the Human up just long enough to give his reasons for not short-listing him, and then done the same for the Gravgurdan. Gronorgh had looked relieved, as had several others, so that had seemed like a good time to end the meeting.

Today, they were down to the Imthiqorakar, who David had decided would *have* to room with someone else if he was chosen, and a Hnng who

David didn't really feel was qualified. He was staring at the files of the two last choices when the door chimed. "Enter," he called without even looking up.

"David?"

At the voice, he jumped up and tried to straighten his rumpled clothes. Somehow it seemed important to not look like a slob in front of Tkal's mother.

"Ambassador!"

She looked pained. "A title? Please. At least call me *tkel ki gan.*"

David ducked his head. "Forgive me, 'Brother's Mother'. This is strange ground for me. I don't know where the path is and—"

"And there is no moon tonight. Tkal always loved that poem. Did he teach it to you, or did you find it on your own?"

"I…I didn't know. I found it in one of his books with a tab saved on it, so…"

Her smile looked like tears. "Every time I see you, I know more of why he chose you. Am I interrupting your work?"

Work? David slapped the screen dead. It felt like betrayal, what he had been studying when she came in. How could he even think of replacing Tkal?

"David, my husband and I want you to eat with us tonight. Our quarters are not satisfactory for cooking, but would you join us in the restaurant at La Grande Étoile?"

"I…"

"We should eat together, as a family. We will not have many opportunities before I must leave. Dgan will be staying for a time, but we cannot leave the embassy on Earth untended for so long. While he deals with matters here, I will return to Tvern to deal with…things that must be done there, so that we may reunite on Earth sooner. Please David, it means a great deal to us both. We want to know you more, to share meals with you, to see you… on a known path with the light of three moons to guide you?"

David suddenly had to shuffle a great stack of printouts on his desk, and the top of his computer screen desperately needed dusting. "I will…I will be there. What time?"

"We have reservations at night cycle 1:00."

And that gave him an excuse to cancel the meeting. He heard the door slide open and hiss shut.

David walked into the lobby of La Grande Étoile. This was not a place David belonged. Silverwood, gold leaf, crystal chandeliers, gilded mirrors, clothing that cost a year's tuition. Louis XVI might be at home here, but not David. He felt very small, and wanted to shrink through the deck to the level below. He tried to adjust his robes and stand straight enough not to look rumpled.

Every time he donned these robes he questioned if he were doing the right thing. Had he had the right to go through with the *fdinel*? Should he have stepped aside and had a priest lead the funeral? Should he now disappear and leave Tkal's parents in peace? Did he honor Tkal or presume on his parents by coming to dinner dressed this way?

The ambassadors sat at a table in the middle of the dining room, tête-à-tête. Were they rehearsing what to say? Arguing? Just checking the menu? Tkal's mother spotted him, and both of them rose and came toward him.

"David, you wore your robes!" Tkal's mother took him by the elbow, and his father put an arm around his shoulder. They guided him back to the table and seated him in a chair between them. It was a round table, but somehow they had managed to arrange the chairs so that it definitely felt like he was sitting between them, not across from either.

Tkal's mother handed him a menu. Paper. It was…no, it only felt like real paper. As he watched, a number of the items on the menu changed colors to warn him that they were not compatible with Human biochemistry. So, the menu was actually intellifiber made to look and feel exactly like fancy paper. This menu, just the menu itself, cost more than most things David owned. And there were no prices on the menu next to any of the dishes. David wanted to bolt and run. He had heard about places like this, even seen them in vids. He had never been in one. How could he know what to order? What if he chose something that sounded like it should be really simple but, well, wasn't? Or something that just happened to be chic at the moment and priced accordingly? A hamburger? A place like this had a hamburger on its menu? David scanned the description. Truffles? The hamburger had shaved truffles in it. Those things were very expensive. Even a dumb burger could be turned into something impossible.

He glanced up to find the ambassadors looking at each other. Tkal's father had a look on his face that David recognized very well. It was that "serious oops" look that Tkal got any time he'd messed up, like the night he'd realized that David never wanted to study diplomacy, and he had eliminated David's hope of escaping that fate, when he'd *thought* he'd been doing David a favor. David tried to duck back behind the menu, but they had already seen him looking at them, so he laid the menu down.

Tkal's father had the same unfailing, highly annoying, radar that his son had possessed. "Why don't I order for everyone, so we can get on with the conversation?"

David was about to object, but Tkal's mother seemed to have his number too. She smiled at her husband, collected her and David's menus, with that innocent look that… So that's where Tkal learned that trick.

Tkal's father signaled the waiter and quickly ordered fish for himself and duck for his wife, each accompanied by an assortment of vegetables. "And for the young man…your stuffed quail with glazed carrots, asparagus, and the wild rice with truffles. Oh, and a baguette.

David gasped. "No, no, I don't need—"

"Don't be silly, David. You're an American. No meal is complete without bread." And with that, he shooed the waiter on his way.

"But—"

"David," Tkal's mother reached over to pat his hand, reminding him of Aunt Katherine. "We have lived on Earth for decades. We know how to eat at a Human table, just as our son knew." Her voice caught, just a tiny tremor, on the last part. "We have our medicine." Each of them withdrew a vial of pills, and an emergency injector. Each took a pill.

David unclenched his jaw long enough to take a sip of his water.

"David, this is not what took Tkal from us. It was not bread or yeast, or Earth or Humans. Tkal was taken by the evil in a heart—evil that had grown and festered to the point where murder was not only thinkable, but doable."

"It was Kvran." David flushed. He hadn't meant to blurt that out.

Tkal's father leaned in. "You know that? For a fact?"

"Well, no, I can't prove it. Yet. But I know it in my heart. It wasn't his hand, but he ordered it."

Tkal's mother reached across the table to grasp her husband's hand so hard the stripes on her knuckles changed color. Her eyes—golden eyes, like Tkal's—darted around the room like a bird of prey.

Tkal's father leaned in close to David and speared him with eyes an almost-Human shade of green. "Son, you must never say that out loud again. Not until a court has proven it. I will not lose another child to that claw. Your mother and I—"

"Ktiral, I thought we agreed not to push that until he is more ready to accept us."

"Right, Fgilal. David, I am sorry. I would have addressed you by your name, but you frightened me."

"Accept you?"

"David, forgive me. I did not think of your feelings."

"That was… That's why?" David breathed in to steady himself. "All those little pauses before 'my husband' and 'my wife'… You were stopping yourselves from saying…"

Tkal's father bowed his head. "We long to be a father and a mother to the brother of our son, but it is, must be, your decision, your choice."

"But I'm the reason he's dead."

"David, you can't mean that. You—"

"He was alone that night because of me. We argued. The very last time I talked to him, we argued. I didn't dance. I didn't join in. It was what he kept wanting me to do, and I wouldn't do it. I argued about the culture exchanges and tried to get out of them. He had to force me. I let him drag me to Epemthu, and then I argued about everything! Breakfast, costumes, money, bread. I ran late, and he had to come looking for me, so we were late for the jousting and got bad seats. Then I just refused to join in. You know what he said? He said, 'You can't get today back.' He was right. I'll never have another chance to do that day right. Then we argued most of the way back, and after we docked, he told me to go back to the pod and wait for him. He had to see someone. If I had been a real brother—a real friend—He would have taken me along, and he'd still be alive."

"No, David. If you had been there, then you would both be dead. And we would have even less information." Tkal's father gripped David's hand hard enough that it hurt. That was also like Tkal.

Tkal's mother pressed her lips together in a very Human gesture. "Who was Tkal going to…?"

Just then the waiter returned with their salads.

Twenty-Six

The Calculus of Pain

David was getting unnerved. Jva had been eyeing him for the last half hour. The look in his eyes was…strange. Almost like hunger. As soon as Enemwenu left the room, Jva came over and sat down in the seat next to David. Not across from him or halfway down the table, but right next to him. That was…uncomfortable. Just as Jva opened his mouth, Xtp entered from its room and Jva became very interested in his homework. Xtp crossed over to the food storage and started rummaging. David tried to engage it in conversation about a poem or anything to keep someone else in the common room, but it said it was tired and only offered half an excuse as it returned to its room munching on dried roots. The instant the door closed, Jva tossed his homework aside. He planted his elbow on the table and spoke only one word: "Armwrestle."

"What? No. I've got homework. You've got homework."

"It can wait. It'll only take a few seconds. Armwrestle me. Come on."

"I don't want to."

"Come on."

"No."

"Don't tell me you're scared. You took on a Gravgurdan warrior, and you're afraid to armwrestle me?"

Oh no. Not Jva. This was what Gornorgh had warned him about. It was already happening.

"Come on." He wiggled his fingers. "I'll let you use both hands."

That stung. A lot. There was no way he was using two hands. He put his elbow on the table and grasped Jva's hand. Jva squeezed hard enough to cause pain.

He called, "Ready? Go!" and David started pulling as hard as he could. At first neither arm moved. David was a little relieved. At least he was holding him. Then Jva smiled and started pulling David's arm down to the table very slowly. There was nothing David could do. He was pulling so hard he was vibrating. His teeth were clenched so tight his jaw was cramping. It was no good. But instead of slamming his arm down and ending it, Jva was dragging him down a centimeter at a time, making it last as long as possible. David was furious, but there was nothing he could do to win. At least he wouldn't just surrender. He pulled with everything he had, until the second his hand touched the table top. Then he nearly yelped in pain as Jva let go and his whole biceps cramped in wave after wave of agony. He was humiliated, and that was exactly what Jva had been hungry for. Jva, of all people. David was still gritting his teeth when he looked up and saw Gronorgh standing, leaning against the doorway to his dorm. He stood there just long enough to frown at David, then went back into his room.

Gronorgh had been right. Absolutely right. And he hated it.

David gathered his things, went back to his room, and tossed them onto his bed. The door chimed. David thought about ignoring it, but when it sounded again, he barked, "Enter."

Gronorgh stepped in.

David took a deep breath, closed his eyes, and hung his head. "Yes."

"I warned you about this."

As David turned his back to Gronorgh his biceps cramped again. He clutched at it reflexively.

"I can help you with that. Basic sports medicine is a primary school subject."

"Please. It hurts. A lot."

"You will get used to it," he said taking David's arm and beginning to massage the biceps.

David groaned. At first Gronorgh's fingers hurt as much as the cramps, but quickly the reflexive contraction stopped like waves interrupted by Gronorgh's big fingers.

"Let me help you. This isn't going to stop."

"I'll be fine."

Gronorgh rumbled, but otherwise held his tongue. This new restraint of Gronorgh's was really strange. He waited a few moments, but when David spoke no more, Gronorgh left without further comment.

When David went back out, Jva was still sitting where he had been with his hands propped behind his head smiling at the ceiling with his eyes closed. Surely this would all blow over quickly. But he really wanted to slap that look off Jva's smug mug.

David held his netbook out in front of him, angling it this way and that to catch reflections of the common room. It looked empty. He sucked his still-swelling lip and tasted blood again. He darted through the door and almost bumped into the table in his haste to get across the room to his dorm before anyone saw him. His eye had already swollen to the point that it was as much responsible for his near miss with the table as was his haste. Just as he reached to palm the lock he heard the last sound he wanted to hear.

"Again?"

He kept his back to Gronorgh. "Again? I'm in a hurry, and I—"

"I don't have to see your face to know. Let me help you."

Silence.

"David. How many times is this now? Three?"

"Five."

"Five? You mean you slipped two past me?"

"One was just a guy who punched me in the stomach as he walked past. I hadn't ever even seen him before. The other one just tripped me in the corridor outside First Contact Protocols. No big deal."

"It isn't going to stop anytime soon."

David sighed. "I suppose you're right."

"Turn around."

David hesitated, then turned around slowly. The last thing David wanted to do was spend time in the gym. With Gronorgh. As his trainer.

Gronorgh grimaced. "Hngrgh. This one took more than one punch."

"They took turns."

"They? How many?"

"Three."

Gronorgh rumbled.

"It really isn't new. It's just new here. Back home it happened a lot."

"Why did you allow it?"

"Allow? I couldn't stop it. I was the smallest and the outsider. I didn't have the size or the friends to do anything about it. I learned to be as uninteresting a target as possible. It isn't working so well this time."

"Because this time you are an inherently interesting target whether you fight back or not. Let me help you. You won't be a great fighter overnight, or strong enough to scare them all away, but you won't look like this every other day either."

"Okay." He was already dodging assault at every blind corner, ducking out of sight of calculating eyes and darting away from fists and feet that flashed out of every knot of people he passed. How could this be any worse?

"You will follow through?"

"I… Yes, I will follow through. At least I will try. This is…strange ground. I don't want to do this, but the administration is already asking questions, and at least one professor seems to think it's you."

Gronorgh made that gravelly sound.

"Yeah. That's what I thought too. If it were you, I would be dead."

Gronorgh sobered. "Hold out your netbook."

"What?"

"Your netbook. Hold it out. I'll downburst your training schedule."

"My what? You mean you already…?"

"Yes. A warrior plans ahead. Hold it out."

David held it up, pointed toward Gronorgh's, and instantly received the information. He opened the file and spluttered. "All this? No way! I can't do all this! When will I study? I've already dropped classes to make room for pod busi— Five times! You want me to eat five times a day? I don't always remember to eat three times a day. I…I…I…"

"Don't panic. Once we start training, your body will crave the extra food. You'll collapse without it."

"Collapse?" David's voice cracked.

"Don't worry. I will push you hard, but I will be careful of your limits. I can be gentle. Or gentle enough anyway. I spent part of my two years of clan-service as trainer for a crèche group. Ninety percent of my crèche were statistically on track to caste as high or higher than their parents." He smiled that Gravgurdan smile that looked like he'd just eaten something disagreeable. "Don't tell anyone. Other Gravgurdanûn would understand and respect that, but the rest of the pod and other aliens…wouldn't."

"Your secret is safe. But I'm not sure I am. Gronorgh. There's no way I can train three times a day. I can't drop more classes. I've never lifted a weight in my life. Well okay, a time or two when I was forced to at school, but it was humiliating." He paused, hoping for a reprieve from Gronorgh. It didn't come. "I won't be able to move. It would be easier to just keep letting them beat me up."

"Would it? And what about when one of them is really serious about it?"

David sighed. "I won't have time for homework *and* my duties to the pod *and* this training *and* the *eating*. The last time I ate this much…well, it wasn't pretty."

"Are you telling me your will is too weak? Before we even start? You promised."

"Did I? I thought I said I would try, and that was before—"

"You haven't tried."

David let out his breath. "Okay. When?"

"Now."

"Now?"

"Now. We'll start with eating," said Gronorgh as he strode across the common room to the cupboards which he flung wide. "I bought you enough Human-compatible protein to last for a month. You will finish it this week. You will drink one of these with at least three of your daily meals until we start training at the start of next tenday."

David looked with dismay at his little bag of snacks surrounded and backed into a corner by a wall of protein. He felt like that. He took the container Gronorgh handed him and drank it down. It wasn't all that bad, but it alone was enough to make him feel full.

"Now eat a full meal and go to bed early tonight. Dai-Soln assures me that you are the sort of student who is always several assignments ahead in every class."

David turned back to the cabinet and started pulling random things out to call a meal, as Gronorgh walked back to his room making a sound that was something between a hum and Mongolian throat singing. David was thrilled Goliath was so pleased. And no, sarcasm never entered his mind.

Finally, the morning David had been dreading came. All weekend he kept trying not to think about it, which only meant he thought about it even more. Today he started training. Thinking about it made him queasy. He was about to humiliate himself completely. But there wasn't any way out of it now. Oh God, he felt sick to his stomach. He grabbed his baggiest shirt and left for the gym where, no doubt, Gronorgh was already waiting for him and watching the clock.

When he arrived, his suspicions were confirmed. Before David was even all the way through the door, Gronorgh launched into a tour and explanation of every single piece of equipment. All David could do was follow along and try to commit everything to memory. And there was a lot of it. Machines and weights and bars and uses and exercises best done with or without certain pieces and reps and sets and rest periods and… Good grief! Who knew exercise could be so complicated? No wonder there were actual degrees in this stuff. And Gronorgh seemed benighted with the belief that David was taking all this in and would be able to spout it all back to him perfectly, from memory, after this whirlwind introduction. David thought he might remember the difference between a dumbbell and a barbell. Oh, and he was sure he knew which one was the treadmill.

And then suddenly the tour was over, and Gronorgh had David lying on one of the machines, struggling to move the bar up. He lowered the resistance weight four times before David could manage even one rep. As little respect as Gronorgh had for David's strength, had he really overestimated him by *that* much? Not encouraging. From there they moved to a leg-press machine where his performance was less humiliating. He could lift enough that he felt better about himself and managed enough reps that he was feeling a sense of accomplishment, until suddenly the weights slammed down as his thighs cramped. All David could do was turn his head and retch. Breakfast was undone in an instant. His stomach was fluttering and he felt dizzy. At first he couldn't tell if his stomach was going to have another go or not. He was so concentrated on ensuring that it did not, that it took a bit before Gronorgh's gravel-laughter registered.

When it did register, David exploded. The humiliation was too much. He staggered to his feet, thighs shaking like jelly that might collapse under him at any moment. His water bottle flew across the room and burst like a thunderstorm against a weight tree by the far wall. Several beings scrambled for the exit. Others gaped.

Gronorgh stopped laughing. *Hhoeghsidrangqoelzhaghaqdhav!* No, please. Control. We will be banned!"

David shouted, "Do I look like I care?" He was about to go on, to launch into a real tirade, when the look of panic on Gronorgh's face stopped him. This place meant nothing to David, but to Gronorgh, it was practically a temple. Being banned wouldn't bother David in the least; in fact, he'd welcome it—never having to return here again—ever. But Gornorgh would be devastated to lose access to this place. David sighed. "Sorry."

Gronorgh struck his chest and held his palm out. "The fault is mine, *Hhoeghsidrangqoelzhaghaqdhav.* I laughed. I should not have expected you to understand."

David glared with suspicion. Then as loud and deep as he could manage while trembling, he demanded, "Explain yourself, *Murglorj'ô.*" The few Gravgurdanûn in this section of the gym had been joined by a number drawn from the high-g section by the ruckus. Almost everyone else had fled. But the Gravgurdanûn had eyes for nothing else.

"Laughing now would be mocking for a Human. Do I understand right?"

David bit off one word. "Yes."

"This is my mistake. Humans do not respect this moment."

David's anger wavered, but did not leave him. The adrenaline of rage was all that was keeping him on his wobbly legs.

Gronorgh rushed ahead explaining, "You see among us, this is a rite of passage. To work so hard this happens. A moment to boast of. There was one boy in my crèche group who took *vingaktuegh* to make himself vomit on our first day of training. Only he took it much too early and vomited as he sat listening to the instructions. Then we laughed in ridicule, but it was the other laugh."

"The rumble?"

"Yes." Gronorgh frowned. "Him we did mock. His school name was *Instructions* from then on. He still lives with that name. To fake something like this is serious." He paused. "But to do this honestly is a badge of honor, a rite of passage, a proof that the will is strong enough to push the body past weakness into strength. My laughter was not mocking."

David searched his face. He looked sincere. But. Could any culture *celebrate* anything so stupid? So humiliating? Yes, of course it could. Cultures celebrated first nursing, weaning, cutting the first tooth, losing the first tooth, onset of puberty, the first injury resulting in blood, baldness, first manufacture of honey, first shedding of exoskeleton… Why not first vomiting during exercise? But just because it was plausible didn't make it real. David longed to do a xenopology search right now, to verify, before accepting this explanation, but with all these other Gravgurdanûn watching, wouldn't that be publicly calling Gronorgh a liar? Mightn't he have to answer such a slight, even from his *Hhoeghsidrangqoelzhaghaqdhav*? And if he didn't, what would *that* do to his status? If he did, what would that do to David's continued existence? He looked nervous, but he didn't look like a liar. Actually, Gronorgh had always despised lies. To lie now would be truly unworthy. And the other Gravgurdanûn had that same sort of look about them. Like honor was at stake, but not the look of ones about to laugh at the duping of another.

David collapsed back onto the machine. "A Human finds vomiting in public embarrassing at best. Being laughed at afterwards is not unexpected, but it does greatly increase the humiliation. I reacted by my culture. I did not consider yours. This is a strange idea. But," he switched to Gravgaln, "I lift your meaning."

That set off an avalanche all around the room. David caught forms of the word *vegh*, 'to lift with the legs,' here and there among the falling pebbles of laughter. Apparently, the joke, substituting that word for the more usual words meaning 'lift by curling' or 'bench press' (for really difficult concepts), had gone over, and the tension was relieved. The other Gravgurdanûn went back to their workouts while Gronorgh scurried to clean up David's mess. Not the vomit. That still pooled between David's feet. No, he was busy with the water, removing all the plates from the weight tree, and lovingly toweling the tree dry, and then each plate, one by one, as he returned them to their proper places. Then he saw to the floor and the walls and any other stray droplets he found. None of this precious metal would be allowed to rust. David was both fascinated by the delicate care he took of this equipment and awed by the ease with which he held these huge plates, some seeming to weigh almost as much as David, holding them one-handed and flipping them around with his wrist, like he was drying dinnerware.

Finally, David was ready to trust his legs to stumble out of this awful place and back to his room to get ready for class. He pushed up and stood to his feet, testing to be sure his legs would get him there. They still felt funny, but he thought they would do.

Suddenly Gronorgh was standing before him, pointing at the pool between his filthy shoes. "Do you want to keep that?"

David's eyebrows shot up. "What? Keep it? The barf?"

Gronorgh just stood there.

David switched to Taisiran, hoping none of the other Gravgurdanûn spoke Dai-Soln's language. "No, I don't want to keep it. It's filthy. A disease vector. The thought of keeping it makes me feel like doing it again. No. That I won't do."

Gronorgh frowned. "It was only a question. Some keep it. Some do not. I threw mine away." He paused. "After a few years." He scanned David's face.

"At the time it seemed *cool.* That is the Human word, yes?"

"In one of our languages, yes."

"At the time it seemed *cool* to have it. But eventually, it seemed childish to hold on to. So the choice is completely yours, even in my culture. But…you should be the one to deal with it. For me or someone else to dispose of it would disrespect you, limit your freedom of choice."

"Yeah," David sighed. "Well, my culture says I should deal with it too, only because it's too disgusting to foist off on anyone else." He wobbled over to the cabinet and found a box of absorber to sprinkle on the mess, waited a moment, swept it up and dumped it—all under the curious gaze of every Gravgurdan in the room, which was to say, practically everyone left.

David's second class let out early, and he rushed back to Green Room, hoping to make a dash for some chips or something, and then hide out in his room till Gronorgh left for Applications of Force. He made it into the food prep and retrieved a bag of tortilla chips, but before he could complete his escape, he heard a door swish open and then voices—Gronorgh and Dai-Soln—speaking Taisiran. "It was going well enough at first."

"Until?"

"Until it wasn't. He vomited."

David crouched behind the counter to listen. He heard the sounds of two bodies, one very heavy, one light, sitting down on the couch.

"This can happen to many beings when exercising."

"Yes, it can, but…well…I laughed."

"Oh no. Gronorgh! I told you this wouldn't work. You don't understand him or his culture well enough to make this work. You've spent all this time despising and none learning."

"I'll learn. I do realize that I—"

"Tell me what happened."

"He was…not doing well. He was becoming angry. I am not sure if his anger was at me, himself, or the situation. Anyway, we moved to the leg press, and he did much less badly."

"Lesson one. Never tell him he has improved by saying 'much less badly.' He will understand 'You were absolutely awful. Now you are just sort of laughable.'"

"No he wouldn't…You really think he…He really would, wouldn't he? Hurgh! This is going to be difficult."

Dai-Soln made frond-shaking sounds.

Gronorgh rumbled. "As I said, he was doing better, taking some pride, maybe feeling better about the experience. Then he vomited."

"In front of you?"

"In front of everyone."

"Many Humans attach shame to vomiting. It is a sign of illness, of weakness. It is considered dirty. Many Humans find it difficult to look at. In fact, for many, looking at it may trigger the reflex producing the same."

"Oh. That explains the water bottle."

"Water bottle?"

"When I laughed—because he had reached this milestone so quickly—he yelled and threw his water bottle across the room to explode against the weights."

"You know what you once said about fire mixed with his water?"

"I was more right than I knew. That also explains his reaction when I asked him if he was going to keep it."

"You'll be lucky if he ever comes back."

"He gave his word! I explained the meaning for us Gravgurdanûn. He needs this!"

"You may have gone too far when you laughed. He has almost no reason to trust you. And then you laugh at just the time when it would be most cruel to him."

"What should I do?"

"Nothing."

"Nothing? How can I do nothing? My actions created this situation where David is the target of every coward on the station. This is the only way to help him. Now, if he won't come back, the attacks will continue until we have another funeral."

"Don't be dramatic."

"I'm not being. You've seen his eye since the last attack. He told me there were three of them, and they took turns beating him. The bruising still isn't gone. I'm expecting broken ribs or a cracked occipital bone or a shattered nose next."

Dai-Soln sighed and his fronds rustled. "Well, there is nothing you can do. If David chooses, he will come back. If he chooses not, then he will not. And if there is one of the *Strengths* at which David excels, it is stubbornness. Even you cannot match him there."

"Stubbornness is *not* one of the Twelve. I believe you mean *willfulness*."

"Same thing."

"No, it…well, okay, in this case, maybe it is."

"The point is, David is so stubborn no one can make him do what he chooses not to…or keep him from what he chooses, except by bringing the two into conflict—which is how he got here, if I am not mistaken. As I have pieced it together, David accepted his government's scholarship only because he had no other way to pay for study here. He wanted no part of diplomacy— only languages. But he wanted languages more than he *dis*wanted diplomacy. Tkal wanted him for the pod, but he still hadn't declared track, so the dean trapped him between losing his funding—and thus his languages—and accepting diplomacy. Again, he wanted the languages more than he *dis*wanted diplomacy. Then Tkal offered him friendship *and* languages *and* that thrice-vile code, and he wanted that combination more than he *dis*wanted diplomacy and *you*."

Gronorgh made a sound.

"We are being honest here. Gronorgh, you have been unspeakable." A pause. "Then he wanted Tkal's memory honored more than he wanted *life*. So he chose to challenge. And he won because he is stubborn."

"My mouth still has the scars to prove that."

"Yes, and then he was finished. He no longer wanted the languages. Diplomacy still meant nothing to him. Tkal was dead. You were still here. The code was broken. He was leaving. We elected him, and it meant *nothing* to him. He was going to give up. I knew it. I also knew our best chance was with him. And his best chance was with us. So *quickly* I had to find *something* he wanted more than escape. He *wants* Tkal's killer. I offered our help and seasoned it with a reminder about duty, which is something he understands and respects, even if he would rather not. Discovering that we had waited too long and could not bring a tenth being on team, until mid term, strengthened that sense of duty. And he stayed. And he still stays. Despite the attacks. Despite your history. Despite still hating diplomacy. Despite being terrified of the position we gave him. He stays because there is something he wants more—justice."

Gronorgh made a sound like a lion deep in thought.

"If you can show him how bulking up and learning to fight will help him find justice, by eliminating a distraction that is slowing his quest significantly, then he will want it so that you will not be able to keep it from him. Otherwise, you have already lost. If I know David, he has already figured out five ways to put an end to this arrangement. Some based on his culture, some on yours. Maybe even a legal option, now that he has this obsession with laws and behavioral codes ever since he challenged you."

"But he vomited his first time. He belongs to the gym, and the gym belongs to him. How can I make a Human—a very willful, guileful, mindcrafty, mnemotic Human who needs the physical strengths to be complete and achieve this worthy goal, understand?"

David stood and stepped out of the food prep. "You stand up, and we go back, now."

Gronorgh and Dai-Soln looked like thieves caught in the act.

"*Now.* Before I change my mind."

Twenty-Seven

Rumors, Lies, and Deceit

David was still struggling to find the courage each time he had to enter his room where Tkal no longer lived. So, in a way, it was a relief when Tkal's mother arrived to help sort Tkal's things. Some of his stuff left with her, for herself and for Tkal's father and the cousins back on Tvern or friends on Earth. Some were sorted to be sold or given to a charity connected to the candle room Tkal frequented on the station. Quite a few things stayed with David, some because they were legally his, like the *fdinel* knives and cups, others because she insisted he keep them, like most of Tkal's books. A few things were set aside for the other members of the pod. And a few things were specifically designated in his *vdeln talnin*, "the final speaking," like his copy of *Dtarln ki Verln*, "The Book of the Eternal," which he had designated to David even before the *fdinel*.

It hadn't taken her long to work her way around to asking David about some of the more spectacular bruises he currently sported. He'd tried to lie, or make light of it, but just couldn't bring himself to do that. "There have been…unforeseen consequences of challenging Gronorgh."

"A Gravgurdan would not…oh." She put that together fast. "Has he offered you help?"

"Yes."

"Have you accepted?"

"Unwillingly, but I don't seem to have a choice."

"My Tkal, our Tkal, was bigger than you, even years ago, but still had some problems with this at one time. He did not train with a Gravgurdan, but he did take some classes, and found that letting that fact be known helped a good deal. And just growing larger helped as well."

"I will remember that."

She seemed to take that as a rebuke, or maybe just sensed that there might be a line nearby that would be uncomfortable to cross, because suddenly the subject changed, and they were discussing whether Chinese or Indian teas were better, until David admitted that he rarely drank anything but iced tea or coffee.

When she left, the room felt vacant. And not just because David really didn't have enough stuff to fill even his side of the room. Most of Tkal's stuff was either gone or boxed up to go away soon. David looked around at the empty room. Did anyone really live here?

The door chimed. Dai-Soln entered with his fronds tucked behind his head. The odd joint of his legs was relaxed, lowering him a few centimeters shorter than David. And he wasn't looking up.

"What…how can I help you?"

"Well, ah, I had been putting off asking, because it was so awkward, but if I delay anymore I won't be able to ask. So, ah, did you find my game among Tkal's things?"

"What? You mean you don't have it?"

"No. Not since that day he ran off with it."

"You mean the day he made me try it out, then snatched it out of my hand and went tearing off to your—" David stopped mid-thought.

"Yes. That was the last time I saw it, and I wondered if you had seen it, or knew where he left it. David, are you…?"

David muttered to himself. "He said… What was it? Which language was he speaking at the time? He was talking about meeting…" David closed his eyes and tilted his head way back. "'There's more than one game in play'…more than… Dai-Soln! When did you buy that game?"

"Term before last."

"More specific."

"Umm…well, I suppose it was…about two or three days before Sven was dismissed."

"Where? Where did you buy it?"

"Where? Oh, from another student, a Tal Chin in the School of Xenopology."

"His name. Do you remember his name?"

"Gol Nezh. He and Tkal were friends for a while. He said he needed the money, and it was a fun game, so I bought it."

"Was it really expensive?"

"Not for the quality. I'd already played the one that Smm, the Hnng trade specialist for now-defunct Yellow Pod, had. So I knew it was worth the price."

David shifted gears. "I haven't seen it. Tkal must have lost it. Message me how much it cost, and I'll pay you back out of Tkal's legacy."

"Oh! No, David, that won't be—"

But David was already halfway out the door.

David sat glaring at the stats for the week. Silver Pod hadn't listened. They hadn't believed the intel Gronorgh had given them. And now they were gone. Well, not entirely gone. They were a "government in exile," which was as good as gone. Unlike the real world where a government in exile could drag on for decades, becoming gradually more and more irrelevant, but sometimes succeeding in coming back to power with outside aid—inside the simulation, you only had till the end of the term. It almost never worked. Still, the pay-off was big enough that some students were willing to take the risk. The points awarded for pulling it off were huge.

The door chimed. That would be Gornorgh. "Enter," David called, and the door slid open.

"Fools!" Gronorgh thundered.

"So who do we send to check on what data they escaped with?"

"What?"

David pushed back from his desk. "Silver Pod. Ex-Silver Pod. We need to know if the intel you gave them, the stuff we collected from Violet Pod's transmissions, went with them or if it's in Violet Pod's hands now. Who should go?"

"I'm too angry." Gronorgh growled. "I'll insult the timid little fools, and— Red-shimmer. Send Red-shimmer. She can talk continued trade to soothe their crushed egos."

David twisted his mouth. "Either her or Enemwenu, to accord them ceremonial recognition."

"Would sending both be too much?"

"I don't know. Do we want to give, or at least appear to give, that much support to a lost cause?"

"They aren't entirely…" Gronorgh closed his eyes and frowned. "With other leadership they wouldn't be entirely lost. Hrrgh. Hopeless."

"I think Red-shimmer is best for this. Why don't you go ask her to take care of it? I need to speak to Enemwenu about something else."

Gronorgh agreed, and left, but there was something about the way he paused at the door. He was suspicious. David wasn't as good at deceit as he thought. Not yet anyway. He quickly messaged Enemwenu for the stats he needed on piracy. He asked for the three tendays before, and the three after Sven's dismissal, another three early in his first term with Green Pod, and another three surrounding Tkal's death. He pretty well knew where everything stood since then.

Enemwenu was efficient and well organized, so the return message came quickly. It showed just what David suspected. He had to track that game down. And he'd start with the Tal Chin.

"I do not want you to 'freak out,' *Hhoeghsidrangqoelzhaghaqdhav*, but we are doing something a little different today," Gronorgh said.

David raised an eyebrow. "Gronorgh? What have you done?"

"I invited someone to spar and train with you today. Another Human. Jva."

"What? No! No way! How dare you? Without even asking me? And you spring it on me now?" David said, gesturing wildly with every word.

"Would you have agreed otherwise?"

"Otherwise? Who said I'm agreeing now?"

Gronorgh calmly nodded toward the entrance. "He is checking in at the office now."

David shot daggers and sparks with his eyes. Flint and steel.

"Trust me. Just trust me this one time," Gronorgh pled.

David gave no reply. None at all.

Gronorgh shrugged and turned. "Welcome, Jva."

"Hello, Gronorgh. Thanks for inviting me. I'll be glad to help my buddy David out anyway I can." Jva was all smiles, but somehow David didn't think helping him was as high on Jva's list of reasons for coming as was the opportunity to humiliate David. Just a bit, just one more time.

Buddy. That would have meant more before that armwrestling match. Gronorgh knew about that. Why would he…? He was up to something. David eyed him, not even trying to hide his suspicion.

Gronorgh went into his coach-instructor mode. "We will start with some light lifting, just to warm up before the sparring."

Jva looked excited. Why wouldn't he be? He was going to get to show off.

"I should explain that Gravgurdanûn may do things a little differently in the gym than Humans do." He led them through some of the more demanding stretching exercises he had taught David. Jva did them, but coming in without knowing what to expect, he seemed a bit clumsy, and he couldn't do some of them as well as David.

"Now it's time to lift," Gronorgh announced. "We do not measure the weights by kilograms or *ngarghîn* when we lift. We measure by *daghin*, multiples of one's body weight, so I queried the database when you checked in, Jva, to get your *daghi*. We will start with some bench pressing at one-half *daghi*."

Jva got a bar loaded with forty-two kilos. David had thirty-three. Jva was doing better than David, but not by a whole lot. Still he had to add a couple more reps to each set to prove he could. Then Gronorgh increased the weight to three-fourths of a *daghi*. David always struggled at this weight, but Jva had expended more than he should have by showing off at the lower weight, and wasn't looking nearly as impressive as he clearly thought he should have.

The same pattern continued though several more lifting exercises, Jva seeming to have to show off in the lighter sets, setting himself up for more and more frustration in the heavier sets when he couldn't outdo David by as much, or sometimes at all. But David stopped watching Jva. He was watching Gronorgh. He was so totally up to something. But what? When this was over, Jva would just say, and rightfully so, that he'd been lifting much heavier weights because he was bigger and had still outdone David.

Then Gronorgh announced that it was time to spar. Jva never looked happier. Well, maybe when he and Ael had announced their betrothal, but that was a very different sort of happy from this look. David set his jaw.

Gronorgh led them into the sparring room and gave the mats a quick inspection. "Okay. Everything looks good. Gravgurdan rules don't have timed rounds. The match is over when one of you submits or is knocked out. Or killed."

David and Jva looked at each other. Neither of them had any intention of going that far. Gronorgh called start and David slid into the stance Gronorgh had taught him. He still wasn't doing it perfectly. He knew that without even looking at Gronorgh, but Jva seemed…disconcerted? David liked that. The match started and David quickly realized that Jva might have fought a time or two, but he didn't really have any training. He was bigger and stronger than David, but he didn't really know what he was doing. Of course, David didn't really either, but maybe he could remember one or two techniques.

Jva made a clumsy first attack and David got in a couple of hits. They weren't powerful enough to stop Jva, or even really hurt him, but they made him mad. Jva lashed out wildly, giving David openings to hit him. Suddenly, Jva yelled, and David saw his chance. He connected with Jva's slack jaw and knocked him loopy—not out, but enough that he staggered and fell to the mat, unable to get back up. Gronorgh stopped the match. Jva couldn't understand what had happened. David was astonished. Gronorgh looked smug, like everything had gone according to plan. He'd set Jva up!

As soon as he could get Gronorgh off to the side, David hissed, "You planned that!"

"Yes, I did. And it worked. Now he will tell this story, and in whatever form he tries to tell it, it still ends with you winning."

"No way. He won't tell this. Not to anyone."

Gornorgh curled his lip. "He won't be able to stop himself. Just wait and see."

Gronorgh watched as David called the meeting to order and launched into his agenda without preamble. "I want to lay a trap for the pirates."

Gronorgh set his jaw and sneered. "Finally. I have plans for just such a strategy. I tried, repeatedly, to get Tkal to do this." He watched David fidget like a pre-casted child in his chair. "What?" He waited for a response, trying to be patient, understanding of cultural differences, while David stared down at his netbook. Gronorgh hissed. "I am not going to like this, am I?"

"No, Gronorgh, you won't."

Gronorgh crossed his huge forearms over his thick chest and growled. He curled his lip, but nodded for David to proceed, and shackled his tongue.

"We are not going to attack openly. We will use subterfuge." David paused. "I want a merchant convoy, some very valuable cargo. Red-shimmer Gold-streak, what is the most valuable thing we currently need? Something that would be an impossible temptation to the pirates. Something that will cripple us if we lose it."

Red-shimmer burbled color. "We desperately need new Traxavoni-Drunzga converters so we can maintain neutronium production. Without those, we can't produce shielding for our ships, not at the rate we are having to replace them. We are at a critical point."

Gronorgh struggled to figure out what the sneak was up to this time.

David nodded. "I want you to order as many as we can afford, as many as Gray Pod can supply." Half a dozen voices erupted in protest. "I don't want to bankrupt us, but I want it to be painful if we lose this shipment. I want it to look desperate."

Again, protest erupted. Gronorgh struck the table with his fist, making everyone else jump. "I see what David is trying to do. This is risky, *Hhoeghsidrangqoelzhaghaqdhav.*"

David glared at him.

Gronorgh opened his fist toward David, palm up. "Allow me this."

David frowned, but nodded.

"Please be careful. This is a very risky course. If this fails, we really will be on the verge of failure. This ruse cannot fail or we will."

"I know. And I want us to do everything wrong."

Silence.

"Red-shimmer, I would like you and Enemwenu to arrange the purchase. And I want you to go to Gray Pod in person. We can't trust this to coded transmissions."

Xtp clicked nervously. "Do you think our codes have been broken?"

"Not yet. At least we don't have any reason to think so."

Red-Shimmer's skin slid through the entire rainbow. "Then, I understand why you choose the two of us. I am trade specialist for Green Pod, and Gray Pod's trade specialist is Alelliawulian, so Enemwenu can help greatly. But if we are seen, will others not guess our purpose?"

David nodded. "Sure. They'll know you're there for trade, but not what you're there trading for."

Shintikaisen jumped in, "But David, Gray Pod's codes have been laughable since their last linguist graduated at the end of last quarter. You said their new one is no good. Violet Pod could break their codes again at any time, or could already be reading them. And they will make it a priority. They will know something big is up if we are sending Red-shimmer and Enemwenu in person."

David's eyes were over-bright. "I'm counting on it." He paused.

Enemwenu entwined hii's tentacles, and sighed. "Then we must work very closely with Gronorgh to protect this shipment."

David shook his head. "No. I need the two of you to do that."

"What?"—or some variation thereof—erupted from every being around the table. Gronorgh frowned deeply and leaned back in his chair studying David through eyes narrowed to slits.

Xtp clicked, "That seems an unfair burden to place on our friends. Gronorgh is the specialist for military issues and…"

"Neither of us is well-versed in military and strategy and fighting," Enemwenu finished.

David twisted one corner of his mouth downward. "Do the best you can. And I do mean the best. This has to look like someone *really* tried. I don't want to lose this shipment."

Xtp spread all its hands, which Gronorgh was reasonably sure meant exasperation. "Then surely you need Gronorgh."

David responded, "I do. But elsewhere."

Gronorgh leaned forward. "If I read your strategy right, this is a *very* risky gambit."

"What do you read?"

"You want to provoke a 'pirate' attack, so I can cripple their fleet."

"Close. I do want to draw an attack. And I don't want to lose this cargo. We can't survive losing an investment this big. But I want them to escape."

"What!?" exploded from mouths and voders alike.

But Gronorgh sneered, then dissolved into an avalanche of gravel. Heads and bodies swiveled to stare at him. They had not fought David. If they had, they would not be surprised. He sobered. "Bold indeed, Firelizard! You want to find their nest and root out the whole tribe! You realize, they may not have an actual base in the simulation."

David's eyes flamed. "I want you to chase them all the way back to one of Violet Pod's planets. I want you to chase them to ground. And I want them destroyed. On the ground. On Violet territory. And I want witnesses."

Silence.

"And if they run elsewhere?"

"If it's to another power, we need to know that. But it won't be. We all know that. If it's to a Violet ally—not good enough. Cut them off. Don't let them land. Force them to run to Violet. There can't be any room for Violet Pod to claim they didn't know, that someone else was responsible."

Gronorgh studied the table top. "We will lose ships. We will lose lives— simulated lives, but the computer takes that into account in the rankings. We could lose status."

David raised one eyebrow in that way that was very typical of him. "Isn't this what you wanted? A pitched battle to prove your ability as a strategist—to prove the warrior knows how to conduct a war? Well, you have a battle, at least."

Enemwenu sighed and wrapped hii's tentacles around hii's head-body. "And if it's a whole war?"

David set his jaw. "Then we will win."

Gronorgh had a great deal of planning to do in order to make that happen.

Nearly everything was in place for outing Violet Pod, and most of David's focus was there, but the rest of life still went on. David almost staggered down the corridor toward home, where his bed and sleep awaited. Gronorgh was possessed. He had drilled David for over a standard hour on one—*one*—technique in some Gravgurdan fighting art. David was so exhausted he could barely even walk.

Gronorgh had finished his session with David and excused himself to go into the high-g section to lift and spar while he composed his homework. Apparently, that was what worked for Gronorgh. He memorized his homework questions and then composed his answers, in his head, while lifting hundreds of kilos for more reps than should be possible for a mere being of flesh. Gronorgh called it meditation. David called it…something else.

A fist flashed out. David darted out of the way just like in the training drill. Crunch and squeal. Zack Kopinski, all 100-plus kilos of him, stood, bent over double, cursing and yelling till he crumpled to the floor clutching an obviously broken wrist. Suddenly David had strength again. He ran.

Zack had tried to smash David's face in. Why? David didn't even know him. But Ryan did. They were thick. David had seen them together often. And ever since Green Pod had started to recover, rising back in the standings, Ryan had been on the outs with Prince Kvran. Could be that. Could be too much testosterone overloading Zack's brain. If Zack had connected that blow with David's face instead of a steel wall… Gronorgh was right about the attacks escalating over time. Maybe David needed…a rumor.

Instead of heading to his room for the nap he wanted, David jogged straight to the cafeteria to put the plan forming in his head into immediate action. He strode in the doors—and *strode* was the only word for it. He got in line, cutting in front of several smaller beings. He had been in the gym enough days to know how this worked. You had to swagger. You had to be rude. You had to draw attention *and* like it. You had to take up more space than necessary. After that, you could be more subtle or more brazen with the boasting part. Sometimes one way worked better than the other. Sometimes it seemed to depend on the effect you wanted. David was going to try subtle, it was really all he could stomach, and hope for the rumor mill to do the exaggerating for him.

He reached over the bigger Human guy in front of him to grab a tray before it was his turn, and when the guy turned to glare, David just raised an eyebrow while holding the tray out to help take up more space than need be. That got a reaction. The guy blanked his face and turned back around.

David was noisy and rude in the serving line, demanding extra portions by semi-shouting things like, "See how much food *your* body needs after training with a Gravgurdan. They're insane. They try to work you to death. Drill the same technique for an hour. Lift till your arms turn to concrete. Then yell at you that *that* was just the warm up. I need *food,* I tell you!" He felt like a real creep doing it, but it was working. He was getting looks, students whispering to each other, gesturing. He tried to walk in a way that said, *Yeah, you remember me. I'm that guy who ate all the firefruits and outdid the Gravgurdan warrior. Yeah, that's me.*

He chose a table with a couple of Human girls, another Human guy, a Traiqi, and a couple of Oezh. Some comedian once said the Oezh were the only species in the galaxy that liked gossip more than Humans. David was counting on the truth behind that joke. He put his tray down harder than necessary, earning more than one glare. He sat and started shoveling the food in. He was making such a spectacle of himself. If this didn't work…

"Manners?" asked one of the girls.

David shoved more food in his mouth before saying, "You try gym time with a Gravgurdan, and tell me how much you eat then!"

The girl who had spoken made a face at the other one, who rolled her eyes, before they both turned their backs to him. But the guy had leaned in, and both Oezh had both their ears angled his way while pretending to look elsewhere.

"You? You train with a Gravgurdan? You don't look like you even lift."

David smiled like he was sharing a secret. "Oh, I just started, but my lifts are coming up." That was perfectly true. "But even with the Gravgurdan, it's not *all* about straight strength. It's also about knowing how to use the strength you have." Also true. He shoveled in more food and mumbled, "And their fighting techniques are amazing." Probably true, David just didn't have the knowledge to judge. He swallowed. "For instance, it is amazingly easy to break some bones…like a wrist, say." True—he'd just witnessed that—but also smoke and mirrors. Everyone at the table should take that to mean *David* had broken someone's wrist.

"Barbarian!" The Traiqi grabbed his tray and left.

David shrugged at the other Human guy, who rolled his eyes at the Traiqi's retreating back.

"How do you…?" the guy started, but got no further.

"Mark, I thought we were going to have a serious conversation!" the prettier girl whined.

Mark was suddenly following the girl across to the garbage chute, apologizing the whole way, while glancing back over his shoulder. The other girl made an exasperated noise, and followed after them at a pace so slow she'd never catch up. When David looked back around, the two Oezh had already scurried off to another table where they had their heads together with more of their kind, who kept glancing at David.

David put down his fork. He felt sick, but couldn't tell if it was from eating so fast or from acting like such a jerk in public. Most of this food would go to waste. One more thing to feel guilty about. Well, at least it looked like mission accomplished.

"Do you have any idea how many places I'm sore? Apparently, there are muscles in places I didn't know existed, but Gronorgh knows. And all of them hurt. Every single one of them."

Ael snorted.

"Did you know there are muscles here?" He ran his thumb down his side, grimacing exquisitely. "All between the ribs?"

"Yes."

"Well, *I* didn't. Not until yesterday. And I didn't believe it until today. Now I can tell you *exactly* where." He moaned and took another spoonful of…something.

"That looks awful."

"It tastes worse. But Gronorgh swears it has something or other that Humans need after intense training." He shuddered and put his spoon back down. "My tongue won't let me abuse it that much. Nasty."

She slammed her spoon down. "Did you really hit Jva?"

David blinked. "He told you?"

"Yes, well, when he's got that many bruises, it's hard not to. He didn't *want* to tell me, mind you, but… David how *could* you?"

"He's bruised?"

"Oh, act like you're surprised. You, training with that monster, and then you have to punch him in the face?"

"We were sparring. He hit me too!"

"But he doesn't train with a Gravgurdan warrior! He said you nearly knocked him out."

"Gronorgh invited him to spar with me. He didn't ask me first. Jva just showed up and Gronorgh sprung it on me. Is he really bruised?"

"Yes. On the face where you hit him. And on his arms and body, and you kicked him in the leg too."

David didn't even remember that.

"I thought you were non-violent, peaceful, a regular bookworm. Now you start picking fights with everyone—Gronorgh, Jva… Cynthia told me you broke some guy's wrist? Some really big guy?"

"Actually he did that himself, but I started the rumor that I'd done it."

"So now you have to go after Jva to…what? Build your reputation? I want this to stop, David. Do you hear me?"

"Yes, Ael. I promise to never spar with Jva again. But he won't be happy when he finds out about this conversation."

And Jva walked in from the corridor. He did have a bruise on his jaw, and there was a little limp to his walk. When he got closer, David could see bruising above his left eye, between the temple and the forehead. Jva pulled out the chair next to Ael and plunked down in it. He reached out and squeezed her hand, before he turned to David. "You owe me a rematch. That wasn't—"

David cut him off. "No can do."

"What?"

"Ael just made me promise to never spar with you again."

Jva dropped Ael's hand. "You did what?"

Ael gave David a look that would make Shintikaisen proud and followed it with a sound that should have come from her as well. "You pig!"

David evacuated to his dorm room, but not fast enough. Something from Ael's plate splattered the wall just inches from his head before he could duck through the door. You could hear them through the walls. And it went on. For millennia.

David had sneaked in the back of the classroom. Dr. Mig Deluv Naktukh flared his nostrils at him, but did not otherwise rebuke him when he sat down in a class where he did not belong. Dai-Soln was near the front of the room, one row behind His Royal Kzati-ness and a couple of seats to his left—a perfect vantage point for watching the show to come. If everything was going according to plan, Gronorgh would be engaging the pirate fleet in battle about now. It should be obvious when… There! Prince Kvran turned to the side and tapped his finger against his ear. Someone back in Violet Pod was alerting him that their pirate fleet had been ambushed. Oh, yes. This was going to be fun to watch.

"Is there an issue of which the instructor needs to be made aware, Your Highness Student Kvran?"

Kvran gave the professor one of his filthy-underling glares, but removed his hand from his ear and nodded acquiescence. Still, David could see how the prince kept fidgeting in most unroyal fashion. As the class went on, Kvran's ability to look poised and royal was stretched thinner and thinner. David watched as Kvran reached for his ear every time the professor's back was turned. Then Kvran snapped his stylus in two. The professor heard the sound and spun around to address the offender just as Kvran leapt from his seat and dashed up the aisle toward the exit with both guards hot on his heals. David had to gag himself to escape the room without attaching the opprobrium of a professor he still might have to sit under some quarter. Besides, David had to get to Gronorgh and the others to see how successful they had been. Watching Kvran squirm and then make a public spectacle of himself fleeing up the aisle was the most pleasant thing David had experienced in a very long time. If the pirate captain had already fled to ground on Violet Homeworld, this would be a very good day indeed.

Twenty-Eight

If by This Hand I Slay

It had taken days to find this store, using every spare moment David could steal from classwork, pod duties, and even sleep. Kvran and all of Violet Pod had been in full-out damage-control mode ever since the pirate fleet landed just outside their capital. The uproar had been huge. There had been defections among their allies and every pod not in their orbit was demanding some kind of reparations or other.

That was the only reason David was still functioning. His grades were slipping, and the others were getting frustrated with his random rescheduling of meetings. More than one being had commented on his falling standards of grooming. But all his time was devoted to finding Tkal's killer.

First David had tracked down the Tal Chin that Dai-Soln had bought the game from. Only to learn that he had possessed the game for mere hours, and had been paid to give the game to Dai-Soln. Getting the Tal Chin to describe the Human girl who had instructed him where to collect the game had been useless. The girl he described could have been anyone. He insisted her hair was "pale" like David's, but David's hair was a rather dark but non-descript brown, so anything short of jet black rated as "pale." She was short, but then all Humans were to the Tal Chin, who averaged around two hundred forty-five centimeters. She was "Human-female shaped." David could only guess what that meant to a Tal Chin, but supposed it had to mean she was curvy—otherwise the Tal Chin might not have even been entirely certain that she was a female. At least he remembered the name and location of the second-hand vendor where he had acquired the game. Getting that cagey shop owner to let slip that the game had been sold to him only hours before it was "picked up" took some doing, but the description of the jerk who sold it to him had been accompanied by plenty of expletives. And once he had warmed to his retelling, the details came in quantity enough. David was not at all sure he believed all the details, as related, but there had been enough truth to eventually lead him to the storefront he now faced.

Cyberheim All-Access Media and Electronics. That name was like fuzzy-legged spiders crawling through his brain. Why did he think he should remember it? No time for that now. He ran his plot through his mind one more time. This should work. Maybe. He hoped. He walked into the store.

"Be right with you!" a voice called in Terran. It was probably facial recognition software set to greet customers in their own languages, to set them at ease and predispose them to spending more credits.

David looked around while he waited for an actual person to show up. This store had a little bit of everything electronic, from games to bugging devices, but very few of any one thing. Strange. Did they deal mostly in secondhand goods? Was this a sort of pawn shop? Great. This was going to be another step backwards in the chain of possession, but still not the end of the line. Difficult, and David wasn't sure where to start with this one.

"Terran?"

David didn't even have to pretend to be startled. He turned around at the sound of a female voice. She was pretty. That just made it harder. He could feel his cheeks reddening. "Uh, yeah."

"Cool. Can I help you?"

"Um, well. You see. A friend of mine had this game, and I, well, sorta misplaced it for him. So I'm trying to find him a replacement. He's not real happy with me."

"Bummer. What kind of game was it?"

"It was a handset. About this big." He gestured too big and shrank it down. "It was mostly black. Human-made. Oh, it was biometric. Sorta remembered who you were and tailored the adventure to you as you went." He paused. "I only played it once. One lousy time. But I lost it, so I gotta try to find another one."

"Do you know who made it?"

"Um, no." David bunched his face up. "Wait, there was this logo on the back. A real stylized T. Kinda looked like a comet or something."

"Oh, *that* game! I remember it. Came in one morning and sold that same afternoon. Made me so mad. I *told* Varghese—he's the manager. I *told* him *I* wanted that game. He *said* he'd hold it for me. He sends me out of the store to bring back food from ZhongHind, the Chinese-and-Indian place one level up. Good egg rolls, great curry. Anyway, I come back, and he's *sold* it—to the first stinking customer who walked in!"

"What? You mean you only had one?"

"It wasn't a shipment or nothing. I bought it off a guy that morning. Gave him too much for it, but he was cute, blond, shiny eyes. Jerk gave me his number, told me to link him when I got off duty. It was a fake number. Won't fall for *that* again. At least Varghese didn't yell at me for overpaying. He usually yells about everything."

David sighed. "I really need to find another one of those games."

"Well, good luck. I've never seen one like it before. Even checked the Thunderstone Electronics catalog to see if I could order one. It's like I just imagined the thing. Couldn't find that model anywhere. Best I can guess, it was a proto. No wonder some jerk snatched it up. I shoulda bought it right then and not waited till shift end. Woulda if I'da known. Oh well. Bridgewater."

Now *that* was interesting. David knew at least two other pods had one of those handsets.

David let her try to convince him to buy a different game, partly to maintain his cover as a customer, and partly to look at her some more. Too bad she didn't seem to be looking back. But just as soon as her manager called her name, David slipped out and darted back to the lifts. Only one game. Bought and sold same day. Then it changed hands a half-dozen times before it ended up in Dai-Soln's hands two days later. So how should David go about finding the handsome blond guy who flattered the sales clerk into paying too much for the game? Records. There had to be info on Blondie. Fake number. He must have used fake ID. That or the store was the kind that didn't really check. If that girl had had real ID on

Blondie, she'd have tracked him down to give him a piece of her mind. So where did that leave him? The manufacturer, Thunderstone Electronics. Red-shimmer did real-world investing. She would know how to find out who owned that company and where it was based. Thunderstone? Torstensson?

Gronorgh was just coming out of his room when he heard a sound like rending metal. No, it was more like a sound made by a living being. One of Shintikaisen's war screeches? No, it had come from—

David's door slid open, and Gronorgh nearly gasped at the sight. Something terrible had happened to David. His skin was purple and splotched, and veins stuck out on his forehead and up his neck. His breathing was very strange, and he looked swollen. Maybe he had been stung or bitten by something in his room. Gronorgh stepped forward to try to see.

"Out of my way *Murglorj'ô*."

Gronorgh was shocked. David had never used that name for him, except in the presence of other Gravgurdanûn. Never. But when David reached out to shove him aside, he stepped back in awe. It was several moments before he could think straight, he was so shocked. Insanity had taken David. He was… O Strengths! All twelve of them! David was already long gone. Just then, Red-shimmer Gold-streak came out of her room. Gornorgh looked down at her. "Quickly, gather the others! I must find Dai-Soln. I won't be able to stop David without him. Get Ael! We need Ael! And Jva too if you can find him. Quick!"

"Calm yourself Gronorgh. What is the problem? Maybe I can—"

"Shut up! Get the others as quickly as you can. David's going to kill someone."

Red-shimmer had never moved so fast in her life.

Gronorgh dove for his room. He grabbed his netbook and dashed back to David's door, sending a frantic message to Dai-Soln who was just across the common room in Enemwenu and Fthofsis's dorm. Dai-soln came charging out with the other two right behind him.

"Dai-Soln, quickly. I need in David's room. Spike the lock."

"No way. We'd both get expelled for that. Why would you—"

"I need in that room. *Now.* David's found Tkal's murderer. He's going to kill him."

"What? Are you sure?"

"Yes!"

"How?"

"He came out here all purple and veins sticking out everywhere—his face, his neck. He sounded like he couldn't breathe. I thought he had been stung, anaphylactic shock."

Ael had joined them. "Oh God. That's not an allergic reaction. That's rage. Oh God! Dai-Soln, if you can do it, spike the lock. Spike it now."

He hesitated only a moment, then turned, and seconds later the door was sliding open. Gronorgh reached out a monstrous hand and shoved the door home, probably breaking the hydraulics. He brushed Dai-Soln aside and ran into the room. Printouts were scattered everywhere, and there was a netbook with a shattered screen.

"Quickly, find what he was working on last." Gronorgh retrieved the netbook with the heel-shaped shatter in the screen and thrust it at Ael. "Here, see if you can get it to print the last file. We'll never be able to read anything on that screen."

Ael checked the docking port which seemed to be undamaged and slotted the netbook into the terminal. It took a few standards to get the damaged device to respond, but she finally got in. The terminal retrieved the file from the netbook and printed page after page of text in what looked like four, no five, different languages in parallel columns. It was a full decode of a code transmission they had intercepted…the day before Tkal died. The first column was what looked like lecture notes from a Xenopsych course written in Standard. The second column… "Does anyone here read any of these languages?" She started passing pages of the decode around as they came out of the printer.

"The third column is an old Alelliawulian poem about a band of alphas hunting wild game," said Enemwenu.

"I think the second column is Madrindiu," said Xtp.

Jva had just walked in. "Here, let me see." He reached for Xtp's page, while Xtp took another from Ael. "Yes, it's lyrics to a pop song that all the Madrindalan have been listening to since the middle of last quarter."

"The fourth column is Hopherl," said Enemwenu. "I think it's a religious text, but isn't the last column Terran?"

"Well, it's Human. And it's written in the same script as Terran, but—Jva?"

"No, I don't know this language. It's—" He dived for the other terminal and started zipping through searches. "It's Swedish."

"Sven." The name came from a half dozen beings simultaneously.

"Here, I've got a translation working. It says something about payment and—" Jva went pale.

"What?" Gronorgh demanded.

"*Jäst.* It's the Swedish word for yeast. He's staying in the hotel on levels three and four, La Grande Étoile."

Gronorgh started looking around frantically. "Is anything missing? Where are the knives?" Everyone understood what he meant. "The cups are here," Dai-Soln called. And here's *one* of the knives, but..."

Gronorgh dashed out through the common room and was out the door to the corridor before it was open all the way. He shouted back over his shoulder, "We have to stop him!"

Gronorgh pounded down the hall so fast his foot falls made the corridor echo and vibrate. Soon he had pulled far ahead of the others. But he was easy enough to follow. Each time the others saw a student, one of them demanded, "Which way?" Somehow they all understood and simply pointed them onward. The corridor ended in a bank of elevators. Several students huddled near the elevators in confusion.

"Did he come through here?" Dai-Soln demanded. He got frightened looks in answer. "The Gravgurdan, did he get on the elevator?"

A Hopherl standing near one of the doors finally answered, "He was... frightening. He threw the Verlain over there off the lift, just shoved him right out and growled at anyone who came close. Is...is he insane?"

"Yes," was Dai-Soln's answer as the others caught up. He jabbed at the call pad. They all tumbled in. "Call the administration. There will be trouble at La Grande Étoile." Then the doors slid shut.

Gronorgh was already in the lobby. He barely took note when the others arrived. He was scanning, looking for David. He was there somewhere. Gronorgh was sure of it. But where? His eyes flitted from person to person. David wasn't among those sitting in the reading area by the big artificial fireplace. He wasn't at the registration desk or by the fake window. Perhaps he had slipped into the bar? Gronorgh was moving that direction when he noticed Ael.

She was looking around, just as Gronorgh had been doing, when she shifted in some way. Suddenly, she seemed much fuller in some places and trimmer in others. The uniform, which had before seemed designed to conceal, now seemed crafted to tantalize. Her walk was different, and Jva stared at her from behind like he had never seen her before. This new Ael slinked up to the Human reservation clerk, and sort of purred, "I'm here for Sven. Sven Torstensson?"

The clerk tried to look displeased, but wasn't quite making it. His face read more like jealousy. He was not much older than Ael or Sven, and whatever Ael was doing to herself, it was working on him. "Second floor, North End Lobby. That's where he'll receive you."

Ael shifted again and became herself once more. Jva knew he'd been staring, and he knew there would be trouble about this later, but now all that mattered was David. "How did you know?"

"I never told you because I didn't want you to do what David's doing right now."

Jva could feel the heat rising in his chest. "Never told me what?"

"How that slug used to leer at me. Blow me a kiss from across the room when your back was turned."

Jva could feel himself starting to boil.

"I knew if he had money, he'd be spending part of it on girls."

The elevator opened onto the second floor of the hotel into a corridor. Opposite the elevator was a sign with arrows pointing to South End Lobby and North End Lobby. Gronorgh led the dash to North End. And there was

David, crouched in a cluster of potted plants. Waiting.

The door opened, and a head of rakishly shaggy blond hair emerged, checking the hall both ways, followed by a pair of broad shoulders. He turned and reached behind him to palm the door shut. It was Sven. Gronorgh was about to yell a warning when David leapt like an animal, flying through the air and spearing Sven with his shoulder. The two of them tumbled across the hall, and somehow David came up with his knee planted firmly in the middle of Sven's chest, digging into the right pectoral. Gronorgh had no doubt that the much larger Sven could have easily dislodged David, if it weren't for the glinting blade David held to his throat. Gronorgh would have been certain David could not move like that, unless he had seen it himself. Did rage turn all Humans into genuine fighters? Was this animal lodged inside every one of them?

Jva could only guess what was going through Sven's mind as he stared up into David's distorted face. He could see the veins pulsing in David's neck and forehead even from his vantage point, and his red eyes. It had to be terrifying, as David leaned in closer, grinding that knee in Sven's chest, with that knife cutting into the tender skin of his neck. Jva swallowed hard when he saw a trickle of blood course down Sven's neck and drip into the froofy hair spilled all around his head. To have that face baring down on him, with David's hot breath spilling over him. No wonder Sven was starting to tremble. He half hoped David did it.

Enemwenu had seen this before. Not again. Please not again.

Fthofsis watched uncomprehending. They were supposed to be looking for David. Why were they stopping to watch this monster attack some other Human? This was not its gentle friend. The being it had talked with in the arboretum. The shy dreamer. This was something other. Strange. Unknown. It did not want to see this, did not want these pictures burned into its mind.

Dai-Soln stepped forward, carefully circling to be fully in David's field of view. He stopped when he was sure he was standing where David could watch him without having to take his eyes from Sven. "David," he spoke softly. When there was no response, he called again, "David," just as gently. "David, don't do this. This revenge has a price too high." Still no response. "David, think of the cost. You'll ruin your entire life. Everything you've worked for. Tkal—"

"Is dead. By *his* hand!"

Shintikaisen slid in behind Dai-Soln, towering over the wispy Taisiran. "Remember Hamlet. Remember the poem I read. Think, David. You're good at thinking. 'If by my hand I slay / My enemy / Do I become / The enemy I slay?'" She paused, waiting for a reply that didn't come. "If you kill him with your own hand, do you become him? A murderer? Will you be just as bad as him? Will the rot in his soul become the rot in yours?"

There was no response, not in words. But hot tears coursed down David's face. Sven winced and tried to pull back against the floor to dodge the tears as they splattered his face. At the first one, he jerked as if it were acid dripping on him, biting the knife deeper into his own throat. He went rigid.

Gronorgh could see Sven's struggle against sheer panic, as every muscle in his body went hard with the barely mastered urge to fight. Fighting was impossible in this position, but the attempt to flee would be fatal as well. Suddenly, the area between Sven's legs went dark, the darkness spreading like blood, but smelling of ammonia. Small whimpering noises started coming from Sven's shuddering chest.

Xtp came up by Shintikaisen's elbow. "David, speak to me." It turned off its voder and began clicking. It went on for several standards, but getting no response, turned its voder back on. "He will not respond. What do we do?" The last was directed to Gronorgh.

All Gronorgh could do was shrug. He could tackle David easily, probably crushing several of his ribs in the process, but would it be fast enough that David didn't slit Sven's throat? Did he really want to stop him? The Gravgurdan warrior understood David's need. He felt some of it himself. But only a small part of David was now Gravgurdan. The Human in Gronorgh, which he had gained in losing to this same Human, knew that David would not survive doing this, not as a whole person. This act would destroy David as surely as it would kill Sven. He couldn't allow David to do this, but he didn't know how to stop him.

He felt a strong hand reach up and grip his shoulder. He glanced back and stepped aside, but the owner of the hand slid smoothly back into the shadow of Gronorgh's broad back.

David was trembling with the effort of not finishing this task. Icy claws pierced his heart and ice water ran in his veins. Thoughts raced through his mind, each swirling into the next like phantoms in the fog. His hand trembled as he decided to gash the throat pulsing beneath his knife in one instant, only to stay his hand in the next. Again and again, the decision was made and unmade. His podmates calling out to him from the fog, begging him to commit an act of mercy that was pure obscenity. Pleading for a soul he didn't have. Asking for a life that didn't deserve to live. And then there was another voice.

"David."

His head shot up, jostling the knife against the soft flesh below. There was terror in that cry. But who cared? That voice. He thought he would never hear—

"David, put down the knife."

David looked around wildly. Where was he? Where?

"David. The knife, put it down. You cannot do such a thing. The Eternal forbids it. Do not dishonor the memory of friendship, of brotherhood, by spilling a murderer's blood with the knife that sealed your brotherhood. The blade will never come clean from that stain."

"Where are you?" he called wildly. "Tkal!" He stood, holding the knife at his side. "Tkal!"

Tkal's father stepped from behind Gronorgh's massive shadow and reached his arms for David.

David stumbled a couple of steps forward, tears streaming down his face, the knife hanging limply at his thigh. "You, you're not Tkal. You're…Father?"

Ambassador Dvarin reached to enfold David in his embrace, to pin David's arms in his own until one of the others pried the knife from his adopted son's hand, when—

Sven leapt from the ground, all his fear and shame transmuted to blind fury. He charged David from behind, grabbing for the knife.

David saw motion at his side. His body moved. His fist, holding the knife, arced and slammed the hilt into a shoulder with all the force of the spin. His knee rose up and slammed into soft guts as his other fist slammed down into spine and ribs with a crack. His other foot was following into a backward kick that would have slammed into skull with full force had hundreds of kilos not come crashing down on him. It was all he could do to breathe under the crushing weight of…

Gronorgh tackled him before he could complete *nivagh shkitav*. Why had he taught David that technique? He had been so clumsy in practice that it seemed ridiculous to teach it, almost a joke, but here, in this moment, David executed with perfect precision—strike following strike. Were he any stronger, or faster, Sven would now be dead. He might still die. Gronorgh finished his roll and brought David up on top of himself before David could be crushed beneath his tackle. Gronorgh's arms covered David's whole torso, pinning both arms from shoulder to wrist. Even another Gravgurdan would have been helpless to escape if Gronorgh used full force. He stood keeping David pinned against himself. Gronorgh only had to take care not to crush David. There was no hope of escape.

But David had gone limp. Gronorgh doubted David could even stand if he set him on his feet.

Tkal's father approached. "Thank you, Gronorgh. I will take my son now."

Gronorgh manipulated David's little body like a rag doll and laid him in the ambassador's cradled arms with surprising gentleness.

Sven struggled to stir himself to his knees. Gronorgh leaned over him and growled, "Lie down, fool. I stopped my friend from killing you, but who here will stop me? Lie there and live until security come for you…or you will have another bodily fluid staining your clothing.

Sven quivered, but otherwise did not move. By the time security did arrive a few standards later, Sven was crying. The medics arrived less than a minute after security, and as they loaded him onto a gurney to cart him away, he cried out in a shattered voice. "I want to talk to Prince Kvran. I demand to talk to Prince Kvran. Help. Help me! He owes me!"

Security had many questions, but Ambassador Dvarin extended his diplomatic immunity around David to usher him away until he was competent to answer those questions. Gronorgh and the rest of the pod were among the least cooperative witnesses of a near murder ever, offering so little information that security was on the verge of arresting the entire pod by the time David returned to explain himself—with a pair of Tvern An lawyers in tow, a husband and wife team who had been engaged by the ambassador.

Twenty-Nine

To Everything…

David entered the office of Chancellor Supradoctor Tal Hatlir. He didn't want to be here any more than he wanted to be confined to his quarters, but he figured it would all be finished after this meeting, so best to get it over with.

"Come in Student David Asbury. Take a seat. This will take some time." The chancellor poured himself a cup of something that smelled like the Chinese medicine shop on level eight. "I hope the smell doesn't offend you, but I have been in meetings, about your case, all day, and I need a mild stimulant." He took a deep draft of the concoction and leaned back in his chair. "I want to make it clear from the start that nothing I say here is negotiable. I have already discussed your case with…" He drew in a breath and proceeded to tick the items off on his fingers. "The head of station security; your lawyers; Sven Torstensson's lawyers; someone who presented himself as a lawyer for Prince Kvran, though I'm reasonably sure he is more a plenipotentiary representative of the Throne himself than a lawyer for the Prince; several different representatives of Earth's government; two members of the Commonwealth Council; practically the entire staff of the Academy's legal department; the head of the station's governing body; and so many others, who had some minor aspect of this case that they had some pearl of wisdom to impart regarding, that I have entirely lost count."

David quirked his mouth and nodded. He had walked into this room sure enough that there would be no arguing his way out of this. Nothing the chancellor said yet had surprised him, except for the sheer number of people involved.

"Let's start at the bottom and work our way up, shall we? First, the Terran Diplomatic Corps has revoked your scholarship. They will not pay a single credit more and may even demand repayment of their investment."

David drew in a huge breath.

"I know. It is unfair, and I have argued against it. I am not sure they have legal grounds for such an action, but you should be aware of the possibility. Second, you will not be allowed to continue at Shel Matkei Academy. Your tenure as a student of this institution is hereby revoked, and you will not be allowed to return to your studies here at any time. This is not negotiable. You will need to vacate your quarters, and the station itself, within three days."

David was very disappointed, but not at all surprised. At least he would have time to say good bye to the pod.

"Third, the Kzati trade representative on Earth has threatened to call off an extremely lucrative trade deal with Earth if you are not banned, for life, from ever holding any position with Earth's government or any subordinate entity with which Earth's government contracts business. It is my understanding that Earth's Commissioner for Extra-Commonwealth Trade Relations is leaning toward signing off on that stipulation. In effect, you could never be employed on Earth. And they have requested that you be returned to Earth on the next available transport."

Now *that* was unexpected.

"However, that may not be possible." He touched something on his console and spoke into the air. "Ishkadhni?"

The receptionist's unintelligible voice responded.

"If Ambassador Dvarin is out there, please send him in."

Ambassador Dvarin? Tkal's father was going to have to witness part of this humiliation? Before he could really formulate a protest, Tkal's father—*his* father—was at his side pulling up a chair. "Of how much of this situation has he already been apprised?" Tkal's father asked of the chancellor without preamble. "Pardons. My manners." He bowed to the chancellor without rising from the chair.

"He knows about those parts dealing directly with his status as a student here and we had just started on his position with regards to his own government."

"Then Chancellor Tal Hatlir, may I have a moment with my deceased son's brother?"

The look that came over Chancellor Supradoctor Tal Hatilr's face was…complex. David had spent an entire term reading his expressions as he taught. He thought he might be looking at anger or displeasure. Worry, perhaps? Reproof? Was that what reproof looked like on a Varktis face? Actually, it could well be all of those, but there was still something else mixed in.

The chancellor nodded to the ambassador. "You always were clever, Dgan. Think well to what you do now…and what comes after."

David had seen a jaw outlined with hard muscle like that before. When Tkal looked like that, he had already made up his mind and dug in for the fight.

Chancellor Tal Hatlir sighed and waved them to the farthest corner of his office.

The ambassador backed David into that corner and blocked his view of the room with his robes covering broad chest and massive shoulders. Tkal had been built like that—not quite as big, but with time, he might have been even bigger. Why had he never felt intimidated by either of them? He should have been afraid of any guy that much bigger and so intense about everything. But he felt safe here, just as he had with Tkal—even at his most insane.

"David, try to look only at me. Try not to look past me. Think carefully about what I am going to say, but you must decide now. Earth has betrayed you. They have cut off your funding. They are very likely to agree to never employ you even if you graduate."

David blurted out, "I won't be."

The ambassador frowned. "We'll see about that." He blew out breath in that way that made Tkal look like a dragon. "They *may*, mind you only may, hand you over to the Kzati for trial on some of the charges they are bringing against you—including slander of the Royal Person. Do you know what that means?"

Death. If convicted, the penalty for slandering a member of the Royal Family was death. David nodded.

"David, you already have a claim, of a sort, to Tvern citizenship, or at least certain rights and privileges very similar thereto. Through Tkal doing *fdinel* with you, as a *fdinel,* you are, in a sense, also Tvern An now. But it is a form of belonging that, while fully recognized by Tvern law, might not be understood, or so interpreted, by an ISC court. Or an Earth court. But by a simple declaration, you could become a full, undeniable and irrevocable, citizen of Tvern, removing yourself from the jurisdiction of Earth courts on this matter."

"What are you saying? Immigrate? To Tvern? Leave Earth? Renounce Earth?"

"Think carefully. By this same document, my wife and I would formally adopt you as our own child. We would become your parents before ISC law.

David did think. His mind raced down a dozen different lines of thought, caroming off different reasons why or why not to accept this offer, comparing dangers, benefits, likely outcomes, futures, non-futures. "Tkal once told me that he felt like he stood between worlds, never fully at home in either, but that he was okay with that." He watched that revelation play in Dvarin Dgan's eyes—sadness, pride, hope and…fear. "I told Tkal that we were more alike than I had ever realized, that I didn't fit anywhere either, but that I didn't exactly stand between worlds, because I didn't have any worlds to be between." He breathed for a few moments, with his would-be adoptive father's eyes searching his face for the answer he, himself, hadn't found yet. He sighed. "I guess it's time for me to share one more experience with Tkal. Where do I sign?"

Mr. Dvarin looked like he might cry. His hand trembled as he handed David the data pad.

David took it and scrolled through the pages. It was clear enough. Was it what he wanted? Was it the right, or even best, choice?

The chancellor called to David, "David, I think I can guess what the ambassador has been saying to you." He sighed. "If I were in his position, I would likely be offering you much the same." He paused. "Dgan, please step aside and let me see him."

The ambassador fixed an intense gaze on David, then bowed his head and stepped aside.

"David, think carefully before you sign that. It is not something that can be undone. I know what it is to be an exile. I did not return home when my people cut themselves off from the Commonwealth. I have been alone out here for a hundred and thirty-seven years. Think carefully."

David looked at the pad, closed his eyes, and pressed his thumbprint in place, signing the document and leaving Earth behind. He looked up at the chancellor. "We now share something."

"Indeed. Perhaps more than you know or are prepared for." He paused and steepled his fingers over his cup. He looked down at the steam rising through his fingers, and sighed, flaring his ear holes. He took a sip. "Well, this changes several things I had left to tell you. And makes a few more irrelevant."

He pulled a data pad over and ran his finger across the screen. He wiped several items and tapped a few others. He steepled index fingers and touched them to his lips. He stared down at his screen. "So, legally speaking, I need to be quite sure of whom I am addressing. You may wish to take counsel of the ambassador or of your legal counsel before you answer. I have been given certain directives regarding the legal entity David Ethan Asbury, citizen of Earth, resident on Shel Matkei Station and enrolled at Shel Matkei Academy on a scholarship from the Terran Diplomatic Corps, that may or may not apply to whatever legal entity you now are, or may apply differently." He grunted. "Actually, I'm not sure that *any* of the rest of this now applies. The lawyers and representatives of the various governments and parties involved will have to hash this all out again, from scratch." He smiled as if that gave him some pleasure.

Ambassador Dvarin cleared his throat. "Mr. Chancellor, I have a question about the status of the student, David Asbury, formerly of Earth, presently of Tvern. I have been informed that he will not be allowed to continue at Shel Matkei."

"That, Mr. Ambassador, is non-negotiable. *I* won't permit him to stay, quite apart from any protests by the various offended governments. He has been a target of physical abuse since the incident with the Gravgurdan. If he stays now, his life would be in constant jeopardy. I will not have another student murdered at this school, under my watch, if I can, in anyway whatsoever, prevent it."

"That, I understand. And quite fully support. David is not safe here and must leave at the earliest possible time. However, I was more interested in his status as regards his academic attainment. I understand that he has taken course loads far in excess of standard full-time class schedules every term he has been here." He paused and inclined his head.

"Ah, I see. It is…not an impossibility…" Chancellor Supradoctor Tal Hatlir sat tapping his earholes. "Yes, well, I can see any number of difficulties, applying mostly to me personally but a few to the school at large, arising from this course…of varying degrees of possibility…and certain very likely benefits accruing almost exclusively to one individual…" He closed his eyes and failed to breathe for several moments. "Well, I might as well look to confirm whether it is even a possibility." He tapped a few commands on his data pad, and spent the next several standards making various small noises as he muttered to himself. He pushed the data pad forward and leaned back in his chair. "Yes, well not quite, I'm afraid. The student designated David Ethan Asbury, is still six course hours short of being matriculable. Had he finished even two more classes before his scholarship patron cut him off and demanded his expulsion, and the need for his *near*-immediate departure arose, he would have… Ah, but that is neither here nor there, and that student no longer *legally* exists"

David sat up. "So, if David Ethan Asbury, of Tvern, were to turn in a number of already completed assignments due over the next several tendays, and perhaps arranged to take some exams, without preparation, during the two or three days before his departure, could such a thing be possible?"

Ambassador Dvarin laid a hand on David's forearm, gripping it much too tightly, but David didn't even breathe.

The chancellor pursed his mouth. "Such a thing…*might*…be possible. I have received no confirmation from ICS officials about whether or not all of Earth's requests regarding David Asbury of Earth require my compliance, and

I have received no communications whatsoever from any government, except from a certain ambassador of Tvern, regarding the entity David Asbury of Tvern; however, voice print and biometric scans should prove that person's right to submit the indicated work for grading purposes." He paused. "Circumstances could occur between now and your departure which would discount everything just said, but if not, the possibility exists for you to leave here with a diploma."

David sighed, and the ambassador let go of his arm in time for circulation to return to the limb. David made his excuses as quickly as possible and dashed for his quarters, pausing only long enough to tell his security escort that he had to return to his room.

The next three days passed in a blur of activity. David hit the *submit* button for paper after paper, assignment after assignment, till everything he had done ahead of time was in queue to be graded. Then he got permission from all but one of his professors to take his final exams immediately, and spent the rest of the first day, and half of the second, taking back-to-back exams without time to study for any of them. Once the last of the exams was submitted, he looked through the assignments he had started, but not finished. Those he could quickly finish, he did. Those he couldn't, he submitted anyway, hoping for partial credits. While he was finishing the last of that, his computer started pinging with returning grades. Most of the backlog of completed homework was receiving the sorts of grades David was accustomed to, the rush jobs and incompletes were getting grades that would have given him an aneurysm just last week. Now David had to look at them as replacing what would have otherwise been zeros averaged in to his grades. His GPA was shot. How bad it really was wouldn't be known until the exams started coming back.

While he waited, he sent a message to his podmates and a few others, explaining that he would be leaving shortly before the end of daycycle the next day, and wishing them well in their studies and future lives. It only took about two hours before his podmates managed to get their demands to see David, face-to-face in his room, heard. The rest of the afternoon and evening was filled up with pings from the computer and chimes from the door as one after the other of his podmates got to say their goodbyes. Xtp and Shintikaisen had been fairly easy. Neither of them made a big deal of it, and each of them had done what they could to be businesslike and make the inevitable as smooth as possible. Ael had been, well *perfunctory* was the only word for it, and that hurt, but she was still mad about the fight with Jva. Jva didn't come at all.

Then Dai-Soln came. He stood outside the door, both sets of knees at full extension, his fronds spread wide. He bent the joints of his legs and swept his fronds back, palming his sword behind himself, in a full, court-style bow, of the sort used to greet dignitaries.

"*Didzai*, David Ethan Asbury, late of Earth, now of Tvern, fiercest of friends, though very intemperate."

"*Didzai*, Dai-Soln, son of Hte-Soln, prince and duke, of Taisirul, wise counselor." David frowned. "So, you've heard."

"David." Dai-Soln gestured to the chairs.

David nodded, and Dai-Soln sat.

"David, I do not know how much access you have had to what is happening out there." His gesture took in events far beyond Shel Matkei Academy.

"Precious little. My access to even the academy net has been limited—not cut off, but restricted, during my house arrest. And since my meeting with the chancellor, I've been too busy finishing all the classes I could to attend to anything else."

"As I thought. Well, I have been following everything I could get access to, both here and through my contacts at the Taisiran court and…elsewhere." He shook out his fronds and rearranged them. "Your actions have…come close to creating an interstellar incident."

"Surely that's an exaggeration? Tell me it is!"

"Only in matter of degree and perspective. David, Sven talked. He talked *way* too much trying to dig himself out. As you surmised, that game was the leak. They were prototypes that were to be released for covert market-testing, but Sven modified them with a spy program that his father's company was secretly developing for industrial espionage. The fact that Prince Kvran got to use it to spy on subjects of the Commonwealth and several other polities, some of whom have actual positions with their respective governments, which may have given him access to real-world secrets—things having nothing to do with the pod simulations. Three governments, my own included, have already accused the prince of conducting espionage against their citizens. Thunderstone Electronics is under investigation and charges against several officers of that company seem likely. The Emperor of the Kzati has…'requested'…that his nephew, Prince Kvran, attend him at court."

David groaned. "He's getting away. He's going free."

"From your perspective." Dai-Soln raised a hand at David's glare, just in time to stop what promised to be a torrent of words. "Mine as well, in part. From *his* perspective, being recalled to face the displeasure of the Throne, with an 'honor guard' escorting him to the border of Commonwealth space. David, he is going back in disgrace. Please, be careful. '*Watch your back*,' as your people say, for the next years, *very* carefully. He *will* want revenge. You have humiliated him badly. He will *not* forgive. And pray he never comes to the throne. That would not be good for you."

David frowned. "Never wound an animal you cannot kill."

"Hmm. Crude image but, well, true." He paused. "David, I do hope you are listening to me. This really is very serious. You have created a very dangerous situation." He paused and rearranged his fronds, yet again. "But realize, you are not without allies of your own. In several different polities, if need arise. I am well-placed on Taisirul. Gronorgh will surely rise quickly through the ranks," he grimace-smiled, "over a mound of broken bodies, if need be. A friend in the Gravgurdan Stronghold is not something a great many can claim. And you have connections on Tvern, which is an important member of the Commonwealth. Fthofsis is sure to be important to the future of its world, whether Fthsaisthf ultimately joins the Commonwealth or not, and they are on the other side of the Commonwealth from the Kzati. Distance can be a great friend…or foe. Do not forget where we dwell."

David wondered what the others would think, if they knew Dai-Soln was volunteering them in this way. But Dai-Soln's own offer could not be so easily brushed aside. How could he reassure him? David had no idea, so he managed to dissolve the conversation into small talk, until Dai-Soln took his leave, offering his forearms, in a grasp that reminded David too much of the day he had grasped Tkal's arms like this.

Fthofsis bobbed in an imaginary wind, waiting for Enemwenu to take the initiative and touch David's door chime. If it waited long enough, its roommate always gave in, but sometimes waiting was too long.

Enemwenu sighed. "This must be done. You will not fly away? We will enter together?"

"Yes, I agreed. The wind will not part us." It paused, then added, "We will not be individuals."

The Alelliawulian slapped a tentacle against the pad by the door, swelled its head-body, and shuffled backward as the door slid open raggedly. It had not been repaired properly after Gronorgh had shoved it.

David stood there. He moved his feet to glide to one side of the doorway, so they would have room to enter.

Fthofsis knew it was its turn to go first, but it hovered just a moment, hoping Enemwenu… No, this was not right. It flew ahead, hoping that Enemwenu really followed it. This was not something it wanted to do alone.

David waved a hand, one of the welcoming gestures. He was acting much like the David Fthofsis always thought he knew. "I am sorry. I don't have the right kind of chair for you, Enemwenu, or any willow branches to share, Fthofsis."

These were the words of the before-David. Was that David still real, still inside there? Did he always co-live with the monster?

David spoke again, "Please, don't stare at me like that. Please."

"David…" they both began. Fthofsis rippled its dorsal wing at Enemwenu, offering hii first speech. Enemwenu did not look pleased. Hii was turning that redder shade that did not mean happiness.

"David," Enemwenu began, curling a tentacle in the forgiveness-seeking gesture. "David, I must ask. Asking, you will not be pleased. Being displeased, do not make violence. Please."

Water appeared in the corners of David's strange eyes as they changed shape and even color. He twisted his arm, trying to copy one of Enemwenu's gestures. David was always doing that. Copying other's ways.

"Enemwenu, forgive me. Your bond parent. That was not for you to see."

"David, I have seen many things, and will see many things, but that was both you and not-you. I am…unsettled. If Gronorgh had done this, or Shintikaisen… This is just their nature, the ways of their cultures. This is not…" Hii paused, twisting hii's tentacles, searching for the right words. "You deceived me. We shared meals. I thought you understood unities, collectives, co-duties, inter-responsibilities. You should have come to us. But at the crucial moment, you became an 'individual' again, and acted most unwisely, without counsel, without help, without thought. Together we would have found a better—"

"My life for my brother's. I found a saying from the Chukchi, one of the clans of Earth, 'A brother is not only he whose face and form are like to ours, a brother's he who knows our joy and pain and understands.'"

"Mmmm… We have similar words. Hii shifted hii's knees, tilting hii's body. "You claim this deed as clan debt?"

"I claim nothing but rage, and the insanity born of it." David extended a hand and curled it downward. "Distressing you distresses me, but the past cannot be changed, only owned." He bent his knees and bowed his head.

Enemwenu began extending a tentacle, then drew it back, and moved hiiself toward a corner of the room.

Fthofsis fluttered forward. "You are truly both of these beings, are you not?"

David bowed his head. "Yes, that was me, too. I didn't know that was part of me, either. How could I expect you to understand, when I don't understand myself?"

Fthofsis could tell David had not let all the gale within him escape. So it waited, and glanced at Enemwenu standing in the corner with hii's tentacles wrapped around two of hii's legs.

Finally, David blew words again. "How many of me are there? I don't know. It was like I looked at that decryption, and I saw his words, Sven's words, suggesting *yeast* as a 'farewell gift.' No one even knew he was still on station, and here he was casually planning Tkal's murder, in print, in text. His family company made the game that was spying on us. His hand volunteered for the deed. I snapped. I became someone else. I became living rage. I found and killed him…only I didn't. I mean, I did, inside, in my heart. There, I killed him. I still don't understand why my hand didn't follow my heart. And then all of you, *all* of you, showed up. Why?"

"To stop you. Gronorgh knew. He saw your face, heard your words, and knew. The rest of us… Some also knew after they saw the papers—Ael, Jva, Dai-Soln, Shintikaisen. Some of us only felt the other's conviction—me, Enemwenu, perhaps Red-shimmer."

"No, I knew," Enemwenu interrupted. "I knew because I could feel your rage. I entered your world, what I knew of your world, and in my own heart, my tentacle reached for the knife. This troubles me. It is too individual, too uncounseled, too divided."

"So," Fthofsis sighed into its voder, "perhaps I was the only one who flew in the fog. There were no clouds of light that day…or since. Only fog…very dense fog. David, I must know. Could you do this to me?"

David sat down hard, but did not speak for a long time. Finally, he looked right at Fthofsis. "Could you do to me, to Tkal, what Sven did?"

Fthofsis flutter-stuttered so that it drifted off-level and had to right itself. "How can you ask? No. Never. I could never do that to Tkal. I trusted and respected him. And you have been my friend. Why would I steal the breath from your lungs and the air from your wings?"

"Then I could never do this to you."

Fthofsis released hydrogen from its flight bladder and sank to David's eye level to peer at his face. The Human writings said again and again that the eyes made a window—a wind's eye—to the winds of the heart. Such appropriate words. But how to read an alien heart through such a small opening!

"Tkal was right about you. About your skill, your talent, and determination. About your fire. About your need for us and ours for you. And even Gronorgh learned that you are dangerous."

"But Tkal would be very, very, deeply disappointed with what I did."

"Yes, he would. But he would also understand. I think…I think he might have tasted the same air for you. And suffered the same."

"Now I wish I had a candle."

"What?"

"Never mind. I don't. And…I…never mind."

Red-shimmer had nearly brought David to tears, and he was pretty sure that the oily sheen that blurred her speech was her version of tears. She had left her voder behind, so their last conversation happened the way all their best conversations had, with David using his coloform shirt.

Gronorgh didn't come.

In the morning, David went to the door to get his breakfast from his guards. Overnight, the rest of his grades had come in. They were disappointing, but he would graduate with a solid GPA, not stellar, like it should have been, but solid. It gave him some hope of a future. His adopted father had already sent word that he was "working on an angle." David didn't know what that meant, but it reminded him of something Tkal would have said. This next few hours would be his last in the room he had shared with Tkal, his sworn brother, for so few months. Then he'd be cut off from this spot, perhaps never to see it again. One more bit of Tkal lost. If he really let himself think about it, he was losing pieces of all of them by leaving here. It would have happened someday, but this was the wrong time, the wrong way. Green Pod would be *two* members down now. Violet Pod might not even exist, depending on how much the rest of *them* knew or were involved.

Soon, his shuttle flight would take him to a liner bound for Tvern, where he would meet Tkal's many cousins. David was very unsure about how that made him feel.

He gnawed on his breakfast and puttered around the room, showering for the last time in this room, dressing for the last time in this room…packing. He had hated this room so much when he first found out he would be forced to come live here. Now he hated leaving it even more. Life was not fair. Dean Haerkarn messaged him a huge download of who-knew-what, but it was supposed to help him in transitioning. He shrugged. Maybe it would. He was even going to miss his sessions with the dean. She'd helped him more than he cared to admit. In fact, he might have been too scared to accept Tkal's friendship without her prodding. Yes, he owed her. No way to repay that now.

He returned his food tray and found his diploma waiting. There was no thrill, no ceremony, no anything. But he had it, and that was what counted for his future. Whatever that might be.

The one real regret was Gronorgh not showing. David had thought that the two of them had come to some kind of growing understanding. Well, some things were real, and some were illusion. That was life.

The computer and his door pinged simultaneously, informing him that it was time to leave. Gronorgh was waiting just outside the door, looming over the security guards, making them look like frightened children. The two of them, a Hiltar and a bear-like Chiurdoun, would have needed a half dozen guys bigger than themselves to restrain him, and the looks on their faces said they knew it for a certainty.

"I will be escorting you to your shuttle, *Hhoeghsidrangqoelzhaghaqdhav.* These," he gestured dismissively at the guards, "will follow."

David set his mouth, hoisted his bags over his shoulder, and nodded for Gronorgh to lead the way. Strange how much lighter these bags were than the ones he carried when he had moved in, and these were much fuller. Many things had changed.

David and Gronorgh walked along in silence, trailed by the guards, until Gronorgh stopped in the corridor, cocked his head to one side, and nodded to David. David nodded back and said, in better, rougher, Gravgaln, "Speak your mind!"

Gronorgh thrust out his chin and returned to walking. "Being in a place like this changes you. It changes all of us. Living in a pod with all aliens, with different societies and cultures and biologies and ideas. The ideas are the worst. They get in your head and change the way you think. We sit around and talk and exchange literature and music and foods. We argue and hate and complain…and fight. But sometimes we fight together, and then we learn to respect and understand."

One of the security guards made a small sound and gestured to the left branch of the corridor. Gronorgh growled, and David snapped "We know the way, if you please."

The group continued toward the lifts, Gronorgh nodded and continued his discourse. "One day, you wake up and look in the mirror above your own wash basin and realize that you see a stranger, or at least someone who will be a stranger to your own family. When I go home, my own father, brothers, and uncles will not recognize me. My schoolmates won't know me." Gronorgh shrugged, not a Gravgurdan gesture. "Even my caste brothers will have to relearn my face, because I have changed. I came here one-hundred percent Gravgurdan, and I thought one-hundred percent Gronorgh, though I realize now that was wrong. I already carried bits of my father and brothers and uncles and schoolmates and caste brothers in me without recognizing it."

The lift doors opened and the guards called for level five.

Gronorgh continued. "But now? Now I am part Trelkairni. You know I actually listen to war screeches on my own now? And I can tell the difference between a good screecher and a bad one. I can even pick out some of the more famous ones in the first measure!"

The warrior inhaled deeply, as the doors opened and they headed past classrooms to the lifts connecting with the lower levels. "And Dai-Soln, well I've spent so much time with him that I am addicted to those beetles he's always snacking on, and I know his Code almost as well as he knows mine. He's the one who taught me to look for strength in small beings. He's so stubborn and has so much fire, that I would have cause to be afraid of him if he were Gravgurdan, even of a lower caste."

"And the others, well, I don't think I realize yet what they have left in me, how they have changed me, but I know it's there. And others of my kind will see it and wonder how I came to be so odd. And some of them may be fool enough to think it weakness and take the chance to challenge.

"The first one who calls me Human will suffer, that I can tell you."

David drew back.

"No, small one, you don't understand. Think with the part of you that is Gravgurdan."

David's thoughts tangled.

"Don't you understand what I'm saying? You're not just Human anymore. You carry a heavy chunk of Tkal around in you. Part of you is Tvern An. Anyone who could carry off that funeral and comfort his parents and convince Tkal to claim him as a brother…Tvern An don't do that sort of thing lightly.

"And you are part Iridian. The effort of learning to use that shirt to speak B-G-2-3, forcing your body to give the subtle signals through your skin to color it this way and that, to be able to speak Red-shimmer's language through your skin so she was more welcome, more included. That changed you.

"And arguing over poetry with Xtp, and your conversations with Fthofsis in the arboretum."

David looked at Gronorgh with surprise. They stopped at the lifts and got on, followed by the guards.

Gronorgh gravel-laughed. "Oh, come on, in a group as small as this? Do you think there are any secrets? Everyone knows the arboretum is your private place, just like everyone knows mine is the high-g gym or Enemwenu's is the museum."

"You knew, and you left me alone there?"

Gronorgh looked hurt.

"I guess I deserve that, but yes I knew, and no, I would never violate another student's private place. I value my own too much. That kind of disrespect would be unworthy even of someone as rude as I have practiced at being." He paused. "It was a way of keeping you out of me. I hated Sven. Really hated him. He was everything that Gravgurdanûn mock in Humans. Proud and arrogant and selfish and always trying to make himself look better at someone else's expense, but never willing to back it up, terrified of someone bigger than himself."

"I had to room with him one quarter. And I was smaller."

The lift delivered them to level one. Now it was just a walk to the port. Gronorgh growled, but his face showed something like revulsion. "When you came along, I judged you by Sven. He had confirmed every prejudice, so you got no chance. I gave you all the scorn I thought your kind deserved. Earth sends us ambassador after ambassador who is utterly incompetent. Fools who know nothing about politics, who couldn't think their way out of an open field, just because they are the biggest, strongest Human males they could find. But when these men, who are used to walking into a room and instantly dominating every male in it, just by their size, arrive on Gramurgh and find they are struggling just to carry their own body through the day in gravity forty percent higher than they are used to, with their heart and lungs struggling to adapt, when they learn that everyone they meet will tower over them and every youth walking down the street can overpower them in any contest, that they can only win against children and the very lowest of outcastes, something inside them breaks, and they are ruined. Some of them hide in their embassies, quivering and cowering, and never come out for their whole term. A couple have," he dropped his voice to a whisper, "committed suicide."

He and David turned and spat simultaneously. The guards gasped.

"You see!" exclaimed Gronorgh. "I openly say such a thing without using it as a curse, like a Human, and you react like a Gravgurdan."

"I just—"

"No, when you fought me, and won, you became part Gravgurdan, a part most important to us. And when I lost, and you wrested the ceremony afterwards, forcing it to submit to your concepts of justice, and I accepted that, I became part Human."

David knit his brow. Each door they passed brought him closer to leaving.

"That is why I will pound the first one who calls me *Human* on my return. He will mean it the way I once would have, as an insult, and he will say it with a sneer. I will teach him, if he lives, to say the word with respect, and he will learn that he can be crushed by a Human, because I will claim the name once he is broken. And when he submits, I will bend down to his ear and whisper your name and tell him that he was humiliated by the Gravgurdan who was beaten by a Human. And when he looks for your name, he will live the rest of his life knowing that he is lower than all Humans, because you are still very small."

And Gronorgh laughed in a way that sounded almost Human. Almost, but not quite. And David growled and attempted the gravelly sound. It was a very weak attempt. But each understood the other.

"I hope someday you may be assigned as the ambassador to Gramurgh. Then you could teach us all to respect Humans as I now do."

David looked up at Gronorgh. "I don't know if I would survive the attempt. And Earth won't have me. I belong to Tvern now." They stopped, and David nodded at the tail of the line forming to board his shuttle to the liner taking him to Tvern.

"Fools," Gronorgh declared flatly, without bluster or heat. "You would survive, small one. The question is whether the Gravgurdan Stronghold would survive."

David laughed.

"You still can't lift your own body weight, and you get tired far too quickly, but you have other kinds of strength. Some of them may not even be among the Twelve. I respect you."

David blinked.

"Bah! Such a useless word. Standard is so weak sometimes. The proper word is *vegnakht*."

David froze. The respect tinged with dread. How could he respond to that?

"You are surprised? You defeated me, and that was when you were still a child. Now you are almost a man, soon you will be. Who will you conquer then?"

"Only myself, I hope."

Gronorgh shuddered. "That's the most frightening one of all. If you conquer yourself, then you are a warrior no one can touch. To face a warrior who has conquered himself, is to face certain death, because he sees every crack and knows the wedge that fits it. Such a warrior can defeat you before the first blow."

David shrugged his slipping bags back up onto his shoulder. "Is everything a fight, a battle, a conquering or a being conquered?"

"Hmm." Gronorgh frowned in thought. "A Gravgurdan should say, *yes!* And give no further thought. Everything is a battle. Every moment another skirmish to fight or fail. Every breath drawn, one more victory. Every failed rep another defeat." He paused. "But your words have weight. I can lift your meaning. There are things, experiences, events that could be described in terms of the battle, but maybe they are better described by some other metaphor, some Human metaphor, or Taisiran, or Tvern An. Perhaps no one way of looking at the world accounts best for everything."

David smiled crookedly at his shoes. "There are more things in heaven and earth, Horatio, than are dreamt of in your philosophy."

"What?"

"More Shakespeare. More *Hamlet*, actually."

"Hhrrrng. Well *this* time he got something right. Strange little man. Of course, he was a Human."

For more information about the languages of the InterStellar Commonwealth
and beyond, see http://awalkerscott.com/languages and the associated pages.